Neighbourhood
of Night

Neighbourhood of Night

Urban Rain II

David Dane Wallace

iUniverse®

Neighbourhood of Night
Urban Rain II

iUniverse books may be ordered through booksellers or by contacting:

iUniverse
1663 Liberty Drive
Bloomington, IN 47403
www.iuniverse.com
1-800-Authors (1-800-288-4677)

ISBN: 978-1-4917-5397-2 (sc)
ISBN: 978-1-4917-5398-9 (e)

Library of Congress Control Number: 2014921632

Printed in the United States of America.

iUniverse rev. date: 12/16/2014

In memory of the love of my life, my ex girlfriend Monica, January 5th. 1978 to November, 7th, 2012 at 9:30pm. No matter how things between us ended, you never left my heart for even a day. I will always love you Baby Bunny, i'll see you in Heaven.

This Book is also for my niece Kate. I love you little Diamond Doll. Thank you for being born.

And For,

Our Canadian National Treasure, the one man that I respect more than any other on this earth. "His Excellence Of Execution." ... ... "The Best There Is, The Best There Was, And The Best There Ever Will Be." ... ... Bret "The Hit Man" Hart. Canada will always love you. Thank you for the inspiration.

This Book is also dedicated to The King Of Harts, Owen Hart. May you Rest In Peace.

The character of Kate"The Gate"Shamrock is a fictitious imagining of the person that my niece may one day be.

While my precious niece(Kate) exists, she is only two years old. For the sake of this manuscript try and ignore the age quandry that her character represents as this book is meant as entertainment at least in part.

Authors note: Monica-Many people do not understand the reasons why things between us ended the way that they did, because at least one of those secrets, the most sinister one, died with you and shall live within me forever. The most important detail of our relationship is that regardless of what many believe, we loved each other, and should have been able to continue on that way.

During the course of the text I will outline a number of the reasons that lead to our falling out and subsequently lead to the events of January 2008. No matter what, I love you, and always will. This book is for you Baby Bunny, i'll see you in Heaven.

Eternal Life!!!

L.A.- The first twenty five pages of this book were written prior to my knowledge of the nightmare that took place on November 7th, 2012. The reason that I have chosen to print the date of her birth as well as that of her passing is so that no human being living or dead will ever be able to come forth and take credit for her legend in whole or in part. This is her legacy. My life, nor my psyche has ever been the same since learning of Monicas passing. I am no longer the same human being.

Throughout these pages I will address both you E.A., and H.A at various intervals throughout the text. Monica was the love of my life, I will never stop loving her and I will never forget the days and nights of our seven years together that our now immortal. Peace and love,

Von.

No fighter will hit you as hard as life-Rocky Balboa.

CHAPTER I:

Lilly Chicoine stood over the body of the eighteen year old man who had just O.D.'d. He had just graduated from High School the previous night. His wallet was full of money. He had been a show off, graciously shoving a handful of one hundred dollar bills in her face as soon as she stepped into his car. Now here he was, dead one day after he was supposed to go on with his life, not a breath in his body.

There was such a thing as making your own bed, and this guy had more than made his. She had prepared a hit for him and told him not to do the whole thing at once but he had chosen not to listen. He had removed the plunger from the syringe and dumped more powder on top of that of which she had already supplied for him.

Now she would have to go to the pay phone downstairs in the hotel and call The Police. She would also probably need to call a lawyer to clear herself of all involvement.

It had been years since she had left David Dane. Things between them hadn't ended well and The Police had ended up getting involved, it had been like a storm, twisting and turning itself into a hurricane, and then spiralling completely out of control, that, and there was another explanation for things happening the way they did.

Dane and Lilly had, had a verbal altercation over the phone and then the sleaze bag that she had been with at the time had encouraged her to call the cops because he himself was afraid that David Dane was going to kick his candy ass, and truth be known, the legendary David Dane surely would have.

It was only a day late and a dollar short that Lilly had realized what a chicken shit little punk that guy had really been. Dane had called him out over the phone and the best that the coward could do in defence of himself was to hang up. What a goof, she had later called him via a third party.

She had also heard through the grape vine that Dane had been charged with one count of utter death threats and ended up spending eighteen very harsh hours in THE HOLE over the entire ordeal. It had been her who had put him there, but there was a dark and insidious secret behind that to, one that both she and Dane had held onto to this day, neither being anxious to discuss what they knew with anyone.

She thought that he had also spent four days in jail as well. Hmm … … … … Maybe now, in the time that had passed they could find a way to work things out. Lilly Chicoine had also heard that there was a Book about the seven years that she and David Dane had spent together, and that it was called URBAN RAIN, it was apparently, a Montreal cult classic.

She's famous. She thought to herself, recognizing herself in the third person. It was a trait that David Dane had always found adorable, it seemed to bring to light Lillys orphanish qualities thus making her even more adorable then she already was by nature.

When The Police arrived Lilly told them what happened and they had filled out a report. She was not going to be charged but she should retain a lawyer for her own safety anyway in case the situation ever went to court. She would do just that, but it would have to be legal aid council for Lilly Chicoine could afford nothing else.

David Dane stood in the glistening heat of Ontario Street. It was twelve am, and the night for this hour was strangely quiet. He had not dropped by the apartment since seven or eight, and he wondered if Marcel or maybe Bill had been by or had tried to call the house line.

There had been a missed call on his cell phone earlier that had come from a private number. Dane wondered if it might have been one of his two closest comrades calling to check in on him. There was no way to tell. He would have to wait for whoever it was to call back.

This night had brought with it many memories. He had fallen asleep earlier and dreamt of Lilly. Somewhere inside of him he had never stopped loving her, and almost all of his dreams reflected it. He was nothing if not haunted, a tormented soul who seemed to be waiting for the love of his life to walk back through the door and rekindle their relationship.

Many a night he had awoken to his own tears wincing in the aftermath of their salt. He had seen her in his sleep so many times and been disappointed when he had awakened only to find out that she wasn't there after all.

He would forever love her, no matter what she had done in the past, or what they had been through together.

There were so many memories between them, so many dreams and special moments that had taken place in a dark and hypnotic neighbourhood known simply as Ontario Street that night itself seemed to own. It also seemed to own Lilly as well as the flair for wickedness that existed within her character, existing like a soulless entity.

Lilly was somehow, bad to the bone.

"You have hair." A punk rocker remarked as Dane walked past him at a stroll. Indeed, the flashy bad boy had grown a head of jet black locks over the past few years. Tonight though, he was dressed to the nines wearing a black sport coat over blue jeans and dress boots.

"You're seeing things." David Dane said in return for a grin.

A Police cruiser rolled past him with the window down its occupants both male cops who had seen David Dane around many times before and knew who he was, both also owned a copy of Urban Rain, it had become an instant cult classic with all of the boys down at the station because most of the book took place on the streets that they patrolled every night. Danes book was a source of east end pride.

They were proud of it, and proud of David Dane for writing it. He was an East End Legend.

There was always an entranced feeling to being on Ontario Street. This neighbourhood and these streets were one of a kind. They made you feel like you were dreaming even though you were awake, and sometimes bad things happened here, sometimes you made it home to a normal brush with reality and other times you simply didn't.

It was 2012, and there had been many casualties of Ontario Street not the least of which was his relationship with Lilly and their friends who had died.

He had given birth to the fame of this neighbourhood, and no matter what he would not let it die. He was happy to be heralded as The Ontario Street Original. There had been good times and bad times, happy times and sad times, but this neighbourhood, this BAD END OF TOWN, was to David Dane, home, and there was no place like it.

"Heads up man." A tall lanky kid with dread locks greeted. Dane did not recognize him.

"I remember you from back in the day when you were with that chick. Alpha Latin." He finally recalled rolling a joint between two fingers and then licking the strip.

Dane nodded. He still did not recognize the stoner who had just approached him. Maybe he was a loner, or maybe he had been around back in the day but David Dane did not recognize him but then again, there were a million faces. It was impossible to remember them all.

"Fuck. How old are you man"?? The punk asked.

"Thirty seven."

"Heads up Mothafucka." He said smiling.

Danes expression was blank.

"You're a hero around here. Everybody knows you. You straight wicked. We all read your Book."

Dane was surprised that this kid, whoever he was, could read at all. "You play base ball"?? Dane asked demonstrating a swing.

"Huh"?? The greasy looking punk retorted amidst an indignant expression that was intrinsic of screwing up his face.

"Anyone ever hit you in the head with the bat"??

"Yeah man. You like the Don Wuan of Ontario Street."

"Don Wuan"?? Dane asked amidst a humoured frown. He had never heard that one before.

"Yeah Boss. You straight up. We love you round here. Peace."

"Happy trails." Dane said in a neutral voice. He was leaning forward on his left toe and squinting with the same eye. It was partial blindness, but he preferred it to having to look at all of this guy at once. He may have been full of compliments and kind gestures but he looked like he had just crawled out from underneath a lump of coal in that sat someplace in Hell.

There was a sudden flash of light in the distance and then the intermittent sound of fire crackers. Dane assumed that it was the same two kids who had been setting off flares outside of his building over the past couple of weeks, it seemed like this neighbourhood never got tired. Outside The Black Domino Tavern there were a group of university students celebrating a birthday.

"It took you long enough to get here." Dane greeted as Bill Ramirez walked up out of the shadows. He was holding a news paper by his side with the stock market page exposed.

"Yeah man. I'm sorry. I had to go speak to my Tenant for a moment."

"Have you eaten"??

"No, not yet. I've been running around all evening trying to do this and that. My stomach's growling so loud that I can almost hear it."

"Wanna grab a burger?? There's not much open at this hour." Dane commented pinching both ends of his nose between his thumb and forefinger in lew of scratching them.

"Yeah man. I'm up for a burger if you wanna go."

Dane was nodding now, agreed.

Ten minutes later and four blocks east Dane and Ramirez walked into an all night eatery that served a wide menu.

"Ah. Hey. Look who here." A tall skinny Haitian said through a mouthful of food. Dane recognized him as a gang member who lived in the area. "It David fucken Dane." He announced.

"Clinton, how the fuck did you get off your leash"?? The Ontario Street Original asked with an intense look in his eyes.

Bill was beginning to fret. He did not want to be in the middle of a shooting spree if that's what this came to. He had enough shit at work, now it looked like he would be involved in this to. His friends reputation had earned him some enemies, there was no motivator like fame and no angst like ego.

"Yeh. He the fuckin white boy who wrote two books."

"Was that supposed to be an insult"?? Dane retorted. He did not want this to go any further, no good could come of it, not here where there were a bunch of innocent bystanders who also served up fries as witnesses.

"Yeah, he write books but he don't wanna know bout my bad side."

Clinton was not alone. There were six other lowlifes with him.

"Man, she look fine." One of the hoodlums said as a stunning blond with big blue eyes, a goddess figure, and a sparkling blue and white top walked by. "And isn't that a wonderful turn of events for me"?? She retorted.

Bill was ordering now and it looked as though he might not get to eat his food in peace. Why did this shit always have to happen when he was around. He made his living as a bouncer, but if this escalated, he would not be compensated for his quandry.

"Dane man, let them run there mouths." He said underneath his breath.

"Yes Sir. Can I help you"?? The Counter attendant asked.

"I'll have a cheese burger and a small fry." David Dane responded watching the group of punks over his right shoulder at the same time. He had seen the incredible blond with the monochrome blue eyes once before. Her name was Jaime, something or other.

"What do you people say, ohhh, i'm out. Cheers." The blond said before locking eyes with David Dane for a second tipping her shake in his direction. She was a ten, a modern day Marilyn Monroe with more looks and hot as hell, like fire!!!

"Man. Rush him"!!!!!!!!!!!! Someone called out.

In seconds Dane was on the ground bleeding and the punks were on their way out the door.

"FUCK. Call an ambulance man." Ramirez demanded.

One of Clinton's boys had stuck David Dane in the back with a shank. "Bill, get me some water." Dane requested in a gravelly voice and then about a day later he woke up in a hospital bed. Bill had been there the whole time and Marcel had been in and out.

"What the fuck happened"?? Dane asked. His voice was lifeless and tired. They had given him Morphine to quell the pain and his brain was swimming in it.

"You got stabbed in the ribs, that's what happened." Bill responded.

"Oh, David. You're awake." Marcel commented as he entered the room. He was carrying a funnel shaped cup with water in it. "It has make many hours that you were asleep." He said.

"Yeah, well, that's Clinton's fault, not mine." The Boxer retorted.

"This is getting serious man. It seems that everyone and their dog wants to take a run at you over this book." Ramirez said. "It's like there's a bulls eye painted on your forehead."

"Or on my ribs."

Marcel chuckled. He was almost laughing now.

"Has anyone called my Mother and told her what happened"??

"I don't know. I haven't, but the hospital might have." Bill answered. He himself looked tired and worse for wear.

"Someone needs to call her right now. Where the fuck's my cell phone"??

"I think I have maybe seen it on the table." Marcel remarked. "Oh yes, it is there." He said retrieving it and handing it to his friend.

Dane immediately placed a call to his Mother and told her what happened.

"Here. Take it." He said handing the phone back to Marcel who placed it back on the table.

"What did she say"?? Ramirez wanted to know.

"She didn't, she was to busy yelling at me for hanging around down there late at night.

"She probably was very upset." Marcel commented.

"Yeah, like my water. Who the fuck knocked it over"?? Dane asked noticing the plastic cup that was sitting on the floor by the bed.

"I will get you another one." Marcel said tipping the stainless steel picture above a fresh cup.

"It's good to see you dude." Dane directed toward Marcel. "It's good to see both of you."

"Yeah man, i'm just happy to see you alive. When we left that burger joint I didn't know what the fuck was gonna happen."

"Glad, for your concern." Dane remarked. "What happened to that salamander"??

"What, the guy"?? Ramirez asked.

"Did he sleaze his way out the back door or what"??

"I don't know. I was to busy keeping vigil over you."

"Yeah." Marcel said with a smile. "It is good that you are okay."

Just then a kind looking elderly nurse appeared in the doorway. "Feeling better I see."

"Better than I was yeah." Dane said. "Thank you."

"If you need anything just push that little button by the bed. It rings directly into the nurses station."

"I will. Cheers."

"Oh … … Well. Maybe I will go. It has make a lot to much time since I slept."

"And what's with that long hair? You look like the mature version of River Phoenix."

Marcel smiled and gave a gesture with his shoulder. It meant that he did not have an answer to Danes question. "Well. I will go." He said.

"I appreciate the concern bro. Thanks for coming to my rescue."

Marcel nodded with his hands held behind his back soldier style.

Later on that night Dane twisted and turned in his sleep. Lilly was there, in his mind as always. There were a series of sea side brown stones shaped like concrete boxes each one hanging off the side of the other with vacant windows that were open onto the air filtering cold darkened winds and the breeze off the sea scape through their openings, it was a sight of both the eerie and the surreal.

Down below there were white and silver capped waves that exploding violently against the shoreline and then frothed against the edges of the darkened beach. Somewhere in the sky a light house beacon swooned and soared above all that could be seen. It appeared to be just past dusk. Lilly stood in the distance with her hair blowing in the current. She was alone. There wasn't a soul in sight.

Inside himself Dane felt the urge to cry, his love for her was as undying as was Lilly's penchant for evil that seemed to grow with each hour that fitful torturous sleep went on.

Soon he appeared standing behind her but she did not turn around to greet at him, her face rather sustained its cruel mask. She was as harsh and as remorseless as the core of evil itself. She wore a denim jean suit over black stilettos with crimson lip stick and a high collar.

"What are you doing here"?? She asked crossly.

"I don't know." He said. "I woke up here but I think i'm dreaming."

"You should have stayed away. All that you're ever gonna get from me is jail because I just used you. You know that, i'm a con. I say whatever I have to to get what I want." She said cold heartedly.

Dane raised his hands slightly in an attempt to embrace Lilly's shoulders from behind.

He could feel his heart beating smoothly and rhythmically beneath the material of his black T-Shirt. All that he wanted to do was hold her and tell her how much he had missed her. There was a fever inside of him. None of that came out of him. He was muted by a nocturnal force. Missing her had been the worst experience that he'd ever had to endure.

"I love you." He said intensely.

She did not reply.

"Being away from you has hurt me so much. I dream about you every night." He said as the glare from the light house spread over the ocean like a silent current of electricity, and with his last word Lilly vanished back into the air from which she had come, a vapour inside of sleep.

The next morning when everything was quiet Dane packed a leather bag and headed for the front doors of the hospital. He felt better, his head had cleared and he wanted to move around a bit. He was sick of being strapped to an IV when he felt there was no further need for it.

Now, with the sun in sight he made his way through the busy hospital lobby and down a flight of stairs. There was pain for a moment that made him wince. It was like a surge of energy running through him. Christ, it was sharp.

He hoped that none of his stitches had come out. He quickly lifted his sweatshirt and reached up and behind him, no blood when he brought his hand into view. Thank God, such an incident would most certainly have sent him running back upstairs. If there were worse places than hospitals then Dane did not know what they were, except possibly prisons.

Soon there were a series of glinting automobiles in front of him parked along several curbs. The shrubbery was magnificent and the trees green. It was great to be out in the world again. Hell had reached its pinnacle for him upstairs in that room. He had been prodded and poked by doctor after doctor, nurse after nurse, and now he was free.

There was a certain mystique about being released from the hospital, even if you weren't cleared for discharge yet. He did not want a repeat of the other night. Sometimes being The Ontario

Street Original came at a price, and sometimes that price could be high. There were a series of bushes surrounding the perimeter of the properly and Dane quickly cleared them.

Now, the next order of business would be locating lunch.

There were several restaurants in the area he recalled, and one of them was a Spanish Diner. Well, at least it was owned by Hispanics. They had always been very kind and welcoming to their local hero often preparing dishes exclusively for the man in the dark glasses.

One of the times that he had stopped by was when he was promoting his Book. He had left over six thousand fliers underneath windshield wipers, in Coffee houses, underneath front doors and anywhere and everywhere else that one could think of. URBAN RAIN had earned him the status of "Cult Hero" in the east end of the city. Finally, in his life, he was a somebody.

"Montreal Legend David Dane leaves hospital." He joked aloud. "To bad he can't stop a knife wielding maniac."

Soon, he heard the squealing of tires and for a moment his mind drifted back four years to a bad time in his life. He thought of how he had been placed in handcuffs inside of his apartment in another city and loaded into a waiting Police cruiser outside of his front doors. He had been charged with uttering death threats against Lilly. They had been on the phone and Lilly had confessed that she had used him and his Family and Dane had lost control of himself. Then there was the matter of the punks involvement in the whole fiasco.

The revelation was so hate inspiring and over powering that Dane had called back and left a death threat on her answering machine. The second incentive was that when Dane had questioned her as to who had been in the room with her and she had said no one, but he could hear it in her voice, feel it in the rise and fall of her breathing. There were those reasons, and "THE REASON," the secret that Dane and Lilly shared.

Someone else had been there alright, he had grabbed the phone from her a few minutes later and told Dane to leave Lilly alone. That's when Dane had challenged whoever it was on the other end. He had told the fucking little punk to come out and meet him, and then the phone had gone dead.

Hours went by where he walked around and around one park after another reeling from what he had heard. She had stolen almost seven years from him and then she had put him in jail. The third prompt for the threat was something that Lilly's Mother had said. Her exact words according to Lilly were-"I want you to leave Montreal in Montreal and that includes David Dane."

All this after having sworn to Dane in phone conversations that he would never lose Lilly when she went to rehab and would always be welcomed in their homes, but Lilly's Mother, just like Lilly, had lied. She had given him her word that he wasn't going to lose her Daughter who Dane would always love and cherish above and beyond anyone on this earth aside from his own niece.

It was, as Danes Uncle had predicted at the time, all a set up. She simply used him to get her Daughter home and then discarded him as though he were so much garbage. He could still hear his late Uncles voice in his head telling him that Linda Chicoine would use him and then toss him away after she had re acquired her Daughter.

Thomas's profiling skills had been right on. She had done just that. He could still hear Thomas's voice saying to him-"Son, and how dare that woman call you up? She's just using you to get to her Daughter and after she has her Daughter back she'll discard you. You're expendable." Absolutely fucking right. He had predicted Linda Chicoine down to the last detail.

When Danes Mother had shown up at the court house to bail him out there had been a message on her cell phone. It had been Danes Father. He was in his office back home suffering a massive heart attack brought on by the stress of all that was going on.

"I loved you." Dane said to the hot, dry, air. There were flecks of tear on his face. He was speaking to Lilly on a spiritual level, he had never forgotten her, and never let her go. The ties that bound the two together were immortal.

However now, he did not harbour any anger or resentment against Linda Chicoine. Aside from believing that one day he would give her a small pay back in the lines of one of his Books, which he had done, he also had many fond memories of phone conversations that he'd had with Lilly's Mother in the past as well as of the day that they had met.

One of the reasons that Linda's words had cut so deeply was because Dane had believed up until that moment that Linda and

Gregory Chicoine legitimately liked him but had then changed their minds for no discernible reason.

Then it crossed his mind that he might've discovered a place on earth that was worse than the hospital. They had stuck him in The Hole for eighteen hours when he was inside, that, had been FAR WORSE than any hospital and they had played cruel tricks on him when they discovered that he was afraid.

In his flashback he saw the big steel door with the small window in it close. There was a guard standing outside who had ushered him in and gave him a garment to wear, that in itself, resembled the most common of hospital gowns.

They had given him a hospital style gown that was made of a sturdier fabric. It almost reminded him of canvas or the material that was used inside of some baby cribs to keep them from leaking when babies urinated.

That Tuesday night had been the most horrible night of David Danes life. He had seen animals that were bred for slaughter who were treated better than he was. The screws played mind games with him until his heart raced so fast that it almost quit on him pumping blood like a machine that was designed for it that was more than simply an organ.

One of the female guards who had sensed Danes nervousness had, as Dane would later discover, staged a conversation with another female guard who said that they were going to keep him in there sunrise after sunrise, sunset after sunset, and say that Dane was to violent to see the judge. It put the fear of The Devil into him. There was no torture worse than being incarcerated or institutionalized, none whatsoever, bar none.

All in all he had learned one thing in his experience. You could easily end up being punished at the end of a long and winding road that you had paved with good intentions. All that he had ever done was love Lilly and protect her and this was how she had thanked him.

The windshield of his memory was flanked with sunlight now. The next frame saw he and Lilly up late one night eating bacon. Lilly had awakened to the scent of the bacon wafting over her head and couldn't resist it, it was making her nuts.

"Fuck. What's that smell. It was driving me crazy." She had commented.

Dane had been so happy to have her there.

There had been nothing to eat in the house and the two were starving but he had located the bacon buried in some ice in the freezer. Back then they didn't live like Kings and Queens but they had each other. He missed those days and he still had dreams about them.

They were and always would be the most special years of his life. They were years that were surreal like the glinting dreams that proceeded them. There wasn't a night that went by where he didn't dream of Lilly Chicoine, sometimes he would dream of her two or three times in a night. The dreams were always intense and took him to places that he had never been before. Each dream was the same in one aspect though, Lilly was in all of them, and each aftermath was the same as well, desperate and empty, lonely and forlorn, crying hopelessly into the fabric of his pillow.

He would wake up aching because she wasn't there, heart broken.

All that he wanted was to see her one more time, to hold her in his arms and kiss her. There was nothing that he wouldn't give to be called her boyfriend for one more day. He would have happily married her had the occasion arisen, despite all the sadness and wickedness. She still meant everything to him. He had suffered greatly on her account, but for some reason that didn't change his feelings for her. Love had a way of keeping you there.

When David Dane loved someone he was all there, no part of him was left outside. There were many who faulted him for hanging on, but that was who he was, he had always taken being Lilly's boyfriend seriously. If he could go back to the place in time where they met he would do it all again just to be with her. Lilly meant that much to him, his Fashion Model Heroin Addict Girlfriend.

If he lived a billion lifetimes he knew that no one would ever replace her or replace the memories that they created together. Why life had taken her away from him he would never know. Being without her was the most wicked dream that he had ever experienced. It was like all of the sunshine had been sucked out of his world and left him in the dark. There would never be a dream of life any greater or with any more intensity than holding her in his arms one more time.

"Hey, aren't you David Dane"?? A heavy set woman asked bringing him back to reality.

"What"?? He asked coming down from the state that he was in. "Do I know you"??

"No, but I read your Book. I recognized you from your photographs. I was just wondering if I could have your autograph."

"Yeah, absolutely.." Dane said soberly, no longer adrift on the sea of memory. He had suddenly come crashing back to reality and to the sun soaked day around him. "You got a pen"?? He asked.

The woman reached into her bag and retrieved a shiny blue Bic felt tip. "To Sylvia." She said.

"Huh. I'm sorry. I'm a little dazed."

"That's my name. Sylvia. If you could sign it "To Sylvia" from David Dane Wallace i'd be so impressed.

"No problem." Dane said, doing just that.

"There you go." He said when he was finished. He capped her pen and placed it back in her hand.

"Thank you. I'm so honoured. I love reading about you and Lilly. Are those stories true or did you fictionalize all of that stuff"??

"Well, like they say. Use your imagination."

"I can't wait to go home and tell my Mother that I met David Dane Wallace." The woman said holding the book with both hands. "Well. I mean. She reads about you to. There's just something in those pages that tells me that Lilly's real and that you actually lived all of those experiences. I was SOOOO SAD when the two of you went your separate ways. I mean I literally shed a tear on every page of your novel."

"Yeah, you and me both."

"I go to Ontario Street all the time and walk around all of the places that are on those pages."

"Yeah. I kinda second that one to. I appreciate that."

"Anyway, thanks for signing my Book. You're amazing. I'll always treasure this. You should write a sequel." Sylvia said backing away.

"The thought has crossed my mind."

Two blocks over and three minutes later Dane encountered a group of Police Officers who were sitting outside having lunch. Four out of five of them raised their hands to salute David Dane in greeting. He had become a local monarch. He was being recognized on sight now, and quickly. The east end loved him.

"This is real man." One of the cops said smiling. Dane saluted him with two fingers and kept going. Just then his phone lit up.

"Hello. Chung Lee's Chinese Wicker Emporium." He answered.

"I was wondering where you were." Marilyn Dane said on the other end. Dane could hear his Father in the background. He had fully recovered from his heart attack.

"I'm on my way home from The Hospital. What a terrific place to get out of."

"I'll bet. What happened"??

"Someone doesn't like my writing style." Dane said stepping off of a curb.

"Oh, why?? What happened"??

"Someone stuck me with a four inch shank."

"Did The Police find him"??

"No cops, i'm in enough trouble. I didn't give them a statement. Shit never seems to slow down does it"??

"I've never seen anyone who was in such constant turmoil." Marilyn remarked.

"Life's remorseless. Are you still going to Korea"??

Marilyn Dane was a professional Figure Skating Coach. She was Canadian Alumni. Next year she was going to Korea to coach one of her athletes. His name was Paul.

Around the next corner just before the intersection Dane heard a loud siren wailing through the afternoon breeze. There were flashing lights everywhere. "What in Christs name"?? He wondered aloud.

"What was that"?? His Mother asked.

"Hold on. I have another line." David Dane said.

"Hello."

"Dane? It's Lilly."

"Oh my God. Hold on. I have someone on the other line."

Dane clicked back to his Mother. "Yeah. Listen. I have to go."

"Who is it"??

"I'll tell you later." He responded. "Lilly." He greeted switching back over. "I can't believe it's you." Dane said almost breaking down. How the fuck did you get this number"??

"I got it from Marcel. His number's in the Book."

"Jesus, you know that you nearly got me killed in jail."

"I know. I'm sorry. I was fucked up"

"Where have you been all these years"?? He questioned.

"Here, there, and everywhere." She said nonchalantly.

"Where are you now"?? He asked. He felt his voice beginning to quiver, as if all of his emotions were flooding back at once. It was shining through in his voice and he knew it, piercing Ontario Streets blanket of night inside of him.

"I'm in lock up."

"Why am I not surprised to hear that"??

There wasn't much background noise. He was surprised. Usually there were cell doors being opened and closed as well as a multitude of female voices. Now, there were none of those things.

"Why so quiet. Where is everybody"??

"I'm in isolation. They let me use a the phone once every few days."

"Why are you in isolation"??

"Because i've been charged with murder."

"What the fuck do you mean murder? Whose murder"? Dane couldn't believe what he was hearing. Lilly had been to jail a thousand times but never for a Federal Offence. This was a whole new bag of beans.

"Another street girl. I was in the room but I didn't do it."

"What was the COD"??

"The cause of death"?? Lilly enquired. "Multiple stab wounds to the head and body." She responded casually.

"Jesus Christ." Dane said looking around. He was completely astonished. "What city are you in"??

"Montreal. I'm back for fuckin what, two days and this happens. I swear to God this city's wanted to put me away for eons."

Dane was rubbing the back of his head with the palm of his hand.

"I heard about the book. Urban Rain. Cool title. So, you're a big shot author now"??

"Yeah, big shot." Dane responded flatly. He was not impressed with himself.

Dane was not even paying attention. She had completely floored him. He was in a word, speechless. There were no words to express his dilemma. He was sick to his stomach.

"I missed you Boo." Lilly said.

"Who's representing you"??

"Right now? Phillip."

"Thank God for that. How is he"?? Dane enquired changing the direction in which he was standing.

"He's good, still Kick Boxes. He won a title."

"Yeah"?

Phillip had been Lilly's lawyer in the past. He and Dane had a strong rapport with one another.

"What comes next"??

"Bail hearing. Phillip says it won't happen. The charges are to serious and the penalty's to high."

"Fu-u-u-ck"

"They brought me Chocolate Pudding from the canteen earlier."

Dane felt emotion rising inside of him. He still loved this woman. She had always and would always own his soul. There was no moving past that. The fact of the matter was that he could not provide her with a lawyer, such a case would almost definitely cost hundreds of thousands of dollars.

"What kind of evidence do they have"??

"My finger prints on the murder weapon."

"Jesus. Compelling."

"Nope, he has nothing to do with it. Actually we're not even speaking right now."

Dane laughed bitterly. "This is gonna run somebody. Thrill my fuckin guerrilla."

"One more time. Please." Lilly said.

"I never stopped loving you. I still dream about you like at least once a night."

"Why doesn't that surprise me"?? The sexy Latina asked. "Do you still lift weights"??

"When they're not lifting me."

"I gotta go. My time's up."

"Wait. When will I hear from you again"??

"Hold on. Let me ask. Guard. When will I be allowed to use the phone again"??

"Oh. They don't know." She answered.
"Lilly. I still love you."
"How many times"?? She asked jokingly.

Dane let a cry and a laugh escape him at the same time. It was all he could do to control his heart rate. This moment had almost brought him to his knees. There was a flash of light somewhere in the distance and then he was momentarily taken back to a night inside of The Black Domino Tavern from around the time that he and Lilly had first met.

The bar was dark and there were multiple dreads seated at each table smoking up. He had been walking around when one of them had chastised him for moving around to much, but Lilly had defended him. She had threatened to "KNOCK ROCKS" with the bitch if she didn't fuck off.

Dane raised a hand to his eyes to wipe away the tears.
"Boo, I gotta go now." Lilly said.
"I love you Baby Bunny."
"You to."
Five streets ahead Dane dialled Marcel's number.

"Oui. Hello." Marcel greeted on the other end of the line. "Have you had a call from Lilly"??

Dane was nodding in response even though that would mean nothing to Marcel. "I have." He finally managed. "She called me a few minutes ago. She's in jail."

"Yes, she has told me something like that." He said.

"She's up on homicide charges. She's gonna need a good fucking lawyer to get herself out of this one. Her finger prints are all over the murder weapon."

"That is shit, monduire." Monduire was French for "My God." There was a stiff pause. "It has make a lot to many times that she has been in trouble."

Dane almost laughed. He loved the way that Marcel worded things sometimes. He had one of the most unique characters that he had ever known, and he was short.

"Next time that you're down on your knees doing Yoga, make sure that you say a prayer for Lilly."

"Oui, okay."

A car rounded the corner momentarily breaking Danes concentration as he looked across the street before stepping down off of the curb and heading toward a local Depaneur. There were sixty million reasons to let Lilly swing, but one reason on the other hand was enough for him not to.

She was and would forever be the love of his life. They had spent so many years together and experienced so much that David Dane would never be able to let go of her. She had stretched his emotions so far that he couldn't come back, but there was also a bond there that could never be broken.

"She has maybe gone to far this time."

"God, I hope not. Who will I have to write books about if that's the case"??

Marcel chuckled. "Oui Sevre. It is true."

"How are your sons"?? Dane asked.

"Oh, good. They are doing well. I think they are doing more money than me." He said with a laugh.

"You're a positive person Marcel. Good that they learned from you."

"Yes, thank you." The French Man said in a humble voice.

"Lilly Chicoine. How do you plead"?? The Judge asked.

"Your Honour my client wishes to enter a plea of not guilty." Phillip Laroche said.

"I'm going to deny bail given the circumstances and severity of the crime as well as the fact that Miss Chicoine has proven to be a flight risk in the past. Do you have anything else to say before we adjourn for the day Mr. Laroche"??

"No Your Honour."

"Court is in recess until nine am tomorrow morning."

David Dane walked through the doors to The Black Domino Tavern at three o' clock that afternoon, across from him was the Father of Clinton, the man who had put him in the hospital with a severe stab wound only days ago, but in this case, Father and son were solar systems apart.

Dane greeted the elderly Haitian with a handshake and then ushered him into a chair. One wouldn't have guessed Clinton's Father to be a year older than sixty, but in truth, he had earned several more candles atop his cake than that.

"I came to this country when I was five years years old" Olden began. "My Father was a proud man. He expected great things from his children. He wanted all of us to work for what we got. There was never a day that went by that he didn't push us to do well. I lost my Mother when I was eight years old to Cancer. So, I did what I could to honour her memory by always being the kind of person that I know that she would have wanted me to be.

My people, my Brothers and Sisters, we believe in God. Every night we would get down on our knees and pray. We would sing hymns and read stories from The Bible. God is great. God is great." Olden repeated.

There were tears in David Danes eyes. He knew this old man and he knew what he stood for. They had known each other for many years, at least six or seven. Dane had even helped Olden move into the house where he lived now, but his relationship with Oldens son was not the same, even at the beginning it had been tenuous at best.

"I tried to teach my son the things that I learned. I tried to read him stories from The Bible but he didn't want to follow me. I've done everything that I know how to do as a Father to guide him, but Clinton is bad."

David Dane was nodding now. There were still tears in his eyes. He truly believed Olden when Olden said that he had done everything that he could to guide Clinton properly and that something had gone horribly wrong. He himself was now wearing the scars of Clinton's wayward ways. Eventually, he knew, there would be retribution.

"My son did something terrible to you I know. Everybody knows. He'll answer to God for what he's done on this Earth. You can't cheat our maker, and you can't go against his teachings." Olden said raising himself to stand up.

"Thank you for coming to meet me Olden." Dane said rising to meet his elder. His hand was extended.

Olden paused for a moment as tears formed in his own eyes. He then embraced Dane as a Father would a son and cried for a moment into his shoulder.

Twenty minutes later Bill Ramirez dropped two quarters into a pay phone and waited for a ring tone.

"Hello." The woman at the hospital switch board answered on the other end.

"Yeah. I need David Danes room. Room 201."

"Just give me a moment." The switch board operator said punching something into her desk top.

"I'm sorry, but Mr. Dane left the hospital this morning."

"Whatdya mean, like discharged himself"??

"I don't know. I just know that he's not here."

"DAMMIT"!!! Bill shouted hanging up the phone. He couldn't believe it. Dane had no business being out of bed yet. His wounds hadn't even had time to heal properly. This was typical him, bad to the bone and stubborn as a mule. He hoped that Dane would have at least gone home as opposed to going somewhere to hang out.

Ramirez eye balled his watch and then sucked his teeth aggressively He had to be at work in a couple of hours which wouldn't give him enough time to visit David Dane. There was likely to be a second stay at The Medicine Motel if Dane didn't take care of himself, and possibly a third.

"Yeah. Excuse me sir. Can I get one of those fliers." Ramirez asked. Bill was good at saving money. He always kept an eye out for specials, this had been a habit of his for a long time.

Now, his mind shifted to work. He would have to go the full distance of an eight hour shift tonight. He was back to working as a doorman again. Great man, and this shit on top of his shift.

He had his own safety to worry about as well as David Danes for the duration of the evening. He hoped that Dane wouldn't be vapid enough to go searching for his enemies in his present condition. Maybe he would try and give Dane a call before his shift started, that at least would help to put his mind at rest. He did not want to finish out his shift tonight only to find out that his friend of thirteen years was back in a hospital bed.

"Fuck." Bill said dropping a flier on the ground. When he looked up there was a Haitian male with three other men standing in front of him. He didn't recognize any of them.

"I tink dat yah know somebody dat we know." One of the three in front said.

"Oh yeah. Who's that"?? Bill asked. He was playing stupid but the obvious answer was David Dane.

The corridor that led into the mall seemed to condense all of a sudden.

"Yah know Mr. David Dane. What, not yah gonna be nice to us boy. We gonna kill you to. We want yah give Dane a message. We don't feel like playin wit him no more. We speakin bout dee odar night."

"Look man. I don't know who you are but if you have a problem with David maybe you should go take it up with him yourself." Bill said, but he was thinking Fire Extinguisher. There was one a few feet away. If he could clear two feet he could probably get to it. "Fuck." He said under his breath.

"Yah just do what yer told and go and tell Dane dat we gonna see him soon."

"Fuck you man." Bill retorted. "Go see him yourself."

"Yah got notten on us. Aint no point in steppin up. We gon gat yah." One of the other gang members said.

"Look man." Bill managed, but there were four of them and one of him. The most muscular of the foursome grazed Ramirez with a glancing blow to the temple before the others jumped in and started kicking him in the head.

He was down on the ground fighting for his life now. The mall had been busy, but not so busy that the group of thugs couldn't hide what they were doing. They were in a hallway that housed the corridor to the mens and womens washrooms as well as a series of tunnels that led to various apartment complexes.

When the group was done they left Ramirez lying on the ground in a heap. He had gashes to his eyes, nose, lips, and head. There was a pool of blood below him. There were shards of shoe lace in his teeth.

"OH MY GOD"!!! A woman said coming out of nowhere. "Call an ambulance. Call an ambulance." ... ... She shouted.

By the time that David Dane came through the door to his apartment he was sweating bullets. Some of the stitches had come out and he was beginning to feel weak as well as nauseated. When he got to his lazy boy he was nearly keeled over. The pain of two days ago had returned and his pulse was drumming in his head.

"Christ." He muttered collapsing into the arms of the leather seat.

As he reclined, he began to dream of Lilly again. This time he was searching a bank of abandoned rooms for her. The place looked like a small Caribbean Island Resort, it's outer perimeter lined with palm trees and white sands. There were people sitting in Cabanas drinking from Coconuts and sipping Margaritas.

Inside of his dream Dane looked up into the sky that was clear blue with hints of puffy white cloud. If you listened closely you could hear the surf in the distance. There were gulls swooning above and then diving low to search for food. Somewhere, a 1957 Chevy idled its engines at the end of a peer. The suns glare was everywhere producing a surreal and powerful glint.

"I'm looking for my girlfriend." Dane said to a stranger on The Boardwalk.

The man turned to look at him and then pointed in the direction of The Beach Side Resort.

As Dane stepped back inside underneath the churn of the multiple white ceiling fans he heard what sounded like moaning coming from one of the upstairs bedrooms. He then ascended the stairs one by one before looking into the first room. There on the bed was Lilly. She was in the throws of passion amidst glistening flesh and perspiration.

"Yeah." She moaned. "Harder." She ordered the young Latin man below her.

Dane immediately rushed into the room to attack his foe but was interrupted by his own brush with reality.

"LILLY"!!!

When Lilly reached her cell that night she was exhausted and had little energy to do anything but sleep. She had been raked over the coals by Detectives and Investigators all day as well as Police

Officers, and Prosecutors, and still she had not met with her Lawyer this evening.

It would be a new Lawyer however as she would need someone with a different background to represent her in a murder trial. There would be accusations flying toward her from every angle. The proverbial shit was going to hit the fan, and she would be centre stage for all of it. The Guest Of Honour.

As soon as she sat down on the edge of the bed Lilly immediately thought of food.

She fantasized about the spaghetti, weiners, Ketchup, and Taco Sauce that Dane used to put together. She would give anything to have a meal like that right now. They used to jokingly call it- "Phaghetti Nummy." Their pet name for their favourite dish.

"What are we having for dinner tonight"?? She asked the guard.

"I don't know yet." The burly male screw answered. "Maybe Pizza Pockets, but I really don't know."

"Fuck. I'm starving." Lilly whined. She wanted her cigarettes, and a point of Smack would have been the order of the day to but they didn't serve that shit in here.

Just then her cell door was buzzed open and a female attorney with short brown hair and pretty features strolled into Lilly's cell. Lilly thought she was hot.

"Hi Lilly, i'm Nancy Mitchell." The woman said extending her hand. "I'm your new legal council."

"Lilly Chicoine." Her client said.

"So. We've got a lot of ground to cover, so let's get started." Mitchell asserted. "Please state your full name."

"Lilly Lucinda Chicoine."

"And you're originally from where"??

"Well. I was born in Brampton Ontario, so, I guess you could say I was from there."

"Date of Birth."

"Jan 5th., 1978."

Mitchell was taking notes. She had a big briefcase and had rested her legal pad on top of it.

"Okay. So, let me just recap. You're full name is Lilith Lucinda Chicoine. You were born January 5th, 1978 in Brampton Ontario. Is that correct"??

"Uh-huh. Yes."

"Alright, now. You're being charged with murder in the first degree. That's a Federal Offence. The victims name is Kelly Mathews. She's from Cleveland Ohio. How did the two of you first meet each other"??

"Well. We're both Heroin Addicts so most of us eventually get to know each other."

"I mean more specifically." Mitchell said trying to speed things up.

"Hmm … … Let me think. Do you have a cigarette"??

Mitchell patted down the pockets of her trench coat before fishing a gold cigarette holder out of one of the outer pockets. "Here." She said passing Lilly a fresh smoke.

"Thanks ah." Lilly said.

"Do you have a light"?? Lilly asked, the cigarette dangling between her lips. The street was coming out of her. The cigarette dangling from her lips gave her appearance a rougher edge. She looked like any street urchin or female hard rock standing outside of a soup kitchen waiting to be served a portion of the late afternoon menu.

Mitchell handed her a book of matches.

As soon as Lilly lit up she continued. "There's a Bus Station on St. Hubert that was just done over. I THINK we met outside of it. Yeah it was outside."

"Then what"?? Nancy prodded. There was a gentle smile on her lips.

"Weeeee … … … … … waited for the guy together."

"The Guy"?? Mitchell asked leaning slightly forward. She looked bewildered.

"Guy, it's code for DEALER."

"Okay, then what"??

"Oh fuck. Well, we worked opposite each other one night. We're both Prostitutes."

Smoke drifted into the air between them. There were only two places to sit inside the cell. The first was a small wooden bench that was attached to the wall and the second was a small cot where Lilly now sat.

"What else. Lemme see." Lilly continued. "That night I think we actually did a client together." She said.

"You mean, had sex with him"??

"Man Oui. Yes."

"What was that like? I mean. Was there any rivalry? A tension? Anything like that"??

"No, you don't really get into rivalries with other girls when you do clients together. It's just business. You wanna get it done and get your dope and that's it."

"Can you think of anyone who might've wanted Kelly Mathews dead"??

"Yeah. Roberta."

"Okay, who's Roberta"??

"She's a girl that we all know. She's not very pretty so she's kind of jealous of girls like Kelly and I who are."

"And you think that might've given her reason to wanna kill Kelly"??

"I saw them fighting that night. Roberta accused Kelly of trying to steal money from her dresser."

"Okay. Was there a physical altercation or was it just an argument"??

"More like a pushing contest."

"Then what happened"??

"I went to the washroom. When I came back there was blood all over the floor and Kelly was dead. I remember that she had no shoes on and that her head was pushed up against the wall. I was scared so I pulled the knife out of her to use as protection. I was pretty high because I had just done Coke. I was still buzzing a bit but I had come down slightly. I was pretty freaked out."

"Do you know what Roberta's last name is"??

"Hmm … hmm … … … It's Clark." Lilly stated. "I remember that because I was there when she was signing for the room. You have to give your first and last name in some of these places. Sometimes they even ask you for I.D. All I have is my Health Card so I give them that."

"How did The Police find you"??

"Because someone heard screaming and called the front desk. Nice ah"?? Lilly asked. "Of course by the time that Charles got there

I was sitting on the floor with the knife in my hand. I have no one to blame but myself for the cops looking at me as a suspect. I should have left that knife right where I got it."

"Okay. Wait a minute. You mentioned another name. Charles. Who's he"??

"He's the Biker Worker who mans the front desk. He's bald with facial hair and tattoos all over him."

Just then the door was buzzed open and one of the guards wheeled Lilly's dinner in on a trolly. There were Pork Chops, Bacon Bits, and a Juice Pack containing Florida Orange Juice.

"Finally. I'm starving." Lilly said lifting the lid off of one of the trays. "Do you want anything"?? She asked.

"No thank you. I ate earlier on." Mitchell responded graciously. "So, Charles enters the room and finds you with the knife. Were you screaming? What state were you in"??

"I WAS SCARED. Fuck. I've never been in that situation before. There was so much blood that I thought I was gonna faint. It was everywhere."

"Alright. So, Charles goes downstairs and calls The Police and you get arrested."

"Man. Oui. Exactly."

"I'm gonna have my Investigator find Roberta. Do you have any idea where she might be"??

"No. She could be anywhere. The last I saw of her was that night. She might still be at The Hotel."

"What Hotel"??

Lilly furnished Nancy with the name.

Nancy liked Lilly. She was cute, very head strong, but in a determined way, don't tell me what to do or i'll show you who's boss. She could potentially be groomed to testify in her own defence, but Mitchell wasn't sure yet if such a maneuver was wise.

There would be a bevy of questions to answer on cross examination, and Nancy wasn't sure that Lilly could handle it. She wasn't even certain yet as to whether or not Lilly was providing her with all of the facts. Sometimes in cases that involved street kids with their own set of codes, it could be very difficult to un earth the real story behind what had happened.

These street kids, they could be tough, and sometimes it was hard to break them even when it was in their own best interest, some of them were dumb as bed posts while others were whitty and stand your ground no matter what like Lilly Chicoine, and you didn't rat, that was THE cardinal rule.

If Roberta had done it, then this kid certainly had to have a mean streak running through her body because the results of the attack were brutal. The Killer had stabbed Kelly Mathews forty eight times seemingly without blinking. It was a definite rage killing that was flagged with all of the ear marks of a brutal vicious over kill in which most likely the victim had known the perpetrator.

"So, what do you do when you're not lawyering"?? Lilly asked quizzically.

"I have hobbies, I run, I also ride horses."

"Wow, i've never actually rode a horse before. I went for a ride on a Pony when I was a kid. My Mother took me there one time. I mean to the place where they keep horses. There were stables and stuff."

Mitchell thought that Lilly was adorable. She was somehow a grown up kid.

"Tell me about your Family."

"Well, I have two Brothers. I know one of them really well because we grew up together, he always protected me and looked out for me. The other I didn't know very well when I first left because he was still to young. I never really got to know my younger Brother until I came back. He's the baby of the Family, and he's very rich."

"What does he do"?? Mitchell asked.

"He's a musician."

"Where were you for so many years"?? Mitchell asked.

"I was here, in Montreal living with my Boyfriend.

Well, he was my Boyfriend then. His name's David Dane. He's a big shot author now. He actually wrote a Book about the years that we spent together."

"Oh, wait a minute. I saw him on TV last week. It was some Magazine show. Isn't his full name David Dane something?? I think he has black hair."

"That's his author name. His Mothers maiden name is Wallace, so, David Dane Wallace is what he went with. The Book is called URBAN RAIN-AN ODYSSEY THROUGH THE DARKNESS OF

NIGHT." Lilly boasted. "Coming soon to a book store near you." She said smiling as if she were in a commercial.

There were monitors outside the cell, and Nancy glanced up at one of them. They were closed circuit televisions that's colour lineage was blue. She and Lilly were visible on six of them.

"Can I bum another smoke from you"?? Chicoine asked.

This time Mitchell pulled the remainder of the pack from her pocket and gave it to Lilly.

"U huh ... ... I get to keep the whole thing." She said lighting up for the second time that evening.

Mitchell smiled, she was somehow happy to please this particular client.

"So, do you think i'll be convicted"?? Lilly enquired. There was a hint of anxiety in her voice and Mitchell caught it. "Not if I have anything to say about it." She said folding up her binder and shoving it into her leather brief case.

"Can I take the tray"?? A tall muscular screw asked through the bars. Lilly had finished eating and was now having a cigarette for desert.

"Ieeeeee ... ... don't see why not." She said.

The Guard took a set of keys from his belt and slipped one into the slot on the wall. There was a short pause and then the cell door buzzed open. "You're finished with everything"?? He affirmed.

"Yep, i'm finished." The little orphan said sliding her tray through a slot in the big steel door.

"Okay, i'm gonna take the cart. Do you want the desert? I was supposed to bring it earlier but I forgot." He said. "I'm gonna go back and get it."

"What are we having? I'm almost full but if we're having anything chocolate then i'd love to have it."

"I think it's chocolate pudding, so i'm gonna bring it."

"YAY"!!! Lilly celebrated. Chocolate pudding was one of her favourites, she had loved it for years, a favourite from childhood. One of her fondest memories was eating chocolate pudding and watching reruns of Little House On The Prairie while sitting next to her Mother, back then, it was like girls night out, only they were staying home.

The name Michael Landon popped into her head for a moment, and she remembered his character Charles Ingles and the little Family that he had on the TV Show. It gave her comfort because it reminded her of a time before all the problems came about in her life while she was still a kid. That was back before things between she and her Mother had gone bad, back before she had so desired to leave and had done so along with her eldest Brother in the shadow of the moonlight.

For a moment she envisioned that night underneath the stars with both she and Julian holding hands as they ran away together leaving a trail of bread crumbs in their wake like Hansel and Gretel, somehow the memory of that night, and the blackness that surrounded it, seemed to glint satanically as if a world of evil awaited her, and indeed it had.

She had gone on to live with her Brother for awhile following that, but then she had found a boyfriend for whom she had given birth to her first and only daughter. Shortly after that, in a nightmare of drugs and bad choices everything had fallen apart, mistakes were made, and a lot of bad things had happened.

Now, here she was sitting in a Prison Cell up on murder charges, awaiting the trial of her life.

"So, it's time for me to go. It was very nice to meet you Lilly. I'm glad that we got to know one another. I'll be back again in the morning. Do you have any requests, I mean food wise"??

"Um … … How about Chocolate ice cream"?? She asked.

"Okay. I'll see what I can do." Nancy said with a polite and kind laugh. "Goodnight Lilly."

"Thanks ah." Lilly said watching her lawyer waiting to get buzzed out.

The following morning David Dane awoke before sunrise, his pillow, the one that he had dragged underneath his head in the middle of the night was soaked in sweat. As he rolled forward he discovered the trail of blood that reached from the top of his shirt to the bottom of it. His sutures were dirty and in need of changing. Some of the stitching had obviously come loose and was dangling, free hanging in loose crimson strands.

"Shit"!!!! He exclaimed.

At that instant, his cell phone which he had forgotten to turn off lit up. It was a Private Number.

"Hello." He greeted establishing contact.

"Yeah, Dane man. It's me."

It was Bill Ramirez.

"You sound like I feel." Dane commented dragging his ass onto his feet. He could hear a multitude of voices in the background along with the faint metallic echo of poorly oiled wheels.

"I suffered a serious fuckin beat down last night man." Bill said. "Well, yesterday."

Dane was tearing away sections of his field dressing now, better change before whatever and why ever got any worse. Fuck!!!

He could feel his head swimming and his eyes were on fire. He could not believe what he had just heard. First he had ended up in the hospital and then this happens to Bill, it was like a cluster fuck of negative karma, always the way, never one thing at a time, everything in a chorus of shit.

"It's no joke man ah. These guys were looking for you. They were threatening you via me."

Dane had come fully awake now and was moving around the room with his cell phone in his hand. The windows were open and the bright hot sun was filtering in through the glass.

"They jammed you up instead of coming to find me … … … FUCKERS"!!! Dane said below his breath.

"They fucked me up man, i'm in bad shape, stitches and all. I'm lucky that those jokers didn't kill me."

"I didn't mean for this to happen. I'm sorry Bill."

"Yeah, those clowns need a good fucken lesson. They better not let me see them again or i'll kill them"

"You and me both." Dane Muttered. The pain was having its way with him again. He was in bad shape, everything out of focus and the ceiling doing laps around his head.

"I don't know man. These little idiots have gotten away with far to much already if you ask me." Ramirez said. "Mannn." … … … Bill said fussing.

"Come and see me when you feel better and we'll go see these guys. I met with Clinton's Father yesterday morning. He's a sweet old man who doesn't deserve to have the scum of the earth that he has for a son." Dane remarked trying to reach for his soda that was on a table three feet away.

"You know Clinton's Father"??

"Yeah, for a few years now."

"It must be a tense relationship given your rapport with his son." Bill said.

"Not at all, Olden and Clinton are as far apart in nature as any two people that i've ever met. As a matter of fact, i'd say that they're polar opposites."

"That's sad to hear that, I mean for his Fathers sake. I've had differences with my Family before but, well."

"I've gone to war with mine. These two are as far apart as you could imagine. Olden has tears in his eyes whenever he brings up the subject of his son. It's a shame that he had to rear such a piece of garbage."

Just then there was a knock on Danes door.

"Who is it"?? He hollered defensively.

"It is Marcel." The voice on the other side came.

Dane turned around and walked toward the door, when he opened it he found his friend on the other side smiling. He was wearing a grey sweater over black jeans and sneakers.

"Oh … … Dane. I hope I have not disturbed you."

Dane was shaking his head while holding the phone with his shoulder at the same time. "Just wait, hold on." Dane said politely raising a finger in a gesture of silence. "Where'd they take you"?? Dane asked trying to multi task.

"Same place as you were." Bill responded.

"Jesus." Dane said before flipping his phone shut.

"It has only make a short time that you were in the hospital. It is maybe to short." Marcel commented.

Danes face was perspiring and Marcel could see the trail of blood on his comrades shirt.

"Here it is mano. I hate hospitals. I think that it sucks that people have to spend any amount of time
in them. They terrify me, the only thing that's worse is the pen."

"Well, it doesn't make a long time that you have spent getting well. Maybe you need to rest."

"I'm alright padre." Dane said, but there were always famous last words. At that moment Dane keeled over and fell to the ground unconscious on the floor.

"Give me a DAMN newspaper man." Bill shouted to the nurse. Just then he saw David Dane being wheeled into the E.R. There was blood all over his shirt.

"Jesus Christ. What the fuck happened man"?? Ramirez shouted over the buzz of Doctors and Nurses who were circulating in the hallway, seeing his friend brought back for a second time was almost as traumatizing as the beat down that he had received at the hands of Clinton's thugs. He also spotted Marcel not far behind Danes stretcher. Fuckin Grand Central Station at high noon.

"Oh Bill, Hello." He greeted. "Dane has collapsed at his apartment so they are bringing him back here."

"Brought. Brought him back here." Bill said correcting Marcel who scoffed arrogantly at the comment.

Somewhere down the hall Dane was dreaming again. This time he was back in jail in another province, the way that things had been. In the dream he was at The Courthouse standing in The Bull Pen with a bunch of thugs and criminals surrounding him, each one with their own hard earned rap sheet, Danes however was cleaner than the board of health.

Just across from him there were two or three screws seated at each table, two of them minding their own business but one of them slipped his hand between his legs and looked across at Dane who was wondering what the fuck was up, unsure of his footing. He had never been through this before. What the fuck was this hacks moonlight, rape??? Dane wondered.

"Does anyone in this place know what time it is"?? The fighter asked turning around to face the other inmates who stood in a collection of murmuring hoards on various sides of the ugly looking room. There was nothing nice about this place, designed to get to your head. It was working.

A tall bald white dude stood up and looked over at him. "They don't want us to know that shit man. That way the time passes slower. We're not supposed to have the comforts of home in here."

"Yeah, no, ah." Dane responded.

"Dane." One of the screws called out. He was big and ugly with pock marked cheeks and a cleft pallet.

"Where we goin here"?? Dane asked following the big man to an unknown destination, but there was no response, just the jangling of keys and the clanging of jail cell doors. The place stunk of something sweet and pungent with no name.

Down three more corridors and two flights of stairs Dane was introduced to Ron Spencer, the lawyer that would represent him in his case. He was a tall lithe individual in his late forties or early fifties with wire rimmed glasses and sharp features. Ron looked like a top criminal attorney, and he was.

He introduced himself and then sat down. They were face to face behind two panes of bullet proof glass.

"So, you're being charged with one count of uttering death threats as well as one count of criminal harassment. Apparently, the reason that you're being charged is because they have you on tape."

"Listen, this woman is capable of a lot more than you know, a lot more then they know. She's no angel." Dane said leaning closer to the transparent partitions.

Ron looked bewildered. He had no idea what to say. He would soon learn that there were clients and then there was David Dane.

"I spent seven years or close to it taking care of this girl. I loved her, I loved her more than life itself. It's incomprehensible to me that i'm sitting behind bars because of her. How the fuck did that happen"?? David Dane asked.

Dane was not impressed and it came across in his tone. There were flaring shadows all over the place. It did not take a genius to figure out that this mess was the cause of Lilly's unscrupulous way of living and nothing more, bad choices, bad decisions, that and unholy drug and thug related fucking nightmares.

"I spoke to your Mom. She'd love to hear from you. She and your Father haven't heard from you since you got arrested."

"The phones on the ranges in this place are battling a case of dead ring tone. It's not like the government gives a fuck about anyones rights around here."

"The phones don't work"?? Ron asked concernedly.

"Not one of them. I've attempted to call out several times but to no avail. They keep the place locked down like no fortress that i've ever seen."

"Have you tried the phones here"?? Ron enquired.

"No, I haven't been anywhere near them."

"Will they let you near them"??

"It's not that, it's that I haven't been on a range here." Dane lamented.

A Range was a bank of cells or a cell block. Some ranges had phones while others did not. Phones had been made available to Dane, just not the kind that worked. They had also made Dane serve Coffee to the other inmates. They had forced him to wheel around a trolly on which a large cooler rested, on top of that he had to deliver breakfast in the form of a brown paper bag full of Apples, Oranges, Bananas as well as Pears.

"So, we need to get you some bail." Ron suggested.

"It would help. I still don't know what the hell i'm gonna be facing in here. The whole thing's a catastrophe. I have no criminal records, but by the time this shit is over, who knows."

"Well, when they see that you've never broken the law before it shouldn't be to bad." Ron said.

Later that afternoon Dane had been shuttled by Patty Wagon to a second destination downtown, there he had faced a female judge who had granted him bail after some deliberation. She was as sarcastic and as arrogant a human being as Dane had ever met, and her behaviour had been abominable, abrupt, rude and ignorant laced with manners that were in short supply. It was as if she thought her whole Court Room a theatre and everyone in it her audience. Everyone was there to fucking entertain her amidst bouts of laughter and good cheer, Christmas time for all sadists.

Good for you. Dane had thought. You woke up this morning and thought you were God. How the fuck did that happen??

Ron however had fought valiantly for Danes freedom. He stood up to this woman in a fashion that nearly made her slink beneath her bench, and her years of law and legal training had just run down her leg. The words "Jack ass" should have been tattooed on her forehead in bright neon pink.

Dane recalled the female judge making a couple of remarkably arrogant comments. She needed time to think.

It would take her awhile. She had even made the comment "No, he stays in jail." Yet Dane had no priors, no previous criminal records to cry over, and here he was being treated as though he were the scum of the earth, low down, and rotten to the very core by this woman who could not make a distinction between herself and Christ.

It would take this woman some ten to fifteen minutes to put her thinking cap on yet only a matter of seconds to remove it, and it was a feet. What a moron.

Later that evening, in the dying sun, Dane had been stuffed into a second cubby hole in the side another Police van that was the size of a dog kennel. The accommodation itself was roughly the size of two ovens one on top of the other with the grills removed for added movement. Dane was being charged with utter death threats, not war crimes against his own people.

That had been the worst part of Danes entire stay in prison. How the law could treat people as they did was beyond him. Canada was in some ways guilty of using psychological warfare against its own people. They had no business doing many of the things that they did, and, after his stay inside, Dane had lost tremendous respect for his own flag.

The whole experience had been particularly reminiscent of a line in a song sung by Michael Jackson called-THEY DON'T REALLY CARE ABOUT US. It was a song that Jackson had written after his brush with the law over child molestation accusations. The line that had stayed with Dane was-"I can't believe this is the land from which I came."

Dane totally understood how Jackson must have felt when he penned that lyric.

About four hours later Dane awoke on a gurney and was starving, there was a sexy nurse at his side. She administered a shot of Morphine via syringe and then left Dane to fall asleep again.

This time The Sandman brought a different package for him. He was dreaming of Lilly lying on a cot in what appeared to be a hut somewhere in a South American location. She was sound asleep and being watched over by natives who were using pieces of sheet metal to shelter them from the silver rain. There was the slightest hint of shadow in the vision.

The next frame brought Dane and Lilly standing in the night kissing, only this time they were a few feet from The Black Domino Tavern. He could feel her lips caress him gently as he cradled her wet hair in his hand. All around them was the track LONG LONG WAY TO GO by POP LEGEND PHIL COLLINS.

A few blocks over he could see them together again as if on a movie screen. She was so beautiful standing there in her bright pink top and red jeans. He had easily remembered the sweet scent of her perfume filling his head.

"You mesmerize me Baby Bunny." He remembered saying. There was dew on the tree tops and Dane looked up just on time to see a rain drop fall and explode hypnotically against the earth.

"I love you." He said.

A cluster of shadows grazed the scene and then Dane saw his late Uncle standing in the dust with his cane. He had developed Arthritis in his later years and needed an aid to help him walk. Dane truly missed him, the two had always been such great friends.

"How ya doin son"?? Thomas asked. There was a surreal haze all around him that closed out at his back. His hair was white and his beard grey, the way that he looked near the end. Just seeing him standing there brought tears to Danes eyes. He had been more than an Uncle. He had been Danes best friend on the planet, and in many ways, a Father figure.

Dane tried to respond but his words were frozen in time.

All of a sudden there was a cluster of voices around him, screaming and hollering for people to get out of the way. Then he saw a gun shot wound patient being wheeled in through the open corridor of The Hospital. Whoever he was, he had lost a lot of blood. There were intravenous bags hanging from poles and sutures saturated with blood falling to the floor.

"Were gonna lose him. GO. GO. GO." An Intern ordered.

"Jesus." Dane uttered as he tried to find his balance on the stretcher mattress.

"Dane man. What the fuck"??

It was Bill. His left arm was in a sling.

"How in Christs name did you find me"?? David Dane asked.

"I don't know. I just kept walking around and around until I found you." He said.

"Glad that you did. I was getting lonely around here. There aren't enough nurses to keep me busy." Dane joked with a smile on his face. In truth, he was in no shape to do anything at all, much less joke.

"Yeah. You should have seen the nurse who took care of me. She was Asian. I'm tellin ya, she was a hotty man."

"Oh yeah." The Author said in an exhausted voice. "Get her phone number."

"Huh. I wish man."

As Dane began to raise himself he saw a familiar face coming toward him. It was Olden, he wore a top hat made of straw over a blazer and dress slacks. His face was serious and his eyes filled with sadness. "I came just as soon as I heard that they brought you back here."

"Jesus." Dane said struggling against the pain. "Who told you. Whoever it was they didn't need to worry you like that."

"I ran into that French fellow on Ontario Street … … Marcel."

"Yeah. My damn, stitching came out. I feel like a stuffed animal."

A Doctor holding a clip board passed between them, his hands were pink.

"You need to take better care of yourself. I'm old enough now to realize the importance of good health. If a man doesn't have his health then he doesn't have much. There's a feeding frenzy in Heaven. We all have to be careful not to end up there before our time."

"If I keep going down this road i'm gonna end up there long before my time." David Dane commented.

"I keep telling him that he needs to take more naps." Bill clowned.

"Fucken smart ass." Dane retorted. "Where's the canteen? I need something to eat."

"I think it's like three floors down man. Can't even get a fucken news paper around here. I wanna check out the stock page."

Bill owned a Stock Market Portfolio. Dane had no idea what the fuck that meant, nor had he ever, numbers and fingers weren't his fortei, nor was anything else related to stocks.

"I occasionally browse through a news paper but I prefer books."

"I'm not surprised. You're an author."

"You two young men have so many years ahead of you. I've wandered around in this life and gained wisdom from almost every experience that i've had. You have a special way about you David Dane. You have eyes that shine bright as fire. You've touched an entire community with your words. We'll never forget "The Original.""

"The Ontario Street Original" Bill said smiling. He was leaning against the outer part of the gurney now.

"Do you wanna towel off"?? A woman a few feet away asked, her husband had just come out of the shower. She was beautiful down to her black nylon panty hose. Both Dane and Ramirez took notice. She wore a blue leather jacket with a white blouse and skin tight jeans that hugged her figure like a mold.

"You should find yourself someone who looks like that." The Former Boxer commented.

"Her with all those curves and me with no brakes." Bill remarked. All three men were laughing now.

Dane was beginning to wonder whether or not they ever served dinner in this place, his stomach was so empty that he thought it might implode. It had been a lot of hours since his last meal and his system was beginning to let him know it.

"I'm getting kinda hungry man." Ramirez voiced.

"Yeah, you and me both. Where's the damn nurse"?

"I can go find somebody if you gentlemen wanna wait here." Olden offered. He was as sincere a person as Dane had ever met. There was no beating his manner or his kindness. There were many people who didn't care about other people in this world, Olden wasn't one of them.

Two minutes later Olden had returned with a nurse and David Dane was putting in his order, he wasn't expecting the greatest cuisine. This was The Hospital after all. They usually served something that was a cross between Cafeteria Food and whatever you called those frozen dinners that you found in the Frozen Food section of The Super Market or the nearest I.G.A.

"They said i'd find you here." The husky and affluent Andrew Dane said appearing out of nowhere.

"Jesus, do you ever stop growing"?? David Dane asked of his younger sibling. "If you have a car here I wouldn't mind having some Dairy Queen or MC Donalds."

"I don't think you'll be needing any of that." A French nurse with a Quebecois accent half scolded as she raised the bed for Dane to eat. "Look what we have here for you." She said.

The meal smelled like crap and looked even worse. There was no way on Gods green earth that he was going to eat that, not even if you forced him at gun point. "This is supposed to be The Hospital, so why am I being tortured"?? David Dane enquired.

"You're not being tortured. This food is good for you. Look at the peas and carrots on that plate. This is all stuff that you never eat. Now's your chance to improve your diet."

"I'm not touching this crap Andrew. You're a fucking lawyer. Make a case for cruel, sadistic, and unusual treatment. This stuff isn't going anywhere near … … … … … …

"Alright man, I have to go." Bill Ramirez said stepping between Andrew and Olden to say "Goodbye."

"Goodnight Bill." Dane responded quietly.

Just then they wheeled a man past them who had fallen off of a scaffold, his head was broken in half.

"Andrew Dane." The lawyer said as he introduced himself to Olden who hadn't spoken a word in more than five minutes, still standing silently with his hat over his heart.

"It's an honour for me sir. Your Brother has told me many stories about you." Olden said shaking hands with Andrew who could on most days block out the sun.

"Oh, and no more of this Andrew shit. I can't stand it. I prefer Lord or Squire." The high powered criminal attorney said. Andrew was as always, dressed to the nines, one of his shoes was likely the sum of most peoples car payments, plus a short vacation in Cuba.

"Hello." Andrew said responding to his ringing cell phone. It was his wife Leilani on the other end. Andrew had married a high end Fashion Model who also moon lighted as a Dental Hygienist. "No, I don't know where the keys to the Porch are. No, I didn't move them." He protested.

"Well, I should be getting back to my card game." Olden said leaning in to give Dane a hug. "You take care and stay well. I'll come back in the morning." Olden said holding the brim of his hat with both hands.

"Goodnight Olden." David Dane answered.

CHAPTER 2:

L.A.-I will be addressing you several times through out the course of this Book. Everything that you've read up until now aside from the dedication was written before my knowledge of the nightmare that took place on November, 7th, 2012. I am not the same man that I was before learning of what took place on that evening. It is my sincerest hope that in reading this as well as in reading The original URBAN RAIN that you will know and understand that this is as much something that I am doing for Monica as it is for my readers.

I once told her that it was my dream to make our story famous. This is how I go forth with that quest, but more than anything else, and my Mother would tell you this, I want Monica to have this as part of her legacy on this earth.

God Bless-You will hear from me later on in the text.

Peace and love,
Von

The quiet and hypnotic Ontario Street stood empty and dark at this hour, it's nooks and crannies, alleyways and alcoves, shadows and dreams were still and silent, unflinching, as if suspended in another time. It was a neighbourhood that had witnessed so much, but most importantly it had witnessed one of the most storied and legendary relationships in Montreal history, a relationship between two people who had loved one another more than anyone had ever given credit to, despite the way that things had ended.

David Dane and Lilly Chicoine had founded their legend on these streets and now people from around the world were reading about them, they were known from Canada to The United States, from England to Aruba, and from Africa to Uganda and everywhere else in between. They were not simply star crossed lovers whose lives had intersected in the night. They were icons.

Kathleen Dane stepped out of her Fathers Porch in front of The Black Domino Tavern and closed its door behind her.

She was tired and had been training for hours. The words "National Hero" were now being used to characterize her standing in The Canadian Female Kick Boxing Community. She was beautiful, charming, sophisticated as well as lethal, the last of which was a trait bestowed upon her by Donovan O Riley, her Irish born boxing coach as well as her legendary uncle, David Dane.

She was frequently referred to as "THE PRIDE OF THE IRISH" by Sports Casters across both Canada and The United States, thus she had been given the moniker-KATE "THE GATE" SHAMROCK. One day she aimed to be a hero and role model to millions. She was her Fathers Daughter and often thought of herself as a Daddies Girl which was emblazoned on several of her designer T-Shirts.

Aside from her role in life as a Female Kick Boxer she had also done some modelling for which her Mother Leilani had been her Instructor. Kate had modelled for Sport and Fitness Magazines and had even appeared on television numerous times when certain stations had chosen to air her fights, on the cover of one such magazine, she had appeared alongside her legendary uncle David Dane.

It had been Uncle David who had inspired her to get involved in Boxing and Kick Boxing because he himself had a passion for boxing and was also known for his ability to fight in the street. It was in this neighbourhood where David Dane and his legendary and iconic girlfriend Lilly "Bad To The Bone" Chicoine had carried out their legendary relationship that was now the stuff of legend around the globe.

Kate wondered where Lilly was right now, it had been awhile since she had heard any mention of her. They had never met, but Kate hoped that one day she would finally have the opportunity to meet the legendary woman whom she had heard so much about, it would somehow be like meeting a character from a movie that had come to life, especially given that it was a film that her Uncle was a 50% star in.

Bubbles rising to the surface of the ocean underneath Gods hot sun. Lilly was dreaming of far away paradises now, seeing all at once the kind of beauty and far off landscapes that she had always wanted to visit, this was the reality that she dreamt of, here in the darkness of her cell.

Outside, below, a hack walked by tapping the edge of a key along each bar as he went as if to announce his presence to the wing turning his head momentarily to see who was doing what, hoping to catch an unsuspecting inmate off guard.

Lilly could see David Dane's eyes beyond her own now. They seemed to be watching her from afar. She could feel that he missed her. "I love you Baby Bunny." She saw his lips say as his mouth moved without sound as if his words were muted.

She had been more to him than any simple girlfriend could have been. She had been his obsession as well as the inspiration that moved him to write with such extreme passion over an experience that had seemingly taken place while under hypnosis, mesmerized.

Many of his friends had commented in a cluster of whispers. She had once over heard his friend Tony say-"I've never seen a man so in love with a woman."

Another friend named Ben had once commented to a colleague-"You don't go anywhere near that girl." Because Danes rages over seeing any man go near Lilly were so bad.

He had lived with her and without her for seven years, and in those seven years that they had been apart Dane had not once been happy. Things had fallen apart and the bottom had dropped out. There was no love on this planet like the love that David Dane had always felt for Lilly Chicoine.

Their relationship had on more than one occasion taken on a flare for the hypnotic. Their world, the drugs, the shadowy people, and the danger. The never knowing in the gathering shadows of Ontario Street what the next hour would bring.

Lilly had been to him what no other woman could have been to any man, and without her, a part of David Danes soul had been lost to Ontario Streets night and its wickedness. Lilly had given meaning and purpose to his life, and without her, all of that was gone, it had simply vanished and now he was alone amidst coiling darkness and voices from the past. No other could have meant to him what Lilly had. There would never be another time like that of which they spent together, nor ever another experience like theirs. It was somehow, what had happened in the darkness of time, at least that's how Dane thought of it.

Olend walked David Dane out through the front doors of The Hospital into the bright hot sun light and shook his hand, somewhere rain drums seemed to play a hypnotic tune.

"Good to see you Olend. Thanks for coming by to meet me. I don't know what i'd do without your friendship. Thank you for being there my friend."

"If I had raised up any better in being your friend I don't see how it could have been. My Father taught me to do right right by others and I know what my son did to you was wrong."

Dane was nodding regretfully now.

Somewhere about a hundred yards off there was the sound of a lawn mower cutting fresh grass. There was a clear blue trouble less sky over head, the birds were singing, and it seemed as if all was right with the world.

"Montreal." David Dane professed gazing up into the pale cloudless sky. He was thinking that if it were any warmer that he might bake, it was that hot in Canada's fashion capitol.

This was a beautiful city, one that's atmosphere was enough inspiration for writing on its own, but coupled with Lilly Chicoine, there was plenty of inspiration to go around.

Lilly was awake now as a screw walked slowly passed her cell door and smiled in at her. This particular French Quebecois guard with the beautiful figure and sandy blond hair with blue eyes had known Lilly for years, they had been fast friends even though they were convict and jailer. This particular guard, or hack as they were called by most of the inmates had often put her arm around Lilly's shoulders in a token of warmth and affection.

"Hey. Good morning." Lilly called out to the familiar face.

"Ca'va." The Guard enquired.

"Hey, when is my lawyer coming to see me"?? Chicoine asked becoming slightly more demanding. She was hungry even though she'd sneaked a number of chocolate chip cookies out from underneath another inmates pillow. There wasn't much of a way to stay full in here if you weren't lifting shit from someone, and that had been a quick job. They had been transporting her downstairs when she'd seen the Cookie wrapper protruding from below the girls pillow.

"Not for awhile, not until after we do rounds. It's gonna be at least three or four hours."

"Hmm … … … hmm." Lilly answered in her cute bunny rabbit tone of voice. Dane had always adored her Hmm … … … … hmms. She wondered where he was now. Maybe they'd give her a phone later on so that she could call him and see how he was doing. She missed him and wondered if he was feeling the same thing. It was to many people a mystery how a simple ordinary man and a drug addicted prostitute could be together, but they had been for many years, even through some extremely harsh times. It was always "Dane to the rescue" as Lilly put it. He had seen things upon things, upon things. To much dope and her dreaming of a way to get more, but they had stayed together anyway weathering one nightmare after another, but when worse came to worse, when the chips were way down, Dane had always been there for her and she loved him for it.

"I need to see Lilly Chicoine." Dane said standing in front of the clerical desk in the lobby of the police station. The Guard regarded him inquisitively for a moment before placing his spectacles on and checking the roster. He looked weather beaten and as though he had seen many years on the force. He was not a rookie. "Sorry, I thought you were looking for an officer. We're not allowed to divulge information about Prisoners." He said. "Can I help you with something else"??

Just then Danes cell phone lit up. It was Lilly Chicoine. She had found a pay phone and had, via Danes forwarding of his own land line been allowed to make a collect call.

"Hey." She said on the other end. "They just served us breakfast. Mine was lousy. It was some kind of fried egg something with sausage but it was almost all cold by the time that they brought it to us."

Dane was stepping out into the sunshine now. He did not want to be over heard by the desk cop.

"So, what's the situation with the charges"?? He asked.

Lilly was rolling a cigarette on the other end of the phone as she spoke to him. She hadn't had a smoke all night and was starving for one. "I don't know Boo. My lawyer's coming to see me later on. I hope to fuck this isn't gonna go on forever." She said.

"Lilly, these are murder charges. They're not just gonna let you waltz out the front doors."

A car passed by David Danes vision as he put on a pair of high end sun glasses, he had paid a small fortune for them, but at least they kept the sun out of his eyes. "How about if I suggest an assistant to your legal team or even a whole new lawyer all together."

"Who's the lawyer"?? Lilly "Bad To The Bone" Chicoine asked.

"You want me to what"?? Andrew Dane would ask several hours later, he was standing underneath an umbrella outside a two hundred dollar a plate wine and caviar restaurant, his choice of the day. He had had a tiresome afternoon and his face reflected his exhaustion.

"I want you to take Lilly's case." David Dane said as Andrew pulled three brownies out of his pocket.

"You want me to represent Lilly in a murder trial"??

A slight drizzle had begun to fall from the sky above. It was about to full on rain, and Dane did not want to get caught in a down pour. There were six waiters within a close radius of them and each one of them appeared to be starting to close up shop as far as the outer eating area went, then there were a few bus boys loading dishes into dish pans amidst the chatter of clanging.

Dane was giving his Brother an, i'm dead serious, I need you to do this expression.

Andrew took a step sideways, the wind blowing his hair around at the same time. He had just gotten his license to practice law in Montreal and here he was defending Lilly Chicoine as Client one.

"Alright, i'll see what I can do." He said.

Two days later Andrew Dane stepped inside of Lilly Chicoines cell that was barren aside from two outfits, an empty book shelf, and a couple of trays with food residue on them. "Hi." She said giving him a quick wave along with a genuine smile. He was now Lilly's lawyer. He could not believe this was unfolding.

"Okay." Andrew said with a sigh as he sat opposite the love of his Brothers life. The cell was small and smelled of some sort of foul odoured cleaning product. It made Andrew wish that he were anywhere but here, other side of the ocean, someplace else.

"I brought you some pens and paper." Andrew said. "In case you didn't have any. Anything that you use them to write as far as this case goes will be subject to the lawyer attorney/client privilege. That means that anything that you say to me is bound by confidentiality." Andrew said kindly. He was looking around for a place to hang his over coat. In this place, there weren't many viable options.

"Hmm … … … … Maybe you could hang it over the sink but then it might get a bit wet. I brushed my teeth but there was no towel to mop up the water with." Lilly exclaimed. There was an orphanish quality about her that Andrew found appreciable. It sort of made her, cute.

"So, okay." Andrew began putting on a pair of reading glasses. "So, you come out of the washroom and you find Kelly Mathews dead in a pool of her own blood is that right"??

"Hmm … … hmm." … She said.

"Apparently there was a woman downstairs who gave a statement and she said that she didn't see anyone else leaving the building. That's basically the gist of it right"??

Andrew was not sure of Lilly Chicoine. He knew that she was a shady character.

"You look a bit different than I remember you from when Dane and I spent Christmas in Halifax. You got a bit older."

"I see." Andrew said reaching into his attache case to retrieve a copy of The Police Report.

David Dane strolled into the community centre at Frontenac looking for a place to sit down and enjoy his Chocolate Shake. It was nearly five pm and he hadn't heard back from his Brother regarding Lilly yet, but he was waiting, anxiously, feverishly, violent inside wanting to know where things were.

Now, he sat here in his favourite end of town reminiscing about all of the special moments that he and Lilly had spent on these streets, he was thinking that if he had one more moment with her down here just the way things had been that he would tell her how much that he loved her all over again.

Just then a familiar face wandered in out of the rain. She was carrying a kit bag over her shoulder.

"What's up Uncle Von"?? Kathleen Dane asked throwing her arms around her legendary uncle. She preferred to call him by his nick name. Uncle Von, which was the short of Von "The Icon." The name that David Dane was known by on Ontario Street.

Dane smiled, his chin dipping proudly to one side. His niece was the apple of his eye and the most important person in the universe to him. "How you doin kid"?? He asked.

"I'm good. I just trained with Donovan over at the other gym. I almost broke my hand on my sparring partners head. She's just to wet. I don't know where they keep getting these girls."

Wet was Boxing for wet behind the ears or showing a lack of experience. Kate Shamrock was good, she was better than good, she was the best. A legitimate bad ass.

"I'm glad you're not complaining the other way. We need you to represent this Family when your Uncle and your Dad get to old. I'm very proud of you, you know." Dane said releasing his embrace.

Kate was wearing a pair of green track pants below a white tank top and running shoes. This was her attire for going from one Boxing Gym to another, and there was one in the community centre. Dane trained there often, but not often enough.

However, if one were to see Kathleen Dane away from her sport they would see her as the epitome of class, style and sophistication. The class and sophistication she had gotten from her Father, and the style she had inherited from her Uncle Von, that along with her innate charisma, a Von "The Icon" trademark.

"Such a bad boy you." Kate said aiming a slow punch at her Uncle as she jestingly displayed her bottom row of teeth. "Where's Lilly "Bad To The Bone" Chicoine???

Danes smile disappeared. "She's in jail."

Kathleen had never actually met Lilly before, but she had heard stories and she had of course read URBAN RAIN.

"In jail for what"?? The gorgeous Shamrock asked. Dane thought that she looked like a cross between Angelina Jolie and Sade around the time that she did Smooth Operator which was one of David Danes all time favourite songs, and videos.

"Murder." Von "The Icon" said flatly.

"Who the fuck did she kill"?? Kate asked, furrowing her brow.

"No one. They think that she killed someone." Dane was looking away now. He was thinking of all of the special moments that they spent together on these darkened streets late at night, after hours when the dealers and the hookers were out. Lilly was and would always be the love of his life.

"Well, who's representing her"?? Kate asked curiously.

Von "The Icon" looked his niece square in the eye. "Your Dad."

"Oh … … … … shit." Kate said pacing one way and then the other. "Well, at least she's in good hands."

"Alright." Andrew said standing up to stretch his legs. "So you don't have any idea who else might have been in the room with the two of you when this went down"?? He asked. He was looking directly into her eyes, watching for movement, a presence, a sign as to whether or not Lilly Chicoine was telling the truth. This was the love of his Brothers life. There was more on the line here then just this case. He wanted to know the truth. Had this woman really committed murder or was she being rail roaded by a corrupt justice system and whoever else was really pulling the strings.

"Anyway, thank you for representing me ah. I'm happy that Vons brother is going to be my legal council. So, are you and Nancy Mitchell going to be working together on this case or will it be just you"?? Lilly asked as her legs swung back and forth below the bench that she sat on.

Andrew sat down opposite Lilly again his posture suave and certain. "Nancy Mitchell was appointed so I assume that now that you have me she'll be stepping down, or they'll remove her. You're in good hands." Andrew said.

He was a professional, and he would represent Lilly Chicoine to the best of his abilities, and those abilities were considerable, he was no longer a small time criminal lawyer with an office in a strip mall next to a veterinary clinic. He was what most people who worked for the media regularly characterized as a "BIG SHOT ATTORNEY," "The Cream Of The Crop," "El Pedron."

"Alright, I wanna go over your story once more from the beginning. The Toxicology report says that you had Cocaine in your system. This is going to be a problem for us considering that it puts you in less than a focused state of mind. Were you able to discern what was going on around you at the time when you came out of the rest room or were you slightly unaware"??

Lilly was sitting on the edge of her cot with her palms flared out on either side of her.

"No, I more or less knew what was going on. Well fuck, I mean it's not like I haven't done Coke before. At that point I had only done half a QT." She said.

Andrew was taking notes. His expression was brilliantly inquisitive.

"Half a QT"?? He asked. He was unfamiliar with the term. He vaguely remembered hearing his Brother drop those letters in conjunction with one another before but he could not recall the context.

"A QT, it's short for-Quarter of Coke. It's sold in small miniature zip lock type bags." Lilly said clasping her hands together back to back. It was a tendency that she displayed whenever she was slightly discomforted. She was afraid. This whole thing was making her afraid.

"Okay, so far what I have in my notes is that you were in the bathroom doing Coke and that when you do Coke you wig out, you're like turned off to the world. Then when you left the washroom you found Kelly Mathews dead with the murder weapon protruding from her. Would that be accurate"?? Andrew enquired??

"Hmm ... ... hmm." Lilly responded.

"No hmm ... ... hmm. Yes or no."

"Yes, that's what happened. I didn't do it. Fuck, I would have had no reason to. Maybe Roberta did it."

"Alright." Andrew said standing up and moving toward the bars. Lilly immediately noticed his expensive dark blue designer blazer and dress pants. She thought that he looked like a movie character in his out fit. She had also spotted the Rolex lurking underneath his sleeve. He was a fashion plate.

"You said that her feet were bare but that she had shoes on earlier. Do you remember what kind of shoes she had on"?? He asked. Andrew was wondering, even as remote a possibility as it seemed to be, that Kelly Mathews could have been killed for her shoes.

"Hmm … … … hmm. I should. I'm the one who sold them to her. They were Nikes."

"Were they old, new"??

"Between. I had them for awhile before I sold them to her so they weren't new."

"How much did you sell them to her for"?? Andrew asked feeling that his own line of questioning was frivolous and stupid, going nowhere, but they needed something to work with.

"Twenty bucks, but they were worth more like forty."

"Do you think that someone could've come into the room and killed her for the sneakers that she was wearing"??

"It's possible but I doubt that would've been the motive. No one in that particular hotel is going to kill someone for their shoes. I mean, things like that just don't happen. It's unheard of ".

Andrew was wondering what kind of a defence such a theory could make. The problem with it was that Lilly was the only one who had claimed to have seen Kelly wearing the shoes. He would have his investigator look into anyone and everyone else who might've seen Kelly wearing the shoes that day. Even still, the item report said that there were two other pairs of shoes in the room. This alone presented a problem because it didn't speak to Kelly being without foot wear.

"Alright, i'm gonna have my investigator speak to the desk clerk as well as to any other occupants of the hotel who might've seen Kelly wearing the missing shoes. What did these particular Nikes look like"??

Lilly looked up and to the right. Andrew thought that was a good sign because it at very least meant that Lilly was accessing the visual cortex of her brain and was thus trying to visualize or recall something.

"They were blue and white. Like the trim was white." She said.

Andrew knew that no judge was going to look favourably upon Lilly given her past records as well as the fact that there was Cocaine found in her blood stream. On top of that The Prosecution had a murder weapon with Lilly Chicoines prints all over it and they could put her at the scene. All of this stood for trouble at best. None of this spelled FREEDOM for his client or a cake walk for himself or his legal colleagues. This was going to take time and preparation to put together. That, and he was going to need a miracle, and Andrew did not know where to get one of those.

Donovan O' Riley strolled into the bag room at The Community Centre Boxing Facility at Frontenac. He had been Kathleen Danes coach since the time that she had begun to take Boxing, Kick Boxing and Martial Arts seriously. He had been born in Dublin Ireland and only found his way to North America a few years ago after he had been hand picked by David Dane to over see his proteges career here in Canada. He was a Ring General, and as seasoned a Professional Fighter as Dublin had ever seen, he had been a part of the old guard, had Family ties to The IRA, and witnessed his only son die at the hands of them after a bar fight that had spilled out of control.

Eight years ago he had lost his wife Heather to Leukemia and had been alone ever since, but Kate had been his salvation. She had given him reason to go on.

If he didn't have "Gate," as he called her, his adopted Grand Daughter, then he would have found his hours at the bottom of a liquor bottle. He would simply be another tired old man buying cigars in the smoke shop and eating his meals at the local diner, lonely as hell and listening to the whispers of the local gaffer as he closed up shop.

He had instilled within her his knowledge which had so far lead her to two straps, offers to do TV commercials and endorsements, and a financial wind fall that she would have little gotten anyplace else, that and International recognition which no one could put a price on. She had become North American Womens Kick Boxing Champion not to mention Canadian Womens Kick Boxing Titlist in under two years bringing him more pride than he knew that he was capable of having.

Her Father was also a good man and supported his Daughter in all of her quests, a lawyer by trade, his only Daughter was a National Treasure as well as a treasure to Andrew, her Mother, and to her legendary Uncle who was now on his way into the Gym with a pair of Boxing Gloves hanging from around his neck. They looked like they had been toyed with by a rottweiler.

"How you doin Irish"?? Von "The Icon" greeted as he embraced his nieces coach.

"You're a healthy lookin lad aren't ya"?? Donovan, who was seventy two years old asked amidst a broad grin. Kate was in the ring sparring. This was her second bout today, even though it was simply practice.

"Watch the left hand." Von instructed his niece. Kate did not look away staying focused on Melissa Anderson who was gloved up in front of her. She wanted to move but Kate was cutting off the ring with such expertise that she had nowhere to go.

"Keep it high and hit." Von shouted through the horn that he was making with his hands so as to amplify what Kate was hearing. It could be harder to hear when your focus was like iron, and God knew that Kate "The Gate" Shamrock had focus.

"Move side to side." Von "The Icon" instructed using his hands as beacons. He was waving them back and forth in a series of paring gestures.

"Good girl." Donovan called out from the other side of the ring post. He was watching his prodigy intently. "Gate. Keep the right hand in closer when she closes in. Move with her." He challenged.

"Excuse me, but aren't you David Dane." A young woman asked appearing out of nowhere. She was no more than eighteen. Dane expected that this girl was a fan of the book, and he was right.

"Yeah, i'm a little busy right now. How can I help you"?? He asked as she produced a copy of his first literary work. His eyes were darting back and forth between the young lady who stood at his side and the sparring session that was going on inside the ring.

"Can I get your autograph"?? She asked fishing a pen from the recesses of one of her coat pockets.

"Yeah, absolutely." Dane said taking the Book from her and signing it. "There you go." He said kindly, handing it back to her.

"You're my favourite author." The girl continued. "Can I give you a hug"?? She asked reaching for the legend who now stood within her reach." Yeah, sure." Von "The Icon" said kindly giving the girl a genuine embrace. This was his nature, he loved people and was known to have a heart of gold.

Kate froze meeting with her favourite Uncles eyes. She was giving him a friendly "HOLY SHIT" expression. "Mr. Popularity." She said as the girl walked out the door and into the hallway where her sister stood waiting for her. "I just met my hero." The girl said.

Dane was inside smiling. "I think they give me to much credit." He said wrapping a towel around his neck and gripping it at its ends. "You better hit the showers. You have to meet Mum in less than an hour."

Marilyn Dane walked onto the boardwalk of a popular eatery in old Montreal, purse hanging from her shoulder. Her Grand Daughter was not yet present but she was expecting her very soon.

It was warm outside with temperatures finally heating up to where they were at the very least liveable. The past few months had been freezing and it was weather more conducive to staying inside with most temperatures dropping well below zero. Nova Scotian winters could be particularly harsh given that they were the sea bound coast with freezing winds often drifting in from across the harbour, and finding home within inlet communities.

In just seconds Marilyn saw Kate walking toward her dressed in diamonds and the latest designer fashions. She was a champion, and always presented as one. She quietly pulled up a chair and sat down with a wistful look in her eyes. "Hi Nana." She began.

"You look nice." Marilyn said admiring her Grand Daughters ring. "Were you at the gym before you came all the way over here to meet me"??

"I was but I cut my sparring session short. Uncle Von was there along with Donovan. I killed my opponent. They can't seem to find anyone in Quebec who can hang with me anymore. The talent pool's to shallow."

A waiter walked by them carrying a tray with a glass of sparkling wine at its centre. He was handsome, maybe thirty six or thirty seven years of age and wearing a bow tie. When he was slightly out of range of them he fished his cell phone out of his pocket and began to call someone.

"Yeah, she's here." He said. He had been the one who had taken her reservation by phone earlier that morning. Kate "The Gate" Shamrock had eaten here a number of times in the past as was her frequent routine.

Tonight, at least, Jerry would be well compensated for the information that he was providing to his benefactor on the other end of the line who seemed to have a particular interest in the female kick boxing titlist.

"So I asked Evan to get The Phantom Of The Opera Tickets for us." Kate was saying several feet from where Jerry now stood.

Evan was Kates fiance, he was an architect as well as an urban planner and had studied engineering at a number of schools. He was extremely handsome and made a rewarding salary that had many times been used to spoil his beautiful fiance far beyond anything that she asked for or expected, for Kate Shamrock was not a materialist person, but a person who valued love and Family beyond all else.

"Well at least that'll give us something to do next week." Marilyn responded taking a sip from her glass of Champagne. She did not want to drink very much because she had driven herself over here and she would also have to drive herself back to the hotel afterwards.

In another five minutes a woman flanked by two well muscled henchmen was standing before their table. Kate immediately looked up. She was not familiar with any of them. The woman looked like a cross between a low end Coke peddler and a barbarian.

"Can I help you"?? Kate asked inquisitively.

The wind blew through the street thugs hair. "My name's Jacky Hannah." The woman said before taking a long pause. She looked mean, and even to Kate "The Gate" Shamrock she was intimidating.

"I want to piss in your face." She said squinting. "I want to piss is your Grand Mothers face to."

Marilyn Dane looked serious. She did not like being spoken to in the manner that this woman was under taking. Who in the hell was she anyway. Marilyn Dane wondered.

"I'm sorry. I don't believe that I know you." Kate said in a half humoured, half taken aback manner. She had never seen Jacky Hannah before in her life, this was their first encounter.

"I'm going to get you in the ring, and then i'm going to kill you." Jacky said. "Then i'm going to send a couple of girls to see your fiance, and they're going to have a good time getting to know him." She said turning to walk away with her henchmen in tow.

"What the hell was that"?? Kate asked looking across the table at her Grand Mother who looked mortified. The wind blew through their hair as both women looked at each other in bewilderment.

"I wanna call Dad." Kate said.

Lilly Chicoine stood up as the Guard opened the metal tray and pushed her meal inside, she hadn't eaten since this morning and she was starving, her stomach growling so frequently and so loudly that it was as if it had a voice of its own. The visit from Andrew had put her somewhat at ease. At least she would be represented by high powered council as opposed to someone less qualified who might end up causing her to spend the next twenty five years of her life in an eight by ten prison cell with a toilet and a sink for company.

Now if only she had Von to hold her she would feel better. It was lonely in here and all that she had were her thoughts and dreams of things that she wanted to do and to accomplish. She also wished that she had a prescription for Methadone, unfortunately that was easier said than done behind the wall. It would be easier to have it then it would to try and kick Heroin cold turkey.

She also wished that she had a quarter of Coke, but that wasn't going to happen either. Fuck, this was a lousy predicament. "Oh for Petes sake." Lilly fussed at the realization that the hamburger that was delivered to her was cold. Couldn't they get anything right??

In moments someone was being brought down the hallway and placed into the cell next to her. It was Holly Briggs. Holy shit, it had been eons since she had seen Holly.

"Hey girl." Lilly began. "What did they get you for"?? She asked spooning up a mouthful of butter scotch pudding onto her tongue.

Holly looked across at her as she sat down on the edge of her cot. "Possession of Crack Cocaine. Mother fuckers, and I was on my way home to. I only had two stones on me. I'm lucky that they didn't get me earlier or I would've been up shit creek with no paddle."

"They should've just let you keep going ah"??

"We're gonna print you in half an hour." A Guard who was out of sight called out to Briggs.

"I couldn't believe it. I got to the corner of St. Laurent and St. Catherine and they rolled up on me. Cock suckers."

"Yeah, I know. They've done that to me before to. I'll be ready to go home and all of a sudden i'll hear someone call my name from behind and it'll be The Police. It's just one of those things I guess, goes with the territory. Hey, did you mule anything in here with you??

"No, I never had a fucken chance. Those pricks."

"Ha, ha. I know ah"?? Lilly said.

Andrew Dane stepped out of the shadows and gave his Daughter a hug, they were standing in the darkness on Ontario Street outside The Black Domino Tavern that's speakers were playing MERCY by STEVE JONES at a volume that gave decibel to the night air.

"That girl really scared me. I thought she was gonna hit Nana although Nana probably would've hit her back. I didn't know what the hell was gonna happen." Kate said releasing her Fathers embrace.

"I don't know about that. I think that she wanted your title and was just trying to give you a scare. If she did any of what you're talking about the only fighting that she'd be doing would be in The Prison Mess Hall at Tanguay."

"Speaking of which. How's Lilly"?? Kate asked concernedly.

"She's being held at The Police Station until morning. She has a hearing in the a.m."

Kate knew how much her Uncle cherished his ex girlfriend even though they'd walked below some bad skies in the past, and she knew that her Uncle Von could not stop loving Lilly no matter what Lilly might have done to him, their history was to long and to storied to simply disregard or walk away from.

In a way it made sense to her. The legendary couple had lived through so much together that it was impossible to over look all of that history or to just turn the page, no pun intended.

There was heavy cloud cover tonight and both Andrew and Kathleen Dane feared that it might rain. The sky was deep and foreboding as though it were about to unleash a fury that man himself could not conquer with its ominous blue lining and thick darkening storm clouds that threatened to explode with their awesomeness at any moment.

"This woman outta be one and done." Von "The Icon" said stepping from within the coiling black shadows behind The Black Domino Tavern. He had been sitting in the park most of the evening keeping track of the walls progress, thinking, amidst trying to find ways to move brick with his eyes, and he was wearing sun glasses although it was well after dark. His Brother had been inside having a beer, chatting and getting to know the wait staff.

Kate looked baffled. "Who's one and done"?? Shamrock asked. She recognized this expression to mean shoot someone in the head once and they'd be done.

"Your friend from The Restaurant. I should make it happen."

Andrew was rolling his eyes. "Lay off the death threats. I know you don't mean it but you should find something else to say anyway."

"Uh-huh" Dane retorted.

"If she shows up again she just might find herself on the other side of a ring made of concrete. I really didn't like the crap that she said about Evan. Leave my fiance out of it." Kate expressed in a venom laced tone. She hadn't known this woman long, but she'd already had enough of her.

"It's to bad Lilly hadn't been there. She would've ripped her face off." The Icon said. He knew that Lilly had a wicked temper and would have no doubt displayed its merits for this woman.

Across the street a sexy mulatto street hooker was working the stroll. Her name was Mikhail. She, Dane and Lilly had been friends for years and walked below a thousand moons together. "How you doin Mick"?? Dane called out.

"Ca, va"?? Mikhail asked. She was decked out in a shiny silver dress with her hair cut short and reading glasses, she looked French as French. She was pure Quebecois.

"This is my niece Kate." Dane said pointing toward his Brothers Daughter.

"Bonjour." Mick called out. She was walking the length of The Stone Park now in her pretty dress and high heels that clicked against the pavement as she moved. She had known David Dane and Lilly Chicoine for years having always been close to Lilly even before meeting her boyfriend who had once been bald, angry, and in a situation that at times he couldn't handle.

"I think that we'd all be better suited to going back to the past then living the shit that we're living today." The Ontario Street Original said wrapping his hand around a can of soda that he had retrieved from his black leather kit bag.

"You weren't happy then either." Andrew responded.

"I was happier than I am now."

"When was your life ever on track?? As long as you've been my Brother you've always had problems. It's not this era or that era it's who you are. People follow patterns and you're no different."

"My luck has always been bad. It creeps up. You can't escape it." David Dane said cracking open his soda. "Cheers." He said raising the aluminum can against the sky.

"Luck doesn't exist. It's not a predeterminer of future events, or past events for that matter."

"Yeah, i'm sorry to hear that. You should come and live my life for five minutes, it's not like you'd enjoy yourself. Then we can talk about bad luck."

Marcel was sitting in his living room watching Jillian dance on his glass table. She was high and most likely drunk to. She was skinny but the edges of her high heel pumps were beginning to dig in and scratch the layer of glass that sat atop Marcels coffee table. She was giving new meaning to the words "Table Dancer." Marcel thought.

"Anyway, I just thought I should ask you. Where is Star tonight"?? Jillian asked. All at once Marcel looked less than happy. "She has go at Graem, and that is shit monduire." He protested. Graem was another older gentlemen that Star sometimes stayed with off and on.

"Well, maybe you should call her and get her to come and see you and then the three of us can watch a movie or something." Jillian suggested. She was so high that she likely did not know where the floor was. She looked like a blond Barbie Doll standing upon a pedestal that stood on four legs.

Marcel had gone into the bedroom, changed, and come out wearing a loud Hawaiian shirt with a pair of rose coloured spectacles. "I AM A GIGOLO MONDUIRE"!! He called out dancing back and forth while snapping his fingers above his head.

"What? You're a gigolo"? Jillian called above the sound of the crazy french rock music that Marcel had turned on. He looked very sexy standing there in his Hawaiian shirt indeed.

In fifteen minutes, the neighbours were at the door followed by Von "The Icon" and his Brother who was dressed in an Armani suit. They had dropped Kate off at home.

"Jesus, what the hell's goin on"?? Andrew asked as he came through the door. There was now broken glass everywhere. Jillian had gone through the table.

"Marcel, you're gonna need a dust pan." Von "The Icon" said surveying the floor. "I don't envy your cleaning lady. She's probably gonna quit." He went on. He still had not removed his sun glasses.

"Andrew, this is Marcel." Dane said introducing his old comrade whose shirt was louder than the music that was playing over the sound system.

"I see." The Attorney said.

"And the young lady lying on the couch is Jillian. She's Ontario Streets answer to the chick who leans backward in The Smashing Pumpkins Video Ava Adore. She looks just fuckin like her." Dane commented. He was now ankle deep in blue shattered glass.

"Marcel, is this responsible adult behaviour"?? The Ontario Street Original asked.

"Well yes, she has done it." Marcel said of the busted coffee table. He was looking around the room at nothing, however attentive. There was a spark in his eye. He was very much alive for someone his age.

"They shouldn't have left that there because they knew I was gonna break it, or someone was gonna break it." Jillian murmured from behind them. She was so high that Dane wondered if she could've come down with a ladder.

At that same moment Andrews phone lit up. The call display said "Leilani."

"Hello." Andrew said. He wasn't sure what he was going to tell her about all this noise. Ready, steady, go. "Yeah, i'm at a friend of my Brothers. I think one of Davids friends decided to do some remodelling. No, no, well, she went through a table ... ... ah-ha ah-ha ... ... she's fine."

"I am not fine. I need another hit of Smack." Jillian echoed from several feet away.

"She needs another hit of what"?? The straight laced Leilani asked. She was wondering where in the hell Dane had taken her husband. "I bought some Bar-B-Que chicken but I haven't cooked it yet." She exclaimed.

Kate had just unlocked the door on Leilani's end of the phone and walked in. She did not live with her Parents however she did have her own set of keys.

Marcel, can you buy me another hit of Smack"?? Jillian asked in her high pitched, sexy voice.

"Where the hell are you"?? Leilani chirped.

Dane was moving around with a dust pan scooping up glass. Marcel was upside down doing Yoga against the wall, he looked like a broom. Dane thought.

"Marcel, she's gonna fall again." Von "The Icon" said watching Jillian who was doing anything and everything other than what she was supposed to be doing. He knew just how bad the drugs were for her. Jillian also tragically suffered from Epilepsy. She had once had open heart surgery.

She was also adorable.

"I am teaching Yoga maybe six times a week now." Marcel boasted from his upside down posture.

Andrew had answered Leilanis query, telling her that he was at David's friends house. He still had not changed out of his suit which now looked tired.

Sometimes Andrew Dane felt as though he spent twenty four seven defending people. Tonight he was assisting in keeping his older Brother out of trouble, and tomorrow, who knew. These were the symptoms of his line of work, be it day to day or night to night. He held up his practice, no pun intended. He also had never lost a case.

Andrew was a success, there was that as well as the fact that he made a large salary to take home to his wife and in the past his gorgeous Daughter who was now able to take care of herself. He could not complain, despite the work load.

"Okay, we should be going." Andrew said. The environment was making him more and more nervous by the minute. The last thing that he needed was to be in a room where there was hardcore drug involvement as well as a girl who did not know when to call it a night.

"Alright Marcel. We're outta here." Dane said standing in the centre of the room. He was still holding the dust pan as Marcel up righted himself and came over to say goodnight. He shook Danes hand and the two embraced. "I will have many women here next time monduire." Marcel said.

Dane shook his head and smiled as he walked down the hallway toward the front door.

"We're lucky that my Brother was able to arrange this visit." Dane said embracing the love of his life. He thought that she looked beautiful standing there with her make up and eye liner on.

One of the other girls had probably loaned her some products as had happened so many times in the past. He was happy to be here with her, still to this day his heart pounded whenever he was in her presence the same way that it had when Lilly first came to stay with him. There was no pulmonary stimulant like love.

"I didn't do it." She immediately offered.

"I know you didn't." Von said genuinely. He had heard it said that when you denied something before being accused of it that most cops saw such behaviour as a sign of guilt. Dane believed this to be bull shit because inferences could be drawn based on behaviour or even environment, if one were in a Police station, then there was probably a reason for it.

He had read a book called Foreign Faction by James Kolar on The Jon Benet Ramsey murder investigation. In the book Patsy Ramsey had denied guilt upon being printed and having DNA extracted from her. She had made the unsolicited remark, "I didn't kill my baby" which to the cops was a red flag because quote "No one had said that she had."

What Kolar had neglected to point out was that by proxy of the very procedure that Patricia Ramsey was undergoing she had every reason to believe that she was under suspicion of killing Jon Benet.

"I'm sick of sitting in here. There's nothing to do." Lilly complained.

"Yeah, I know. I'm gonna see if they'll allow you to have Books. If they say it's alright then i'll bring you some reading materials. Maybe The Halloween Books." He suggested. Von was speaking of John Carpenter and Debra Hills infamous series about a Baby Sitter being stalked by her deranged half Brother as his Psychiatrist tried to put a stop to it.

The films were a favourite of the famous couple.

"My Brother knows what he's doing Baby Bunny. You're in good hands. Andrew's never lost in a courtroom. If you wanna sign a waiver or a permission release of some sort that discloses the details of your case to me then maybe I can do a little investigating on my own."

"Okay." Lilly said exhaling slightly.

There was a screw out in the hallway and he was keeping vigilant over Tanguays most well known couple. He had been there for years and Von had seen him many times before. Whenever he would drop off money and a letter for Lilly, this particular hack would always staple both contributions together.

"I called Phillip the other day to thank him for everything that he's done." Von said of Lilly's original lawyer who had always stood by her side.

Phillip had always been someone that Dane held in the highest regard, a class act who had always done whatever he could for Lilly not to mention as an acting liaison between she and Dane on days when Lilly was in court. On top of it, he was a helluva nice guy.

"Phillip is a good lawyer." Lilly echoed.

Dane went back in his mind for a moment to a night where The Police had brought Lilly home to him instead of taking her to jail. It immediately reminded him of how long they had both known each other not to mention what an emotional road they'd been down together.

He could still envision her standing there in her little yellow jacket with the hood on the back. She had looked nervous intertwining her fingers with her hands back to back seemingly unsure of what Danes reaction to the situation might be, not knowing whether he would allow her to claim his apartment as her home or not.

It made him realize how much he loved her, and of how much he had always loved her and always would. No human being, no force had ever been as powerful or as intoxicating as Lilly Chicoine, she had over taken his mind, body and soul ever since the day that they met in the rain.

"I never thought i'd be in a mess like this. I guess they still can't find Roberta." Lilly disclosed.

"Who's Roberta"?? Von asked. The name only rang the faintest of bells.

"She's the girl who would've had a motive if any to wanna kill Kelly Mathews."

Dane was arranging chairs in the conjugal room for them to sit down on. They were smooth, made from an orange plastic material. He remembered these chairs being here from years gone by.

"Did you tell Andrew about her"?? Von "The Icon" enquired as he sat down with Lilly doing the same across from him.

She was bright eyed and attentive. She looked well slept. He also thought that she was absolutely beautiful sitting there in her red plaid shirt and blue jeans. Lilly had always been gorgeous.

"Hmm … … hmm." This hmm … … … hmming tendency of Chicoines was something that Von had always found cute as well as adorable. "He's having his investigator look into it but when he called earlier they still hadn't found her yet." Lilly professed.

In moments there was a guard at the window pointing to the face of her watch as if to signify that the two famous lovers did not have much time left together. The visit had been slated for thirty minutes, and they had used most of it up.

"I'm gonna call Andrew as soon as I get to my cell and have him draw up those release forms. I know this place isn't exactly The Waldorf." Dane said taking visual stock of his surroundings.

"Okay. So, how's your famous niece that i've heard so much about? I've seen you guys all over TV together. I hear that she's a woman not to be messed with. What is it that they call her"??

"Kate "The Gate" Shamrock." Von "The Icon" answered proudly.

His niece was the apple of his eye, when Kathleen was still a Baby Von had sent her one e-mail per week and constantly showered her with gifts and toys. Spoiling Kate had been one of his favourite pass times, and still was. Kate was an angel.

"Why do they call her Kate "The Gate"?? I've never gotten that." Lilly enquired.

"The Gate, is the line up at a show or a sporting event. Kate draws a crowd. The Promoters count on her to draw revenue and bring in money. Therefore, because of her name and drawing power, she's Kate "THE GATE" Shamrock." Von explained emphasizing his nieces moniker.

"Oh, now I understand. I saw her on TV when I was back home. She's beautiful. She looks like a movie star."

"She's had offers from film companies. She just hasn't had time to respond to any of them yet." Dane said beaming from ear to ear. "Plus I don't think that that's her style." He said. His niece was without a doubt his favourite subject on this earth, she, along with Lilly Chicoine.

"I love you Boo." Lilly said as the bell sounded for the visit to end. "I love you to. We're gonna get you out of here, I promise. Heads up." Von "The Icon" responded leaning in to kiss the love of his life on the lips. Her lip stick tasted like cherry.

SHADOW PLAY BY CONTRACT KILLER echoed over the loud speakers at The Black Domino Tavern as Kate Shamrock walked through the door to meet her Instructor who was seated near the far end of the room. Donovan, against the advice of his doctors, was enjoying a cigarette.

Donovan wore a tami on his head and a clover leaf green vest over a white dress shirt and black dress slacks. There was a boiler maker on the table in front of him that was frothing at its brim and to its left was a pack of Camel Cigarettes, minus one.

"Ah, me Gate. I was wondering when you were going to show your face." He said standing to greet his protege who seemed somehow driven to distraction. Kate looked like she was half miffed, half bewildered. Donovan O' Riley did not know why. He had been here since eleven o clock this morning. It was now three.

"Hi Donovan." Kate greeted throwing her arms around her trainer as a white sweat shirt hung from her right wrist in sleeve and shirt tail. She had left her bag at home and was thus tooling around carrying her laundry. There was a square bandage on her forehead, a bi product of this mornings sparring session.

There weren't many tough girls left in town, but she had found one today in her training mate.

"What's on yer mind"?? O' Riley asked her. He could see her wheels turning, and usually, when she was like that, something was wrong. He had seen her big heart suffer before. Kathleen Dane was one of the kindest, most positively raised young women that he had ever known, but now, something was troubling her.

"I had a run in with someone yesterday while Nana and I were out having dinner."

Donovan was now the one who looked bewildered. He had not heard about this yet and had no idea what Gate was talking about.

"We were sitting there and this woman came over to our table. She looked like Conan "The Barbarian. She said that she wanted my title as well as including some other expletives which I don't care to mention. I'm so hungry I could eat a horse." Kate said pulling up a chair and sitting down.

Donovan's face had taken on a more serious expression. "Did she give a name this lady"??

"Jacky Hannah." Shamrock answered.

Donovan gave no reaction. "I've never heard of her." He said. "Did she seem to be new in town"?? He half joked, his facial expression giving away to a light smirk. He was familiar with most of the names on the roster here in Montreal. Jacky's was not one of them.

"Bad, bad girl her." An alien voice came from across the room. It was a male sitting alone with his back to them. He wore a black leather jacket over biker chaps with long greasy blond hair.

"Who the hell are you"?? Kate asked unseating herself and heading across the floor to the strangers table in a straight line.

Who was this guy?? She wondered to herself as he stood to face her.

He looked her up and down, one way and then the other. His eyes were all over her like a cheap suit. "Boy, you sure are a tough little lady." The thug said. He was sipping on a bottle of Jack Daniels that he had brought into the bar with him. He looked like he might've crawled out from underneath a rock.

"Who are you"?? Kate asked boldly. She was assessing the dirty boy pound for pound, wondering if worse came to worse whether or not she'd be able to kick the holy fucking hell out of this mother fucker.

He took another pull from his beer before beginning to speak. Now though, his demeanour changed slightly. He seemed less sleazy and more serious.

"You see, Jacky doesn't have time for a puppet like you. Thing is, she wants your title, but that's the easy part. She also doesn't have time to get ranked. So, here's what's gonna happen. You're gonna sign of the dotted line or we're gonna start taking your Family apart piece by piece."

Donovan O' Riley was now back on his feet listening to this from just feet away. His eyes were half smouldering. He should have stepped in, but he wanted this abhorrently reared horses ass to finish what he was saying first.

It was at that moment that Andrew Dane walked through the door. He was standing behind the biker with the greasy hair balling up his fists clenching and then releasing as if taking part in a warm up regimen. Was this scum bag giving his little girl a hard time??

She had seen her Father and was making eye contact with him now. Her expression seemed to say that she was able to handle it and that her Father did not need to get involved. However, his face said something quite different.

"You tell Jacky to come and see me at The Frotenac Gym Community Boxing Centre tommorrow morning at eight a.m.." Kate said closing the distance between herself and the biker while raising her hand in her Fathers direction.

She had things in hand, and besides, she was aware that if her Irish Papa decided to step in that he might lose his license to practice law and she refused to be responsible for that, not now, and not after a lifetime of working hard to get to where he was.

The Biker looked her up and down again before taking a final pull from his bottle of Jack Daniels that he held by the neck. "I'll give Jacky your message." He said turning to brush up against a violent looking Andrew Dane who was standing not a foot his junior in distance.

The two men locked eyes for a moment and then the guy with the greasy hair and the chaps walked out of the bar and disappeared into the grey afternoon.

"Who was that"?? Andrew Dane asked throwing his thumb in the direction of the door.

"I don't know, and I don't wanna find out." Kate said. The intensity was still in her eyes. She had not been prepared for what had just happened.

Ten minutes later Kate's fiance Evan Baker walked through the door and kissed her fully on the lips, he had just come from work to find his future wife standing there upset and all he had wanted was a cold beer. "What happened here"?? The handsome architect asked. He was also a former fitness model.

"Someone wants my title, and they don't wanna go through the rankings system to get it." Kate Shamrock said. She was ready for war. If this bitch wanted a piece of her then that's exactly what she would get, whether or not it would be for one of her straps was another story.

"Donovan, I want you to find out all that you can about this Jacky Hannah woman." Kate offered. "See if she's been ranked anywhere before."

"Aye Gate. Will do." The trainer said lifting his jacket from the seat behind him and pulling it on over his shoulders. If this woman wanted Gate to fight, then fight Gate would. That's what she did, and she was spot on. It was not easy to defeat Kate "The Gate" Shamrock.

"Why is everyone standing here"?? The Ontario Street Original asked coming through the door with a look of bewilderment on his face.

Andrew explained to him what had happened as well as its impending aftermath.

"Someone needs to cut this woman down." Von "The Icon" said ominously. He was also known as "The Knife Of Thug Life," and for good reason.

His morality as well as his judgements came from over twenty five years on the street, not from a more civilized echelon of society like his Brother who was class, loquaciousness and sophistication from head to toe, a monarch of self respect and dignity.

"I think this woman needs to find a more suitable pass time. I know some people who own a cement company." Von said grabbing a bottle of beer from a tray that was going by. He was holding it by the neck. "Jimmy, that's the second one in five days, and I never drink." Von "The Icon" said. He was speaking to the bar tender.

"Evan." He greeted tapping his nieces future bow on the shoulder as he swallowed a mouth full of beer thats glint from the light outside was reflected in the lenses of his sun glasses.

"I don't fuckin like people coming into this bar and threatening my Daughter."

"I don't like people coming into this bar and threatening your Daughter either. These are my streets, and I want her off them. Why the fuck do you think I want someone to cut this bitch"??

Kate was zoned out, thinking about her predicament. This woman was only going to get worse, better was not in the cards. What a bitch. This was stressful, but she was a champion, and she would react to this lowlife like one.

"Uncle Von." She said. "Will you come to the gym tomorrow morning with Donovan and I, and bring some of your crew."

"Uh-huh." Von "The Icon" said. "I don't know if this woman is gonna like Ontario Street Politics. Her band of bullies might not make it through the night. If she has a fuckin brain in her head, and if she wants to keep it there, then she should stay in bed tomorrow morning."

Andrew Dane was at this moment wishing that he was not a member of the bar, at least not the one that issued legal licenses. When things got out of line, and in his world that meant the act of up setting his Daughter, Hell may rain on earth with himself as the catalyst.

Evan was nodding.

"I love you Daddy." Kate said giving her Father a hug as well as a peck on the lips. He was and would always be her hero, never had she idolized and respected a man more in her life for all of his accomplishments or for the things that he had done for her during her life.

Second on the list was her Uncle Von who had always been there for her and never let her down. As rumour had it he was working on a Book about her. She wondered what it would be called.

Andrew was on the phone now. "No, I don't want my client speaking to anyone, least of all The Police.

No, I want her kept away from the other prisoners. Put her in Administrative Segregation. Tell them i'll pay for a TV and whatever else out of my own pocket. I want her to invoke her right to remain silent on everything short of what she wants for dinner. Please make sure that she has cigarettes as well as chocolate, candy, soda, whatever. This is the love of my Brothers life. I don't care, put it on my tab."

Von was listening to all of this from just feet away. He was holding his bottle of beer by its neck. "What in Christs name was that"?? He asked after his Brother hung up. "The Police want to question Lilly. They have new evidence. I said no fucking way."

"What?? What new evidence"??

"I don't know." Andrew said looking around. He was clearly not happy.

Von appreciated all that his Brother was doing for Lilly. He just hoped that it would be enough to save her from a twenty five year prison sentence. He didn't believe that she had done it. Lilly wasn't capable of shanking someone to death.

He thought for a moment, remembering all of the days and nights that he and this woman had spent together, and of how much she had always and would always mean to him. Calling her the love of his life wasn't saying enough. If there was a title, or a crown to be worn, then Lilly Chicoine was The Lady Of His Heart.

When Andrew Dane got to The Police Station he was ushered into a debriefing room with four chairs, a lamp, and one table. There was a Sergeant named Morella waiting for him. There were two file folders on the table top, and one of them had Lilly Chicoines name on it. It also read, down sizing. Andrew Dane did not know why.

"Alright, council. We've got a video tape. It's in evidence but I had one of my men draw up a report with respect to what's on it. There's an image of a male walking up the stairs shortly before the murder takes place but we can't positively identify the face. We're wondering if there's any possible way that your client might recognize him. The only problem is that there's a light bleeding into the frame that leaves the face slightly out of focus." The husky French Italian Sergeant said. He was standing to one side of the room straight and statuesque before the table.

Andrew was already wondering if this might be a set up, a way to get Lilly to open up and talk. "You should have notified me before you asked to speak to my client. Under no circumstances do you ever again in the future try to engage my client without my prior authorization. Are we clear"?? Andrew Dane asked. He was in no mood to put up with cheap fuckin parlour tricks. He would have these cops badges.

"I want a copy of the actual footage, not a report that was drawn up in place of it."

"We want access to your client first." Morella insisted. His body language indicated that he would bargain, but only in exchange for what he wanted. He looked like a thug in a uniform standing there in his stripes. Andrew Dane was pissed. None of this bull shit. They had a right to view the actual footage. Mother fuckers, trying to get him to serve his client up.

"No, we'll subpoena the tape. That's disclosure. You have no right to withhold that tape from my client, or from me." Andrew Dane said. He was ready to climb over this table and pull this mother fuckers tongue out through his ass. "I'll be in touch." Andrew said, lifting his brief case off of the table and storming out the door.

The next afternoon at three P.M. Lilly Chicoine had another visitor. This time it was Marilyn Dane. It had been years since the two had seen each other, and for Lilly this would be a bit of an awkward reunion because she knew that what had happened in 2008 had been rough.

"Hi." Lilly said smiling and putting on her best face when what she really wanted to do was cry. She had fond memories of this woman who had once treated her as though she were one of her own children. Lilly loved Marilyn, and was in all truth, regretful about the way that things had turned out between them.

"I thought you'd be happy to have a visitor this afternoon." Marilyn Dane said smiling as she came through the door. She thought that this ordeal must be a nightmare for Lilly. Marilyn wore a sky blue blazer over black dress slacks, and her hair that was bleached blond was tied up at the back.

"You look nice." Lilly complimented. She was, in all honesty happy to have her secondary Mother figure here visiting her. However, this was a window visit and not a conjugal so there were no hugs.

"I put some money in your canteen so that you'd be able to get some pop, chips, cigarettes or whatever." Marilyn said. She had deposited a hundred dollars in total.

"Thank you. You didn't have to do that though." Lilly said genuinely. She remembered The Christmas that she had spent in

Halifax as well as the three other Christmas's that she had spent with David Danes Family in Montreal. Marilyn had always been good to her buying her lots of gifts and giving her the occasional hug. Her boyfriend had also gone out of his way to make sure that her Christmas's were a beautiful time for her, he always wanted everything to be special.

She recalled the time when Von had gone around to five different stores in order to find all of the C.D.'s that she wanted. That had been very sweet of him. One of them had been The Depeche Mode CD Violator. Lilly, however, could not recall the rest. It seemed so many moons ago now.

"How are you making out in here"?? Marilyn asked concernedly. She hated to see Lilly locked up like this as she had always loved Lilly as though she herself had given birth to her.

This was a horrible place and Marilyn could sense it in the air. She wondered how even the most hardened of convicts could stand to be incarcerated. If there was a Heaven and a Hell, then this was Hell. Her own sons four day imprisonment had been a nightmare that had altered him psychologically forever.

"So, are you in town for long or is this only a temporary visit"?? Chicoine asked. She had lit up a cigarette behind the bullet proof window and was now using her hand to fan the smoke in another direction.

"Hey, are you allowed to do that"?? Marilyn asked frowning. She did not want to see Lilly "Bad To The Bone" Chicoine dragged off in shackles and bracelets, despite her nickname.

"No, not really, but they never catch me."

"Hey, put that away. If they see you they might cancel this visit as well as any future visits as well. I won't be able to come and see you anymore." Marilyn said trying to scare Chicoine into putting the cigarette out.

The only problem was that there was no scaring Lilly out of doing anything. She was way beyond fear. This dare devil side of her personality had existed since child hood. It seemed that Lilly Chicoine had no fear of anyone or anything, and particularly detested rules and authority, it was part of what made her who she was.

"Okay, i'll put it out on my shoe." Lilly agreed. Normally her resolve would have been like iron, no negotiating and absolutely no compromising whatsoever. When she had made up her mind she had made up her mind and that was that.

It had been this problem very early on that had lead to her falling out with her own Parents who had in all reality wanted the best for her, but the fighting had become to intense and Lillys will was to strong. She had wanted to leave and had after awhile done just that.

"Hey, there's a Guard coming. Kick the cigarette butt underneath your side of the ledge." Marilyn ordered. This was her nature.

Lilly obliged her.

"You being a good girl"?? A familiar looking screw asked turning her gaze toward the back of Lilly's skull. She was wearing a light coloured uniform shirt over well pressed dress pants.

"Uh-huh. What time are we having dinner"?? Lilly asked the guard.

"I don't know. I'll have to ask." The hack responded. This was a big fuck you and Marilyn knew it. She could tell by the look on Lilly's face that this was utter defiance. The screw hadn't caught her and Lilly was somehow pleased with herself over it. Marilyn shook her head in mild disbelief but was in truth humoured by Lilly's rebellion against authority.

Marilyn Dane herself had no love for Law Enforcement Officials firmly believing more times than not that they abused their power and in kind abused innocent people. She had often expressed to her eldest son that she quote "Did not trust them."

This opinion had been born of so much of what she saw on television and/or read in the papers. They were just to quick to draw their fire arms or not to resist the urge to use their tasers. She believed that many Police Officers should be put in jail themselves to see how it felt to be on the other side of the wall.

"Oh, by the way, please tell Andrew that I said thank you for the television set that they put inside my cell. Fuck, I would've gone crazy without it, and thank him for putting money in my canteen. That was nice of him."

"Oh, you're welcome." Marilyn said warmly. This girl who sat across from her had sparked a genuine emotional reaction from her. She truly sympathized with Lilly's plight and wished that things had been better for her. It was just as if Lilly Chicoine was one of her own kids.

"Thank you Marilyn." Lilly said. "Have you heard from Von today? I tried calling earlier but his phone went into voice mail." … … … … …

That morning Von "The Icon" had stood in the ring at The Frotenac Community Boxing Club with two of his thugs standing on the floor to either side of the low risen canvas but Jacky Hannah and her goons had put in a complete no show, no message. Kate had been there to, ready with gloves on but there had been no sign of any of Hannah's people, they had done nothing to initiate contact nor to tip their hand in any way.

The twenty five year veteran of the street was bewildered. This woman had gone far out of her way to get Kate to fight her and yet when presented with a golden opportunity she put in a complete no show. To Von "The Icon," Ontario Streets Last Outlaw," this made zero sense. Why the fuck would Jacky pass up her opportunity???

"I don't get it." The Ontario Street Original voiced at supper time that night. Now, he and Kate were alone in the gym. The window to the eastern side of the room was growing black and night was almost upon them.

"This lady goes out of her way to confront you and Mum outside of a restaurant. She has you followed, then she decides not to cease her opportunity to confront you in an environment that fosters her cause. Is she suffering from Multiple Personality Disorder"?? The King of The Street asked.

He was, as usual, wearing wrap around sun glasses when it was not a necessity. On his back he wore a black leather jacket with a thin orange stripe down each sleeve over a black sweater and blue jeans finished off by black sneakers with three white stripes down each side.

Kate stood for a moment in pause. She was gazing at her Uncle now as if she were day dreaming. She thought of this man who had loved her unconditionally since childhood. He had sent her an e-mail every week when she was still a baby for her Father to read to her. He had bought her gifts and showered her with more love than she ever thought possible, he had offered himself as her best friend when she was only six months old, and for all those things, she loved the man who stood before her now with every fibre of her soul.

"What"? Dane asked reacting to the far away look in her eyes. It was a look that he didn't see often.

"I love you Uncle Von." She said. "You're the best there ever will be."

"Hey, that's nice. Thanks." Von "The Icon" said. There was a warm smile on his face. "I love you to."

Just then Kates phone lit up on the other side of the room. When she got to it she immediately noticed the words PRIVATE CALL on the display window.

"Hello." Shamrock said into the mouth piece. Her expression immediately turned to one of horror.

"What is it"?? David Dane asked.

Kate put her hand over the mouth piece. "It's the hospital. Evan's been shot." She said with terror rising from her aura.

Von "The Icon" looked mystified.

As soon as they got to The Hospital Kate went directly to the desk and enquired as to which room Evan Baker was being kept in. "He's in The O.R. The Duty Nurse had responded.

"Is he gonna make it"?? Kate asked with so much desperation in her voice that Von "The Icon" was afraid that she might faint as he stood at her back. He knew who was behind this and now he knew the reason why Jacky Hannah and her people had no showed the rendezvous, because they had never had any intention of showing. This was all a set up.

It had all been a smoke screen to keep Kate away from her fiance while he was being shot. Apparently he had been lying on the floor of their home for awhile and had lost a fare amount of blood and had to be given a transfusion.

Dane suspected that he could very well have been lying there for hours before anyone found him.

"Please tell me." Kate begged desperately. "OH GOD, IS HE GONNA BE ALRIGHT"?? Kate demanded turning around to embrace her Uncle.

"It's alright. It's alright." Dane said, cradling the back of Kates head with the palm of his hand as she cried into his chest. He could not believe any of this. He had seen many of his own friends die young. His friend David Jacobs had been shot to death outside of a strip club.

His friend Paul had fallen to his death when he and two other people had been trying to allude security after a robbery and had fallen two stories from an under ground parking lot and hit his head. His former friend, Kerry, had died of Diabetes at 30yrs old, his friend Blair of the flesh eating disease.

Blair Coffee had been one of the most brave and emboldened street fighters that Von "The Icon" had ever had the pleasure of knowing, and he was an incredibly loyal friend as well often calling out or challenging anyone who dared to oppose his friend and mentor. Dane would never forget Blair Coffee for that.

Blair had always looked up to David Dane as a big brother as well as a personal roll model. Dane had been told this just weeks after Blairs death, and the revelation had brought him to tears.

He had lost his friend Mary who was a World Renowned Super Model when she'd been sitting on a park bench on a date and a drunk driver had come out of nowhere and ploughed into the bench that she had happened to be occupying. She had died instantaneously.

His friend, Norm, who had been a Boxing Instructor back in Halifax had died just days after he was attacked by several men carrying base ball bats following a confrontation with them outside a Motor Lodge in Halifax for verbally abusing his wife. Norm was also a brave and heroic soul who would have fought Satan himself if only Satan had bothered to ask.

Then there was the death of a legendary and iconic Maritime Gangster who had been murdered due to his involvements with organized crime.

This particular individual and Dane had been at odds for years but had ended things with a handshake and a mutual respect for one another in front of a popular Halifax Shopping spot. Dane had also been flattered to the point of tears when he had heard of a compliment that this particular individual had paid him through a mutual acquaintance some fourteen days prior to his death. Dane was genuinely saddened to hear of this legends passing and wished to this day to extend his warmest condolences to this individuals Family and friends despite their intense rivalry.

Dane had lost his friend Shane to a drowning accident when Shane had been only eleven years old when his raft had separated and the fisher mans over alls that he'd been wearing had filled up with lake water dragging him below the surface of the water and ending his short life.

Danes friend, "Trey," as he called himself, his real name was Cort, had allegedly died when he was shot to death over testimony that he was supposed to give but never made it to court for(This however, was unconfirmed).

Then there were The Ontario Street related deaths of Angelica, who had died of Aids, to Jenny, who had either died of Aids or an OD, and there was also Blast who had died of Aids who to David Dane was more an acquaintance than a friend.

Then more recently, another childhood friend named Marc had fallen asleep at the wheel and gone into a ditch where he later died.

Dane and his niece were sitting together in a waiting area now. Kate was beside herself and Von was taking small sips from a styrofoam cup that contained piping hot Coffee.

Kate was resting her head on her uncles shoulder as he sat slightly forward holding the cup between his fingers. He had removed his sun glasses. He also wore black leather cut gloves on his hands that had holes cut into the knuckles street fighter style, they had been a trade mark for years.

In moments a Doctor wearing a sanitation mask appeared before them. He was holding a clip board in his hand. Kate immediately looked up and into his eyes. She appeared totally exhausted. She couldn't believe that any of this was real.

"We've stabilized him." The Doctor informed the pair as Kate let out a yelp of relief. She was off her head terrified, unable to form a complete sentence. "Can I see him"?? She asked right away.

"No, not yet." The Surgeon responded flatly. "His vital's are good but he can't have any visitors yet. We have to do our best to keep The Patient calm. He's been through and incredible trauma, and he's lost a lot of blood. We had to give him a transfusion." Dr. Emblem said. "Your Fiance's a very strong man. If he's a fighter, he'll pull through."

"It's alright baby. It's alright." Von "The Icon" comforted putting both his arms around his nieces shoulders, but inside he was so fucking enraged at whoever had done this that he felt like shooting them himself. They had shot Evan which was bad enough, but on top of that they had hurt Kate, and to Von "The Icon," that was not acceptable..

When Dane awoke the next morning he was stretched out across three seats and cradling his right arm. At first he did not know where Katie was.

When he finally stood up and looked around he found her wrapped in a blanket slumped over between a rubber plant and the wall. Her face was expressionless. It had been a trying night, and he was glad to finally see his niece getting some rest no matter how discomforting the position.

Just then an auburnish nurse with high cheek bones walked by. Immediately, Von was taken back to the mid nineties and the memory of a gorgeous, sexy, strawberry blond Dutch model named Kendra that he had dated for a time. She had been a very sweet girl, and he wondered to himself what had become of her.

Kate moaned as she yawned and stretched still half underneath the blanket. "What time is it"?? She asked. There was no clock anywhere in the vicinity of either one of them and there was still darkness at the Emergency Room doors, past them, and in the parking lot outside.

Von "The Icon" glanced at his watch. "It's three am angel. Go back to sleep."

"Did The Doctor come back to see us"?? Shamrock asked, her eyes were blood shot and her face was drained of all of its colour. She looked like a cross between a zombie and a super model. Dane thought to himself.

"Not that I know of, but I just woke up myself. You want some Coffee"?? He asked.

Kate was shaking her head now. "Someone should call my Dad and let him know. At least that way he can tell my Mom and she won't have to hear it from anyone else."

There were two ceiling fans whirring above their heads.

"I'll drop a dime on your old man as soon as it hits five or six am."

"You think our friend had something to do with this"?? Kate "The Gate" asked.

"Do Bears shit in the woods"?? Von responded. His voice was stronger and more awake now. He was coming around.

"This was or this is … … …" Kate said correcting herself. "Her way of getting me to defend my title, so she'll have no problem getting me into the ring. It worked." Shamrock said with a determined look in her eye as she stood up from her seated position on the floor and began to stretch on her feet.

"You're setting a precedent." Von "The Icon" said raising his chin. His hands were on his hips.

Kate looked around for a moment. She had never thought of that. Giving this bitch what she wanted could cause others to follow her down the same path. What a predicament she had found herself in and it was just beginning.

The next morning at nine am, Andrew walked through the door to Lilly Chicoines cell. He had just received a voice message regarding Evan's situation on the way into The Prison driveway and was still in disbelief. It never ceased to amaze him how life had such lousy timing.

Here was Lilly on trial for her life, and there was Evan's life hanging in the balance. This really was one hell of a fuckin quagmire.

"Hey." Lilly greeted smiling. She was sitting on her cot with one knee raised to her chin.

"I have some good news." Andrew Dane began. He was about to tell her about the surveillance tape when his phone lit up. The call display said "BELL PAYPHONE."

"Hello." He said answering the ring which was the theme song from televisions 24 starring Kiefer Sutherland.

"Yeah, it's me. Evan's in The Hospital. He's been shot. Kate's here with me." David Dane said. His voice was quick and shaky. He was on his final nerve.

"Yeah, I just got your message on the way in here. I'm in Lilly's Cell." Andrew explained. "Can I speak to Kate"?? The Attorney asked. He was at this point extremely worried about his Daughters frame of mind. He knew how deeply in love Kate was with Evan and what this must be doing to her. He also wondered who the fuck was behind it and whether or not any of this had to do with this woman who had been putting pressure on Kate to defend her title.

"I'd let you talk to her but she's asleep on the couch in the visitors room." Dane responded. He was himself wondering how

Lilly was holding up at the same time. "I can go wake her up if you want but I think it's better that we let her sleep." He said.

Andrew breathed agreeably into the phone. "I do to." He said. "Lilly's here. Do you want to talk to her"?? He asked.

"Yeah I would." Dane answered.

"Hey Boo." Lilly said into the mouth piece. She was smiling. It was nice to have her boyfriend to talk to first thing this morning. She had been cooped up in here for days other than the couple of visits that she had received from Von and his Mum and these thick walls were beginning to truly horrify her. "How are you"?? Lilly asked.

"I'm alright gorgeous. How you doin"?? Von asked. He was really concerned about her psyche in the environment that she was being kept in, he himself had only been a Prisoner of The Hole for eighteen hours and that had almost destroyed him psychologically. It was in all honesty one of the most frightening experiences of David Danes life, bad ass or not.

"I'm good. Your Brother's helping me. I hope that i'll be out of here soon, fuck, these walls get to you after awhile. "Where are you? I hear funny buzzers going off in the back ground." Chicoine observed. She was moving her arms about restlessly above her head.

"I'm at The Hospital." He said. He was not prepared to unload anymore crap onto Lilly Chicoines plate then she already had to deal with. There would be plenty of stress associated with her current hell without him dumping anymore fuel on the fire.

"What are you doing there"?? Lilly "Bad To The Bone" Chicoine asked. She was upright on her knees purposefully rolling a cigarette while she held the phone to her ear with her shoulder. This was and had always been a frequent habit of hers.

"I'm here with Kate. She's having some tests run." Von BS'ed her.

"Oh, well tell her that I said hi." Chicoine said before telling her boy friend that she loved him and handing the phone back to Andrew Dane who had been standing at the far side of the room. He was angry, upset and confused, not to mention concerned for his Daughters safety.

"Yeah, when Kate wakes up tell her that I love her and that i'll drop by The Hospital to see her later on."

"Alright." Dane answered. He then hung up.

CHAPTER 3:

L.A.- I hope you are enjoying the murder mystery that Dane and Lilly are involved in. I want to take this time to address how things between you and I ended. People say angry things to each other but they do not always mean them. Monica and I unfortunately ended in the same manner, but truth be told Monica and I had many verbal arguments over the years yet ended up back in each others arms the next morning, these are the things about us that people do not know. It also amazes me how one person, one insignificant lowlife can change the course of someones life, i'm speaking of course of whoever the coward was who was on the other end of the phone with me on that fateful night that lead to Monica and I saying goodbye forever. He didn't give his name, and I doubt he ever will. I called him out once yet he chose not to accept. I am now calling him out again.

That one particular individual that I will address as well as speak to directly later on in this text. This whole thing was none of his business, but he contributed largely to the falling out that Monica and I suffered in the end. Now, and for all of eternity, I will live with the darkness surrounding her death as well as the dreams and the aftermath.

What Monica and I lived on Ontario Street as well as in private is, was, and forever shall be sacred to me. She gave me the experience of my life. She was an experience, my life has never and will never be the same without her.

I will address you as well as E.A. later on in the text. Hope you are enjoying URBAN RAIN II-NEIGHBOURHOOD OF NIGHT.

Regards,
Von "The Icon,"

When Leilani Dane walked into The Hospital waiting area later on that morning she was fashionably dressed and carrying her purse underneath her shoulder, she had just received the news about Evan and hopped a cab to The Hospital directly afterwards.

This had come as a major shock because she had never heard of Evan being involved in anything outside of his business and had not yet been made aware of the situation between her Daughter and Jacky Hannah. Leilani was still sitting on the fringes in shadow like the rest of the world waiting to be informed, inside she was a bundle of nerves waiting for the storm to unfold.

When she arrived in the waiting area she found her Brother in law seated in a chair with her Daughters head resting on his shoulder. Kate was fast asleep.

Dane greeted Leilani with a nod. "Andrew called you"?? He asked. His leather jacket was folded up and being used as a mock pillow behind his head. He hated hospitals, and what was worse was when you had to use one as a temporary residence, for however long.

"He called me about an hour ago." Leilani chirped. She had a small if not tiny voice, and Von had always thought of her form of speech as chirping. He wondered if his Brother was going to be here soon, he could use the conversation.

"Do you want Coffee"?? Leilani asked. She now had her purse between her thumb and her fore finger and was fishing a ten dollar bill out of it.

"No, i'm fine." Von "The Icon" responded as Andrew Dane showed up out of nowhere. It was as if Von had closed his eyes for a split second and when he opened them again he saw his Brother standing before him. Dane was wondering if he was hallucinating. "Morning Councillor." The Boxer greeted.

"Do you want Coffee"?? Leilani immediately asked upon seeing her husband.

"Hey." Andrew said addressing his Brother as he leaned in and kissed the sleeping princess of the cheek. She was dead to the world.

"No, I don't want any Coffee." Andrew Dane responded. He was now gazing at his Daughter wondering what his one and only angel had been through over the past twenty four hours.

He knew that hearing that her fiance had been shot must have been like she herself being shot between the eyes with a diamond bullet that's fragments embedded in her precious soul. Kate had always been a Daddy's girl, and now she needed her Father more than ever. As a child, she had always looked to him when problems had gotten to heavy, now, Andrew hoped that this situation wouldn't be any different.

This was a real choice situation. Von thought sarcastically as he stood up to move around. Evan had been shot, Lilly was in jail, Kates heart had been broken, and this Jacky Hannah character who was more likely than not behind the attempt on Evans life was walking around scott free. Mother Fucker!!!

Leilani had disappeared around the corner now into the area where the Coffee and vending machines were located, there was also a water fountain there flanked by two rubber plants that had been strategically hung from the ceiling as decor.

It had just occurred to Dane that no one had bothered to notify his Mother that any of this was going on, yet she was staying at a Hotel not far from here. "You wanna call Mum and let her know what the fuck is up." Von "The Icon" asked his Brother who was now seated to Kate's left.

"I already left her a voice mail and a text. She hasn't responded to either one yet." Andrew said stretching his arms and yawning. "She probably isn't even out of bed yet." He surmised yawning. He was exhausted beyond comprehension between worrying over his Daughters well being as well as Lilly's case, both were a drain on the funds of his psyche.

He had informed his client that they had footage of someone on a surveillance camera. She seemed to be elated by the revelation but had no thought to offer as to whom the spectre might be.

THE HOLE, where Lilly Chicoine was being housed was a man made hell that was designed to destroy one physically, emotionally, and mentally. It would not take long for such a facility to destroy one completely, but in this instance, such confining quarters were a necessity.

There was to much chance of other inmates or guards getting to Lilly and then testifying to something that they heard or said they might have heard later on in court. She had to be segregated from other prisoners. That was that.

"How's Evan"?? Andrew Dane asked. He was looking over at his Daughter who was still dead to the world. He hoped that she was dreaming of calm oceans and exotic landscapes, because when all of this was over, he intended to take her to a place with such attributes.

"I don't know." Dane said temporarily removing his arm from behind Kate's head so as to stretch it. He was slightly nauseated and felt close to becoming sick to his stomach, lack of sleep had never agreed with him. He had been up a thousand nights, one nocturne burning into another until his body wouldn't work for him anymore, but now he was getting older and all the kings horses and all the kings men, couldn't put Von "The Icon" back together again.

He was immediately reminded of when he and Lilly would stay out five days at a time cause Lilly was Coke tripping. Dane had often followed Lilly around for security reasons as well as just to be with her, it was a surreal time that he could never get back.

He remembered her bragging one time to another girl that "My boyfriend's been out here with me for five days and he doesn't even consume. He's never been high a day in his life." She had boasted to the jealous looking female who sat across from her.

Lilly had then looked across at him sitting in the field on De Lorimier and said "I love you Boo." Boo, was street slang back then for boyfriend. Dane did not know what it was now.

Then there was the time that Lilly had been loaded into the back of a Police Cruiser on Papineau at about five am in the morning flailing and screaming, and accidentally kicked the arresting officer in the back of the head. The cop had not been impressed. Dane himself had been mortified, he did not know what they might do to her for that, and to this day, he had never heard of the incident again.

Just then Marilyn Dane made her way into the waiting area and took a seat across from both of her sons. Leilani had since returned with a Coffee and a Kit Kat Bar and placed them on the table before her laying them out strategically as if setting the table for dinner.

"I came as soon as I got your text." Marilyn said with a worried expression nestled in her brow. "What the hell happened"?? She asked. There were tears drying in her eyes and her mascara had run.

Von "The Icon" did not flinch. He did not want to tell his Mother who had done this nor did he want to drag her into it, to much information, to much baggage. He would handle it himself. How, he did not yet know.

The next night as the moon rose over Ontario Street, Olend Marx stood in the neighbourhoods shadows talking to his son. What the two were saying could not be heard unless one was standing close by but it looked as though Olend was handing something to Clinton as Clinton reached for the inside of a bag thats colour was blue.

Suddenly there was a yelp as Olend felt a knife being driven into his chest. "Ah ... my." He attempted as he fell face first to the ground clutching his chest with a trail of blood pouring out of him below the glistening moon light.

"Jesus Fuckin Christ." Dane hollered as he watched Olend Marx being wheeled into EMERGENCY sixty minutes later. The Ambulance attendant who was pushing the gurney immediately noticed Danes reaction as he stood up and asked him if he knew the identity of the man that they had just brought in.

"Yeah, yes. This is Olend Marx." Dane said gripping the edge of the gurney with one hand while pouring over his friend with the other.

"He's a friend of mine."

"Alright, listen. I need you to tell The Triage Nurse the identity of your friend." The husky french man stated. They had searched Olends pockets as soon as he was discovered but found no sign of any identification. He had a puncture wound to the lower left chest as well as to the abdomen.

Kate was awake now and immediately rushed to her Uncles side. "Who's that"?? She asked, never having seen Olend Marx before. "Friend of mine." Dane answered seriously.

Andrew Dane was looking over the back of his chair. Leilani and Marilyn were seated before him. Leilani's eyes were shut. There was still no word on Evan.

"Yeah, my name's David Dane." The Fighter said to The Triage Nurse who was sitting in an enclosed booth behind a window. "The gentlemen who was just brought in is Olend Marx." He said. Then he spelled it for the twenty something year old desk attendant. She was fishing around in her coat pocket for something.

When she retrieved what she had been looking for Dane realized that it was a Beret.

Christ, a man had just been brought in covered in blood and this woman was worried about pinning her hair up. What the fuck were they using as Hospital Protocol these days????

"Are you the next of kin"?? The Triage Nurse asked with a clear view of Olend who was just feet away.

"Yeah, i'm his Brother." Dane said sarcastically of his Haitian friend who was lying only feet away bleeding to death. The next thing that they'd be asking him was whether or not Marilyn Dane was Olend's Mother.

The Nurse took stock of Dane for a moment but gave no reaction. She then went on and typed something into the space bar on her computer terminal.

Two days later Jacky Hannah stepped into her coaches office inside of the boxing club that housed her training. She was wide awake because of the buzz that she was experiencing from the line of Coke that she had just powdered her nose with, copped two baggies, cut one up.

It had been a slow burn but it had just kicked in. Sometimes it took a few minutes. There was light mascara run at the sides of her eyes and her fingers boasted a display of chunky gold rings each with an inscription on it.

She was not married, but her boyfriend Danno had always acted like a husband. He was from Brazil, the low end slums better known as "The Barrio." Danno had, had to gouge, claw, kick, bite and scratch to get everything that he'd gotten, even to earn his place as a member of a gang better known across the world as THE SHINING PATH.

"Sup Marty"?? Jacky asked greeting her rat faced coach who looked like he'd been dragged face first through most of his fifty five years on the planet. He was from Rio, and had snuck into Canada's borders illegally using false documentation.

Marty wore a stained white T-Shirt over blue track pants and white sneakers. He looked like the ass end of a used up gigolo. At a time, Marty had been a pimp, six girls and a stable that turned a decent profit every night. Marty had never known an honest day in his life. Beat the slums, rackets and any measure possible to turn a profit. Money made sense, nothing else mattered.

"You doin your cardio as regular as you should be? I can't keep up with you these days."

"Uh-huh." Jacky said

Someone has to worry about the books down here. It's better if I don't have to chase after you. Danno tells me that you're goin after Kate "The Gate" Shamrock, tells me that someone got into trouble over it, her lover or somethin."

"I wouldn't know anything about that." Jacky said walking across the floor and straddling Marty before she kissed him on the lips. "But I know this." She said as her trainer squeezed her ass cheeks." If I get Shamrock in the ring with me i'm gonna break her fuckin little neck and then i'm gonna paralyze the cunt.

She'll end up getting more than she bargained for. I don't think there's a damn thing that she could do to me if I was workin it toe to toe with her, she's to much of a pampered Prize Fighter. I don't think she's got what it takes to put it in the wind with me." Hannah said in a half seductive, half, nonchalant manner.

"You gonna give it to me before Danno gets back or what"?? Marty asked firming up Jacky's position on his lap. He had been doing the twenty seven year old Hannah behind her boyfriends back for two years. She was a great lay, and nasty as hell in the bedroom.

"Yeahhhh." … … … … Jacky said before grabbing his face and kissing him again.

Lilly was sitting alone in her cell reading a book. It was then that her Mother entered her mind for a moment. She thought of the many tough moments that had existed for the woman who had given birth to her, all of the trials and tribulations, the harsh times, and the things that she believed made her Mother a warrior.

Linda Chicoine had grown up in the slums of Portugal with no money and had to sometimes walk twenty miles to the nearest air port to go to work just so that her Family would have bread to eat. She had been very strong, and Lilly truly respected her for that.

Later on in life, after coming to Canada, Linda, and Gregory Chicoine who was the only Father that Lilly had ever known had worked their asses off every night of the week cleaning offices, homes, and even church halls. They had done all of this, every bit of it, so that their children would have a better life. They had also done it so that they would one day own their own home.

It had been a long and arduous road but they had made it.

Greg Chicoine, Lilly's only life Father had gone on later on to work in a meat packing plant as a respected supervisor while her Mum, Linda, had become a well liked Daycare worker who was exceptional with people. Von had once referred to Linda as cool and charismatic.

Lilly was very proud of both of her Parents to this day and despite all of the fighting she loved them with a pride that words could not do justice for.

Beyond that, there was Julian, Lilly's older Brother, he had always loved her and looked out for her, he was a genuinely nice guy who had spent most of his adult life as a starving musician, he also, in most situations referred to himself as a minimalist. Lilly was not sure as to what exactly that meant.

Then there was her youngest Brother, Nicholas. who was the success story of The Family. Lilly had grown up not knowing him because she had lived away so much and the second reason was that Nicholas had only been a baby when she left, Nicholas was a world Famous Concert Pianist and Piano Teacher who owned his own academy that had a variety of students to its credit, he had such a turn over, and the client base had been so steady that he was in demand world wide. Nicholas's house looked like a candidate for LIFE STYLE'S OF THE RICH AND FAMOUS.

Nicholas Chicoine had done very well for himself indeed.

When Von "The Icon" returned to his building he found the Night Watch Men Max sitting behind his desk eating a salad, there were five monitors sitting below the marble before him each alive and blazing with imagery. Every monitor displayed a different echelon of the buildings interior from back to front and was inclusive of high definition footage as well as a zoom feature that allowed one to zone in on whatever or whomever they were interested in seeing close up.

Max was once thought of as a genuine male show piece, but had since put on a ton of weight, ate far to much and looked like a shell of his former self. They called him Papa Persia in the wake of his anti Canadian comments that began with slandering Canadians and finished with Max slandering everyone else as well. His usual commentary of Canadians was that they were a stupid, ignorant bunch who could only be counted on to worsen Max's already deteriorating opinion of the country.

Dane had often commented that he looked like a character from a Michael Mann film always dressed in pin striped suits, pastels, and white ties, beyond that, he was a useless piece of shit better huddled to the floor with the furniture.

"David." Max began in his customarily smooth, suave tone of voice. Silk over an ocean of calm. "What's going on"?? He asked the Boxer who looked like he had just gone eleven out of twelve rounds with Evander Holyfield.

"You're gonna be goin on a plane back to where you came from if you keep talking to me."

"You could have at least brought me some coupons." Max said. "The ones from A and W are the most useful to me." The Watchmen said smirking inappropriately with a loll of his head.

"So you still running around here trying to illicit personal info on me from the other tenants or have you found a new pass time"?? Dane asked the smug Persian who sat before him.

Max ran a hand through his thick jet black hair while one of his feet rested gingerly on the edge of the console placement. "Why would you think I would do that "?? Papa Persia asked feigning disinterest in what he was trying to convince Dane to be a manifestation of his own subconscious mind.

Dane paused for a moment. "Are you really enough of an idiot to think that I don't know any better"?? Dane asked making a cross with his fingers. "You need to get out of here more often. The monitor signals are killing your brain cells." He said.

Sooner or later there was going to be holy hell to pay if this band of idiots didn't quit their games.

Just then a gorgeous blond with massive breasts walked in and greeted both men with a vague smile.

"Disneyland." Von said half smiling, but in truth, he was so fucking tired that he could have cared less about women, not now, maybe after a week of sleep and a hot shower.

"Okay buddy. I have to go and do rounds." The well dressed Iranian said lifting himself from his seated position, and in the process, he farted. This was another repulsive habit of Max's.

"Jesus that's disgusting." David Dane said before exiting stage left and disappearing upstairs where he would retire for the next nineteen hours.

In his sleep that night Dane saw himself walking through what appeared to be an aquatic theme park full of twisting slides and roller coaster rides. In some of the wading pools at the bottom of the run Von "The Icon" saw what looked like porno graphic live sex scenes going on between the males and females who were in the pools.

The whole thing was taking place at night, everything playing out below the underwater high beams that were used to illuminate after hours activities, shining, glaring, dream lights.

The bulbs underneath the water appeared to be round and florescent, there jagged light wavy and distorted below the tiny ripples created by the water itself making zig zagging lines and dreamy little shapes underneath the surface of the pool.

As Von walked along the perimeter of these extreme scenes he saw more and more men and women fornicating or in the early stages of foreplay. There also seemed to be something cruel about what was going on only he was not sure what it was and could not put a finger on it.

In a few minutes the nocturnal focus changed and then there was a well lit underground parking garage with a limousine sitting in its centre with its motor idling. After a few seconds had passed one of the doors to the limo came open and Lilly Chicoine stepped out wearing a three quarter length red dress and an array of diamonds that shimmered and shined in the foreground of the dreams back light.

It was somehow Lilly who owned this theme park, it was her who was somehow unconsciously bringing this dream to life. This would make roughly dream one million and one brought to him by The Princess Of Night herself.

Later on that evening when Dane awoke the remnants of the dream were still with him, his mind was unable to shake what he had seen inside of sleep and it was still troubling him.

Now, here alone in the dark of his bedroom with the venetian blinds drawn he wondered how Lilly was. He knew that being in lock down twenty three hours a day was not easy on anyone, and apparently, while you were kept in there the door only opened when you were going somewhere. This was likely not the way to go if one wanted to stay sane.

In the kitchen a few minutes later Dane took a glass from the cupboard and poured himself some Diet Coke that frothed at the brim.

If Dane had a nickle for every can of soda that he drank he would have been a millionaire many, many moons ago. He was a fucking addict. He could not live without Caffeine.

Just then the call display lit up and the phone rang. The screen said ANDREW.

"Hello." Von "The Icon" said into the mouth piece. It was not his Brother on the other end, but rather his Mother. She sounded tired and badly in need of rest.

"Yeah, it's me. My batteries dead. I'm just calling to let you know what's going on. They just moved Evan downstairs. They're prepping him for surgery. I guess there's a fragment of the bullet that's lodged by his heart. It looks like it's gonna be touch and go so we're gonna say a prayer for him." Marilyn Dane said sadly.

"So you don't know who might"ve wanted to do this to him, do you"?? She asked with slight accusation. Marilyn believed that her son probably knew what was going on, he always did, at least according to her frequent and often times unfounded suspicions.

David Dane, mastermind, she thought to herself. This wasn't the first time that she'd rendered such a thought.

Von hated lying, but in this situation the inevitability was that it was a necessity, there was no way around it.

"How's my niece"?? The Boxer asked trying to divert his Mothers attention from the matter at hand.

"Oh, she was crying. Andrews holding her right now. They're sitting together in the waiting room. Leilani went to Kates apartment to bring Kate some clothes for after they let her take a shower. I just hope they'll let her in after all that's gone on over there."

"Yeah, I know." Dane said sympathetically. He could not believe the A to Z of this situation himself. Kate had titles, and through endorsements etc, she had money. There were no lengths that some people would not go to in order to line their pockets with fresh green backs, and quite obviously, Jacky Hannah was one of them.

"Donovan just walked in." Marilyn Dane said.

Von hoped that Donovan would not accidentally open up and spill the beans with regards to The Jacky situation. "Can I speak to him"?? Dane asked. He was a bit nervous about not getting to Donovan before Donovan said something to Marilyn that he shouldn't say.

"He's right here. DONOVAN"!!! Marilyn called out. She was holding the phone up in the air now. "David wants to speak to you for a moment."

"That damn Jacky. We'd likely not be here if it wasn't for her." Kates Coach blurted out on his way to the phone.

"Who's Jacky"?? Marilyn asked. She had an inquisitive frown on her face. She was wondering who this mystery woman was and how she might be tied in to the attempt on Evans life. Then it came to her. Jacky was the woman who had come over to confront Kate while the two of them were in old Montreal.

In all the excitement, the incident had completely slipped her mind.

"Jacky's me bloody arse." Donovan offered. He was wearing a black suit with a green tie topped off by an Irish Tammy Cap. "Hello lad." He greeted into the mouth piece.

"You spilled the beans Dono." Von "The Icon" said addressing Donovan by his nickname. It was a David Dane original.

"What beans have I spilled accidentally lad"?? He asked.

"Telling my Mother that Jacky was behind this. My Mother was a Politician. You never know whether or not she could one day be called to testify in court. That's why you don't give her information like that."

"I apologize David. I didn't mean to do anything that I shouldn't." Donovan said shining up an apple against his suit jacket. It had been over twenty four hours since he'd eaten and his stomach was starting to let him know it.

"Don't give her any more details." Von "The Icon" said on the other end. "This end of things sucks. The next thing that you know she'll be shooting at someone else if she doesn't get her fuckin way."

"What do you think that we'd best do"?? Donovan asked. He was open to suggestions.

"If she takes this woman up on her challenge then she's setting a precedent that says that if you want a title shot than you can side step the rankings by shooting at a member of my Family. If she ignores this woman all together then Jacky may decide that one vic wasn't good enough to get Kates attention. So we're at an impasse."

There was a shard of light eclipsing the blinds in David Danes living room. It was temporarily blinding him now. "Twenty four hours." He said.

When Lilly Chicoine awoke the next night she was beginning to hear voices that spoke of unspeakable atrocities, most of them emanated from the darkened recesses of her mind etched in blood tones so horrifying that they made the hairs on the nape of her neck go straight and curl at their ends tipped with electricity.

She had been in Solitary Confinement for weeks and it was starting to takes its toll on her psyche. She was mortified and felt abandoned by this solitude. If only she had one friend.

"Mummy." She called out, but no one was there. Then she heard a key being turned in the lock on her cell door so she looked up. There was now light in the doors opening, if only a sliver. She had been in the dark for hours, thinking, hallucinating, pining, dreaming, and now finally someone had come to open up the gate way to which the outside world existed.

Lilly missed the greens, and blues and reds and purples. In here everything was black, white and clinical silver. There wasn't a single beautiful rainbow or calm ocean to speak of.

She was so lonely and wished for Von to be here with her so that he could hold her and protect her from the dark as he always had in the past both on Ontario Street as well as anywhere and everywhere else. It reminded her of a line in one of their songs, Bring Me To Life by Evanescence-Call my name and save me from the dark.

"Chicoine." The Hacks voice came. He was a tall gentlemen with short wavy hair and a thin moustache. "We're moving you to another section of The Prison." He explained.

Lilly was excited. Fuck, it was about time. Now maybe she would get to see some other people. This confinement was killing her.

As Lilly exited her cell and followed the guard down the hallway she immediately noticed that her brown eyes were sensitive to the light. She thought that this exact sensation must have been what it was like when one was coming out of the womb upon being born and taking the first breath of life.

"In here." The Guard said as he opened the door to another cell, only this time the cell was much smaller and a lot darker. "NO." Lilly plead turning around to beg the guard for another accommodation.

"This is all that we have right now." The Guard said.

As Lilly walked slowly inside she thought of all the times that she had come home and Von had put his arms around her and told her that he loved her. Lilly would get into her jogging pants, well, actually they were Von's jogging pants as well her pink T-Shirt and sit down on the mattress Indian style while playing with a piece of Kleenex examining its texture over and over with her finger tips as if it's lining was made of Heaven.

This was a ritual that she reserved for after she'd done her hit because she enjoyed the sensation of the Kleenex against her skin.

Soon, Von would put his arms around her and tell her how much that he loved her. After that they would both cuddle up together in front of the TV like two snuggling rabbits and watch one horror flick after another until it was first light, then her need for drugs would begin again, over and over.

It was a beautiful memory, and Lilly held onto it, minus her joans.

Now, here in this cold, dark and evil place Lilly "Bad To The Bone" Chicoine missed those surreal moments and she wished that she had Von to put his arms around her one more time.

"What the fuck is that supposed to mean"?? Von "The Icon" asked venomously the next morning. He had just received word that Lilly had been moved and was complaining of signs of psychosis if not Dementia, a revelation that had frightened the east end legend to death.

He was furious, not only was he furious at Prison Officials but he was also enraged at his own Brother for allowing such a cluster fuck to take place. How in the name of sweet fucken Jesus was he supposed to accept that the love of his life was being treated like an animal who was being bred for slaughter?? He himself had been a victim of THE HOLE and was thus all the more sympathetic to Lilly's plight.

"Andrew, you're supposed to be her fucken lawyer. It should be you who's looking in on her and making sure that these types of things don't happen. Do I need to find someone else to take her case"?? Von "The Icon" raged. He was so sick of this. He was beginning to wonder if Andrews conduct was deliberate or accidental.

After all, this was a Family that was predicated upon fantasy, one after another, and one of those fantasies was that Lilly Chicoine had caused Jonathan Dane to suffer a heart attack during the four days when David Dane had been locked up because of her.

This "FANTASY" was just that because via Jonathan Danes own words his heart attack was caused by plaque in a heart valve. In other words, had the attack not taken place when it did it would have not beyond a shadow of a reasonable doubt, but beyond the shadow OF ALL DOUBT have taken place within a VERY SHORT WINDOW OF TIME!!!!!!!!!!!!!!!

Nonetheless, Lilly was doomed to be blamed for Jonathan's heart attack until eternity closed its doors.

Dane wondered what it was with people, when even when confronted with incontrovertible proof against a theory they still chose to ignore it. He even wondered if Andrew Dane had seen this thing coming and instead chose to let it happen anyway.

"You're off the case." Dane hollered. He was furious, and the sound of his own voice only served to cement the anger that he was feeling. To Hell with Andrew. He would get Lilly a different attorney. This was bullshit and he was in no longer going to foot the bill for it.

This was once again his Fathers side of The Family bringing him undue, unwanted, and unnecessary grief when he did not deserve it and would not put up with it. He was also going to call The Prison right away and threaten them with a fucking lawsuit the parameters of which they had never ever heard of before starting with the fact that they were causing the love of his life to suffer what could be irreversible brain damage.

It was as always Von "The Icon" coming to Lilly's rescue and one more time he would do whatever he had to do to protect her as contrary to popular belief amongst idiots, had been the case from day one.

In fifteen minutes Von was on the phone speaking to The Prison Warden. He then informed him that if Lilly suffered any permanent psychological scarring do to where she was being kept, and could it be proven by a psychiatrist then The Prison as well as its staff were going to face a multitude of charges including a Civil Litigation that would appear in the news papers. Fuckin cock suckers.

The country of Canada and its miserable rotten, stank ass no good for nothing government was again up to something of which it had no right. It also stood to vastly characterize and demonstrate why the country itself should be run by small regional factions instead of huge crooked, over powering, tyrannical Government bodies whether they be Provincial or Federal who would do anything that they could to over power you, rob you, or screw you!!!

It was without proper or for that matter any justification at all that The Canadian Federal fucking Government were using war measures against their own citizens and should on those grounds alone face extinction.

L.A.-It is at this moment that i'm going to break in order to address you in light of a real life comment made by someone that I did not appreciate. I want you to know and to rest assured that I will always and FOREVER BE MONICA'S ETERNAL KNIGHT IN SHINING ARMOUR.

I still to this day fight for Monica and defend her. I will ALWAYS LOVE HER WITH ALL MY HEART AND SHE WILL ALWAYS TO ME BE AS I USED TO CALL HER-MY BABY BUNNY.

It is also my intention to bring The LEGEND OF VON "THE ICON" and MONICA "MAYHEM" to the level where should our names be mentioned in the east end of Montreal that there will be a multitude of people standing up and cheering because we made their neighbourhood as well as their community world famous.

Monica's name will never be forgotten by Montreal's east end. I will see to it.

Later that afternoon with the blazing sun shining in a barren tangerine glow over Montreal, Von "The Icon" stormed through the doors to The Prison where he managed to get one of The Hacks to allow him to visit with Lilly, albeit it be against standard regulation.

When Von finally walked in to Lilly's cell she all but broke down and collapsed into her boyfriends arms. He had never seen her in the state that she was in now. She presented as someone who appeared to be suffering from malnutrition not to mention solar deprivation. She looked like a POW as opposed to someone who was being kept in a Canadian Prison, this was not The Bangkok Hilton, but for the state that Lilly Chicoine was in, it might as well have been.

She looked awful, and all that David Dane wanted to do was lift Lilly up and take her home. Once again, for a moment he felt like Prince, somebody, and in this house of horrors, in a dream of wickedness where The Devil seemed to cackle at every turn, Von "The Icon" was all that she had once more. He was in Lilly's mind, once again, her white knight.

"I love you Boo." The most funny of all bunnies managed. She was wasting away to nothing.

"I love you to. Oh Christ"!!! Von "The Icon" lamented emotionally as he attempted to lift her up. He was fighting back tears, the emotions inside of him rising up so intensely that he could hardly breathe.

He was himself in a state so desperate after seeing her like this that he thought that he might actually attempt a Prison break. The conditions that the love of his life was being kept under were barbaric. Once again the lyrics from The Michael Jackson song- THEY DON'T REALLY CARE ABOUT US came to mind.

It was in The Prison Mess Portion of The Video, and Michael was turning to walk away from a table when he sang a lyric that David Dane had always felt a great kin ship to. The line was-"I Can't Believe This Is The Land From Which I Came."

"Aw God." Dane uttered with one arm cradling the sick and emaciated Lilly Chicoine. Dane loathed and despised governments, and situations such as this were the reason why.

He hated to believe that sleaze bags who wore suits and hid behind their Cabinets and fancy fucking lawyers were allowed to render decisions against weak, helpless individuals who had no power whatsoever to fight back, yet it seemed that that was The Canadian Governments right of entitlement.

Being a Politician in Canada seemed to mean more times than not that you were a power hungry low life scum bag who had nothing better to do with your time than to push people around and make them feel helpless, weak, or inferior.

It had occurred to him at that moment that he was all that Lilly Chicoine had on this earth. He was again her saviour as he had been so many times in the past often showing up at the last minute to save the day.

Holly Briggs had several times referred to David Dane as SUPER MAN. He had also been honoured when Alyssa M had referred to him as her quote "HERO" after he had slapped a certain punk across the face for making a lewd comment in regards to her.

To show her gratitude, Alyssa had wrapped her long, sexy legs around David Danes waist and sang BETTE MIDLERS "WIND BENEATH MY WINGS" as he sat with his back to her chest in The Stone Park. It had been at a time that he and Lilly were not together.

Von "The Icon" had in his years on this Earth been heralded as a hero by many and had even mentored young up and coming Body Builders who were in need of his guidance and expertise. He was also himself known to coach Boxing to students who were always more than proud to learn from him and had always been willing to offer his guidance as well as his moral support whenever needed.

"I don't feel good Boo." Lilly murmured.

At this point Von was surprised that Lilly was able to speak a word however precious at all. She had withered and wasted away to almost nothing and Dane believed that Andrew Dane was partially to blame for it. He had let this happen, his lack of judgement, or his vendetta over his old man.

"It's okay Baby Bunny, i'm here, i'm here. It's alright." Von said in a consoling voice. He HATED PEOPLE who hurt Lilly, disparaged Lilly, or did anything to upset Lilly. The two of them had so many special memories during the days and nights that were now immortal that no matter what come Hell or high water, life or death, their bond could never, and would never be broken by anything. He would love her forever and no matter what. Lilly owned his soul, and she had made his life special.

The next afternoon Marilyn Dane again postponed her flight back to Nova Scotia so that she could spend one more day at her Grand Daughters side. It was now into the wee hours of the morning and the darkness outside had not yet lifted, Evan was out of surgery but not out of the woods.

They had managed to remove the bullet but there were still several other procedures that had to be undertaken. He had been awake for a few moments and Kate had gone in to see him. She said that she thought that he looked weak and pale and that his usual well kept sun tan had greatly dissipated and that his colour was low. She was desperately afraid for him, speaking to Doctors on and off to see what she could learn.

Andrew had gone home early to retire for the night because he had to work at eight am the next morning in the dead heat.

Even with the A.C in The Court Houses blasting the temperature was still well above any bearable degree, there was the heat, dead and dry, and he had been exhausted from having been at The Hospital for a number of nights in a row now, and emotionally and physically, he had nothing left to give.

It was sickening, one major catastrophe after another. These things always seemed to come in threes. There had been Evans shooting, Lilly's incarceration, and Davids friend who had been brought into Emergency with knife wounds.

"Is there anything new that you can tell me"?? Kate asked when she ran into one of her fiances Doctors in the corridor. She was so tired that her every movement was beginning to become a chore. She felt weak in the knees and her stomach that had been doing loops all evening was now beginning to churn. It felt as though she were attempting to carry a washing machine to term and was having labour pains.

"No, there's nothing new." The Doctor had responded. That had been ten minutes ago and now she was searching for a glass of water. At some point while it had still been daylight she had seen a fountain somewhere but now she could not remember where she had spotted it.

This was likely still A-WING Kate registered. There were gurneys huddled against each wall below Morphine Drips and Colostomy Bags that were full of God knows what. It was night, no Doctors on the floors and only the odd nurse doing rounds.

"Excuse me. Do you know where I can get a glass of water"?? The famous female kick boxer asked. She was definitely not going into the washroom and using one of those little styrofoam cup things. Yuck, all she wanted was her usual Evian Water regimen and she'd be satisfied.

"No where to get water but the sinks. There might be a water fountain on the first floor but I don't think I remember where it is." The elderly lady said. "Then there's the gift shop if you like that water in a bottle stuff. Only thing is I don't know if any of that's open til after ten am."

"Thanks." Kate said with a broad smile across her lips. She hated this environment.

If she had her way she'd prefer the comforts of a cardboard box in an alleyway to the inside of a gloomy hospital. Nonetheless, if she had to be here because her fiance was in serious trouble then so be it. She would survive with or without water, or the comforts of home.

"There you are. I've been looking all over for you." Leilani Dane greeted. She had gone home and come back despite the perils of her being worse for ware. Standing here in the shadows she looked her Daughter in the eye. "Is he going to make it"?? She asked.

"I don't know." Kate answered.

She did not know of another answer that she could offer her Mother who had been sleeping between the visitors room and the waiting room off and on for days.

"Evan was always so polite to your Father and I even when we were first getting to know him. I remember the time that we were moving into our new condo and Evan took the day off work just to help us juggle the furniture load." Leilani reminisced.

Leilani and Evan had been close right from the very beginning when Kate had introduced them often reminding Kate that she hoped that she and Andrew would one day have Evan for a son in law, it was either that or they were going to adopt him, one or the other.

"I remember when we first went out and he took me this really trendy Indian Restaurant." Kate said. "We ate so much spicy food that we spent the entire night sitting on the floor in the kitchen sipping Champagne because we couldn't get our mouths to cool down. I would've settled for Burgers and Fries but Evan had to take me to the best restaurants with the best menus because he said that I was the best and should never have to settle for anything else."

"Kate, do you know who did this to Evan"?? Leilani asked exhaling slightly. She felt and had felt for days that her Daughter knew who had done this but that for some reason she was covering it up.

Kates smile had dissipated. She did not want to have this conversation, and based on her Mothers level of curiosity she was going to have a hard time getting out of it.

"Can we talk about this some other time"?? Shamrock asked.

The situation alone was enough to set her angst on fire. She wanted to kill Jacky, and discussing the situation any further would only serve to exacerbate that blood lust.

"Okay, we can talk about it later." Leilani chirped. She had immediately picked up on her Daughters reaction and was not prepared to take things any further. There was something else going on here but Leilani was still not certain as of yet what it was. It would be one day much, much later that she would find out.

When Andrew Dane stepped out of his Jaguar in old Montreal Von "The Icon" was waiting there to meet him. The sun was dying, and the pink orange glow that stretched out above the horizon was casting its shadow everywhere making the lights of the surrounding businesses seem a dim blur in the gathering dusk.

"When did you get here"?? Andrew Dane asked still wearing the suit that he had worn to work. He had not had time to go home and change, and his hair although dishevelled, was still neat.

David Dane was not smiling, as a matter of fact, he looked more like a bad dog standing there wearing sun glasses over a black leather jacket and dark coloured blue jeans. His expression yielded a quiet if not lethal rage. "About half an hour ago." He said. His voice was emotionless but it was glaringly obvious that he was far less than happy. "Lilly's hallucinating."

"Look, I tried to make sure that she didn't talk to the other inmates, but as far as your loyalty to this woman goes I can't stand to listen to it. I can't stand another minute of it. You have all this respect for her but you don't have a fuckin ounce of respect for Dad and he's the one who's been financially supporting you all these years." Andrew Dane espoused.

It was in these situations that Andrew had disdain for his Brother and for everything that came out of his Brothers mouth. He could not stand the thought of how Von "The So Called Icon" had all this respect for this goddamn woman yet not a stitch of respect for Jonathan or the money that their Father had given him many times over.

There were two sides to every story, however trying to convince Andrew Dane of that was like trying to convince a bear that he should shit in an out house.

"You and I didn't have the same relationship with our old man growing up. You're never going to accept that, and as far as Lilly goes you know absolutely nothing about our relationship or what it was predicated on.

You view things, everything, from the outside. You refuse in your assessment of whoever not to mention whatever to be fuckin subjective. If Dad had been so nice to me then what do you think that all of this anger and animosity is about. It didn't just fall outta the fuckin sky Andrew."

Von said raising his voice on the last sentence. This was a recurring theme, and it had over time repeated itself exhaustively.

"Dad worked every day of his life to give you money." Andrew said becoming breathy. His voice was now wrought with underlying emotional anguish. "You fuckin put all of these other people on goddamn pedestals, people like Uncle Tom, Lilly, and Chris Markem. People of questionable character ... ..."

"Hey." Dane interrupted warningly.

It was the same argument as always, it never changed. One side of The Family liked their people while the other side of The Family was for the opposite. Things would likely exist in this vein forever. There would never be a resolve.

"Uncle Tom was of questionable character"?? David Dane asked. "Where the fuck did you get that"??

Andrew then offered a personal opinion of their late Uncle.

"Uncle Tom was one of the nicest guys that i've ever met. He was my friend." Dane said tearing up. It was him going to bat for one of his own heroes again, the one that he related to, the one who had stood by him, not the one who had thrown him out of his house at two o' clock in the morning.

What the hell did this kid know?? He had spent his life getting his knowledge from a Book while David Dane had spent twenty five years on the street. He was getting damn tired of listening to this, and of hearing from people who had no street smarts.

"You know I used to sit there and think of what it would have been like to have had Uncle Tom as a Father. I thought of what a nightmare that it would have been.

I thought about what it would have been like to have him in the house instead of Dad." Andrew said defiantly.

"First of all I knew Thomas a whole lot better than you did." Ontario Streets Last Outlaw said.

"I spent every single night on the phone with him for years before he died and I can tell you without reservation that he wasn't of questionable character. He was a class act, and I think his career speaks for itself. Look at his past. Thomas was involved in Covert Operations, V.I.P. Security for people like Prince Charles and Lady Diana. Thomas even received a medal from JFK before he was assassinated. He was a Man Of Honour if there ever was one and you have no right to dispute any of that, nor can you."

"Like fuckin hell I don't." Andrew Dane said. "Then you worship all these fuckin people and you have nothing good to say about our Father who supported you financially for years. He gave you money to pay your rent. He also put food on the table for you and your goddamn girlfriend. He gave the both of you money to eat every day while Lilly was out raising Hell … … … …

"WHAT"?? Von "The Icon" raged. If the person standing before him had not been his own Brother then he would have thrown a punch and hit him square in the jaw. He was getting angry now. He did not like disparaging comments about the love of his life, especially from someone who had never really gotten to know her.

"What the fuck did you just say"?? Dane repeated again. His blood must have just maxed out at a hundred degree's. Who did this kid think that he was??

"Who are you"?? Dane questioned condescendingly. "You've never once walked through Hell with us. Von "The Icon" and Lilly "Bad To The Bone" Chicoine are world legends. Can you say the same thing for yourself"?? He asked with a steely anger smouldering like a heatwave in his eyes.

He had his own relationship with his Father. No one was going to tell him, or order him for that matter to feel a certain way about someone when he did not, however his younger sibling was becoming an expert at it and had seemingly been for quite some time.

"You also mentioned Chris Markem. You know ABSOLUTELY NOTHING about my coach and have no right whatsoever to offer commentary on him at all. None. Not a shred.

Chris was a second to none Boxing Coach and I learned more from him in a day then i've learned from most people in a year. He taught me everything that I know about style and pinache and he also taught me how to take care of myself. As far as i'm concerned, he's a legend." Von "The Icon" boasted.

"Our own Father is the legend. He's the one who gives you money all the time and pays your bills. He's the reason that you're not dying in an alleyway or in a cardboard box. He went to work in the woods from the time that he was seventeen to support himself. Can you say the same?? You don't even have a fuckin job, and if you're going to accept someone elses charity then I think that you should at least give them some goddamn respect."

Dane turned sideways to watch Andrew Dane walk past him and take a seat behind the wheel of his Jag that was sitting in a No Parking Zone. The conversation was over, however abruptly.

Von looked sad and as though he could not believe what he had just heard from his younger sibling even though it was a dialogue that had been repeated a thousand times, add nauseum.

105

"Charity case"? He repeated below his breath.

This was one of the most disgusting tirades that he had ever barren witness to, particularly the part at the end. What a statement. Andrew had no remorse and today he had made it obvious.

"Hey, you got a big mouth, ye know"?? Dane said as Andrew closed the door behind himself and powered the window down.

"You have no right to talk that way about Lilly and I or our legend." David Dane said.

"Yeah, well you know what I think about that legend." Andrew said before slamming the door and speeding off.

Von watched as Andrews Jag disappeared into the absence of light that had overtaken the evening. There were tears welled up in his eyes.

Sundown.

The next morning as Andrew Dane stepped away from his vehicle across from The Black Domino Tavern he noticed a group of neighbourhood regulars as well as a number of members of The Ontario Street Originals Street Gang chanting a familiar ballad– "WE, WANT, VON!!!!!!!!!!!!!!!!!!!!!!!!!!!! WE, WANT, VON!!!!!!!!!!!!!!!!!!!!!!! !!!!!!!!!!! WE, WANT, VON!!!!!!!!!!!!!!!!!! WE, WANT, VON!!!!!!!!!!!!!!!!!!!!! WE, WANT, VON!!!!!!!!!!!!!!!!!!!!!!!!!!!

Andrew immediately surmised that they must have heard that he was no longer representing one of their sweet hearts in Lilly Chicoine and this chant was its subsequent result. He could feel the heat and the hostility from the crowd. He had fallen out of favour with them, and his disrespect of Von "The Icon" and Lilly "Bad To The Bone" Chicoine had been the reason.

The Legends of Ontario Street were coming out in support of two of their own and the roar was deafening. "WE, WANT, VON"!!!!!!!!!!!!!!!!!!!! "WE, WANT, VON"!!!!!!!!!!!!!!! "WE, WANT, VON"!!!!!!!!!!!!!!!!!! "WE, WANT, VON." Every chant louder than the last, and then as Andrew stepped onto the curb carrying his briefcase … … … … "WE LOVE LI-LLY"!!!!!!!!!!!!!!!!!!!!!!!!!! Beat, beat, beat, beat, beat. "WE LOVE LI-LLY"!!!!!!!!!!!!!!!!!!!!!!!!!!!! Beat, beat, beat, beat, beat!!!!!!!!!!!!!!!!!!!!!!!!!! "WE LOVE LI-LLY"!!!!!!!!!!!!!!!!!!

As Andrew stepped inside the Bar the first person to greet him with a handshake was his Daughters Coach Donovan O' Riley. He was seated at a table next to one of The Slot Machines with both of his palms now resting on the wooden hand rails of the chair.

Andrew immediately thought that he looked exhausted. He had circles underneath his eyes the size of quarters as if he had been awake for days, and given the situation, he very well might have been.

"Ye want somethin to drink lad"?? Donovan asked through his thick Irish tongue. He looked mean, but there wasn't a mean bone in his body. This was the effect that he had on people. They often read him that way although he was a kind hearted gentle soul who just happened to be extremely proficient with his fists.

He had seen the crowd on his way over here and there were a lot of them.

Apparently Andrew Dane had done something to piss them off, and whatever it was, they weren't happy nor the least bit content. It looked as though something had gotten them fired up if not set them into a frenzy.

He had been in a hurry, no time to stop and ask questions, however now, he had a few.

"So you're not to popular with some people right now"??? Donovan enquired. There was the faintest hint of a friendly however inquisitive smile on his face. He was not just curious, he was fascinated.

"Yeah, i'm not representing Lilly Chicoine anymore." Andrew responded below his breath with just a hint of self consciousness. He had set his briefcase down and was now taking a seat across from his Daughters Coach. This had become the hangout spot for the younger echelon of the Family.

Just then a roar of applause and adoration erupted from outside of The Black Domino Tavern as Von "The Icon" pulled on the bars front door handle and stepped inside. He was wearing a black sweater with two buttons at the top over blue jeans and a pair of wrap around sun glasses.

Donovan thought that Von "The Icon" looked like a hit man as he walked across the floor and sat down with a grin on his face. It was an expression that was indicative of satisfaction. He would always be their hero. That was that, and he was damn proud of it.

"Phillip wants your files." Ontario Streets Last Outlaw said.

"Who's Phillip"?? Andrew asked sitting there in his blue blazer. He had a less than thrilled look on his face, non plussed, and pissed as sour grapes.

This was all the end result of one thing or another, but most likely it was the end result of a Family Feud that had gone on between his Father and Mothers side of The Family for decades, neither could get along with the other. It was like Palestine versus Israel, East versus West, The United States versus Osama Bin Laden or Christ only knew what else. There was rage, fury, and an unparalleled anger that never seemed to be satisfied. It was if nothing else a modern day version of The Hatfields and The Mccoys.

"Phillip Laroche is Lilly's former and current lawyer. You have such a seething hatred for the love of my life that I have no other choice but to reappoint Phillip." Von said.

This would not have been necessary if only Andrew Dane, Jonathan Dane as well as the rest of their clan would let sleeping dogs lye, but no such luck.

There was going to be a rehashing of January 2008 until the taste of the words coming out of their mouths was enough to permanently parch them.

"I can't keep doing this." Andrew relented. "If we weren't the bi product of the same people we probably wouldn't even be talking to each other. We can't agree on anything." He said dropping one forearm gingerly across the arm rest of his seat. There was no changing his Brothers mind, nor was there any changing his own.

They had differing points of view on everything from A to Z. Their only mutual common bond was their love of a Daughter and a Niece who they happened to share. Kate was their mutual love, aside from her, there was none.

"I'll turn my files over to him as soon as I know where to go. Do you have an address for his office"?? Andrew asked.

The next afternoon Phillip Laroche walked into The Court Room carrying a briefcase with Lillys files among its contents. He had seen Andrew Dane that morning and had a heart to heart with him. It was not an easy situation, and given the history Phillip believed it was best that he resume his duties as Lilly Chicoines lawyer even if it would mean putting in some extremely long hours.

It also helped that Phillip had known Von "The Icon" for many years and that the two had an extremely positive rapport with one another. Von had even gone so far as to send Phillips Boss a letter of recommendation several months ago stating that he had always been pleased with Phillip's work ethic well as his personal and professional demeanour. The gesture had meant something to Phillip and he would not soon forget it.

"Are they going to move me"?? Lilly asked sitting at the front of the court room. She was wearing prison greens although Montreal's detention centres had no dress code. This was an out fit that one of the other girls had given her. It was to big but it would do for now.

"I'm going to request that you be given a psyche eval as soon as possible. That's probably the quickest way to get this done." Laroche said leaning in closely enough to whisper to Lilly.

If they felt that Lilly was suffering psychologically due to her quarters or suffering symptoms of Dementia as she had reported then they would have no other choice but to move her to gen pop or at least to another cell even though gen pop was against Phillips better judgement.

"Hmm … … … hmm." Lilly muttered. "No more Segregation. Fuck, I can't even watch television. I'm in my cell twenty three hours a day. They brought me a TV and now the damn thing doesn't work. Last night I thought the wall was talking to me." She said.

"You're having auditory hallucinations"?? Phillip asked just above a whisper. His eyes were turned upward toward the Judge who was seating himself in his booth.

"No, I thought the wall was talking to me." Lilly repeated. She was beginning to wonder if Phillip had something wrong with his hearing. Fuck, he thought that she had some fancy disease when all that she was trying to tell him was that she thought that the walls were talking to her.

"That's what an auditory hallucination is." Phillip informed her. There was a vague however warm and understanding smile on his face. I guess Lilly's not familiar with that term he thought to himself. His concept of Gen Pop 101 was obviously different from hers.

"Can you tell The Judge that I need to be moved immediately, that these walls are really getting to my head and that I want to see my boyfriend"??

What did she think this was, a country club??

"Annnnd … … … … I need my cigarettes, like now." Lilly half requested but was at the same time demanding. She did not look overtly pleased about her predicament sitting there in her over sized green jogging suit and white runners. If she had her way they would've been delivering from MC Donalds or Pizza Hut about an hour ago.

"I don't think that this particular Judge does cigarette requests." Phillip said. "But i'll ask him." The suave, handsome Laroche jested. He had many times been told that he resembled Canadian Political Superstar Justin Trudeau. Most women thought that Phillip was gorgeous or at worst extremely good looking. He was in his own right, a stud.

"All rise." The Judge requested standing before the court in his shiny black robe.

Lilly and Phillip obliged him.

"Court is now in session. The honourable Judge Vallencourt presiding.

"Let the record show that Miss Chicoine is present along with her legal council." Judge Richard Vallencourt said as he placed his spectacles on his face.

"Mr. Laroche. How may I assist you this morning"? He asked.

"Your Honour i'd like to request that my client undergo a full Psychological Evaluation as soon as possible. She's currently being kept in Administrative Segregation and has informed me that she's experiencing signs that are related to Dementia as well as Auditory Hallucinations. I request that she be transferred out of Ad. Seg as soon as possible."

The Judge who was looking downward at a memo that was on his bench shot a sharp glance at Phillip.

"I'll request that she be moved first thing in the morning." He said. "As for The Psychological Evaluation i'll appoint someone." The sixty something Judge approved.

"Yay"!!! Lilly celebrated, and that was that.

The next day at four pm Evan rose from his coma, he had been sleeping soundly and when he awoke he found his fiance doing exactly the same thing in the chair beside his bed. There were circles around her eyes and she was clutching the bottom end of a sweater in her left hand, it had an insignia on it although Evan could not see what it was.

"Hi." Evan managed.

"You're awake." Kate exclaimed rubbing her left eye with one hand. She was afraid that she'd never hear the sound of her fiances voice again. There were tears in her eyes.

Just then Von "The Icon" stepped into the room from outside in the hallway. Andrew Dane was in tow. The two Brothers had, had a long talk the previous night and agreed to bury the hatchet despite the fact that both agreed that Andrew would no longer represent the iconic Lilly Chicoine.

"It's good to see you." Von said addressing Evan who was sipping water through a straw with the assistance of his fiance who had seemingly been awake forever. The two looked like a couple of giddy school children sitting on the play ground The Ontario Street Original thought to himself.

"The Man." Evan said smiling in the direction of his hero. His eyes were full open.

"I'm glad you're awake." Von "The Icon" said in response as he lifted a chair and then put it down. He and his nieces fiance had always been very close, they had become friends shortly after they'd been introduced and stayed that way ever since. Von had once helped Evan build a house.

"Fuck, i'm so glad he's awake." Kate beamed turning around to address her Father and her Uncle who were standing at her back watching this form of a reunion, both were wearing traces of a smile.

"I need to speak to you down the hall." Von said leading the way back into the hospital corridor. If this had been the way that things were all the time then maybe there would be less fighting and more peace within their Family, however, that was seldom the case.

Von recalled one such scenario when he was still a child when his Grand Father and his Grand Mother had been fighting for days, this and that had taken place amidst screaming and hollering leaving his Father and his Grand Father face to face on opposite sides of a rocking chair in his Grand Parents apartment nearly coming to blows, it had, in Danes opinion been the fault of his Fathers side of The Family for getting involved in the first place.

It was an ugly memory and Von "The Icon" had never forgotten nor forgiven his Father's side of The Family for it, and to this day, he did not particularly like certain individuals in that camp.

Had it been he himself in the situation then things would likely have spiralled out of control with the police being called as an end result, such instances had taken place in the past.

When he and Andrew reached the waiting room they sat down taking turns stating their case as to why they each believed their side of The Family to be right. It just seemed that in these instances no truce nor alike way of thinking could ever be reached. Andrew had his opinion and Von had his. It was seldom that Von didn't wonder if one day he and Andrew wouldn't be the modern day version of his Father and his Grand Father standing on opposite sides of the room ready to go to war.

Vons Grand Father, Tom Wallace Senior, had been a rugged old Scotsman who was afraid of nothing and no one. He had once been rumoured to have walked onto a Farmers property in Scotland and wrestled a Bull to an unknown conclusion.

Tom Wallace had also served in The Air Force during WWII and had been said to have flown The Mosquito. The Wallace clan had always been known for their fearlessness, much like their namesake Sir William Wallace who had been a fearless warrior, in many an instance, The Immortal Von "The Icon" had carried forth the tradition.

"I think that it'll always be like this. It started long before us and I personally don't think that it will ever stop." Von surmised. He was sitting in a plush leather chair with his hands folded in his lap.

"Look, you and Mum, Uncle Tom and Granp have always thought the same way and so have Dad and I. You may not like Dad but you at least owe him your love and respect."

This was more of Andrews opinionated hypocritical rhetoric. If Andrew was such a staunch believer in the rights of people to have their own opinions and points of view as he had espoused in the past then he should at least practice what he preached. Von had far different opinions of what it was like to be raised as Jonathan Danes son then Andrew did, and none of them were pleasant.

This was the legendary personality conflict between the two Families coming to light, neither side could see eye to eye with the other. It was a feud that went back almost fifty years and still raged today like a wicked inferno of tempers and emotions, there was no off button and no fix. Things were what they were.

As far as Von "The Icon" was concerned his Fathers side of The Family was green and inexperienced, and they lacked the knowledge and experience that a man of his own status had acquired after having spent so many years on the street.

On the flip side of the coin the other side of the Family believed that Von as well as his Uncle were not sophisticated or politically correct enough as they so required one to be, it was in many ways, had been said and surmised that his Father and his clan saw themselves as aristocrats yet nothing could be further from the truth, it was ego and its off spring that was destroying the entire Family from their end, despite accusations to the contrary.

Thomas Wallace had been a Military man who frequently spoke his mind while Von "The Icon" was from the street and couldn't have given a rats ass what others thought of his opinions, to him, freedom of speech was a self given, self granted right of passage, otherwise we had become the dictatorship that Steven Harper so desired Canada to be.

David Dane believed that "POLITICAL CORRECTNESS" was an unofficial form of brain washing, mind control method, or way of bringing about a hidden agenda without the low life Canadian government having to tip their hand and reveal themselves to be who and what they really were, a bunch of two faced criminals who masqueraded as a fair and upstanding governing body.

Here were a bunch of people who granted you FREEDOM OF SPEECH but then tried to rob you of expressing or voicing your opinion in the very same breath under the guise that what you had to say did not suit their Political Agenda or self given right of blanket authority.

These people were scoundrels who did every fucking thing on the sly not bothering more than once in a hundred years to offer reason or justification for any of their actions and yet they blamed other regimes for being dictatorships, this one was evil, that one was bad, yet here they were doing their own people dirty just the same, and above and beyond that, Canadians did not have the right to bare arms

Von "The Icon" loathed sneaks, and yet that is what he believed The Canadian Government to be comprised of from top to bottom, self serving loathsome pit vipers out to line their own pockets with green backs at the cost of destroying their own citizens.

You were allowed to voice your own opinion, that is just as long as it concurred with their agenda, but if it did not, or if what you had to say in any way offended anyone, then you could lose your job, your position in life, or even your home. It was as though offending a person was the ultimate crime or sin, even if it meant that lives would be saved, one such example of tyranny was September 11th, 2001. Had it in this case not been for The American Government allowing a bunch of wicked snakes to habitat within American borders then three thousand five hundred lives would have been saved. This is tragically what The Americans had been forced to endure and they didn't deserve it and should not have had to put up with it.

Canada had also nearly undergone a full on terrorist attack before RCMP and other detachments apprehended a bunch of felons in a house somewhere North of Toronto. Regardless, those people never should have been permitted within Canadian borders in the first place, but had we not permitted them entry, then we might have accidently offended someone.

Von also did not understand the allowances made for every day actions. No one seemed to think or believe that it was wrong for everyone to just hop from one bed to another instead of having a serious, meaningful relationship where two people were monogamous to one another.

Society had adopted a mentality called-FRIENDS WITH BENEFITS where two people could just be friends, fuck, and then onto the person down the hall with the same mentality being applicable.

It was mind sets like this one and others similar to it that made The Iconic Street Legend wonder where the hell we were going with all of this. What stupidity would we adopt as common sense next?

Then there was the vindication that we had found for not communicating verbally, by phone, or even out the window anymore. We called it- TEXTING.

This was another form of social disease that had been lapped up by the masses as though it was butterscotch on ice cream. It was also the most irritating, disruptive, anti-social behaviour encouraging habit that had ever been invented by a technological engineer.

It was a habit only served to pulverize proper or traditional communication while distracting the inhabitants of North America and The World from just about whatever else they should be doing including participating in normal, healthy relationships while at the same time endangering our lives as well as turning us into morons.

Less was more, if it had not been for all of these new social mediums the inhabitants of North America would have been far better off both mentally and spiritually and they would probably have been getting along a whole lot better with one another as well, in the end, we had fucked ourselves.

Dane had long since lost count of how many friends as well as Family members that he had lost because of Face book, each one back stabbing and discounting the other over petty, trivial bullshit. It was the ruination of our society, and the very catalyst for the destruction of privacy.

We were better off without our text messaging, friends with benefits, or the God awful social networks that were destroying our relationships not to mention our lives. How much more of this foolishness were we going to be forced to endure?

How much more nonsense would we allow to replace COMMON SENSE?

Von "The Icon" believed that if this day and age had a theme it would be to find out how much traditional common sense we could replace with such total and utter stupidity that we ourselves looked like idiots for accepting it.

We would invent one completely asinine trend after another, claim it as brilliance, live by it, subsequently contributing to the down fall of our society all the while defending it with a flaming sword. Had we lost our heads????

The strange thing about us was that we were supposed to be a society that was in a constant state of advancement, yet instead we were on the decline, all that was supposed to have helped had only instead hindered us and caused us to fight and drift away from one another permanently desecrating our relationships.

There was no good coming of our so called ascension or upward movement that was more an act of self sabotaging, rear ending, or inherent self blind siding. I.E.-We had become a bunch of fools.

Technology was not our friend but rather a wicked enemy to be feared. If any good had come of the last twenty years or so it should have been the knowledge that to avail ourselves of new rules instead of embracing the old ones was the mechanism of our inherent destruction. RULES WERE NOT MADE TO BE BROKEN. They were set in place for a reason as Mother Nature intended them and to breach them was to ask for trouble. PERIOD.

"Olend." Dane said as he entered his friends room at the hospital. He had just left Andrew in the common area to watch television. "What the fuck happened"? The Fighter asked as he took a seat next to his friend who had a bunch of tubes tunnelling out of him.

Olend offered a weak hand gesture before resting his palm back on top of the blue blanket that was covering him. He was frail and to out of it to be able to respond to his friends enquiry.

"Did you see who did this to you"?? Von asked hoping for a response.

The oxygen pump was making a hissing sound at Danes back.

Once again Olends attempt to gesture was in vein. He looked weak with his eyes only half open on the shadowy room. "Mmm Hgf." He attempted.

"What"? Von asked leaning in more closely in hopes of hearing whatever it was that Olend Marx had to say, which was in the end, to no avail.

Just then Kate entered the room behind him. "Uncle Von." She beckoned calmly before yawning.

"Yeah hunny." Von responded turning away from Olend momentarily to take stock of his niece. He was so proud of her for being as strong as she had been through all of this.

Kate had always made him proud, and the strength with which she had handled this situation was one more example of that. Kate

"The Gate" Shamrock was a fighter in every aspect of the word, that and a champion.

"I love you." She said wrapping her arms around her Uncles neck from behind.

The next morning in the sun rise Massoud walked into the lobby of the hospital and put his feet up on a seat that served as an island between two tables. He was best known for having taught The Iranian Military how to kill, and he was, as Von "The Icon" had called him, "The Black Ninja."

Von had often joked that maybe one day Persia would retire the tank and instead employ Massoud as a full time substitute for the armoured vehicle, after all, he was very likely just as lethal, and he was here, waiting.

"Good morning Von." Massoud greeted with a warm smile and a hand shake.

"You wouldn't fuckin be saying that if you'd slept in that chair." The Boxer said embracing his close friend who looked fresh and awake as though his quiet dreamless sleep had gone uninterrupted.

"You need to meditate." The always calm and relaxed Massoud said. "I'm here to see your niece. I don't want her anger to fester so I am going to teach her about the disciplines of Kung Fu." Massoud offered with his hands on his hips. "When i'm done i'd like you to meditate with me."

This was Massouds way. He was a gentlemen whose class, manners and good nature had made he and Von "The Icon" fast friends. They had met very late one night in the lobby of Vons building. Max had introduced them.

"Kate's in The Chapel right now. Lemme call her. I'll see if her phone's on."

Kate and Massoud had never met each other before. Today would be their first meeting.

Late that afternoon below the reach of Frontenac's Brewery Von "The Icon" stood with his hands loosely mimicking a fisted posture while doing a shadow boxing routine. This was his customary way of releasing energy as well as that of letting off steam, blow by blow.

It had been a long week and the stench of hospitals and prisons was beginning to take a psychological toll on him. He hated both of these facilities with a fucking passion.

He had, had enough of institutions. Ontario Street was his sanctuary. These streets had grown on him. They had become as much a part of him as his hands, legs, arms and feet and he loved them although he was in all legitimacy probably the only person in the neighbourhood who did not speak french, however, his grasp of The English language had made a French Community world famous, go figure.

"When's your friend coming back"?? Kate Shamrock asked from her seated position on the ground. She was doing stretches on the cement. She had been in The Hospital Chapel when her phone had lit up and her Uncle was on the other end. He told her that he had a friend that he wanted her to meet, someone who could teach her many disciplines, and then the three of them had convened in The Hospital lobby.

"He went to grab some juice. He'll be back in a minute or two." Von "The Icon" said. "He's an insidious criminal minded bastard." The Ontario Street Original blurted out.

"Who"?? Kate asked with a bewildered frown as well as a humoured smirk crossing her face at the same time. Whatever was coming, it was going to be good.

"Steven Harper. I keep thinking about what that prison is doing to Lilly." He said.

"I finally found a store that had carrot juice." The Health Conscious Persian said returning to where they were sitting. "This is a unique neighbourhood."

"Aw, believe me Massoud, after awhile these streets will become like an extra limb. I couldn't live without em. I love this crazy place." Ontario Streets Last Outlaw said, and it was true, he did.

Von "The Icon" without Ontario Street was like peanut butter without jam. He would forever cherish his memories of this white french ghetto and the memories that went with it.

He and Lilly had been through so many nightmares and dreams together in this neighbourhood that these streets were like a member of the Family, one that you simply couldn't live without.

Just then a K-9 walked by and barked leaving a trail of fur in his wake.

Von immediately thought of his late great best friend HUNTER and of all the love that HUNTER had bestowed upon he and Lilly. Von only wished that HUNTER as well as THOMAS were able to be here today to read his book. Well, Thomas would have read it, Hunter would have sniffed it, and then maybe tried to eat it.

"Love ya son." He heard Thomas saying to him from the recesses of his mind.

Von "The Icon" had been so proud of his late Uncle as well as of his accomplishments in The Canadian Armed Forces. He had been a hand picked Body Guard for Prince Charles and Lady Diana as well as for Pierre Elliott Trudeau. As a Cadet the esteemed Thomas Wallace had also received a medal from John F. Kennedy.

Thomas had been a mans man, he was someone that other men felt comfortable around as well as looked up to for his rank and achievements in The Armed Forces. He also had a kind nature which was to the liking of those who spent time around him. Once, many, many moons ago, he had been called The Warrant Officer with a heart of gold. His youngest son, William, now trained commando's.

"I told your uncle that I wanted to meet you today." Massoud began. "I know that you have accomplished a great plethora of accolades in kick boxing and that you're also independently a Martial Artist."

"What I came to see you for was because after hearing about all that has befallen you I know that you must be living with a great deal of anger. I want to give you a way to circumvent this anger in hopes that you will be able to use your inner chi to over come the situation that you're in. My Sensei was a great man. He taught me many disciplines and always guided me down the proper road in life." Massoud continued. There was great warmth and admiration in his eyes when he spoke of the man who taught him.

"Where is your Sensei"? Kate asked. She was standing full up now giving her newest mentor her undivided attention.

"He's in Persia." Massoud said proudly displaying a photograph of his trainer and friend performing an aerial kick. The photograph looked to have been taken in a large stadium or in an air plane hanger. Kate could not discern which of the two it was.

119

"He certainly has no trouble getting the elevation that he needs from his kicks. I can do some of that fancy high flying stuff to. I used to watch Seagal and Van Damme as a kid and i'd emulate them, although I always thought that Van Damme was a bit of a dick. Ken Shamrock is my MMA and Martial Arts hero, thus the nick name." Kate boasted handing the photograph back to Massoud. "I met him while I was in Hawaii. There's a picture of him standing under a tree with his arm around me in our living room."

"Who is he"?? The average in appearance, dark haired Massoud asked. He was unfamiliar with the name that Kate had just mentioned and was curious, however somewhere in the recesses of his mind the name rang the faintest of bells.

"Ken Kilpatrick, AKA KEN WAYNE SHAMROCK." Kate said. "He's a Former Ultimate Fighting Champion and UFC HALL OF FAMER. He's also a Former WORLD WRESTLING ENTERTAINMENT Superstar which is definitely how Uncle Von identifies with him best." She said turning to look over her shoulder at her Uncle who was two feet away. He was smiling.

"So, he's a Martial Artist"? Massoud enquired.

"That and an MMA Fighter." Kate answered.

"I've never heard of him." Massoud commented. "But then again I haven't been in Canada for to long."

"Ken Shamrock is from The United States, he owns and operates a school out in California called "The Lions Den. His Brother fights as well, Frank." She explained.

A light breeze circulated between them now.

CHAPTER 4:

Charlie Brown was an aspiring porn star and seasoned male model. He was also Von "The Icons" second cousin by marriage. He had built a life for himself, he was a Father, a business entrepreneur and a small time career criminal amongst other things.

There had been many trials and tribulations in Charlies life not to mention that he had financial responsibilities that were becoming harder and harder to meet, each week becoming more expensive than the last, it seemed as though every time he turned around there was another creditor after him or woman asking him to take responsibility for a child that he had made during one of his drunken stupors or Coked out hiatus's from reality.

He had at very least done well for himself in one of his ambitions. His career as a model had taken him to Rome, Paris, Switzerland, The Big Apple, New Zealand and even Thailand. Over time he had made some money which he reinvested in drugs and later blew on gambling or dope that he had used himself.

He was by nature a con man in life. He wanted to go places, and if drugs, porn, modelling or other shady ventures could do it for him then so be it, scruples were a luxury that he could ill afford to entertain, but if Charlie Brown had, had a bumper sticker on his car it would have read-"My jooks is blackmail-Check it out."

He had come from wealthy law abiding parents but unfortunately did not share their luck in the arena of status or affluence, on the side, he was himself an immoral sleaze bag. Theirs seemed a hand better dealt, and nurtured in the womb of a different time.

Charlie also had other crosses to bare. He was behind on his Credit Cards and had a slew of outstanding debts that spanned both ends of the border as well as The United States. It had seemed for awhile that gambling would benefit him. He had once made some money at the track and for awhile believed that he knew how to pick horses, it had been an illusion. He had placed over a hundred bets after having one big pay day but lost on all of them. He had created a false image for himself, and it had back fired horribly.

"Good morning cuz." Charlie said pouring himself a glass of pineapple juice over four ice cubes. Von "The Icon" was on the other end of the phone. He had coughed a couple of times but was now able to hear himself over the twitch in his throat.

"If you make it out here you could come to Kate's next fight." The Ontario Street Original said moving a box aside with the in sole of his foot, this was down and dirty, he had expected the worst from his cousin but was trying to put up with him regardless which would in the end be a thankless job.

"I'm gonna have Eva with me." Charlie said half expecting the response that was forth coming.

"I have a refrigerator that she'd fit into nicely, that is if I were to cut her in half."

Eva was Danes aunt on his Fathers side, she was a candidate or at least runner up for bitch of the year.

When Kate was a baby, Dane had threatened to cut Eva's hands off if she ever lifted Kate out of her crib again. As a matter of fact, it would likely have brought about the same result if Eva had lifted Kate out of anywhere shy of a pit full of rabid dogs.

"Try to be nice. You can at least attempt to get along for a couple of days."

"I don't attempt to get along with anyone, least of all Eva Nicolette."

"Well, it's only for a few days. Think you can swing the bat"??

"Don't give me any idea's." Von said with a light smirk. He then hung up.

"Idea's about what"?? Andrew Dane asked strolling into the room. He was dressed in a dark coloured blazer over a white shirt and dress pants. His work day had not yet started, but he had a list of clients to see who would be coming at him like The Guns Of Navarone.

"Idea's about Eva Nicolette."

"You need to lighten up." Andrew said standing in front of a mirror with a gold tapestry running the length of its perimeter. He was late. None of this mornings case load was going to thank him for his tardiness.

"They moved Lilly to Gen Pop. No more single cell." Von said resting his hand, finger tips first, against his forehead.

"Good." Andrew responded efficiently. "So, I hear that Ontario Street's holding some type of pow wow in your honour tonight.

Kate said something about free boo's and a hand full of radio personalities." Andrew espoused fixing his cuff link.

"Yeah, they wanna thank me for Urban Rain but what this is really for is to help raise money for Lilly "Bad To The Bone" Chicoines legal defence."

"So what are you gonna do, sing and dance"??

"Nah, i'm gonna do my best Sinatra impression and then they're gonna let me go home."

"I see." Andrew Dane responded. "Listen, i've gotta get to work. I'm already late. There's milk and cookies in the fridge in case you get hungry."

"That's thoughtful of you." Von said reaching into his bag and retrieving his electric razor.

Milk and Cookies. Von thought jestingly.

That night underneath a black sky Von "The Icon" stood in the cab of a pick up truck with The Ontario Street Original's surrounding him on the pavement. It was a humid night, and aside from his own brethren, Ontario Street's most famous personality was also flanked by media as well as radio disk jockeys including Richard Dee's from UP ALL NIGHT, JOHNNY ACE from SOUND SYSTEM, AND BILLY WHITE from THE BREEZE.

"Because you're a King." Kate Shamrock said in response to the reaction that her legendary uncle was getting from the crowd. She was looking up at him as AC/DC'S SHOOK ME ALL NIGHT LONG played on into the dusk.

"They're having a good time with their hero." Someone else said.

"It's nostalgia." Sheryl commented with a tear in her eye. She had known Von "The Icon" for so long, ever since his early days with Lilly when the name and reputation of The Ontario Street Originals was still young. The Iconic Duo had meant so much to this neighbourhood and it's surrounding sub divisions. They had lived and died for one another on these streets. All the trials and tribulations, all the darkness and rain, all of the looming shadows and the things that went on after dark.

"Hey Von" SEXXXY EDDY said coming out of the crowd. He wore a leopard skin vest over a bare chest with blue jeans and snake skin boots. He to had been robbed of his space to move. There was a host of media and beautiful women all around him, the best looking of which was attempting to suck the tongue out of his mouth.

"There's still a lot of thunder on those lips." Von "The Icon" said of his wrestler buddy.

"Solid as a rock." Eddy said remarking on his friends physique.

Before long two unidentified men were pushing their way through the crowd, one was taller than the other but both could easily be identified as thugs who looked like they'd seen a few years on some bad streets.

The music drifting over the amplifiers had changed and was now a slightly sinister riff which Von could have sworn that he'd heard someplace before.

"HEY DINO." The shorter of the two thugs called out. It had taken a minute as well as one or two double takes but now Dane was able to identify both of these dangerous looking individuals. Their names were Scott Paris and Troy Barclee. They were friends of David Dane's from about a thousand moons ago.

"Who the hell are these guys"?? SEXXXY EDDY asked inquisitively. He had never seen either one of these hoods before in his life, then again, why should he have, he had never been one to spend much time in this neighbourhood.

"They're not from around here." Dane commented. "They're Outsiders."

"Oh." Eddy responded before turning his attention to the blond who had been occupying his tongue. He had himself done well lately. He had made it into the ring with W.W.E. LEGEND-ROY WAYNE FERRIS A.K.A., THE HONKY TONK MAN, as well as LEAPING LANNY POFFO who was the Brother of the late MACHO MAN RANDY SAVAGE. He had also hung out and partied with W.W.E. LEGEND BRUTUS "THE BARBER" BEEFCAKE who was the life long best friend of THE IMMORTAL HULK HOGAN, not to mention assisting Micky Rourke in his training as he prepared for his starring role in the big budget Hollywood block buster, The Wrestler.

"You don't know, why we're here." Scott Paris said leaning into the side of the cab that Von "The Icon" stood upon, it was a familiar line, and he'd heard Paris use it many times in the years before.

The Ontario Street Original was shaking his head now. His face was expressionless.

"A little birdy told us that you might be lonely down here." Barclee exclaimed. He was a big bastard, maybe six feet seven. He had long wavy hair and a satanic looking pinch.

"You been talking to Jason Ronin"?? Von "The Icon" asked. "He phoned me about eight weeks ago. He was in fuckin China or somewhere."

"Shoulda known better. The cuisine over there isn't very good."

"I think he was getting married."

"He's over there studying Martial Arts to." Paris said leaning over the edge board of the cab. He had a martini stir stick in his mouth. It was something of a trademark.

Jason Ronin was a French Canadian born Martial Artist, Restauranteur, and frequent world traveller. He and Von"The Icon" had been close ever since they were kids often getting into scrapes with the local thugs or dope dealers for speaking their minds whenever they felt like it even to their own detriment.

"Bend over and touch your toes, and i'll show you where the wild goose goes." A voice came from behind the pick up truck.

"There's only one human being alive who would greet me with that line." Dane said turning to face his six foot four inch child hood buddy who was now all grown up.

"Gimme a hug you bastard." Jason said standing there wearing a sports shirt with a tidy collar.

Von obliged him stepping down from the pick up truck cab and embracing his life long chum. He had missed the kid that he always thought to be his non blood brother.

"Where's Manny"?? Dane asked, his eyes scanning around for Jason's usual partner in crime.

"He's sitting in the car about a block over. He just got back from Kurdistan." Jason said lighting up a cigarette. "These fuckin jeans are killin me. I been in em all day."

"It's probably crotch wrought." Von offered jestingly. He was still presiding over the crowd now.

"If it is then I got it from you."

"Fuckin prick." Von said catching a beer that someone had thrown toward him. "Tell Manny to come see me. I haven't seen him in a long time."

"Wait, I think he has his cell phone." Jason said flipping his own handset open. "Fuck, there's enough static on this thing for me to wanna buy a few million shares in Bounce." Jason proclaimed.

In moments a husky looking dude with a thick beard was walking toward them.

"What's up Von"?? Manny greeted. He was as always, smiling. There was a long history between these two that dated all the way back to the early nineties.

Von and Manny had met many years ago when they'd trained together along with Mannys younger sibling at a Y.M.C.A in Halifax. It was the same Y where Von had met Chris and Jack Markem as well as Richard and Robert all of whom had appeared in Urban Rain.

"Fuck, I can't get these jeans to stop clinging to me."

"To bad you never had the same luck with women."

"Yeah, when they found out who my friends were, they ran." Jason continued.

"I wouldn't be to hard on Manny." Von quipped slapping Manny on the back. "How's your Brother"?? Von asked the man from Kurdistan.

"He's good. He still driving Limo's. He gets loads of bitches."

At that moment a current of air passed between the three friends who were standing together. The night was beginning to cool off.

L.A.-At this point I will again pause to address you. I know that you may feel objectionable to me publishing Monica's name at the out set of this manuscript, but you will learn here and later on why I have chosen to do so, there is a reason, that reason being that I want Monica to have her fame.

I know how Monica and I parted, I also know that in the end that circumstances between you and I were not the best, but Monica was the love of my life and she will never leave my heart, nor its ruin. There is not a day that goes by that my Mother and I don't talk about her and think of the good times that we spent with her, especially The Christmas's that she was with us as a part of the Family.

Monica is still in my dreams every night when I fall asleep. I never got a chance to say goodbye nor to tell her that I love her once more forever. I will regret that for the rest of my life.

I will never forget the many early mornings when we would sit in one of the parks on Ontario Street and watch the sunrise together in each others arms, or the haunting memory of watching her walk through the door to our apartment late at night. She was and will forever be everything to me. Monica was an enigma, i've never met anyone who carried with them the ambiance that she did. Monica had a dark and original charisma that was all her own, it's one of the traits that makes her a legend.

There were many times that Monica and I exchanged angry words only to end up in each others arms the next morning. She will always be the lady of my heart, no matter what. I won't let anyone take that away, despite influences, and despite how things ended. No one will ever know what i've been forced to live with, and endure.

I would like to one day be able to visit her graveside and bring flowers. I am troubled by the fact that I have not been there. I also would like to have dinner or Coffee with you and E.A or H.A someday, but i'll leave that entirely up to you. I am on Face book under DAVID DANE. You will see my photo there. I now have a full head of hair and am wearing sun glasses. You E.A, or H.A are welcome to connect with me anytime. If you do not then I will understand. I only ask one thing of you. Please remember in your mind and in your heart that no matter what, Von loved Monica and always will.

When David Dane passed out later that night he thought of how his Aunt Eva had once betrayed him. It had been shortly after the wake for one of Danes relatives who had died at a young age.

There were bad times that brought about bad Karma and bad memories, and this had without a doubt been one of them, maybe even the worst of them all.

About three weeks before Eva did what she did Dane had checked himself into Night Ridge Hospital over a potential black mail situation that had occurred in his life. They had treated him for severe anxiety and let him go inside of forty eight hours after pumping him full of pills, asking him to sign some forms and releasing his clothes. By the time that Dane had reached his Parents house in Halifax he was worse for ware hardly able to recognize the floor from the ceiling, his condition had caused him to become afraid of everything, of the shadows dancing on the walls to the scent of sulphur rising from the air.

He was paranoid, and then it had it seemed, been advantageous for the wicked and evil Jonathan Dane to take advantage of David Danes predicament and weakened state of mind.

Giving Eva specifics of the order of blackmail had been a mistake. She had sat there with a smug if not sneaky expression on her face and let her vibes do the talking.

As soon as Dane had dropped the particulars of the situation on her she used smirking, grinning, and timely facial expressions to let Dane know exactly what she had in mind, then it was mental telepathy, that and a unique talent of Danes thought of and referred to as being a sensitive.

She, this witch, was gonna try and communicate with the hospital under the pretence that she herself was Dane. BITCH!! Then, because of his local, Halifax, not Montreal, he would be the suspect, nice and clean.

Here he was, all the way in Hali, so if a letter or what not surfaced in Montreal it would appear that Dane himself had sent it. Finally, his fear had gotten so forceful and intense that Dane had sent communication through to Night Ridge Hospital to let them know that Eva was coming.

Later, a few months later as a matter of fact, Dane contacted a friend of his who was a seasoned Psychiatrist and actually divulged Eva's full name so as to have it on the record. What Von "The Icon" loathed more than anything about this woman was that she claimed to be a Holy Roller.

"You thump your Bible." Von had remembered cursing aloud with a smirk of his own on his face.

Von was truly grateful for the friendship of this particular Psychiatrist and thought of him as top of the line (HOPE YOU ENJOYED YOUR COPY OF URBAN RAIN AND PROPS TO

YOU MY FRIEND. THANK GOD WE HAVE DOCTORS LIKE YOU).

Then Eva added insult to injury when she uttered the exact response to Danes Mother upon being confronted that Dane had predicted that she would beforehand. Eva's song went a little like this–"I was taken aback." Dane had predicted that Eva would use exactly that wording. What a coincidence!!

She also said something about a back and forth not being necessary.

What was necessary was someones boot up this woman's ass.

"You know that you're my everything." Von said tugging his ROLEX watch into place as he greeted his niece with a peck on the forehead. He was almost ready to go, a can of DIET COKE and he'd be the fuck outta here.

Kate was reading the morning paper with her ankles resting on the edge of the Coffee table. "How's Lilly"?? She asked flipping over the front page.

"I'm gonna go see her after lunch. Phillip arranged for us to communicate through the window. I'd invite you to come but prison handshakes suck." Ontario Streets Last Outlaw said moving quickly about the room, in truth, he did not want his niece exposed to such an environment, nor did he feel that Andrew would have appreciated it either.

Lilly was someone who had always been surrounded in darkness and mystery and shadow, and her current predicament was no exception.

"I like your hair like that." Kate said still focused on her paper. "Evan's being released this afternoon."

"I hope they get him the right home care." Von said.

"Then you're doing what, after you finish your visit with Lilly.

"I get to go have dinner with Charlie and your great Aunt Eva." Dane said with a tempered smirk on his face. He was looking forward to Eva the way an atheist looks forward to Sunday mass. She had needled him in ways that he couldn't discuss with his lips parted, what a total and utter smug piece of garbage.

"By the way, there's a nine millimetre Beretta sitting on top of the bread box." Shamrock said casually.

Von had stopped smiling. "I guess I forgot to put that away." He said.

"You were using it for what"?? Kate asked with a smirk of her own on her face.

"Skeet shooting." Von "The Icon" lied.

"Where, in the kitchen"??

"Bathroom." Von "The Icon" responded.

When Von walked through the doors to the visitation room Lilly was already seated behind the window wearing lip stick and make up. She looked sinsational. "I was just reading about you." Lilly "Bad To The Bone" Chicoine said to her gorgeous boyfriend.

"I didn't think they had my Books or the newspaper in here." Dane jested.

"Hmm … … … they don't, but one of the screws left a copy of THE MONTREAL GAZZETTE lying face down on a mercury thermometer. It was two for one day."

"I don't even wanna ask what the fuck you did with that."

Lilly shot her tongue upward against the top of her mouth and gave him an "You know how bad I can be" expression. He had seen this look a thousand times in the past.

"So, I hear you got a heroes welcome on O Street."

"Yeah, they shook me all night long." Dane said in reference to the AC/DC song they had been playing in his honour. He was fumbling with a piece of maple fudge that he had retrieved from his pocket now.

"They love you to ye know." Von proclaimed. "You look adorable. My Baby Bunny."

"Little Bunny is still the Bunny that they won't let out of jail." Lilly said in a soft fuzzy voice that she was putting on. "WHY, won't they let Little Bunny go home"?? She asked in the same fuzzy but serious voice.

"Phillip and I are gonna fix that." Von said. "You're not hearing voices anymore I hope"??

"NnnnnnnnnnnnnnnOOO." … … … Lilly said again playing the Bunny.

At that moment a screw walked past Lilly and sneezed before disappearing out a side door. There was little sunshine in the room, and the portly hack was likely going outside to get some, after all, being in here was like an endless walk through Hell.

"Kate wanted to come and see you but in all honesty I don't know how Andrew would feel about me bringing her to a place like this." Dane said wiping a bead of sweat from his brow.

"He doesn't wanna defend me anymore." Lilly said in a voice that was both sad and self conscious.

"You know that I love you more than my own life." Dane said genuinely.

Lilly looked downward nodding slightly.

Von's eyes were watering now. Lilly's visible shame and sadness had caused him to tear up. Lilly had stolen his heart so many, many moons ago, and she hadn't given it back since.

"If I could i'd trade places with you … … … I love you Baby Bunny."

Suddenly, Lilly jumped up. "That's her. That's Roberta Clark." Lilly shouted. She had hopped to her feet and was now pointing toward the conjugal room across the way.

When Jacky Hannah saw a forest fire she tried to make it worse. It was all over television that Kate "The Gate" Shamrock's fiance had been found almost dead in his living room, had surgery, and was now on his way to a full recovery.

It was also point of interest for Hannah that a spokesman had said that Evan would be going home this morning. Maybe it was going to take one more crack for little miss hot shit to learn that her Family wouldn't be safe until she put her title or titles on the line against her tormentor, but it wasn't until Jacky turned around to see who was standing behind her that she got the shock of a life time.

There wearing skin tight blue jeans and a grey tank top was Kate "The Gate" Shamrock. Her eyes looked like two smouldering heaters from the depths of Hell.

"Hello Jacky." She began. "I have several things that I wanna get off my chest before I walk out of this tawdry little shit hole that you call a boxing club." Kate said clenching her fists into a ball. "Let's start with my future husband. I know, that you're the one responsible for Evan going to the hospital. I also know what kind of a whore you are behind closed doors. If you ever." Kate went on emphasizing the R at the end of her sentence "And I mean, ever, go near anyone that I love ever again, i'll walk into this club and put two in your fucking head."

Jacky's face was like stone. There was no give to the expressionless evil that seemed to occupy her iris's. As a matter of fact, she hardly seemed human.

After locking eyes with her nemesis for a few more seconds, Kate Shamrock turned toward the clubs front door and walked out into the blazing afternoon heat.

"Please state your name for the record." The Chief investigator said.

"Roberta Clark."

"Why are you here Roberta"?? Detective Solomon asked with an expression of confusion coming and going from his face. The room was a maze of shadows, only one light burned.

"Because he mesmerizes me." Roberta exclaimed.

"Who mesmerizes you"?? Solomon asked.

"Turn off the tape recorder." The Senior Detective ordered his protege who stood only four or five feet away from him underneath a veil of shadow.

"Now it's dark." Roberta whispered below an ocean of deception.

"What the fuck"?? Garrison asked. He thought that Roberta looked like she'd just been found walking along the shores of the dead sea. It was as if her soul was turned off.

"Do you know where you are"?? Detective Drew Solomon asked.

Roberta gave no response.

"Do you remember being arrested two nights ago"?? Solomon pressed but he could see no visceral reaction coming from her, nor could he hear one. It was as if he were talking to a statue.

Garrison displayed a frown in his partners general direction. He was wondering what in fucking hell was wrong with this young woman who seemed to have become catatonic.

"I wanted to introduce myself to you." The short man with the slicked blacked hair and the grey skin began. He was wearing a black garment almost akin to a cloak over flat shoes.

"Do I know you"?? Von "The Icon" asked standing with his back to the prison's front door.

"I'm an actor. I met you once many, many years ago outside your house." The little man with the wicked eyes said. His voice was as straight as the edge of a knife and equally as sharp.

"I don't remember you."

"Are you sure"?? The Kubuki looking character continued.

"I think i'd remember someone like you." Von "The Icon" commented, transfixed.

"My name is Cyril Mathews."

"What can I do for you"?? Von "The Icon" asked intensely.

"I've seen your picture in the newspaper. I also know you from Ontario Street. I'm a connoisseur of people. There's an artistry to every person."

"That's terrific. What can I do for you"?? Dane asked becoming agitated by the presence of this stranger with the unholy eyes.

"I shoot films. Some of them have girls in them."

"Did you follow me here"?? Dane asked wondering how the fuck this guy knew where to find him.

"I didn't need to follow you. I knew where you'd be."

"How the fuck did you know that"??

"I saw you."

"You saw me"??

"In my head. I was watching you."

What the fuck was wrong with this guy?? Dane pondered.

"I make movies." Cyril Mathews said. He produced a card and handed it to Dane between two fingers.

Dane was returning Cyrils smoulder now.

When Dane got to the small sit down Restaurant where he had arranged to meet Charlie Brown and Eva Nicolette he found them already waiting for him, no surprise, no friendly warmth, just their faces. They had chosen a booth and each had drinks sitting on the table before them.

"Hi." Eva began in her best i'm your friend with a knife in your back voice. You poor wounded animal. I'll pray for you, was what was coming across. It was as if you were pathetic and sweet Eva was making sure that you somehow knew it, willingly or not.

"Charlie, I need to make a phone call. You wanna order me a Sprite or a Seven Up." Von asked.

"Yep." The thirty year old responded. His fuckin voice cracked like he was still going through puberty.

"He doesn't know what I have in store for him." Eva said as soon as Dane was out of ear shot. It was as if her comment had been an attempt to make up for her crows feet and lack of self esteem around someone the caliber of the legendary Von "The Icon," she was insecure, and it was readable.

"Just chill out. If he senses that you're up to something he'll bolt on us and we won't have any fun."

"I had to call my brother. He's at work, he sends his love though. He's an emotional bastard." Von said returning to the table.

"So, those people are done with black mailing you"?? Eva taunted.

"Yeah, you know how to get a persons blood boiling don't you Eva"??

"I don't think that I said anything verbally." She went on.

Dane was sucking his lips backward and smirking at the same time. Eva was pushing it.

"So, are you training often these days"?? Charlie asked.

"I try to hit the gym at least three times a week, unless it's hitting me back."

"Good lookin out. I always keep up my fitness." Charlie said, right as rain, self assured, however juvenile. It was a fuckin veneer, locked in his own closet of self illusion.

Just then Danes phone lit up. "Just a second, I have to take this." He said.

"You have a collect call from … … … … (Lilly). The Operator said. "You may press one now to accept the charges, or answer the following question with only yes or no. Will you accept the charges"??

"Yes." Dane responded.

"Thank you. Please go ahead."

"Hey Boo." Lilly began on the other end. Where are you"??

"Rosie's Diner." Von responded.

"With who"??

"My Aunt and my cousin."

"The Aunt that you told me about, the one who tried to make us look bad after that wake"??

"The very same."

"Someone needs to put this bitch in her place. Phillip is bringing me in for a second bail hearing tomorrow."

"This woman really gets underneath my skin." Dane said looking across the room at his aunt who was sipping Champagne, if he had his way, he would fucking kill the cunt.

"Well, if I make bail tomorrow night ... ...

CHAPTER 5:

Monica, this chapter is especially for you Baby Bunny. I am crying like Holy Hell as I write this. You will always be number one to me. I love you with every fibre of my body, heart, and soul. My love for you is undying. God Bless You Bunny Rabbit. Eternal life!!!

After the wake Dane and his aunt were sitting side by side on the couch along with another relative whom Dane was just meeting for the first time, it was sad but more of a tragedy for those who had known the victim well, his Parents, particularly his Father, was inconsolable.

It had taken Dane, in his infinite wisdom, well over two years to discern the real reason why Eva had turned her back to him in the conversation. It was an act of disrespect against him as an author as well as against his book because this same relative had just read URBAN RAIN for the first time. It was also an act of disrespect against Monica and their story.

Along with this insulting behaviour, this aunt had been giving off heirs via smirks as well as gestures. Dane also firmly believed given the text of something else that had gone on before all of this that his aunt was mocking or belittling Dane because she understood that Dane still had feelings for Monica despite all that had happened, mother fucker.

Then he was sure at one point that Eva had been thinking something else. Danes cousin Charlie was extremely good looking, given the pathology, and this woman's innate propensity for sheer vindictiveness, Dane was more than 95% certain that this woman was thinking that Charlie could go "On there" and talk to Monica. There, being, Face Book.

Did this foolish woman have any idea what Dane would have done in retaliation for something like that??

Dane had recently been called "A Sensitive," by a friend who was touted as being a psychic.

If Dane knew you well enough, it didn't take him long to read your face or your body language.

So my dear aunt. My business is witchu.

Eva had insulted Dane as well as Monica beyond comprehension, and now she was going to FUCKING PAY FOR IT!!!

That night, in the shadows of Ontario Street, the gorgeous, sexy, stunning world legend Lilly "Bad To The Bone" Chicoine pushed her way through a crowd that was hanging from the rafters. She had made bail, and was now being welcomed home by a series of rabid cheers as well as a deafening roar from The Ontario Street Originals Street Gang, even the surrounding community had come out to see her. Lilly, as was the case with Von "The Icon" was a hero in Montreals east end.

They were ecstatic, one of their two sweet hearts was back in the fold with Ontario Streets Immortal Legend Von "The Icon" watching the scene from behind his mirrored sun glasses.

LI-LLY!!!!!!!!!!!!!!!!!!! LI-LLY!!!!!!!!!!!!!!!!!!!!! LI-LLY!!!!!!!!!!!!!!!!!!!!! LI-LLY!!!!!!!!!!!!!!!!!

LI-LLY!!!!!!!!!!!!!!!!!!!!! LI-LLY!!!!!!!!!!!!!!!!!!!!! LI-LLY!!!!!!!!!!!!!!!!!!!!! LI-LLY!!!!!!!!!!!!!!!!!! LI-LLY!!!!!!!!!!!!!!!!!!!!! LI-LLY!!!!!!!!!!!!!!!!!!!!! LOUDER, LOUDER, LOUDER, LOUDER!!!!!!!!!!!!!!!!!!!!!!!!!!!! LI-LLY!!!!!!!!!!!!!!!!!!!!!!! LI-LLY!!!!!!!!!!!!!!!!!!!!!! LI-LLY!!!!!!!!!!!!!!!!!!!!! LI-LLY!!!!!!!!!!!!!!!!!!!!

They were literally going crazy with one "Lilly" chant following the next. Then came the chorus, WE LOVE LI-LLY!!!!!!!!!!!!!!!!!!!!!!! BEAT, BEAT, BEAT, BEAT, BEAT, WE LOVE LILLY!!!!!!!!!!!!!!!!!!!!!!!!!!!

She's famous, Lilly registered psychologically referencing herself in the third person as she often did when assessing her own situations, it had been a habit of hers ever since the days when she squatted in abandoned buildings and slept outside in the cold at night. She was the most hardcore angel alive, bar none.

"I love you Boo." Lilly said embracing her boyfriend underneath the glow of the Icarus moon.

"You know, it sounds to me like some people are happy to see you." David Dane said.

"Yeah, I guess so ah." Chicoine responded placing a cigarette between her perfectly shaped lips.

Dane thought that she looked gorgeous standing there in her dark blue denim jean shirt over sun blasted blue jeans and bright yellow ball cap. The outfit finished out over a pair of nylons and shiny black stilettos that shined in the after glow of the vapour lamps that loomed above.

"What's the name of that song"?? BAD TO THE BONE CHICOINE asked of the music that was emanating in a storm from The Black Domino Tavern, it was familiar, she had heard it someplace before, maybe a movie.

"That's DREAM WARRIOR'S by DOKKEN."

"Mm ... ... I've heard it someplace before." Lilly said blowing a ring of smoke into the warm night air and watched it drift into the limitless black sky overhead.

"Nightmare on Elm Street 3. Tonight, you're the dream warrior." Von "The Icon" said as Lilly eye balled Eva as she crushed her cigarette with her foot at the same time. If this woman wanted to defame a legend then she was going to have to pay for it, that legend being the legacy of Von "The Icon" and Lilly "Bad To The Bone" Chicoine.

"So, you're my boyfriends aunt." Lilly began walking across the street.

Dane was eye balling Charlie to keep him from interfering.

"Look, I don't want any trouble." Eva squirmed now realizing the true nature of her invitation to this event.

"Hmm ... ... Hmm ... ..." Lilly said in an adorable tone. This woman was responsible for belittling herself, her boyfriend, and Urban Rain. There was going to be Hell to pay twice over!!

"I've been fucken waiting to knock rocks with you." Lilly proclaimed.

"I'm not here for that. I ... ...

"You're lucky that I don't decide to bust your head open on the curb for the way that you disrespected our legend. Get outta my sight and don't ever let me catch your BIBLE THUMPING ASS in this neighbourhood again." BAD TO THE BONE CHICOINE FINISHED as she loomed over the pathetic Eva Nicolette who was trembling with fear brought on by the bad ass who had just confronted her.

LI-LLY!!!!!!!!!!!!!!!!!!!!!!!!!!!   LI-LLY!!!!!!!!!!!!!!!!!!!!!!!!!!!!!!!   LI-LLY!!!!!!!!!!!!!!!!!!!!!!!!!!!!!! The crowd roared on. It was a magical night indeed.

Five hours later, as the darkness was turning to light, Jason Ronin ran into Charlie Brown four blocks over from Ontario Street. "I hear you're a man with a lot to say" Ronin commented upon seeing Charlie. "I also hear that you're pretty chummy with two of my best friends enemies." He began placing a cigarette in his mouth.

"I think Jay is gonna kick your ass." Manny remarked in Charlies direction.

"Oh, well, just because Von doesn't like certain people doesn't mean that i'm gonna break off my association with them." The idiotic Charlie remarked in the face of what was soon to be devastation.

"No ah"?? Ronin questioned firing up his smoke. The match that he had used ignited with a flare sound as its brightness came to life. "I think that's a pretty shitty deal for someone whose supposed to be Von's cousin." Jason said shaking the flame out.

"Why should I stop being friends with someone because Von doesn't like them? There his enemies, not my enemies. He's living twenty years ago, those people have grown up, they've moved on."

"That's not cool." Manny said. He was getting pissed off. This punk should have known better than to mess with Von. "So, why do you call yourself his cousin then"?? Manny asked. "You may as well call yourself his enemy. I mean, if someone was enemies with Jay or with my Brother I wouldn't be friends with him."

"Look, I don't answer to the two of you." Charlie flexed.

"I'll be the judge of that." Jason Ronin said. "You know it's to bad that my Mother isn't here." Ronin said. He had just dropped his cigarette and was now stepping on it.

"Oh yeah, why is that"?? Charlie wanted to know.

"Because my Mother, she's religious, she goes to church ye know."

"So what."

"So if she was here she could pray for your fuckin ass."

The sky was beginning to show its first lines of colour now.

"Oh yeah, and why would she have to do that"??

"You think you're a cold blooded killer"?? Ronin enquired. He was disrobing of his spring jacket now. "I just bought it. I don't wanna get blood on it." He said with a fresh smoke dangling between his lips. "I hear you know how to pose for pictures and use your cock. How about your fists"??

Charlie was beginning to look a mite nervous now. After all, as he had once said himself, street cred wasn't really his thing, and in all actuality, Charlie had spoken the truth that time, BITCH!!!

"One two, there's my shoe, three four there's the floor." The handsome, dashing Jason Ronin said as he kicked Charlie so hard that he almost broke all five of his toes on one foot.

"Fuck you." Charlie said standing up and charging at his opponent on all cylinders.

"What is that, a modelling move." Ronin asked using a basic Kenpo technique known simply as DELAYED SWORD. He had brought the soles of his palms down across Charlies shoulder blades before stepping on his toe and elbowing him in the jaw.

"CRACK"!! Ronin yelled out. He was fishing below a car for a length of rubber tube that he had seen just moments ago. When he retrieved it he looked across at Charlie and said-"Bend over and touch your toes, and i'll show you where the wild goose goes."

"Jay is kicking your ass." Manny said.

"I'm gonna take a picture of this for Von so he can have the fuckin thing bronzed for posterity." Ronin said releasing his cell phone from the recesses of his coat pocket and turning it on. In moments the screen came into view. "Did you know that people are watching movies on their cell phones these days"?? Ronin asked the fallen Charlie. "Just last week I watched KICK ASS, and what a coincidence, I just kicked your ass."

Charlie was making noises on the ground, and then he farted.

"Pew, nasty. Manny, let's take our pictures and go before he decides to finish his thought."

"Good idea Jay. We don't need to stick around for this mess."

"Say cheese." Ronin said snapping a photograph. "Cheers."

As Lilly had left Ontario Street the previous night she and Kate "The Gate" Shamrock had locked eyes for the briefest of moments as Strange Love by Depeche Mode played somewhere in the night. It was an expression of mutual respect between two female warriors who had many common bonds. It would be Kate who would soon go forth and carry the torch in Lilly Chicoines honour for tragedy was about to strike the unsuspecting. It was now the morning of November 7th, 2012.

CHAPTER 6:

THE BIG SHADOWY CLOCK THAT GOES TIC TOCK:

L.A.-The following is a fictitious imagining of the events that took place on the night of November, 7th 2012. You will also find that there are facts mixed in along with non truths in this chapter. Monica was and always will be my favourite person on this earth along with my niece Kate. I loved her with all my heart and I would have GLADLY given my own life for her on that highway. I want more than anything else for you to know that because when I go to my grave, that is one of the few things to me that will matter.

Regards,
Von "The Icon"

"Good morning Boo." Lilly said to David Dane as she called him on the phone the next morning. "What's today's date"?? She asked.

Dane rolled onto his back and looked at his watch. "It's November 7th, 2012." Dane espoused. "Where the hell are you"??

"I'm at my Brothers house."

"You're in Ontario."

"Yeah, I wanted to come and see my Mum and my Brother before I have to head back to Montreal tonight."

"How did you manage to get your sexy ass all the way out there"??

"I drove. I have a Drivers License. I got it after we broke up with each other."

"I didn't even know that you had a car."

"I have a Nissan Maxima." Lilly said fishing around for a cigarette.

"I wouldn't know a Nissan from a caravan." Von "The Icon" said.

In moments there was a knock on Von's door and then he had to go. Somewhere in the back ground "I Wanna Make The World Turn Around" by The Steve Miller band played faintly beyond a door.

Today, Lilly's Mother was taking her shopping and then she and her Brother Julian were going for lunch.

"You're up early this morning Councillor." Dane said as Andrew power walked through the door holding a magazine between his thumb and fore finger. It's bold lettering read "CITY," and just beneath it was a photo of Andrew himself seemingly presiding over a series of sky scrapers.

"This photo is a very accurate depiction of your self opinion." Ontario Streets Hero jested. He was still in his robe and hadn't bothered to brush his hair yet causing him to look as though he'd just stuck his finger in an electrical outlet.

"Think so? I think it actually underscores the way that I truly feel about myself." Andrew responded jokingly.

"How's Princess Kate"?? Von asked with regards to his niece.

"She's good. How are you"??

"Like I just went ten out of twelve rounds with Floyd Mayweather."

"You should take a couple of Tylenol."

"Nah, then i'll fuckin pass out and I won't get anything done today."

"Where's BAD TO THE BONE CHICOINE"?? Andrew asked.

"Lilly, is in Ontario."

Just then there were a series of loud harsh thumps on the door.

"Who is it"?? Dane asked leaning over his shoulder.

"Oh, C'mon, lemme in." Marilyn Dane echoed from the hallway.

"Open the fuckin door." Von said.

Andrew walked about four feet and then obliged him. "When did you get here"?? He asked their Mother who looked like she'd been up for the better part of ten days, there were circles beneath her eyes, some Mascara had run and then chipped in tiny fragments.

"I just flew in about an hour ago. It was a bumpy ride."

Dane was non plussed by all of this, had it not been for Lilly's phone call, he'd still be in bed.

"You guys make yourselves at home. I need to take a shower."

"How's Dad"?? Andrew asked as soon as he and Marilyn were alone. Things between David and their Father were not good, so Andrew usually left the subject alone when his Brother was around.

"Your Father's up at the building painting. He's workin his ass off." Marilyn said amidst a frown. She and Jonathan were both landlords with a penchant for being hands on when it came to detailing their properties. The frown itself was not necessary nor relevant to the topic but she still wore it anyway, it was an old habit that never seemed to find residence elsewhere.

"He's had a heart attack. He should be more careful about doing stuff like that." Andrew said concernedly.

"Yeah, well, we've gotta make money." Marilyn responded. The frown seemed a permanent resident of Marilyn's face at this point. She was wearing it, and she would be damned if she was going to take it off. Jonathan Dane had at one point given his wife the nickname-GROUCH, and to some degree, it served her right.

By the time that David Dane was out of the shower they had changed the subject, however, that was not going to prevent "Ontario Streets Last Outlaw" from going into a tirade about his old man who to him was nothing more than a sicko and a sociopath, over and over again, it wouldn't end.

"I overheard you guys in there. You talk about Jonathan like he's the fuckin Sultan Of Brunei minus the mega-bucks."

"Aw look, I didn't come all the way out here to listen to this. I'll get on a plane and go home if that's how you're gonna behave. I have things to do, i'm stressed. You're Father and I are working seven days a week to keep you and you're being disrespectful."

Dane was pulling a pair of jeans on below a black satin shirt and mirrored sun glasses.

"See, that's just it, you forget how Jonathan treated me when I was sick. I came home because I wasn't well, my anxiety had just reached the point of no return and he decides to take full advantage of my condition, then you take me to a fuckin Doctor and tell him that i'm schizophrenic. I've never been schizo a day in my life."

"Yeah, well, you know what I mean." Marilyn said. The frown could not escape her. It was being held hostage.

"When the fuck did you get a degree in psychiatry"??

"Alright." Andrew Dane chimed in.

"I was in that fuckin house. I know what went on." Von proclaimed staunchly. "Oh, you're gonna clam up now."

"You're a big burly guy with big shoulders. You were sittin behind your Father while he was on the computer, intimidating."

"How the fuck was I intimidating?? I'm the one who had to worry about being electronically impersonated the whole fuckin time that I was home, at your request I might add."

"Look, just stop alright, enough." Andrew again interjected.

"He wanted that fuckin receipt for the lawyers consultation. I had to fly all the way back out here with you in tow in order to secure that piece of paper."

"Oh, you were imagining things."

"You have a non verbal learning disability, I was imagining nothing." David Dane said.

"Well, you weren't well. We had to take you to see a Doctor."

"No, I was perfectly well. I just didn't happen to agree with your point of view on how things in the house were proceeding."

"Oh, C'mon, your Father and I had to sign contracts saying that we wouldn't electronically impersonate you so you'd have enough security to live in our house."

"Bull shit, I had every reason not to trust your husband. Past behaviour is the best determiner of future behaviour. Just ask Dr. Phil. Then Dad's sister decides to chime in and have her little party at my expense. They both opened up on me."

"What's Charlie doing out here?? Andrew said he got a call from him but wouldn't take it."

Andrew had stepped into the kitchen to make himself a sandwich.

Von was fucking with the channel selector now. He couldn't seem to get the volume to rise.

"Charlie, yeah, that's another one who needs a foot up his ass. I heard that his Mother slapped the stork who delivered him."

"Yeah, I always knew there was something about that little prick that irked me." Marilyn commented, she had not liked Charlie long before his problems with her son. She believed him to be both cocky and arrogant as well as pretentious "Her kids always have to be the best. She puts them in in everything so that they can be competitive and then she runs everybody else into the ground."

"The only reason that he's not dead is because he's Family." Von stated.

"There's no lettuce in this house I take it." Andrew said fishing around for a pair of scissors.

"I ran out two days ago."

Marilyn stood up and moved about the spacious apartment, she was not sure if the air conditioning was on but it felt like it was. From somewhere, cold rising in waves.

Andrew was cutting a line along the edge of a package that's lettering read "JAMBON." French for HAM. Dane had always thought that the name "JAMBON" sounded like it belonged to a French Rock Band.

"Hi Nana." Kate said coming in from the hallway. She had used her own key to get in.

"How's Evan"?? Ontario Streets Last Outlaw asked.

"He's better. He still has tubes in him but he's starting to eat on his own."

"That's good, I haven't been able to eat since I saw your aunt Eva. They should put a warning label on her that says-Induces Vomiting."

"Oh Christ." Andrew said, he was between a mouth full of sandwich and a glass of milk.

"I never got to spend that much time around her." Shamrock said.

Dane's eyes went one way and then the other.

"You were right about Lilly. She's beautiful." Kate stated.

"You two met"?? Von asked.

"Sort of, we passed each other in the shadows during her home coming."

"Lilly loves you, I want you to know that. Thinks that you're a woman not to be messed with." Dane said. He was looking for a photograph of her.

"Here, I want you to keep this in your wallet." He said having found one. It was a small snap shot of he and Lilly sitting on a couch side by side, they looked cozy together. "She'd be very proud to believe that you were carrying this."

"I'll have to get a picture of Lilly and I together someday." Kate espoused. She was proud of this legendary bad ass that her uncle had spent so many years with. She was something of an enigma.

"Lilly's like you, she's fearless." Dane said.

"I still have the garnet ring that she gave me for Christmas." Marilyn said. "I've always thought of her as one of my own kids."

"Yeah, your Grandmother and Lilly are very close, she even bailed Lilly out of jail a couple of times."

"I did all kinds of stuff." Marilyn said as though she believed that she was not being given full credit. "I bought her all kinds of Christmas presents and comforted her when she was upset. I've always been understanding of Lilly."

"Lilly saw you on T.V." Ontario Streets Last Outlaw said. "Believe me Katie, she's very proud of you and she loves you."

"Tell Lilly i'm buying her dinner whenever you see her." Marilyn offered.

"I will. She's in Ontario right now visiting her Mum.

As Lilly walked down the mall next to her Mum she thought of all the beautiful places that she'd dreamt about for so long, there were paradises and islands that she'd seen in her imagination that she desperately wanted to go to. Maybe one day she'd visit some of those places with her Mum, Dad, and Brothers or with David Dane.

Today, she was receiving a special gift. It was a locket that her Mother had specially inscribed just for her. It said-TO MY BEAUTIFUL DAUGHTER LILLY. I WILL ALWAYS LOVE YOU, LINDA, and inside was a photograph of Lilly and her Mum cheek to cheek.

They just needed to wait until it was ready, and that's what they were doing now. Well, Lilly was eating ice cream and her Mum was examining a dress in a store front about two feet away.

"What do you think about it"?? The glamourous Linda Chicoine asked.

"M … … … … hmm … … … … It's very pretty. Are you going to try it on"?? Lilly asked taking another bite from her ice cream cone which was coming apart, she was worse then a kid.

Ice Cream, had always been one of Lilly Chicoines favourites. She especially like Chocolate Sundae flavour that came in the tub. Dane used to buy it for her with the groceries. Lilly would always celebrate whenever he gave it to her. She was happy because of little things sometimes, a trait that Dane had always found cute and adorable.

"Linda Chicoine had forgone answering Lilly's question and instead bought the dress as a gift for her special daughter. "I love you Lilly." Linda said gazing into her daughters eyes. "Both Gregory and I love you. We always have."

Lilly stood up and moved away from the bench where she'd been sitting. There were tears of emotion welled up in her eyes, she had always loved her Mother to. She was in her own right, a mommies girl.

"I love you to." Lilly said breaking down.

H.A.-At this point I want to break in order to address you. Ye know over the years Monica would talk about her Family at different times and address them in different lights, but you were the one person that she never wavered on. Monica was always proud of her big brother. She used to tell me about the time that you guys lived together and about how you used to have jobs at WENDY'S. She would always laugh whenever she told me about the patties(I won't go any further with that here). Monica told me that you always supported her, even when you couldn't. I'll always have respect for that.

Back in 2001, we were having a conversation about you, and I believe her exact words were-"I love H. I love my big brother. He's awesome."

I know that later on in time after you and I got to know each other by phone, that things between Monica and I became tumultuous and then disintegrated. Things got the way they were because I could never let her out of my heart and I couldn't part with her, the days and nights, the good times and the bad times, the happy moments and the sad moments, were to hard to let go of. You'll read about many of them in these two books. Those days and nights that we spent together on Ontario Street and elsewhere are forever immortal. There will never be a time like that again.

Monica and I had a legendary relationship. To this day I have not let her go from my heart, like a winged dove suspended in a cage of sunlight. I still cry whenever I think of her. She will always be special to me to the degree that no other woman will ever be able to fill her shoes, no matter what.

Like I always say when I think of situations. Try and remember the good times.

Regards
Von "The Icon"

After paying for the locket and placing it around her Daughters neck Linda and Lilly Chicoine went to a sit down restaurant and ordered dinner, sparing no expense.

"I'll have a T-Bone steak and french fries." Lilly said taking a pull from her Orange Crush.

"I like the design on the outside. They did a good job on it." Linda exclaimed noticing that Lilly was all the while enamoured with her new piece of jewellery as she rocked kiddishly back and forth on the seat admiring her new locket.

"I'm gonna wear it every day." Lilly said.

"I hope you will."

At that moment Gregory Chicoine appeared out of nowhere. He was just on time if only a minute or two late. "You got your hair cut." He said immediately observing that Lilly "Bad To The Bone" Chicoine now had short hair.

"Hmm ... ... hmm, and I have a new locket." Lilly boasted, proudly displaying her new piece of jewellery for her Father to see.

"That is very nice. I like it." Gregory exclaimed through his thick Salvadorian accent.

"Excuse me." Linda said tapping their waitress on the shoulder. She had a camera in her hand between her thumb and forefinger. "Would you mind taking a photo of my Family and I"?? She asked.

"Sure, no problem." The waitress said positioning the camera in her hand to take the shot.

Lilly was standing now wearing a brown pull over and black dress slacks. She looked absolutely beautiful, as always. Even on the worst days of her life, Lilly had always been gorgeous.

"Say cheese." The waitress said smiling as she snapped the photograph of the attractive trio.

"There you go." She said handing the camera back to its owner.

"Thank you." Linda said.

Andrew Dane turned to face the news media and their lenses. He was as always fascinated by their interest in him. He was not a celebrity, at least not in his own estimation. It seemed though that on this quiet November afternoon that he had once again caught the attention of the public eye and was now the centre of a spectacle.

What did they want now, he wondered. Had this something to do with upcoming murder trial of Lilly Chicoine or was this a less conspicuous rendezvous??

"Excuse me, Mr. Dane. Have you heard anything at all about the upcoming trial of Lilly Chicoine"?? One reporter asked while shoving a microphone in Andrews face.

"Is there any chance of you returning to your duties as Lilly's council"?? Another member of the Montreal Media Department asked as she forced her way between two beefy looking security officers.

Andrew Dane had to think for a moment. He knew how important this trial was and to what degree his Brother as well as Lilly might be counting on him. It was possible that he could at some point assist Phillip Laroche in Lilly Chicoines defence.

"I have no comment at this time." He responded surpassing the media onslaught and heading for his black Jaguar which sat idle facing the curb.

"David." Andrew said sitting in behind the wheel. He was on his cell phone now. "I'd like to return to my duties as Lilly's lawyer."

"It's November seventh." David Dane said greeting Olend at the doors of the hospital. "I know the food's lousy. At least you won't have to live with their excuse for fruits and vegetables anymore."

Olend looked around at the brisk afternoon. He was ready to leave. He'd seen enough over the past few weeks and the thought of anymore doctors and nurses poking and prodding at him was enough to make him sick. Over the past eight of nine days he'd begun to feel like a pin cushion. Pleasing to him was the thought of his warm bed and whatever he had at home in the fridge.

"How the hell did this happen to you"?? Von "The Icon" enquired. He was not happy that his elderly friend had been the subject of a brutal knife attack.

"I was in the wrong place at the wrong time." Olend said straightening the length of his brown blazer which he wore over grey dress pants topped off by a white hat.

"Who did this to you"?? Ontario Streets Last Outlaw asked becoming more assertive.

"I didn't see his face. The night was to dark. I only caught a glimpse of the fellow walking away."

"What was he wearing"?? Dane asked.

"Pair of those baggy hang downs and a ball cap." Olend lied.

Dane believed that Olend was holding out on him. It was then that he began to wonder if Clinton had been the knife man, it made sense, and would have given Olend more then enough reason to keep his mouth shut.

"I'm going to go home and shut my eyes on Gods prayers." Olend exclaimed. He was exhausted and simply wanted to feel the linens of his own bed against his skin. This ordeal had been enough, his son had stuck him with the sharpened end of a knife and now Olend did not know where or when he might see his own flesh and blood again.

What might Clinton, his boy, do this time? Would he finish the job and try and kill him for certain in order to silence him. It was a possibility.

If his son decided that he might one day be named for what he had done to him then Olend felt that he might actually go through with it. Clinton was dangerous, he had run long and hard in gangs and killing was not foreign to him, it was on many levels, a way of life.

"I called you a cab while you were still inside, it should be here in five or ten minutes." David Dane said removing his black shades and hanging them off his shirt. "You sure you don't know who did this to you"?? He asked accusingly.

"I never saw the mans face." Olend responded. "So many of today's youths are troubled. They're starving or they need money for drugs. My Father used to preach to the young people in his congregation. He tried to make every one of them see the light of God. There was one who needed a demon removed from inside of him and my Father helped him.

He was just a young boy, only nine or ten. One night his white eyes turned to dusk and a demon entered him, it almost tore away his soul. My Father was one of God's hands, i've always believed that. He did so many special things for people, he cured the blind and the crippled. He performed only once an exorcism and the demon released the boys soul." Olend explained viscerally flashing back on the day that it happened. "Seeing that boy in the state that he was in frightened me to my very core but my Father, he loved us, and he wanted us to see Gods true power, to experience for ourselves the power of Gods kingdom."

Dane who was a skeptic was listening to all this, Olend had spoken of his Father Damius many times before, it would however take a lot for him to believe a story involving actual possession by a demon.

"You should never stray away from Jesus." Olend said gently touching Dane's cheek with his finger tips.

Dane pulled away just slightly. He was not sure about stories involving exorcisms and/or demonic possession although he'd run up against his share of wickedness in his time on the planet.

Just then Olends cab pulled into the curb.

"I'll call you to go for Coffee in a day or two." Olend espoused seating himself down in the backseat. He was happy to have a comfortable place to rest his back.

"Thanks Olend." Dane said genuinely gently closing the door for his friend.

As the cab drove away Dane thought of the many moments that he and Lilly had spent at this particular hospital, it was a favourite haunt of theirs.

On one such night Dane had been deathly ill with a fever of God knows what and he had brought Lilly along with him to this place to see a doctor.

Lilly had on that particular evening curled up in his arms like a bunny rabbit and gone to sleep not making a sound.

They had spent the entire evening in the waiting area slumped against the arm rests of a chair. It had been a long evening that bled into the next morning without Dane having gotten to see a physician, he had left with constricted tubes and coughing so forcefully that he thought he might puke up his tonsils, it was horrible.

When he and Lilly had gotten back home Lilly was dope sick and Dane was so near death that he thought that he might actually succumb to his Bronchitis which had worsened with lack of rest.

"Baby, i'm sick." Lilly had moaned.

Dane was by that time so ill that he thought that her cries were part of a dream that he was having.

He did not recall how she had found her hit that morning.

"We're going to kill her on film." Cyril Mathews said of the stripper/adult film star that he had just hung up with. "Next week, in the quiet room. We're going to give her some pills. Her name is Samantha Wilcox." He said speaking into his other phone which was a cellular.

"If I can have you do it then I will. If you're not fucking available then we'll have to use someone else." The little man in the black cloak said in a straight voice.

There was crackling on the other end of the line.

"I don't want to reschedule it. If I can't get you then someone other than MONSTER will have to kill her. I met their local celebrity for the first time the other day. If we could get him to come and work for us then we could make a film based exclusively on him. He could fuck whoever he wanted then bash her head in for all I care. We could call the parent company ICON INDUSTRIES."

Just then someone else walked into the room and closed the door.

"I have to hang up now. I have someone in my office. I understand that. Give me a call."

That afternoon, Dane walked into an adult cinema and sat down in one of its two viewing rooms which were currently unoccupied, he was alone. It was not for the pornography that David Dane was here but simply for the distraction of its offerings, it was a means of escape. He could feel the tension that was bottled up inside of him as he sat in one of the cinema's twin rows with shadows produced by the screen washing over his face as moans of pleasure echoed throughout the mini theatre that wreaked of semen and mold, mildew on top of decay.

His Father had put another scare into him just over an hour ago when he's subtly threatened to use Danes former black mailing situation to his advantage once more, threatening to twist things, turn them to his advantage. It was a threat that made David Danes blood run cold, fear inside, nothing left to hold onto.

As one image burned into the next on the soft screen Dane began to think of all that Lilly had been involved with in Montreal as well as the career that her life choices had led her to. There was something about this afternoon that in retrospect would one day seem hypnotic to David Dane for this was the morning of the day that Lilly Chicoine would die.

No one was coming in, and no one was going out. He was completely by himself in this room full of erotic sexual images and shadow. The words-DEATH TOLL AND DARK DREAMS ran through Von "The Icon's" mind without cause.

After close to two hours of hardcore xxx features Dane stood up and walked back out onto the street into the sharp morning air. Across the street from the cinema there was a strip bar and two or three pizza joints lined up row on row, always open for business, twenty four hour jooks. We never close.

As Dane walked into one of the pizzeria's that read "PAPA'S PIZZA'S" in bold black lettering he paid for a can of Coke and then walked slowly into the restaurants shadowy recesses to sip it. There was an empty pool table sitting in front of him, no Q up, no shot to miss.

"Hello" Dane mouthed quietly into his phone responding to the lit screen that he had nearly missed.

"Where are you"?? Marilyn Dane asked on the other end.

"I'm in a food joint." He said.

"Did you get something to eat"?? She asked. "No, i'm not hungry. I feel sick to my stomach. Dad upset me again."

"Uh-uh-uh. I told you to get off that. You're Father's not doing anything to you, he's under a lot of stress, he's workin seven days a week to keep you. We're all busy."

"He manipulates you. He tells you that he's an angel and then he leads you to believe that he's not doing anything wrong when nothing could be any further from the truth."

"That's your paranoia taking over." Marilyn sang into the mouth piece.

"That's not paranoia. The sonovabitch is selling you horse shit and you eat it up like it's cotton candy every time. How many times do I have to tell you that he's up to no good before you listen to what I have to say"??

"Listen, i've gotta get back to work. I don't have all day to listen to this. You're venting on your Father and I and we're the ones that are keepin you."

Just then a soda machine made a dispensing sound somewhere in the shadows.

"I'm gonna start to walk home. I'll call you later on." The Ontario Street Original said.

"Goodbye." Danes Mother said hanging up, and for now, that was that.

Ten minutes later Dane sat down on a bench that sat at the foot of a fire station, he was again thinking of Lilly. She had been his obsession for so long, night after night, moon after Icarus moon. Had it not been for the Latin Goddess who had captured his heart then there would surely be no URBAN RAIN. Maybe, one day Dane would write a sequel and call it-URBAN RAIN II-NEIGHBOURHOOD OF NIGHT.

Just then Claude F.(The Man With The Moustache) walked by and sat down next to him.

"Maybe I am go for da work." He said. "Every day is I am wake up and find something for da work, maybe I do the painting or the dry wall"

"Yeah, work is not exactly the easiest thing to come by in Montreal, neither is money, but then again that situation was the same wherever I went in Canada, and i've lived all over." The Ontario Street Original said. "Do you still do construction"??

Claude, the urban stud sighed. "I am for da work go to Longueille but just for try. I have one girl, she's dance now for da club in Gatineau. She make maybe five bills a night and sometimes she is give me one or two because she want." The Urban Stud commented.

Claude was bad, but somewhere underneath the lethal exterior there was a heart and a sense of maturity that knew right from wrong. He was better than most people might have given him credit for simply because he looked so intimidating, it could be misleading, that was if you didn't know him.

Dane thought that Claude looked as sinister and as dangerous as ever sitting there in his reflective ball hat and trade mark black track suit with an open jacket. He had BAD ASS smouldering dead in his eyes as if his heart were made of it, but in truth, yes and no, if he knew you, liked you, and you didn't cross him then he was alright.

"I see Francoise the other day and he was go. He have no money so maybe he go up north for da work but just for try. My girlfriend she wonder how I make my money. She can maybe for one night make a lot, for me is not as easy. Okay, I go." Claude finished standing up and walking away into the afternoon haze.

"Laters dude." Dane said watching his friend walk away.

Julian Chicoine lifted his guitar from its case and set it down on the table with his pic next to it. He was expecting Lilly, if she showed up on time he would play a song for her as well as for his own Daughter.

"She's here." Lilly said in her best unintentional orphanish voice as she walked through the door. She was again referencing herself in the third person, old habits died hard and bad asses did to.

"I'm glad. I was just readying some music to play for you. I hope you like G N R cause i'm gonna play DON'T CRY." Julian said.

"She does." Lilly said sitting down on the edge of the couch, above her head was a picture of Bob Marley and beside it a photo of Genesis in concert, to the left of both was a picture of Julian's adorable five year old Daughter who was in the next room having a snack.

"Okay." Julian said calling his Daughters name. "We're ready."

In a matter of second's Julian's Daughter entered the room and sat down on her Aunt Lilly's lap.

Julian Chicoine was readying his microphone and amplifiers now. He was a very good musician who possessed considerable talent. "I just need my bench." The husky Latin male with the beard and miniature pony tail said tuning up, readying himself, getting into the zone.

His eyes were darting around now but he could not seem to locate his bench.

"Ah … … … found it." He said lifting the wooden seat from behind a crate full of cables and wires.

In a moment he had tuned up and was both playing and singing DON'T CRY BY GUNS AND ROSES for his two favourite Princess's in the whole world.

Lilly was singing along. DON'T CRY was one of her all time favourites and her big Brother brought his very own style to it. There was a certain Latin flavour to all of his singing.

Julian paused for a moment adjusting the elastic band that was tugging on his pony tail, then he continued. "I'll still be thinkin of you, and the times we had." He sang.

After Julian was done playing he placed his guitar back in the case and lifted his Daughter to sit on his knee. "So, what have you been up to"?? He asked directing his question at his Sister who was rising to her feet.

"Not much, I mean I haven't gone to pick up my Methadone today but I should probably go and get it sooner or later. I have the Nissan so i'll drive over there and get it before five." She said picking a piece of thread from her slacks before disappearing into the kitchen.

"Daddy." Julians Daughter said giggling. She was nonchalantly brushing the front of her Fathers nose with her finger tips. "Did you watch cartoons today"?? He asked her.

"Yes," the little girl nodded jumping down from her Father's knee and heading to play with her dolls that were lined up on the couch. She was touching her chin with the tip of her finger as she pondered which doll to dress up as if there was a question mark in her mind, and indeed there was. She would now have to decide which one wore the blue dress and which one wore the orange baseball cap.

"Do you guys have any plans for later this evening"?? Lilly asked from the shadows of the kitchen.

"I have to go and help Daddy bring some boxes up from the basement. He says they're to heavy for him to lift by himself."

"I see. Okay, well, thank you for the mini concert." Lilly said returning from the shadows.

"I love you Aunt Lilly." The adorable little blond girl said stretching her arms out in her Aunts general direction.

"Aw … … … … Mmm … … … hmm … … … … … Aunt Lilly loves you to." Chicoine said reaching for her niece whom she gave a mucho hug to before putting her down.

"Always love you." The little girl said watching after Lilly as she vanished out the door, and into history.

L.A. AND E.A.-It is at this time that I will address you both as a unit. I hope you now understand that regardless of the situation between us that I never stopped loving Monica and never will, our ending was remarkably unfortunate, and had all of the factors been on the table then things might have been different. Monica was and always will be a part of my Family and of me, no matter what.

Every time that I think of her coming into my life I realize that in part that it was somehow meant to be that she would give me the experience of my life as well as inspire my first and third books, I am BEYOND emotional about that fact.

It was as if fate put us together so that one day I would be the care taker (At least in part), of Monica's memory as well as the author of our story and that's something that I take incredible pride in.

I will never again be able to sit with Monica and watch the sunrise over Ontario Street, I will never again have the chance to hold her in my arms and tell her that I love her once more forever and that is what hurts worse than anything else. I would have gladly taken her spot on that highway but life did not grant me that opportunity. I loved her and always will, no matter what, forever!!!

After all, my roll was always to protect Monica and to defend her life, but now tragically, I am to late for once. I could not be there to protect her as fate would have it and it was the one time that she needed me more than ever. It always seems that everything has to go wrong and that it cannot go right.

I will address you again later on.

God Bless,
Regards,
Von "The Icon"

As darkness fell that night David Dane rested a hand on his Brothers shoulder. He was standing behind him. "I need you to drive me to Ontario." He said looking tired as well as bewildered. It was as if he'd been sleeping and just awoken to strange news. There were shadows all around them.

"What? Now"? Andrew Dane asked. He could not believe what his Brother was telling him. He'd just worked for nearly twelve hours and now this.

"Yeah, Lilly just called. She's in the parking lot of some bar having car trouble."

"Well, can't she call a tow truck"?? Andrew enquired not yet resigned to the reality that he was going to have to do this. If he stayed awake for another minute he'd need an energy drink to keep his eyes from closing, he was beyond any beat down, broken, over worked and exhausted, all of this to much.

"I'm sorry, it can't be helped. Lilly's stuck and she has no money." The Ontario Street Original informed him leaning in to lift his leather jacket with an orange stripe down each sleeve from the couch. It was as if somehow his voice was not his own.

"I can't do this, but it looks like i'll have to." Andrew confessed.

"I'm sorry, I know you're tired and this is an imposition." Von "The Icon" said. He felt bad about having to do this to his Brother, but there was no other choice, the mountain had risen up, and this was the end result.

"Let's go." Andrew Dane said folding, there were a mass of shadows behind him, it was as if wickedness and sin were somehow closing in and taking hold, for this was a night that no one in David Dane's Family nor Lilly Chicoine's Family would ever forget.

"Grab my car keys." Andrew Dane requested. He had been sitting on the arm rest of the couch and just stood up, he was still wearing his work clothes.

Dane tossed the car keys into his Brothers hand and signalled him by raising his chin. "Let's go." He said heading for the darkness that lead to the door.

In ten minutes they had hit the highway and were headed North bound. Dane hoped that whatever Lilly was doing that it wouldn't cause her to drop out somewhere or go to sleep, if that ended up being the case, then Andrew would likely shoot him. "If you're thirsty then you can have one of these." David Dane said passing a can of Diet Coke to his Brother whose eyes looked heavy and grey. It was to some degree like he was dreaming awake, not far off sleep, just making due.

"Thanks." Andrew said cracking open one of the cans by pulling its tab back with his finger tips. "I'm gonna resume my duties as Lilly's lawyer." He said.

There was mild shock on Von "The Icons" face, he was not expecting this but was pleased with the revelation just the same. "I think that you and Phillip Laroche could work well cohesively. You guys can be like Lilly's Dream Team." He said.

"I'm no Lee Bailey or Johnny Cochran, but i'll try." Andrew said passing a car that was in the other lane. "I'll give it my all." His voice seemed to guarantee.

There was somehow an apology in his words. It was as if an "I'M SORRY FOR LEAVING HER SIDE" was inclusive of what he was saying.

There had been fighting in this Family, even war, but now at least Andrew was going to put aside some of the differences between his side of The Family and David Danes and do what was right, regardless.

At that moment an eighteen wheeler rumbled past them and headed for a turn off that was lined with brown/orange vapour lamps. The night was growing dark with the evenings shadow turning to a deep black dusk, somewhere in the distance, plumes of smoke like a brush fire burning out of control.

For a moment Dane was suspended in time. He thought of how he and Lilly had met, of the life that they'd lived together, mesmerized, under hypnosis.

It had begun outside of a seedy tavern on a wet and rainy day and now here they were all these years later. It seemed that they had heard The Devil's voice echo from the alleyways, streets, and alcoves of The Neighbourhood Of Night better known as Ontario Street, but they had survived it all, come through it, and lived to fight another day.

That's what life was about, one more hour, one more minute, one more breath. The big shadowy clock that goes tick tock.

"Turn off here." He said.

Andrew was looking passed the windshield now trying to see through someones high beams. "Fuck, it pisses me off when people do that."

Just then Vons phone lit up. It was Lilly. "Fuck, are you coming or not"?? She asked impatiently. Dane had heard this tone a thousand times before. Lilly Chicoine was not, and had never been a woman of patience, she was a woman with her mind made up, hardcore to the bone, and no one runs her.

"We're on our way. Andrew's driving. We should be there in a couple of hours. We're doing the best we can Baby."

"It's fuckin two hours i'm waiting already." Lilly complained. This was her frequent lament.

She was off her edge, maybe a bit fuzzy from Methadone. "Try to get here as fast as you can. I have to go cause i'm at a pay phone and I think someone wants to use it." She said.

"Uh-huh. I love you Baby Bunny." Dane said as the call crackled to its end.

As they headed further along the highway Dane thought of the time that two Pigeons and their unborn babies had come to take refuge on their balcony, they had sat there for the better part of two weeks unmoving, just sitting on their eggs, and Lilly had placed an umbrella over them when it rained. They had named the pigeons, Frank and Albert, and Lilly had taken a very special interest in them. "I love you." Lilly had once told them just before their newborns came into the world. It was an adorable scene with Dane watching Lilly tend to the pigeons with love in his eyes.

"I hope that Lilly and Kate get to know each other." Von "The Icon" said.

There were streams of white light washing over the hood of the car now.

"I'm sure they will." Andrew responded amidst yawning.

Somewhere in the universe Waiting For The Miracle By Leonard Cohen began to play, but this night would be no miracle, it would be a nightmare delivered in vibrant shades of technicolor. The songs melody was hypnotic as line after line of its chorus ran through David Danes mind winding and turning amidst rhythmic beats.

"I'm hungry." Andrew Dane said.

"Yeah, I could use a snack myself." Von agreed as they rolled past two twenty four hour eateries. "I don't think we should stop, Lilly's waiting. We need to get to her first." He said.

Just then there was a burst of static over the radio saying something about an accident that was in their vicinity.

"What the fuck did they just say"?? Andrew asked fiddling with the station.

Dane's expression had turned to one of seriousness. It was the same expression that he had worn eight Christmas's ago when Jonathan Dane had purposely upset Lilly and made her cry, it was a memory that always seemed to stay with David Dane, haunting him and tormenting him in flash backs that played themselves over and over like a movie on a screen. At some point Marilyn Dane had walked across the room and told him that quote-"Your Father doesn't even want her here."

Those words had cut into Danes soul like a scorched knife searing soft flesh and he had never forgotten them. After all, it was Lilly's house and she was the love of his life.

Dane would have died for his street angel girlfriend. She had always meant everything to him.

"Mam, can you hear me"?? A young gentleman of foreign decent called into the window of Lilly's Nissan but she was despondent, lying there motionless.

In a matter of a minute or two another car had appeared on the highway and soon there was a shadow standing in its headlights that looked more like an image from a bad dream, eyes closed on sleep.

"LILLY"!!!! David Dane shouted as he recognized an item of clothing that sat against the cars rear window over lapping a square stereo speaker that belonged to no one.

"You know her"?? The stranger asked amidst an expression of terrified bewilderment.

"Oh Jesus Christ. SOMEBODY HELP US"!!!!! Dane cried as he discovered Lilly's body behind the wheel of the sedan. He immediately reached through the window and felt for a pulse but the rhythm was not there, nothing, hollow metal droning representing that which was dire in his head

Andrew Dane was dialling 911.

Shimmering glass and streams of blood in the night.

Somewhere in the recesses of Danes mind PRETTY WICKED THINGS by DAWN RICHARDS echoed over and over as if to give ambiance to this nightmarish predicament- I heard thunder, looks like lightning. The song played. It was as though its lyrics were built on the fear and trauma that was reflected in Danes heart.

Now, moment by moment, in a series of melodic drumbeats Dane recalled several pivotal moments in their lives. He saw them meeting again for the first time standing in the silence and rain as if he were a third party watching the scene from the window of a moving car.

He remembered their first kiss in the shadows behind THE BLACK DOMINO TAVERN followed by the night that The Police had brought Lilly home wearing her yellow jacket with the hood on it.

"Her vital signs are weak." Someone said as Andrews hands pulled him away from the window of the car. "Come on." Andrew said consolingly as he was leading him somewhere. Where, Dane wondered. What realm were they in.

Then DAWN RICHARDS haunting track again. There were people and faces and shapes with white shirts moving in clusters. They had culminated here in this foreign place for what reason and to do what. They weren't speaking to him, just making laps or doing rounds. Why, and what was all of this commotion about.

Somewhere there was a pulse of hot silver light and then someone said something about last rites.

"… … … hear me"?? Andrew Danes voice echoed through the hollow cavernous reaches of Danes subconscious. "Try to calm down." Andrews voice said gently. He was somewhere else amidst time and space.

"I love you Boo." Dane imagined Lilly saying.

It was all flowing back in a stream of night, each image without a soundtrack, playing itself out. It was somewhere inside, deep in the pit. He and Lilly were together in a shadowy spot behind a tavern on Ontario Street waiting for Lilly's Dealer to put in an appearance. Almost sun up, and the wait was growing uncomfortable. "Remember no matter what Lilly says, Lilly loves you."

"I love you to." He had responded pulling Lilly into his arms. They had, had a fight the night before and now this was the two of them making up. Dane thought that she looked adorable standing there in her little blue fisher mans hat over her neon pink top and red jeans.

"Hit her again." A woman's voice commanded as electrodes struck flesh somewhere outside of memory. There were now two places. Here and there, wherever there was. Somewhere one clock ticked away, ticked away.

"I never learned to live without you." He remembered having told her once. "You leaving is like an oxygen mask being removed. I need you to breath. I love you Baby Bunny."

"I know." Lilly had responded softly cocking her head to one side and raising her thumb in the air.

"You really love me don't you"?? Lilly had asked one morning in 2002 after they'd been out all night.

Then there was a second pulse of light and it was Christmas Day 2004 all over again with Dane and Lilly sitting in the back seat of Jonathan Danes car. Jonathan had jammed on the brakes several times in a row to give Lilly a scare, the continuous inertia of which had almost given all four of them whip lash. Dane had from that moment on never felt the same way about his old man whom he despised for having treated the love of his life that way, for making her cry, and for wounding her so deeply that she could hardly talk.

It was undeserved and it had left Lilly in tears. In retrospect, and if he could have rewound history, Dane would have stopped speaking to his Father right then and there instead of years later, however, he had protected Lilly verbally and gotten her as well as himself out of there.

To her credit, Marilyn Dane who was sitting in the front seat had ripped into her husband for what he had done and later physically consoled an emotionally wounded and speechless Lilly by giving her a lengthy hug.

None of this was good enough for David Dane, that morning had haunted him to his present mind space and he had declared a bloody holy war over it, NO ONE, NO ONE on this planet had any right to hurt Lilly like that despite what her faults may have been. She was, had been, and would forever be the one person along with his niece that he cherished above any and all else on this earth, then, to this day and for eternity.

"Clear." The woman's voice called again from the other reality that currently existed.

"I'm sorry baby. He had no right to treat you like that." Dane had said when he and Chicoine had reached the elevators of their building, but he could get nothing out of her, Lilly was despondent, huddled safely within herself, what had happened had wounded Lilly so badly that she could not find the words to respond. Dane had wanted to kill his Father in cold blood at that moment but he had restrained himself, taking the high road.

"I love you Baby." He had told her over and over again that same afternoon when they were alone trying to make it up to her.

It was to Dane almost like a verbal coma, Lilly had been so struck by what had happened that her emotional hurt had suspended her ability to speak.

Marilyn Dane would comment years later that she would never forget the look on Lilly's face that morning and that still to this day it troubled her.

In Danes minds eye he saw his Mother walk into the kitchen and embrace Lilly who was standing there in her house coat wearing what to this day Dane would characterize as a-How could you do this to me expression on her face, her expression also carried traits of utter disbelief. When Dane was reminded of this moment his temper would reach a temperature that was WHITE HOT!!!

"Clear, we still have no pulse." The woman's voice blasted.

"Open it." Dane had said to Lilly as he handed her her Christmas present. It was a set of C.D.'s that she had asked for that Dane had personally gone hunting for, he was very proud of his gift and very proud to be called Lilly's boyfriend, which was in a way, a status symbol.

"I love you Baby Bunny. Merry Christmas." He remembered saying as he wrapped his arms around her. He loved her more than words could ever declare. She was his everything.

For a moment Dane had thought that Lilly looked sheepish or cowed as if she was afraid that her gift might be something other than what she had asked for or might embarrass her. She had once again reminded him of an orphan.

"It's something that you asked for." Dane coaxed. He would never have let Lilly be unhappy on Christmas morning, or any morning where he could have helped it for that matter.

Finally, Lilly opened her present and her face that had displayed a range of emotions that morning was now happy. She was very pleased with her new Cd's. "Thank you baby." She praised him as she stepped forward to give him a hug.

"I love you Baby Bunny." Dane said kissing his girlfriend square on the lips.

"She's still flat lining." A male voice from the other reality said.

That Christmas night Dane, Lilly, and Danes Parents had driven round and round looking at Christmas lights and Nativity scenes. The snow was beautiful, fresh powder with white crystals of ice on top. Dane recalled Lilly wearing a white parka over black jeans and a maroon watch cap, the two of them had sat in the backseat holding each other in their arms.

The male Doctor in the other reality shook his head as he began to unhook Lilly from the heart monitor that she had been strapped to. "She's gone." He said flatly.

"Time of death 10:27PM." Another attendant said. "Patients name, Lilly Lucinda Chicoine."

Five nights later as crisscrossing spotlights swooned over Ontario Street Von "The Icon" stood amidst a crowd of two hundred that had gathered to bid farewell to Lilly Chicoine, they ranged in age from eighteen to seventy five and were inclusive of The Ontario Street Originals as well as Kate "The Gate" Shamrock, her Father, and Marilyn Dane.

"First of all, I hope that you know how much you meant to me." David Dane said as tears streaked down his cheeks. There was a microphone in his hand.

There were signs and placards everywhere. They bore such sentiments as LILLY "BAD TO THE BONE" CHICOINE 4 LIFE!!!!!!!!!!!!!!!!!!!!!!! VON AND LILLY FOREVER … … … ONTARIO STREET LOVES LILLY CHICOINE … … … … … FROM DUSK TIL DAWN, LILLY CHICOINE LIVES ON … … … … … …

Somewhere in the night DON'T CRY BY GUNS AND ROSES stormed over a set of loud speakers adding ambiance and tragic flavour to the evening.

"I'll always remember you as the girl that I met in the millennium." David Dane went on. "You came to stay with me when I had no one else, you became all that I had, and then you became the love of my life. You always gave me an adventure no matter where we were or what we were doing, and even at the worst of times, you made my life fun. We spent a thousand days and nights on these streets and then we became their legend. You are a legend. Lilly you and I saw and experienced things that few have ever been through or will ever see and we forged a bond that death itself could not break, all that we lived through lets you know that. I'll never forget you Baby Bunny, i'll always love you. Death can never do us part." Dane said covering his face with one hand as he broke down on his final words. The force of Danes tears was uncontrollable, his whole body was shaking, unearthed by the passing of his girlfriend. "I'll love you forever." The Ontario Street Original said.

Kate "The Gate" Shamrock was crying a few feet away. She had never seen her Uncle so emotional.

Amongst the gathering of people were Alyssa M, Star, Marcel Monduire as Dane called him, Nick Monroe, "The Casanova Killer" Nick G(Lillys Councilor), Sheryl H, Claude F.(The Man with the moustache), Hedea, Mikhail, Tiffany whose I.D. Said Dale Frost, Suzy/Judy Q, Barbie, J.P. And Crazy Nadia, Carolyn, Mary Andre, Katia, Brando, Alexandra, MJ, Emanuelle, Jillian, Stephanie B. and a host of others.

"I have something that i'd like to say to my Uncle." Kate said lifting a twin mic from its case. The ice blue spot lights were everywhere now, making laps, crisscrossing, over lapping, swooning. The crowd was silent but for the sound of David Danes emotion and Guns N Roses.

"Ever since I was a baby you've always taken care of me." She began. "I also know how you took care of the incomparable Lilly Chicoine." She said her voice echoing over Ontario Street. "When I think of you, I think of hero's." The female champion went on.

Von "The Icon" was trying to shield his eyes but the emotion was over powering him.

"When I was still a baby you wrote to me every week and you never let me forget how much you loved me. Well here, tonight, I want you to know how much I love you." Kate Shamrock said raising her fingers to meet with her lower lip. "I have undying love for you, and I have undying respect for Lilly Chicoine, and for the legend that you both created on these streets. You'll go down in history, you truly will, you gave a love to this neighbourhood that it never would have had if it weren't for the two of you. God Bless you Uncle Von. Thank you for the inspiration." Kate said breaking down fully as she embraced her favourite Uncle. "I love you to Princess." He managed.

DON'T CRY by GUNS AND ROSES BLASTED ON.

L.A.-This is the point in the book where I will present the eulogy that I have prepared for Monica. I did not get to go to her Funeral, so I will instead present my eulogy here. I hope that you as well as Monica are honoured by it. I have little experience with eulogies, but I will try my best.

Dear Monica,

You know, there's a song called "Lovers In A Dangerous Time" and every time I hear that song I think of us. Ever since we met that day in the rain, my life has never been the same, and it was on that day that you took hold of my heart and never gave it back. I treasure you, and I treasure that quiet afternoon when our lives intersected for the first time.

I will always think of you as the girl that I met in the millennium. You came to stay with me when I had no one else. As I said above, you became the love of my life, and then you became all that I had. I have never loved anyone the way that ill always love you, I have never loved anyone so completely or with all of my heart.

As I told you so many times over the years you're the love of my life and the enigma of my soul. You shadow my thoughts constantly. You are the private dancer in my dreams and the legend that I long to hold one last time. I love you so much that the years that i've spent without you seem for nothing, meaningless. I'd give all of my tomorrows for the chance to hold you one last time.

You still come to visit me after sun down. I will see you there.

I will never again have the opportunity to watch the sunrise over Ontario Street with you or to tell you that I love you once more forever. I wish that I had been on that highway to protect you as I have so many times in the past, but this one time, that was not to be. I can't believe that you're gone.

I treasure all the moments that we shared together so many moons ago, all the quiet moments, all the kisses in the middle of the night, all the things that we said to each other. Those days and nights are now immortalized somewhere in the whispering, echoing winds that blow across the fields and parks surrounding Ontario Street.

You know i've always thought that you were the most beautiful Latin Angel that i've ever seen. I remember calling you a Goddess on more than one occasion, and you were. I can remember a time when everyone wanted you but I had you, to me that was always surreal.

You gave me the gifts of URBAN RAIN and NEIGHBOURHOOD OF NIGHT with your inspiration. I'm extremely emotional about that. It's as if fate brought us together knowing that one day there would exist these books. I want to forget the bitterness and hate and the moments of anger that existed between us in the end, for me that was evil intervening in our lives.

At the conclusion of this manuscript there is going to be an Ontario Street Hall Of Fame and you are going to be the first ever inductee. I will need to save some words for that.

I can only hope that if there's a book store up in Heaven that you're in there reading both of these books and smiling, because we made it Baby Bunny, we did it, all those days and nights, all of our troubles and hard times paid off. There are two books about our lives now. We are The Legends Of Ontario Street.

As i've told so many others in the past. If there hadn't been any Monica, then there would exist no URBAN RAIN or NEIGHBOURHOOD OF NIGHT. I know now why we came together. It was not only so that we could share the love that we did, but it is because I was meant to write our story as well as to be the keeper of Ontario Streets memory, and yours.

We were, as the song says, lovers in a dangerous time.

I love you with all my heart Baby Bunny. I'll see you in Heaven.

Rest in Peace.
God Bless you Monica.
Eternal life!!!

"I'm sorry about what happened to Lilly" Nick G. Said with his hands on his hips. "I always tried to do my best for her."

"I know that. I'm eternally grateful for all the kindness that you've shown toward Lilly and I over the years. She always liked you." Dane said truthfully. Nick had a heart and a soul, and he was nothing if not a great guy.

There was a very somber expression on Nick's face. "I had hoped that one day she'd get out of it for good before her life style claimed her but things don't work out that way."

"I don't think that you ever get out when you're that far in." Dane said standing at the foot of the stone park. "I keep wondering if that had something to do with her accident."

Most of the crew had cleared away and gone home for the night. The Lilly signs remained, they were perched against the sides of The Black Domino Tavern as well as on the ledges of the picnic benches behind them, painted blue, red, green, and many other colours.

"These streets will never be the same without her, from now on they'll have to do without Lilly Chicoine." Nick said. There were tears in his eyes. He usually tried to remain emotionally detached from his clients, but this one time he could not help it.

"She gave me my first book. There's a part of me that will always believe that that's why we were brought together. I think I was meant to write our story."

"Thank God that you did. It's good closure."

"I'll never have closure. You can't forget the kind of things that Lilly and I have seen. You can't say goodnight, and I don't think that i'd want to."

"Well, you always did a good job. I know that you tried your best. Very few people in this neighbourhood are likely to ever forget the names Von "The Icon" and Lilly Chicoine. Nick assured.

"I'm just sorry that Kate and Lilly never had the chance to get to know each other. I wanted so badly for them to be friends." Von said reflectively.

Somewhere over head there was a light thunder clap followed by a lightning bolt that ripped through the fabric of the sky softening as the silver pulse of energy hit the earth. It was as if Lillys way of saying "Thank you" for the street ceremony. I love you.

"I think it's gonna rain soon." The Casanova Killer said. He had been given that nickname due to his Martial Arts abilities coupled with his good looks. "I should be getting home." He said.

"Thanks for comin Nicky."

"Don't mention it." Nick said shaking Danes hand before dismissing himself into the night.

"Von." A female voice followed Nicks dismissal. "I can't believe she's gone." Alyssa M said.

"I know, neither can I."

"She was the first person that I met when I got off the bus from Toronto."

"I remember." Dane said wistfully. He had written that moment into Urban Rain. "These streets, none of us will ever be the same again. I spent seven years getting to know Lilly Chicoine inside out, back to front. There will never be a day that goes by where I don't think about her ever again."

"My biggest rival ever." Carolyn said from two feet away from them. "She brought me so much competition I don't think that i'll ever recover from it."

Dane smiled. "I remember that. You guys used to compete over everything."

"Yeah, but I always respected her." Carolyn offered. She still looked exactly like Sandra Bullock.

"I am very sorry that it has happened." The very genuine and sincere Marcel said. "It has make a long time that we have all known each other."

Dane was nodding solemnly. "Thanks Marcel."

Alyssa slid her arms around Danes torso. "Cmon, i'll walk you home." She said.

L.A.-This is the point in the text where I will present the eulogy that my Mother prepared for Monica. She to was moved by her death. Here it is.

Life is a journey, no one knows when it will end. You were taken tragically without warning and I know that we will never see you again, but these words are meant to express how much I treasured the times we shared. I remember you spending Christmas with us in Halifax, it was a special occasion having you there. I enjoyed shopping for your gifts and seeing your face when you opened them. I remember the Christmas dinners that we shared in Montreal. I remember the long trip back to Montreal by car and the singing that went on for hours. The garnet ring you gave me will stay with me forever as a symbol of our friendship. You will always be a member of our Family regardless of how things ended May you rest in peace. We'll never forget you!!

MARY ANN.

"I keep thinking that if we'd gotten there sooner that I could've done something." Von said to the shadow who sat feet away from him in the darkness. "When you live your life the way I have you tend to see things for what they really are. Lilly was careless, we all know that, but she wasn't stupid. She came from the street. I keep seeing her face lolled against that head rest." He said raising a handful of fingers to his face. It was as if there was emotion rising inside of him as he tried to quiet it.

"Hey, you loved her." Alyssa said. "Just look at the people in that neighbourhood. They all know that."

Somewhere, pale blue light like energy flashing against a wall.

"In the time we were apart, I never had any desire to go on without her." He said truthfully. "I would make up these lies and tell myself that she was dead so that I could go on living, but it never worked. I had failed at my relationship, despite how hard I tried."

"Hey. Hey. You did your best for her." The beautiful and charismatic Alyssa said standing up. "The first time that I saw you look at Lilly I knew that you loved her. This isn't your fault."

"Sometimes in life I think that people end up apart for no reason. I've always felt that way about Lilly and I."

For a moment Dane remembered a night when Lilly had poured Talcum Powder all over the floor as a base for her rave dance, she'd been trying to entertain Dane but he'd been up for so long that he'd yelled at her, and told her to get out, to this day he loathed and despised himself for having been so mean and rotten.

If he now had his way, he would invite Lilly to come and dance on his floor forever. He also decided that he would be willing to trade all of his tomorrows to hold Lilly in his arms one last time, even if only for a moment.

"I love you Baby Bunny." Von said breaking down completely.

"Von, you guys were very special to each other. I've been up and down the roads with Lilly and she told me over and over how much she loved you."

"I should've been a better boyfriend." He sobbed. "I should've done more for her."

"You did everything for her. There's no minus in this equation. Stop beating yourself up."

"You know I can remember so many nights on Ontario Street where we'd watch the sun come up together. We'd either be sitting in the park or i'd be following Lilly up and down Ontario Street. She'd always be complaining because she had money but couldn't find anyone to cop from."

"COP," was street slang for buy drugs.

"I would've taken the heart out of my chest and given it to her. I'd gladly have given my life for hers on that highway, if there was anything that I wanted her to know, it would be that." Von said.

"I believe you. I know that you would have gone to any lengths for her no matter what."

At that moment Kathleen Dane interrupted their conversation as she stepped into the shadows of the room. She had entered with her key, pushed open the door and tip toed inside. "I thought i'd come by and see if you were alright, but if your busy I can come back another time." She offered gingerly turning her thumb backward in the direction of the doorway.

"Not at all. Hunny, I want you to meet somebody." Dane said introducing the sexy Alyssa by her first and last name. Then he introduced his niece who needed no introduction.

"To say that I was proud to have you in my corner tonight would be an understatement. You honoured Lilly and I both. I love you." Von "The Icon" told his niece. "I ah, have something for you." He said pulling a square garment box from below the shadow of a coffee table.

"Is it a gift, for me"?? Shamrock asked, her blue eyes shimmering.

"Yeah." Dane said pulling a jacket out of the box by it's length. It was black and white and had writing on the back, Alyssa already knew what it was, they had discussed Kates gift earlier.

It said-ONTARIO STREET ORIGINALS on the back, and on the sleeve, was Lilly's name.

"I want you to have this." Dane said helping his niece put the jacket on over her expensive designer sweater and black dress pants that she had worn to Lilly's Ontario Street wake.

"Thank you." Kathleen Dane Shamrock said as tears streamed the length of her cheeks, she felt so honoured to have been given such a sacred patch, Kates beautiful blue eyes were sparkling with both pride and emotion. She knew how much Lilly Chicoine had meant to her Uncle Von, and of what a legend she was now a part of, she would keep Lilly Chicoine and her memory in her heart forever.

"She would've wanted you to have this." The Ontario Street Captain said as Alyssa walked across the room and threw her arms around the fighter. "Welcome to the Family." She said as Kate broke down completely in a sea of emotion.

"I can't believe that she's gone." Marilyn Dane said as a cab pulled up to the curb.

"Yeah, well she was very reckless." Andrew Dane said still in his work clothes. It was the day after the wake at around six pm "I'm gonna try and get a hold of the Toxicology report when it comes out. I'll pull some resources, see what I can do." They were on De Maissoneuve West and the traffic was heavy.

"I have to go home and face the music." Marilyn Dane said of her duties as a Real Estate Broker. She had lost her room key hours ago and had to wait for the Bell Hop to make a new one.

"I still remember the garnet ring that Lilly gave me." Marilyn said seating herself down on the backseat of the cab. "I had her in my home, I bought Christmas presents for her." She said tearing up.

"Be careful on your way to the airport." Andrew said, his foot was half on the curb, half off leaning in.

At that moment Marilyn Danes phone lit up. "Hello." She said momentarily composing herself as best she could, the call display said unknown name, private number.

"It's me." Dane said on the other end. She could tell that he'd been crying. "I keep thinking about Lilly's accident." He said becoming emotional. "I worry that she suffered."

Andrew Dane had heard his Brothers comment. "At that speed, I doubt it." He said into the mouth piece.

There had already been an online newspaper article with a line that David Dane would never forget. It said- Chicoine was pronounced dead in hospital, and there was a picture of her car with the doors ripped off because the EMT's had used the jaws of life to rescue Lilly from the vehicle.

It said rescue crews had worked tirelessly to extricate her from the vehicle. The video image seemed to burn hypnotically over and over in and out as if part of a nightmare. Dane also took note of the image of the pink and blue lights on the side of the fire truck and of the two accident investigators standing behind the remains of the vehicle. The whole thing was horrific, and Danes mind could not put it down.

"It's gonna take a long, long time to get over something like this." Marilyn said to her grieving son. She knew how much Lilly had meant to him and that every single moment of his life was tied to hers. There was even a Book.

"I had a dream about her last night." David Dane said amidst heavy crying. "I was standing in The Stone Park and Lilly walked over to me and kissed me, but then I reached for her and she faded away." He said breaking down heavily.

"Aw … … … …" Marilyn Dane sympathized. "I know how much you loved her. Just think of the seven years that you had with her, of all the good times and the special moments. She meant everything to you and you loved her. There's no one on earth who loved her more than you did. You were her Guardian Angel."

"It's funny how you'd give all of your tomorrows for one more hug, one more chance to hold the person that you care about." Dane said. He was as broken as Marilyn had ever seen him. This was the love of his life, he had many times in the past called Lilly his wife. They had once been engaged.

"Marry me." Dane remembered whispering a hundred times as his lips had caressed the top of Lilly's head somewhere in the middle of the night.

"You have your memories, no one can take those away from you no matter what. They're forever. Look at all the things that you did for her, all the times that you took her clothes and money when she was in jail. You were her saviour. There was no other boyfriend on earth like you."

"I just wish I could hold her once more, just one more time." Dane said out of the darkest place that he'd ever been in. It was cold and shadowy here, not at all the inviting apartment that he used to reside in. The place had changed, it didn't feel like home to him anymore.

Just then there was a knock on the door. It was the always thoughtful Kate "The Gate" Shamrock. As usual she was putting all else ahead of herself and had brought her favourite Uncle a Casserole dish. It was still piping hot. "This is gonna stop now." The Angelina Jolie lookalike said. "You're gonna eat if I have to spoon feed you."

Dane took a towel from the drawer and yanked the top off of the glass microwave bowl.

"You cooked this"?? He asked.

"Yup." Shamrock responded.

"I'm proud of you, you know that"?? The Ontario Street Original praised. There were tears in his eyes.

"I'm proud of you to." The beautiful, exquisite kick boxing titlist said, her Uncle was the greatest. There wasn't another Uncle on this earth who could compete with him, he was her champion, and he had never let her down.

Dane was digging into the casserole with the prongs of his fork now. "Mm … … … I'm starving." He said more out of trying to please his niece then out of actual fact.

"Annnnd, I brought you a special dessert." Shamrock informed him.

"Mm … … … If this is cheese cake i'll pass. I don't need to get fat." Von "The Icon" said through a mouthful of macaroni and sun dried tomatoes.

Kate was smiling. "I brought somebody with me. This should cheer you up." She said.

At that moment there was another knock on the door.

"What's up Uncle Von"?? Evan Baker said taking a seat next to his hero. "I had to come over when I heard that Kate made casserole. I love the way she prepares food."

"Yeah I know, thank God she can stand to cook for me or i'd be dying of starvation. I'm very lucky to have Kate as a niece." Ontario Streets Last Outlaw said downing a mouthful of noodles with a glass of water. "Here, grab a plate." Von invited handing his guest some silver ware and a plate.

Just then Danes phone lit up and he answered it still chewing on his dinner. "Hello." He said.

Kathleen was smiling.

"Mm … … … … It's your Father. He's on his way up. He's a neanderthal. He almost walked into the wrong building." Dane said jestingly.

"Oh, you brought me some of my favourite dish." Andrew said putting his briefcase down and digging in with a fork, he hadn't eaten since this morning.

"Have some casserole." Von said comically on the heels of his Brothers helping himself to some of the meal. "I'm sorry about what happened to you." Von directed toward Evan. He had become more serious now his inflection changing.

"Yeah, well, not as sorry as I am about Lilly. I should've been at her wake."

Kate's smile had evaporated. "You're not supposed to stand up for long periods of time, not yet anyway."

"You did the best you could and I appreciate your condolences regarding Lilly." The Icon said.

"You from what I hear were a world champion boyfriend. You always did whatever you could for her."

"Well, I loved her. A lot of people don't understand our relationship but we had some beautiful moments together. I would've given a hundred years for five more minutes to say goodbye to her."

"No complaints here. You were the greatest I understand." Evan praised with a great and genuine warmth.

"I'm glad that you guys have the relationship that you do. I love sitting here and being a part of you." Shamrock said picking up macaroni with her fork end.

"Mum just left for the airport. I saw her off." Andrew said.

"I'll call her in a few hours." Dane said switching the television on.

"Gimme that." Kate said stealing the clicker from her Uncle who had stuck his tongue inside of his cheek as an acknowledgement that this was a joke between them. "One of my fights is supposed to be on channel twenty four in an hour Kate said. She had turned on the tube and was now channel surfing.

"Where's Donovan"?? Dane asked. He was en route to the sink with his plate now.

"He's in Ireland, that's why he wasn't at Lilly's wake." Kate answered.

"There you are." Andrew said pointing toward the TV screen.

"That's the commercial for my fight."

"Can I get a hug before I go"?? Kate's Irish Papa asked.

"If I can find one in these tired arms. I haven't slept well in days." She said embracing her old man who towered over her at six foot three.

"We're gonna be at The Black Domino later on if you wanna drop in on us." Von "The Icon" invited.

"I'm kinda tired so I think i'll go home and turn in. I've also got a meeting at nine am that I have to be bright eyed and bushy tailed for. I'm outta here."

"Goodnight Dad." Kate said. "I love you." And indeed she did. Andrew Dane had been the best Father in the world. He had always showered her with gifts and praise and love.

"Goodnight sweetie." Andrew returned, he then disappeared out the door.

As the synthesizers from Joseph Renzetti's "Don't 'Cha Know That" crept seductively over the airwaves, Von "The Icon" casually strolled across the floor of The Black Domino Tavern and sat down opposite his niece. "That's from the 1980's film Wanted Dead Or Alive starring Rutger Hauer." He said.

"That should be your theme song." Kate suggested. "The suave riff suits you."

"Aw Jesus Christ." Dane said as he saw Charlie Brown walk through the front door of the bar. "What the fuck are you doing here"?? The Ontario Street Original asked reaching for the 9 millimetre Beretta that was tucked in his waist band.

"Uncle Von, NO, don't shoot em." Kate commanded reaching forward with one hand as if to block her Uncle from de chambering the pistol, at the same time there was a vague smirk on her face as if she somehow unconsciously knew that he wouldn't really go through with it.

"This is the second time he's been in here today. He tried to sell Marcel some Protein Bars earlier that he quote "Got off this guy.""

"I need to talk to you big boy." Charlie said through clenched teeth.

Now it was Von who was smirking as he got up off his seat. "Step into my office." He said as Kate watched Charlie follow her Uncle over to the far corner of the room into its sinister recesses. "What can I do for you"?? The legend asked mockingly. If it hadn't been for Kate, this clown would likely already have been loaded into the back of an ambulance with a bullet in his chest.

"You know what Eva and I are gonna do with certain information." Charlie began.

Von "The Icon" gripped the bridges of his chin between his thumb and forefinger. "I'm gonna tell you what, I know that Jason already put the boots to you, but if you go ahead with your little blackmail scheme insteada leavin town … … … … … I'm gonna kill you." Dane hissed venomously into Charlies ear. His eyes were smouldering. "You better go back to sellin stolen protein bars or you're gonna end up so full of holes that they'll be able to use you as a strainer," Dane said walking away from the punk who stood before him amongst the scent of cigarette smoke and stale boos.

"Look who it is." Ontario Streets hero said as he watched a familiar face enter the room. There was a a wicked grin on his lips.

"So, my nephew got hurt because of you." Eva Nicolette said. There was an evil smoulder in her eyes and her arms were customarily folded, she looked like the wicked witch, of the, in this case, east.

"Yeah, and if you don't turn around and walk out that door you're gonna get hurt to, being a woman is not gonna help you out of this situation."

Just then a familiar looking figure walked through the same door through which Eva and Charlie had entered, it was Jonathan Dane. He looked positively evil amidst his white hair and simmering blue eyes that bore not a single trace of decency or mercy. He was for all intents and purposes, a sociopath.

"Hail, hail, the gang's all here." David Dane said, now he really felt like firing off some rounds.

"Oh Jesus." Kate said. Now, without a doubt there was going to be trouble. "Uncle Von, NO" Kate said standing up in order to physically restrain her Uncle for the second time in five minutes. "You and Grand Dad are not gonna fight here." She said. There was white smoke in the air around them.

"I want chu out of here." The sexy Alyssa M said appearing from behind Eva Nicolette.

"You goddamn sonovabitch." Jonathan said glaring at his son who was being physically restrained via his Grand Daughter. "I'm so F'N mad I could friggin kill." He said.

"Get em outta my sight." Ontario Streets Last Outlaw said ordered. The fact that his patience was waning, trickling down, was apparent in his voice, his restraint was limited, and if Jonathan Dane and his Family did not remove themselves soon they were going to find that out.

"I said, get out." Alyssa repeated.

"Are you gonna throw me out"?? Eva asked challengingly.

"I'm not much of a fighter, but if you bother my best friend anymore I guess we'll see." Alyssa answered closing the distance between herself and the wicked witch who stood before her.

"You've got a BIG EGO"!!! Jonathan Dane lamented. He was furious, there was no friendship and no rationalization between he and a son who had stopped talking a long time ago. This was a vendetta, it had started with Danes Father and his Grand Father and now here it was in Von's living room all these years later.

"Listen, Jonathan, if you don't turn around and walk out that door i'm gonna show you that you're to old and to withered to dance with someone this many years younger than you." Dane said looking toward his vain arrogant old man.

"Just because i'm older than you doesn't mean that I don't have plenty of piss and vinegar left in me."

"The piss part I agree with. Soon enough you'll be wearing a fucken colostomy bag to go to the bathroom although I don't know if they make colostomy bags for snakes."

"Uncle Von, C'mon." Kate said pulling her Uncle away by the shoulders. "I want em outta here hunny." Von said to his niece.

"Well, you know what we're gonna do to you." Eva threatened in a wicked voice, and then there was that smirk, the smirk that she had been known to wear for a thousand moons before David Dane was ever born, it was like a trade mark hence the word be used in as negative a light as possible.

Once, when Eva hadn't been chosen for something she had gone around the Family telling them that she did not know why she hadn't been chosen, and that quote "Everyone liked her better anyway." This to Danes ears had been absolutely amazing, because in reality, the whole Family despised this black mailing bitch!!!

"Now you're leaving by force." The sexy and attractive Alyssa M said physically man handling Eva.

"I'm gonna deal with you." Jonathan Dane warned his legendary son. "I've never known hatred … … …" He remarked of his sentiment, which to The Immortal Von "The Icon," wasn't worth much.

"I'm shaking in my boots" David Dane said. "You're so old that when you went to school they didn't even have history." The Boxer quipped, trash talk and treachery.

"You just wait, i'm gonna make you so goddamn sorry that you won't have a leg to stand on." Jonathan Dane said. He was practicing his best "I'm so goddamn angry that i'll do anything to get even with you voice" Nice guy, and he was so full of piss and vinegar over someone elses ego that he had forgotten to remember that he had one himself. This world was full of hypocrites, and Jonathan Dane was absolutely no exception.

"What the fuck's he doin here anyway"?? The Ontario Street Original asked.

Charlie had exited the bar and Dane was now wondering where the sonovabitch had gone to.

"Kate, get me a drink hunny." Von "The Icon" requested.

There was a smattering of static like radio's and then The Police were there. "Okay, everyone here is going home for the night." The first of the six officers voiced, he was tall and skinny with a gruff voice and had a thinning hairline, to much cologne, to much aftershave, in that order.

"Fuckin rat." Dane exclaimed, now he knew where Charlie had gone in the wake of his absence.

"I remember you." One of the elder officers said in a friendly voice. "You're Lilly Chicoines boyfriend,. We used to see you at Frontenac all the time."

"Yeah, I was." Dane said somberly. "She was killed a few nights ago."

The cop had paused with his pen on his pad. "I knew Lilly from out here on these streets for years. She was a nice kid." He said. "I'm sorry to hear that. Who are these people"??

"My old man, and two of my relatives. The piece a trash who just walked back through the door is my cousin, he's a protein fiend, amongst other things."

"Okay, the three of you are leaving, if you come back here tonight you'll be placed under arrest." Officer Devon Simons said. He remembered Dane now, he was the one who had written the book.

"I'll sue your goddamn department." Jonathan threatened on his way out the door.

"Listen, we gonna let you go, but if you cause us any more trouble we gonna arrest you tonight." The junior officer said. He looked cross, as if he'd had a bad day and was in no mood to be messed with.

"I'd go quietly if I were you. I don't think you or Eva would mix to well with the Bubba's or the Marge's." Dane said as Jonathan walked past him. They locked eyes for a moment but then Jonathan did as he was told, complying, no room for an arrest warrant.

Kate was standing over the bar with her face covered with one hand. She did not want to be here listening to any of this. She was also glad that her Uncle had not been caught carrying a concealed weapon which had been another of her immediate concerns.

"I'll see you later big boy." Charlie warned on his way out.

"I hope so." Dane said nonchalantly.

Someones radio squawked and then Jonathan, Eva, and Charlie disappeared out the front door.

Danno Santiago sat at the edge of his living room couch. So much had happened in a few nights that he did not want to remember it, think of it, or hear word of it in his ears. He had once been a member of The Shining Path, then he had been the one who put people to rest. He did things for money, for power, and for his Queen. Six nights ago had been no different, as if poisoning a woman's drink had mattered, he thought as he sniffed a line of Heroin up his nose.

Now he waited for his Queen to come home. He also believed that she may be cheating on him with his business partner, if he found out that she was, he would kill her.

A moderate breeze blew in through the open window cooling the skin above Danno's hot blooded exterior, inside he was torched, not ready to pay the rent of all that had gone on in his life.

"Where the fuck were you"?? He asked as Jacky strolled through the door.

"I had to go and see somebody." She said removing her jean jacket and couch tossing it as she walked past him glare in her stare and an impenetrable arrogance that would have miffed a saint.

"You were gone a long time. You should have called me if you had known you were gonna be so late."

"I'm sorry Baby. We're gonna get Kate to do what we want her to do. Fuck the rest of it. I'm gonna tell her soon what we did to Lilly Chicoine, that should set a fire under her ass. Then there's the other thing, the thing that they don't know about."

"I want you to come home earlier." Danno said adjusting his penis through his grey jogging pants.

"I said I was busy." Jacky said with unwarranted sharpness.

"You better be fuckin telling me the truth about where you are." Santiago said falling backward into the arms of the plush white sofa. The buzz had hit him.

"Are you my fuckin keeper"?? Jacky shouted angrily. Her awesome temper was rising to the surface.

She was waiting for a response, seething, but Danno was to out of it to fight back.

Jacky made a primordial sound kicking over two CD racks and an exercise machine. "You want me to fuckin leave you forever"?? She threatened. "Then i'll go to the cops and tell them that you fuckin killed Lilly." She hollered loudly. If anyone had been standing outside their apartment door then they might have heard what Jacky had just said, careless and stupid but she didn't seem to care.

Danno was still lying against the couch, his tan skin visibly perspiring. He was not ready at will to answer his lovers verbal onslaught.

"YOU FUCKIN COCKSUCKER"!! Jacky yelled bifting a ceramic cat at the wall. "I should fuckin stab you to death." She said, her rage a palpable inferno.

The influence had not let go of Danno.

"Just then there was a knock on the door. Jacky froze. It was as if the hollow thump had brought her back into reality. What if someone had heard what she had said?? What if that someone had called The Police??

"Who is it"?? The kick boxer asked, but their came no response.

Soon there was a second knock, louder this time. It was as if the person had punched the frame of the door rattling its entire casing.

"It's Karen, your upstairs neighbour." A voice finally came.

"Go away, we're busy"!! Jacky shouted.

"You're making enough noise to wake the dead. My husband and I are trying to sleep."

"I'm coming." Jacky said nearly tripping over some of the debris left behind from what she had thrown. She and Danno had known Karen as well as her husband and her two kids for a long time.

"Yeah, what'dya want"?? Hannah shouted throwing open the door.

"What's all the yelling?? We can't sleep." Karen said exhaustively. She was still rubbing the sleep out of her eyes. "Who's Lilly"?? She asked.

"Why don't you come in and have a cup of Coffee"?? Jacky asked, her face straightening morbidly, stretching into a grimace that was still turned off.

"I really need to get back upstairs." The twenty seven year old girl said.

"Get in here." Jacky ordered through clenched teeth. Her face, amidst a heavy sheen looked like something from the depths of Hell, an inferno unto itself.

"What the hell is goin on"?? Danno asked having awakened from his opiate induced coma. He had walked into the entryway of their apartment to find Jacky holding Karen with one hand placed over her mouth and the other wrapped around her neck.

"The little bitch knows that we killed Lilly. She overheard me. Now we're gonna have to kill her." Hannah exclaimed. There was fire in her eyes, a component of viciousness that was not seen on the face of most average human beings. "We need some rope." She hollered. "Hurry up." She ordered as Danno ran into their bedroom returning with a length of cord.

"Tie her up." Jacky ordered placing a dry cleaning bag over Karen's head. "Shut the fuck up or you're gonna make this worse on yourself." She said to the mother of two.

In a minute Karen was gasping for air, her face turned purple, and then she, like Lilly before her, was gone. "That's it." Jacky said coaxingly. "Suck all of that air out hunny."

"Let's drag her downstairs." Jacky suggested lifting up on Karen's cadaver from underneath the arms.

"What if somebody sees us"?? Danno asked incredulously.

"We're on the first floor. I'll bring the car around. We better get her out of here before Alex comes looking for her." Jacky said. Alex, was Karen's husband.

Within five minutes they had dragged Karens body out the door, around the corner, and out into the night unseen. Karen had tape around her wrists and feet as well as the length of cord that Danno had brought from the bedroom bounding her wrists to her ankles.

"Help me lift her into the trunk." Jacky said attempting to position Karen's corpse in such a way that it would be easier to fit her small body into the medium sized storage space. "Grab her feet."

Danno obliged his Queen lifting their victim feet first off of the ground.

"There." Jacky said dumping the body of the woman into the trunk of the sedan with Danno's help.

"We need to drive her the fuck out of here and then clean out the trunk of the car." Jacky said for a moment flashing back to six nights ago when she and Danno had walked into a tavern called The Snake Pit and seen Lilly Chicoine for the first time up close.

Lilly Chicoine had been seated alone at the bar and Danno had approached her telling her that he believed that her car was in the way of a friend of his, it was only then that he had found the opportunity to slip narcotics into her drink. She had left her tumbler just sitting there un guarded as she moved around the room sticking her head in and out the door, it was not until she got outside that Lilly had gotten the surprise of a life time that began when Jacky had appeared out of nowhere underneath a mask but that had been moments after downing the remainder of her drink.

"Let's go." Jacky said turning her key in the ignition of the automobile.

Danno quickly surveyed the parking lot to ensure that no one was watching before getting in next to his lover who was seated behind the wheel. "Go." He commanded.

Soon, he and Jacky were on the highway with dark orange vapour lamps glaring above. "We really need to ditch this car." Santiago said looking out the back window as he leaned over the head rest. He had watched C.S.I and programs about DNA. They had killed this woman in their apartment and now her corpse was in the trunk, there was likely to be some kind of DNA left behind.

Of course Karen and the kids had been to their apartment many times before tonight so her DNA being there was explainable, it was the trunk of the car that they had to worry about.

"How is that gonna look, us getting rid of the car right around the time that Karen comes down to investigate a noise and disappears"?? The seedy Hannah asked pulling into another lane.

"It's better than The Police finding Karen's DNA all over the trunk. How are we going to explain that?? These investigators have tools like Luminol and shit that picks up fibre DNA. You know that in The OJ case that they found invisible fibres from the Bronco on Ron Goldman's shirt."

"We'll make a decision later on, right now we need to focus on finding a place to ditch this body."

Just then a Mac Truck whizzed by them at a high rate of speed.

"Let's boot it." Hannah said.

Von "The Icon" stood amidst the coiling shadows of his apartment with a 9mm Beretta trained in front of him. "One more time and i'm gonna put two in your fuckin head Eva." The Fighter said to the darkness and dreams around him. "You've pissed me off for the last time." He said gripping the 9mm revolver with two hands and aiming it at the wall that he wished was Eva Nicolettes head instead.

"Who are you talking to"?? The gorgeous, sexy, and seductive Alyssa asked emerging from the bedroom. She was fully clothed wearing a beige blouse over casual dress pants.

"This scathing ritual, is a bi product of a group of relatives who never cease to mark their territory with my rage." The bad ass said.

"I love you." Alyssa said slipping her arms around the iconic hero from behind. She had never slept with the legendary Von "The Icon," but she would if he asked her to.

"I love you to." Von said, and indeed he did. Alyssa had been one of the kindest, most awesome, truly supportive females that he had ever known, and it didn't hurt that she was a ten in the looks department either, something of a Juliette Lewis lookalike, short hair and small entrancing eyes that made you want to take her to bed every time you saw her.

"I miss Lilly." She said.

Von lowered the gun. "We all miss Lilly. I think that i'm somehow trying to avoid thinking about her so that I don't break down again." He said tearing up, it was like a raw nerve.

"I didn't mean to do that." Alyssa said genuinely. "You both mean the world to me. You guys were the first friends that I met when I came to Montreal."

"I just never thought it was gonna be so hard ye know." Dane said breaking down completely.

"Hey, you were always there for Lilly. You never let her down. There may have been ups and downs, but God knows that you guys lived for one another." Alyssa said consolingly.

"Except I wasn't there on that highway." Dane said leaning over the edge of the couch. "If I could've traded my life for hers than I would have and I wouldn't have needed to be asked twice."

"That's not the way that life works. We don't get to be there every time that our loved ones are in trouble. You did the best you could, always." Alyssa reassured him. "Did you ever know that you're my he-ro." Alyssa began singing Bette Midler's Wind Beneath My Wings to her champion who turned around to face her. He was embracing her now, holding her as closely as he could.

Just then the telephone rang. It was Marcel. "Oh, Von. How are you"?? The kindly french man asked.

"I'm alright. Alyssa and I were just talking about Lilly, that's why i'm a bit fucked up." Dane said realizing that he sounded a bit off.

"It will make a long time it will take you to get over that." He said. "That's what I have called you about. Is now a bad time"?? He asked.

"No, not at all." Dane said politely sitting down on the couch with Alyssa holding him with her head resting against his shoulder.

"I have had loss in my life. You are very young. I know that you loved Lilly.

I was thinking that maybe tomorrow we can take a Coffee together at The Train Station if you would like. It will be a good time for me because I don't have Yoga class."

"That sounds great Marcel. Thank you." Dane said. "Can you hold, I have another call."

"Oh, Oui." Marcel responded.

"Hello." David Dane greeted into the mouth piece. He was not expecting to hear from the person who was at the other end of the line.

"YO"!! Scott Paris shouted into the mouth piece. "I just found another one of these." He said to someone in the back ground. It's not like she didn't know, why the fuck would she have come home from the bar with me otherwise."

"What the hell are you talkin about now"?? Dane asked his long time comrade.

"No, I don't wanna fill out a survey. Go bother someone at the bar."

"What"?? Dane asked incredulously.

Marcel was still on the other line.

"I'm sorry Von. Go ahead." Scott Paris said.

"That's Von "The Icon" to you. Where the fuck are you"?? The fighter asked lifting his leather jacket from a table top. It read ONTARIO STREET ORIGINAL'S on the back.

"I'm at the eights or the domino or whatever the fuck it is that you call it."

"The Black Domino." Dane said turning to look at Alyssa who had passed out on the couch a few feet away, her legs were draped over the arm rest.

"SCOTT"!! Dane heard Troy Barclee shout out in the back ground.

"Hold on a second." Dane said clicking back to Marcel. "Can you call me back"?? He requested of the french man. "Oh, oui." Marcel responded agreeably.

"You're still in town"?? Dane asked going back over to Paris.

"I think so, at least the guy in the mirror at The Sheraton looks like me." The thug said.

"What are you guys in town for"??

"Like half a million and change. Troy has an Uncle who passed away."

"Oh yeah." Dane responded. "Jack and Jill went up the hill and I shot them both in the fuckin head, turn about's fair play. Is this Uncle Reuben"?? Dane asked of a fictitious character that they both knew did not exist.

"That's the one." Paris responded with a light grin on his face, he was holding a tooth pick between his first finger and his thumb as if he was about to pitch it.

"You have a surprise for me"?? Dane asked.

"No more of a surprise than you've ever gotten in the past. Troy and I talked to some people and no one's happy to see you back home. They're not happy unless they're unhappy."

"You make sure you tell them how much I love them to. How many times can you consort with the enemy and then come wailing to me that you're pissed off because i'm angry."

"Apparently they don't see it that way. They believe they can be friends with whoever they wanna be regardless of anyone elses relationship to them."

"That's why I left." Dane said speaking of a mentality that had caused him to leave Nova Scotia back in the nineties. How the fuck could you claim to be someones friend and then consort with their enemies who wanted to leave them for dead?? Twisted logic, broken thinking.

"So, are you gonna come down here and drink with us or are you gonna be an ass hole"?? Paris enquired briefly glancing over his shoulder.

"The latter, I don't drink anyway, one beer every now and then. I have a 9mm Beretta in my waist band that says I should know better." He said.

"I have one of those, it's in storage. Bring me yours so that I can make sure that you don't shoot yourself with the damn thing."

"I'm not that clumsy. You'd probably spill beer all over yourself and then kill the bar maid because she wouldn't give you a cat bath."

Paris was laughing now. "CAT BATH" was code for blow job.

"You want us to swing by later on?? We'll bring girls with us."

"Nah, I already have company." Dane said turning around to appraise Alyssa's condition on the couch. She was moaning slightly with the back of her hand against her jaw, relaxation posture.

"What's her jooks?? I know you." Paris said. "Your niece just passed me my cigarettes."

"Stones and pieces."

"You know what they say about rock stars." Scott said. "They're better in bed than Coke heads."

"That what they say"??

"I've always found that, then again, different strokes for different fokes."

"I wouldn't know. She's just a friend."

"Don't keep it that way. I gotta go. I'll give your niece a kiss for you." He said seriously.

"Uh-huh."

"Ciao." Paris said.

Massoud stood in the golden light of the morning sun rise practicing advanced Kung Fu. He was a master in three disciplines, taught four, and had been referred to on more than one occasion as a ninja. "What do you want to know about The Martial Arts"?? He asked the beautiful Persian woman who now stood side by side with him, she was wearing a chador. (Standard Persian womens garment).

"Whatever you want to teach me. All I know of Martial Arts is what I saw on TV in Iran." She said.

"Martial Arts are everywhere in our country, you were born here so you don't see that." Massoud said performing a series of hand techniques that in succession were referred to as a kata. He was dangerous, far more so then most in his field.

"I hated TV in Iran, so I went out and bought a satellite dish." Massoud said laughing.

Sayeh was laughing now as she did leg stretches. "That's cute." She said.

"How are your Mum and Dad"?? Massoud asked doing a backward somersault and ending up back on his feet, this was standard calisthenics for him, he had always been remarkably flexible.

Sayeh moved her hair to the side with one hand and then scratched her nose with her finger tip, her demeanour had suddenly adopted more emotion. "They're still being held captive by those people. They won't let them go until they pay them." She said.

"So why don't your Parents pay them?? They have money." Massoud responded.

"Because they don't want to give money to evil men. My Parents are very religious, they'll die before handing over anything that they've earned to a bunch of lowlife rebels."

"I think that these men are more than rebels. I wish that I was there so that I could teach them a lesson." Massoud said drawing a sword from a satin wrapped interior.

Sayehs Parents had been taken hostage by men wearing masks one night while she as well as her Brothers slept, they had remained, but her Mother and Father were taken as Prisoners.

"I need water." Massoud said. There was perspiration dripping from his brow, it was very hot below the early morning sun that's heat dripped with golden rays.

"Mohammed." Rashid greeted as a thirty something year old friend of his came to introduce himself to their training session.

"Good morning. Happy to see you Sayeh." Mohammed said extending his hand to the girl.

"I'm so hot from all this that I need a swim to cool off." Massoud said slightly out of breath. His right hand was extended.

"Last night I was reading when I heard an explosion outside, it was only children playing with fireworks but it reminded me of back home. I kept waiting for the air raid sirens to start." Sayeh reflected softly.

Massoud was wielding the sword a few feet away from them now, educated posture.

"Massoud trained our Military back home." Mohammed said flipping a cigarette out of a pack. "You want one." He asked of Sayeh who was now done with her stretches.

"No, I don't smoke." She responded, her beauty radiating in the dawns early light. Sayeh looked like a Persian Princess complete with gorgeous brown eyes that shimmered like smouldering diamonds in the suns early morning fires.

"Can I join you guys"?? Kate Shamrock asked showing up sight unseen. "Of course." Massoud said gesturing for the female champion to sit down, but there was something in his gesture, something strange.

"This heat is killer." Shamrock commented sitting flat on her butt with her arms stretched out behind her, palms flat, getting ready.

"I don't think we've met before. My name is Sayeh." The twenty five year old goddess said introducing herself to the famous Shamrock who smiled affably before shaking her hand. "Kathleen Dane." The Champion greeted her warmly, but what was it about both of these people that somehow lacked merit??

Massoud at times gave her the creeps, and not for any particular reason, just one of those things.

"How is David"?? Massoud asked his voice dipping into his diaphragm.

"He's alright. He's still very upset about Lilly, he really loved her."

"Kate, may I ask you something"?? The always polite Massoud enquired.

"Of course you may." Shamrock said looking up at Massoud from her seated position on the ground, her ankles were crisscrossed one over the other, slight pain in both.

"Do you think it would be a good idea if we invited your Uncle to train with us?? I think this can be, how do you say it in your language?? Hold on, let me check my collection of words. Hmm ... ... Massoud said fishing his cell phone out of a bag.

"Yes, therapeutic, and by the way this very quiet man is Mohammed." The Black Ninja introduced.

"Hey." Kate greeted. She thought that Mohammed was also a bit eerie, something off about all three of them, not registering, cheque not quite clearing.

Mohammed had deep set eyes, sharp features and an almost hypnotized demeanour. He looked like a killer she immediately registered, one of these brain washed weirdos who went to day school minus recess to learn how to become a suicide bomber, head full of shadows and dreams. He was the poster boy for someone who might walk into a train station or a crowded mall with dynamite strapped to his waist and pull the rip cord.

"Hmm ... ... maybe we can reach him on his cell phone." The educated and charming Massoud said.

"He's probably not up yet." Danes niece said looking at the graffiti on the wall a few feet away. The four of them were in a park just off of Ontario Street that was tucked away behind some buildings, there were swing sets and a sand box plus a picnic table.

"Then I will wake him up." Massoud said ending his sentence with a deep and intentional laughter.

"Yes, David." The Martial Artist said. "It's Massoud. Can I ask you something"??

There was an nondescript moaning on the other end of the line.

"Hmm ... ... Hmm, I think we woke him up." Massoud said placing a finger tip over his mouth. "I just heard something break." He said as a lamp hit the floor on the other end of the line.

"Has your Uncle ever been up this early before"?? Massoud jested.

"Not unless he was forced, neither Dad nor Uncle Von have ever been great early risers.

"He's growling now." Massoud reported. He was still waiting on the line.

"Where are you"?? David Dane finally asked, he honestly couldn't recall the last time that he'd been up this early, to make matters worse, there were work men at the door. "No, i've never had a can of paint shoved up there before." Massoud finally heard the foreman of the painting crew say.

"What's going on"?? Kate asked as she watched Massoud walking back and forth with his cell phone to his ear. She was still seated on the ground basking in the warm glow of the sun.

"We're sitting in the park just behind Dufresne, Frontenac and I don't know what the people around here call it. There are childrens swings and a couple of benches as well as a picnic table." The Black Ninja said, one hand on his hip, the other holding the cell phone.

"I'll be there in forty five." Dane finally said rolling over next to Alyssa who was sound asleep next to him. They had slept together, but that's all they had done.

When Dane finally arrived he immediately took stock of Mohammed looking into his eyes and then past them. It was well within the reaches of Danes imagination to believe that this sinister person was capable of terrible things. He thought it, but he said nothing, after all, this was Massoud friend, not his.

"Good morning." Mohammed said. "Pleasure to meet you."

Dane nodded but said nothing.

"Okay, so, we are all going to train together, Hmm … … … … hmm." Massoud said ending his sentence with his trade mark laugh that sounded wicked even on its face. "I'm ready for you all." He said adjusting his sash at the waist of his gui as he stretched and bent from side to side.

"Good morning angel. How you doin"?? Dane greeted his niece who sat only a few feet away. "How's Evan"?? He asked hoping to hear that he was improving. It had been a tough road, and there was still a lengthy battle to be won.

"There are three different types of back kicks." Massoud began demonstrating. He turned his back to his audience, torking his hip, and then brought his heel back in a stealth, slender motion.

"He's better." Shamrock whispered not wanting to interrupt Massoud lesson. "What about his hero"?? She asked smiling as her gorgeous eyes shimmered in the morning sunrise, sparkling oceans of calm, blue mixed with flecks of green diamond.

"I'm getting there, I miss Lilly. I wish I could have taken her place on that highway." He said fighting back a river of tears that the two of them would have ended up crying over.

This was engulfing, the night in whispers and all the moments that they shared together under the silence of Ontario Streets veil of shadows, twisting alleyways and smoke filled taverns. No one would ever know the half of it.

There would never be another Lilly Chicoine, nor another Ontario Street. This was a story about two legends who had met by chance outside of a bar on a stormy afternoon many, many moons ago, it had taken on many twists and turns leading up to Lillys death, and it would likely lead beyond.

"I love you." Dane said to his niece. He was trying to manage a smile.

"I love you to Uncle Icon." Kate said with a pinched smile that was both pride and adoration for her favourite Uncle on this planet.

"Whenever you're up to it maybe we could watch Halloween together." Shamrock said. She knew how much John Carpenter and Debra Hill's series had meant to her Uncle and his late girlfriend.

"Thank you Diamond Doll." Dane said leaning in to peck his niece on the cheek.

"Time." David Dane said. "That's what life's all about. The big shadowy clock that goes tick tock, one more hour, one more day, one more breath." The fighter said almost breaking down again. "You know she once told me that she was afraid of dying. That upsets me now." He said.

Jacky Hannah stood above Lilly Chicoines headstone at Strode Cemetery dumping out the contents of a clear vile. It was all that remained of the drug that Danno Santiago had insinuated into Lillys drink on the night that she died, and sooner or later, hopefully, it would be the very reason that Kate Shamrock would agree to defend her title. "Last call for drinks Lilly." The evil woman said as the last drop from the vile fell to the ground exploding against the earth.

"When the time comes we'll let Kate know that all of this could have been avoided if she'd done what she was supposed to do." Danno who had just done a line of Coke said. "In your honour baby." The killer said building a mouth full of saliva and then releasing it onto the ground.

"I can't wait to see the look on Shamrock's face when we tell her that Lilly died because she refused to put up her strap.(Strap-Slang for Championship belt).

"You can walk right up to her after The Police do a toxicology report on her and you can tell little miss muffet who sat on her tuffet eating her curds and way, that i'm the big bad spider, who sat down beside her, and poisoned her friend Lilly away."

"I'd like to see the look on her Uncles face when he finds out to."

"Maybe he'll wanna dance with me." Danno Santiago said doing a short dance number by swivelling his hips from left to right. "I wanna do another line. It's starting to rain. You know I read in his Book that it was raining on the afternoon that he met Lilly. I just sold my copy on E-Bay." Danno said spooning another nail full of The Devil's Dandruff up his nose.

"Oh yeah, i'll have to check that one out someday." Hannah remarked sarcastically.

Danno was laughing now. "Let's get back in the car. This shit is doing more than just making me high." The scumbag said. "I can twist these hips in plenty of other directions." Santiago said adjusting his crotch and then making his eyes wide in a manner that made him look sleazy as well as bizarre.

"Remember when we were down in Rio and I cut that eighteen year old boy after I watched him have sex with you?? I still have the tape in my safe." Danno said. "I let Gus have a copy of it to." He said sniffing one more line up his nose before getting into the passenger seat of their car.

Gus was a friend of theirs from the states, he had died in a boating accident just over a year ago.

"So long Lilly" Hannah sang eerily as she stepped in behind the wheel. "Sleep tight." She said as she palmed the car keys with one hand.

Von "The Icon". Ontario Streets Vindicator In The Night.

ONTARIO STREETS CAT

Von "The Icon", Ontario Streets Last Outlaw

Von "The Icon", The Ontario Street Original

PART II:

PHOBIC

David Danes dream began with a view of a park exterior that looked as though it were being shot from the window of a car with a hand held camera. "See you again." He muttered inside of unconsciousness as bursts of static invaded the night inside of this sinister brush with non reality. First he saw the glowing fountains, frothing at their wading pools, a man and his dog passing by.

This was the park at the foot of The Jaques Cartier Bridge across from the big church that loomed like a gate post at the centre of Heaven, been there a thousand times, him and Lilly, so many nights.

There was for a few moments only the sounds of an idling car motor as well as the static in tune with the dreams sequence of events before voices came to join whatever was going on, whatever this was, inside, that he was for whatever reason meant to see.

They were awful and Satanic, as if The Devil had planted them there to teach him to fear … … …" To prove that there is life on other planets. Thousands of years ago extraterrestrials left hieroglyphics for us to find … … … … … and was himself professed to be the son of God. These things that we know now only serve to further … … … … … … … …

Then there was a flash of Lilly standing in the night back in 2000 wearing her denim jean suit and ruby red, fire engine bright, cherry lipstick with a fendi bag and spike heeled stilettos. Her face was mute but her darting eyes were all purpose and vigilance.

"I love you." He heard himself whisper before he cuddled her then and kissed her on the cheek.

She gave him a smile with her beautiful lips tight.

He made a crescent shape around her with his motion before sitting silently on the divider by the road again before the Satanic voices returned. They were, he and Lilly, at the far end of the street, near Dufresne and Ontario. It was well after midnight.

"Evil on this scale is immeasurable … … … … … the rings on his hand symbolizes … … … … … … Pontius Pilate … … … … … … … … was himself the son of God." … … … … … … … …

There was one more burst of static from the scene put on by the car encircling the park and then he woke up.

Cyril Mathews walked past a long faced doberman sitting half in shadow before a woman of no more than twenty five who had come to see him. "I've been expecting you." The little man with the long nails, black heart and carefully applied silver flesh tone said.

"I want to do this for my Family." She said.

"You're Samantha Wilcox." Mathews said crushing a cube of salt with the palm of his hand and watching it fall through his fingers. "What religion do you believe in"?? Cyril asked.

"I'm an atheist. My Father used to go to church all the time before he killed himself but I could never get into studying the Bible."

"Have you ever seen any of my work"?? Cyril asked sliding a photograph of a masked man across the table. "This is Monster, he's the one you'll be working with. You won't meet him until the shoot." He said ominously fishing a pen light out of his desk.

Samantha lifted the photo up applying lip balm at the same time. As soon as she saw the wickedness in Monsters eyes there was a surge of fear as well as euphoria inside of her. "I don't want to die slow, that's the other reason why i'm doing this."

"We'll have whatever drugs that you ask for on hand. You need to be certain that this is your final decision. On the day that we do the shoot, there won't be any turning back." Cyril Mathews warned her.

"My sister is here." Samantha said examining a text message that she had just received.

"I'll have Alexander let her in."

Alexander was one of Cyrils house watch men. He was tall with wavy hair and a powerful build.

In five seconds the door to Cyrils inner sanctum opened up and Jacky Hannah walked into the room accompanied by her husband. "I love you Sammy." Jacky said kissing her younger sister on the right temple. "Thank you for introducing me to Cyril."

"I don't wanna be there but I want a tape of the finished product." Jacky demanded flatly.

"You'll have whatever you need. You've shot with us before back when we were doing Apartment Wrestling films. You know the routine, I can't have anyone in the room other then the model's while we do the shoot but I can get you an advanced copy of the final product."

"I want it before my sisters burial." Hannah said. "Can I see you for a moment outside your office"??

"Please excuse me." Cyril said standing up behind his desk.

"What do you want"?? Mathews asked when they were finally alone in the hallway.

"My finders fee for Samantha. I brought her to you." Jacky said aggressively.

"We don't do that anymore."

"Well make a fuckin exception or i'll take my little sister and walk out of here."

"You won't walk out of anywhere. I'll give you three hundred dollars from the safe but that's all that you're getting, pay outs aren't even scheduled for another week."

"I brought you the only piece of ass that's ever been willing to die on film. Your company is gonna make a fortune in underground so fork over the cash or we're history, and I want eight hundred."

"Five is my final offer." Mathews bartered.

"Fine, i'll accept that." Jacky said standing outside while Cyril with drew money from the safe in another office.

When he came back Jacky was waiting for him with her arms folded. There was a scowl half a mile long on her face, down both cheeks, and seemingly all the way through the back of her skull.

"Let's go." Jacky demanded as they reentered the office. She had made her bread, pissed off The Devil, stoked his fires and would be walking out the door with five hundred dollars for her hand.

"When are we doing the shoot"?? Samantha asked, still seated across from Mathews.

"We're going to give you Ether during the final moments." Cyril said. "I need to wait for it to get here so it should be by this time or so in two weeks." He said petting the doberman on the skull.

"Alright, that gives me enough time to get ready." Samantha said turning to look up at her sister who stood only a foot or so away from her.

"Good girl." Jacky said petting her sister quickly on top of the head and then looking away. It was as though she were addressing an animal.

"Let's go." Danno said raising himself up on the other side of the room.

"Let's go." Hannah agreed.

"That's some nasty swelling." Alyssa said applying a cold compress to David Danes bare shoulder.

"Ouch, yeah I know, it's been like this for a few days." He said struggling against the agony that he was in. "If I could afford to spare eight or nine hours i'd go to a hospital."

"You need to make time." Alyssa said emphasizing the second part of her sentence.

"Who's here"?? Dane asked lifting himself from his seated position on the edge of the bed. There had been a brief however loud knock on the door. It was late and who the fuck could it be??

"Can we come in"?? Dane heard Troy Barclee call out from a number of meters away, still behind the door.

"Holy fuck. YEAH"!!!! He answered as the big man and the smaller big man walked into his house. They were each carrying a case of beer and boasted a french blond to each an arm.

"We would've brought you one to but we heard that you already had company."

Alyssa was giggling now. "Who are these guys"?? She asked emerging from the bedroom behind her best friend. The compress was now in her hand.

"Alyssa, this is Scott Paris and Troy Barclee." Dane said lighting up the toaster.

"I told you how many times that i'm not interested in these surveys." Paris said into his cell phone. He then hung up. "These people call me like ten times a day. I can't seem to get them to put me on their don't ever bother me again or i'll show you a razors edge list."

"I doubt that they have any list with a heading like that." Dane answered.

"Tell him he needs to go to a hospital, his shoulder's fucked." Alyssa stated looking for the loaf of bread that they'd purchased last night, nowhere to be found.

"Doctors and hospitals make me squeamish." Dane said. "Anybody want butter on their toast"?? The fighter asked taking stock of their cupboards. He could find nothing, no bread, no danish's.

"Fuck the butter baby. We can't even find the bread." Alyssa said dryly.

"By the way. I saw your niece on her way to the gym. She said tell Uncle Von that I love him." Scott Paris relayed. "Mm … … … … … By the way, we have a mutual counter part." Paris stated.

"Who"?? Von "The Icon" asked.

"Jacky Hannah."

David Dane almost passed out, listening, but not quite believing what he had just heard. "How do you know Jacky Hannah"?? He asked, astonished.

"She used to run a string of Brothels Down South while we were living in Florida" Scott said. "She was into everything. Every cop in the state used to run her rap sheet and then spend three days sleeping. Danno, that's her boyfriend … … … … … … …

"Guinea pig." Barclee interjected. "I had to split his head with a tire iron once because he owed seven grand to a friend of mine. The seven grand was money that Jacky needed to pay back her supplier so Danno borrowed it from Christoff."

Von "The Icon" could not believe any of this. "Who's Christoff"?? He asked.

"Christoff is a loan shark." Paris informed him.

"How did you know that she knew us"?? Dane enquired. He hadn't made the connection just yet.

"Kate "The Gate" Shamrock" spent about an hour talking to us at The Domino the other night. She dropped Jacky's name a couple of times." Barclee informed him. "Suffice to say that Scotty and I were more than just slightly alarmed that the two of them knew each other." The big man said laying a kiss on one of the blonds who sat next to him. She was nibbling on his ear lobe now.

"I'm not at the centre of your universe. Who's Jacky"?? Alyssa asked spreading peanut butter onto a cracker with a knife.

Dane looked one way and then the other. "Jacky is the unfortunate bi-product of Kate's success as a kick boxer." He said reaching into a grocery bag that was leaning against the side of a floor cabinet.

"I found the bread." He said.

"This is the man that you were looking for." Detective Drew Solomon said placing a photograph in front of Roberta face down. "He's the one that you see in your sleep." The haunted looking Detective persisted through a mask of perspiration. "I know that you can't think of anything else, and neither can I, because I see him to." Drew said honestly.

Roberta gave no response, hands neatly folded into a tent on top of the table. She wore a rosary around her neck, dangling in beads.

"You saw him. I see him every night. He's the man on the tape isn't he"?? Solomon went on. "We both see him, and we both know that he does terrible things to people."

Garrison was statuesque standing near the west wall, his posture was unflinching.

"You can't dream without seeing him can you Roberta"?? Solomon continued with a hollow echo. "He's there whenever you close your eyes isn't he?? I know, because he's there whenever I close mine."

She was losing focus now, her eyes starting to open and shut systematically like an alarm system set to a timer. It had likely been weeks since she really slept, the reaction to the drugs she had been given to help her was nil.

"He's in the dark with me." She whispered tugging on the string of beads. "He won't go away and he's wicked." She cried below laboured, frightened, terror laced breathing. "I see his face."

"Who is he Roberta?? You know his name." Solomon pressed inside the shadowy little interrogation room. His white dress shirt was stained with perspiration, clinging, attaching itself to him like a second skin. There was no ventilation.

"He won't let me tell you who he is. He says i'll die for it."

Garrison was fascinated, he knew what working on this case had done to his partner psychologically. He had watched this girl and whatever she knew become an obsession.

"He can't get to you in here. We're protecting you. We have all the locks and all the keys, and he doesn't know where they are." Solomon reassured her.

There was a low buzzing sound in the room, like a cooling system regulating itself.

Roberta now sat forward glaring into Solomon's eyes.

"Who is he Roberta"?? Garrison asked interjecting himself into the conversation. There was night like the absence of all things good around him, stealing away his perimeters. "Tell me his name. C'mon hunny, I know you know who he is." Garrison pushed before Roberta launched a mouthful of spit towards his face.

"Alright, that's enough." Drew Solomon said. "Turn the tape recorder off."

"MOTHER FUCKERS!!! NO GOOD FOR NOTHING FUCKING COCK SUCKERS"!!!! Roberta hollered standing up and backing herself into the west wall. "HE'S HERE!!! HE'S ALREADY IN THE ROOM WITH US!!! HE'S LAUGHING AT THE TWO OF YOU"!!!

Solomon looked as disturbed as Roberta did unbuttoning his sweat stained shirt before removing his tie.

"Get Holbrook in here to give her a sedative." Garrison half ordered.

Holbrook was this Police Divisions resident medical physician, he was a thirty two year veteran.

"Jesus Christ"!!!! Garrison exclaimed as Roberta yanked her shirt off exposing her sagging breasts and self mutilated flesh, there was bruised skin as well as fresh scars running to her naval and underneath her belly.

"C'mom, hurry up"!!! He shouted as Solomon momentarily disappeared from the room returning with Holbrook soon after. "I have Thorazine in this syringe. Hold her down"!!!! He commanded.

"DAMMIT"!!! Holbrook hollered as Roberta sunk her teeth into the back of his wrist.

"GRAB HER"!!! Solomon shouted reaching around from behind so as to get a steadier grip on Roberta's torso. "I've got her. Go ahead." The senior Detective commanded.

"Okay, Roberta. You should be feeling a bit more relaxed in a few seconds." Dr. Holbrook said reassuringly as he removed the blade of the needle from his patients arm. "You're going to feel a bit warm and fuzzy but that's perfectly normal." He told her as her body went limp in his grip, muscle by muscle feeling the effects of the drug, everything shutting down now.

"There you go. Just relax. It's alright. You'll be feeling better in no time."

CHAPTER 7:

Jonathan Dane lifted a rifle from the trunk of his car, he had at one time been a woodsman and a hunter, drifting from that to operating heavy machinery such as cranes, ploughs and fork lifts to make a living for himself.

It hadn't taken Jonathan long to find employment growing up, he came from a town with a population of fifty or sixty but had later immigrated to small city life having left the dwellings of the country behind.

If Jonathan Dane had a rival, other than his eldest son, it was change. You could take the boy out of the country, but you couldn't take the country out of the boy.

When he was eighteen years old Jonathan Dane had found his niche in the corporate world having spent almost forty years with the same company before changing business venues. After that, he had worked steadily for about another twenty years before being offered a package and accepting it at the advice of a financial adviser, he had then retired.

"David's got a big ego"!!! Jonathan lamented as he set one more rifle onto the pile.

"Oh, c'mon Jonathan, get real. He's from a different world than you are, one's from the street and the others from the corporate world, you'll never see eye to eye with each other." Marilyn Dane argued.

This was Jonathan's frequent disposition towards his eldest son as well as a sign that he had never fully accepted city life. David Dane had often surmised that Jonathan would go fuckin ape shit living in a place like Montreal where ego's were as common place as The Metro that ran underground from one end of the island to the other every fifteen minutes.

Big cities fostered heavy competition resulting in plenty of big egos to go around. David Dane also came from a world of bodybuilding, boxing, crime syndicate figures, and thugs who constantly tried to throw their weight around, and when they did, you had to be ready to push back.

You weren't going to find humble crop tenders, church goers or women wearing bonnets anywhere in Von "The Icons" world, that was simply the reality of it, like it or not.

If you didn't have a big ego, if you didn't believe totally in yourself, you perished. Many of the individuals in David Danes world were akin to animals or sharks, if they sensed weakness or smelled blood, you were a goner.

"Even when I was in school I could never stand people who had BIG EGO'S"!!! Jonathan bitched.

"Jonathan, we go through this every time we talk about David. I keep telling you, he's not from the same world as you are, his associations are different. You gotta remember that there's thirty years between you guys. There's a generation gap. It makes a difference." Marilyn said.

"I have to go put these in storage." Jonathan Dane said of the pile of guns that sat at his feet.

"Alright, call me on your way home, I want a blue berry muffin from Tim Hortons." Marilyn requested before disappearing into the garage and back up the stairs from which she came.

"I'll see you when I get back." Jonathan finished.

Monica-I hope that all in all you know how much you meant to me, I hope you know how much I will always love you no matter what, and regardless of the circumstances surrounding the way that we ended that never should have been.

This is your series, as I said at the outset, I am dedicating this Book as well as URBAN RAIN to you. You will always be the owner of my heart as well as the keeper of my soul in genuine light and love.

The years that we spent together, I now cherish, I cherished them even back then as I used to tell you every day. It's all like a dream in my head, a rain storm or a whirl wind, it all seems so surreal.

One day I will tell my niece Kate about all of our memories and about all of the sacred moments that we shared together in the days and nights that are now immortal, through the crispness of the cold or underneath Ontario Streets warm skies in and out of its smoke filled taverns and darkened alcoves.

I can still see your lips moving in silence, talking to me. I still remember the way that you pursed your lips and smiled when I kissed you in the middle of the night when we were alone below Ontario Streets blackened skies, together, as always.

One more moment, one more day, one more breath.

I can still remember how special it was being alone with you down there. You always have and always will mean everything to me. I will always defend your name as well as your honour. I will never allow O Street to forget you, or us.

Sometimes when I dream about you, when i'm holding you, when we're alone in my sleep, I can hear a pin drop, I can feel the night again, I can see all of the bits and pieces of the time that we shared. No one will ever be able to duplicate the era that we spent in Montreal's east end. Only you could have brought that special charisma to those times, only you could have been the star of that stroll and done it with the style and finesse that you did it with, you are and were that special. My number one bunny.

I will always love you.
Von.

P.S.-Monica, you ended up being the true star of your Family, the true icon and the true legend, and there is no one else, and I mean NO ONE, who can hold a piano key to that. Just saying.

L.A.-I hope you are enjoying NEIGHBOURHOOD OF NIGHT-URBAN RAIN II, all that I do in this book I do for the sake of two people, Monica and my beautiful niece, Kate. I want you to know that whatever your opinion at the conclusion of this book that I tried my best. I know that at a certain period that things were not well between you and I, and that we weren't getting along, but I loved Monica with all my heart and still fight for her to this day. I will let NO ONE!!! speak ill of her.

There is a bond between Monica and I that death itself cannot break. We shared an experience as well as an era that will never be forgotten nor can you just simply put away. Your Daughter meant more to me than any words can or will ever do justice to, no matter what, as I always told her, I would have given my life for her on a moments notice, and always defended her at the risk of my own safety.

We have all been through a plethora of difficult times with Monica. I will never accuse her of being the easiest person to live with, I think you know that, but I love her and I cherish her memory above and beyond all else. She will always and forever be, my Baby Bunny.

At this moment I want to take the time to remember someone else who meant a great deal to me, my Aunt Mary O' Mann who is up in Heaven. You were the kindest, sweetest, most genuine person that I ever knew and you constantly filled my ears with wisdom. I know that this earth will never see another person like you, you exemplified all that was positive and good in this world, they don't make human beings of your quality anymore. I only wish that you could have lived to see me become an author.

I can just imagine you now, you are probably somewhere in Heavens highest tier walking arm in arm with your son Michael who was taken from this earth to soon. I know how truly proud he was of you.

If any soul on this planet deserves to be called a saint, deserves to be heralded as a human being that was truly special, then it is you.

I love you Aunt Mary.
God Bless you.

Sheryl H walked to the edge of the wharf in old Montreal, she was scheduled to meet David Dane in about ten minutes and she wanted to prepare herself adequately, both emotionally and spiritually. This would not be a light conversation. Lilly was dead, and Sheryl had known her boyfriend/husband for a long time, almost from the beginning of this whole thing back in 2000.

There would likely be tears, and she knew that discussing this topic was not going to be easy, it was in her head now that things were going to be tough and she wanted to ready herself for the onslaught of emotion from a friend that she loved so much.

As she looked off of the pier Sheryl watched the white capped waves make laps over each other before laying flat and drifting out to sea in a million adjoined blankets of salt silvered ocean water.

Standing there in the shadows of the big warehouse Sheryl recalled the moment when she and David Dane had first met, it had been in a MC Donalds at Frontenac while she was having breakfast with Lilly. She now thought of those days on Ontario Street as being a part of a golden era. Things were not the same down there today, no one looked out for each other the same way or thought of themselves as part of a Family, back then everybody watched each others back and took care of each other, now it was dog eat dog or rip somebodies eyes out to get what you wanted, no more all for one and one for all. Those days were over.

"Hey." Sheryl called out as she saw Von "The Icon" walking toward her underneath the clear blue morning sky. He looked unslept and sported matching circles around each eye, there was a set of jangling house keys in his hand.

"It's good to see you. I'd hug you but I know how you feel about hugs." David Dane said.

"Yeah, well, you know, it's the things that happened when I was a kid. I've always associated being hugged with being smacked across the head." Sheryl said.

"I'm sorry about that," Dane said squinting in the glare of the cold morning light.

"I wanted to say that I was sorry about Lilly. I know that you guys were close and everything." Sheryl said genuinely, her expression occasionally giving way to a self conscious smile. "I still remember the day at Frontenac when you walked into MC Donalds and sat down with us. I can't believe that. I can't believe that Lilly's really gone." Sheryl who looked like a thinned out Whoopi Goldberg said.

"Me neither." Dane said looking wistfully across the water. "Ontario Street will never, ever be the same without her. Lilly brought a special atmosphere and charisma to the neighbourhood that you can't just buy in a store. I think it had to be something innate, something that came as part of the package." Dane said. "I had a dream about her the other night. I dreamt that I got a call on the intercom system from a woman but I couldn't hear what she was saying because of all the static, so I went downstairs. When I got there, just across the lobby through the glass doors I saw a woman standing in the forecourt outside in the daylight. She had a grey trench coat on and I could feel my heart drumming in my chest, and when she turned around, it was Lilly." Dane said through a heart full of emotion.

"She was special, I mean, I know how much you guys loved each other. We all knew it." The kind hearted Sheryl said.

At that moment a large wave rose and collapsed against the shoreline underneath the legs of the reef.

"I wish I could've said goodbye to her." Von "The Icon" said.

"We all do." Sheryl agreed as The Ontario Street Original lit her cigarette for her.

"We all loved Lilly. She was my friend.." Sheryl said. "She was such a dare devil, I guess that time and tide finally caught up with her. I used to tell her that she had a dangerous personality. It's like when she used to do Coke and Heroine we used to tell her to do one drug, not two, but I guess she never listened. I don't know what she might've been on that night"??

"My Brother's trying to get his hands on Lilly's toxicology report." Dane reported wondering if Andrew had succeeded in his quest yet.

A gull soared past them and then rose into the limitless sky again. The scene reminded David Dane of a song by Mister Mister. Broken Wing, he recalled. At the same moment he remembered a dark and misty night back in 2001 when Lilly had arranged to introduce a dealer to a portion person for a reasonable finders fee. There had been three cars sitting in front of The Black Domino Tavern well past sun down awaiting Lilly getting into one of them. Lilly had told Dane that she was going to the destination with him or not but that if he wanted to join her then he could. Dane had gone. He wasn't going to let Lilly accompany this three car motorcade an hour out of town without him there to protect her. In his minds eye Dane could still remember the intensity of the love that he felt for Lilly sitting in the back of the four door sedan with Lilly seated next to him with her head resting comfortably on his shoulder. He would do anything for her, even put his life on the line.

About an hour or so later the three cars came to a halt in front of a quiet and secluded park that was nestled away in an alcove. Lilly had made her money and walked away unscathed with Dane next to her. His love for her was so intense that Dane often felt as though he was on the brink of crying whenever she was in his presence.

"She'll never get to appreciate any of this ever again." Dane said in a melancholy voice. "She'll never get to watch the sunrise again or be able to sit by the ocean. It's funny how you'd give all of your tomorrows for one more hug or one more chance to hold the person that you love and be able to tell them what they meant to you."

"Lilly knew what she meant to you. I still remember you guys out there every night, all the other girls used to get jealous because Lilly was being so well taken care of by her boyfriend and they didn't have that. She used to brag about you. You and Lilly were special. You guys brought a quality to Ontario Street that no other couple ever has."

"Thanks Sheryl." The Ontario Street Original said warmly.

"What was it that you always used to call her"?? Sheryl enquired. "Your Bunny or something."

"My Baby Bunny." David Dane said.

Just then a familiar looking black Jaguar pulled up at the far end of the pier. "I think that's Andrew" David Dane exclaimed looking in the direction of the suns glare.

"You're lucky you told me where you were going." Andrew Dane said when he reached his Brother. There was a blue file folder in his hand. "I have Lilly's toxicology report."

Dane could see the expression in his Brothers eyes. I have something bad to tell you, and you're really not gonna like it. "They found traces of GHB in Lilly's blood stream." He said.

"Did they say how long before her accident it was ingested"?? Von "The Icon" asked.

"One hour, maybe two." Andrew said flatly. He did not believe that Lilly Chicoine had done this to herself. "The autopsy report suggests that it was taken with some alcohol."

"I've never heard of Lilly taking GHB." Sheryl said. "Heroine, Coke, the occasional stone, but never GHB."

"Somebody did this to her." David Dane said with a frown of extreme concern on his face. He had walked several paces away moving underneath the shadow of the warehouse that stood near the edge of the boardwalk. "Why"?? He wondered aloud.

"Could she have seen something"?? Andrew surmised. "I mean we know that Lilly was involved in some bad shit, or maybe she pissed somebody off."

"Nah, I don't think so. It's more likely that it had something to do with this case." David Dane concluded. "I mean they wouldn't do that to her if she owed money, they'd just shoot her."

"I'm Sheryl." She said introducing herself to Andrew whom she hadn't met until now.

"Hi, nice to meet you." The lawyer said shaking her hand, but he was only half paying her any thought to busy with the situation at hand.

"What was the name of that bar that we went to meet her at"?? Dane pondered aloud.

"I'm not sure." Andrew responded. "You're the one who took the call."

"Wasn't it The Snake Pit or something"?? Dane recalled. "Yeah, because I thought of Jake "The Snake" Roberts talk show segment on Superstars back in the eighties when she mentioned it. "It was called The Snake Pit." He said.

Silver lightning flashed between two clouds as Andrew closed his overcoat that was worth as much as some peoples house payments. "It's gonna rain. We should probably get out of here." Andrew said.

"Lucky I brought my umbrella." Sheryl commented. "Be prepared."

"Someone needs to pull the camera footage from the night that Lilly died, if they still have it." Von "The Icon" suggested.

"They've probably all turned over by now." Andrew said in response to his Brothers suggestion. "I'd be willing to bet that most of these places only maintain their footage for about twenty four to forty eight hours before the tapes start a new loop."

"It's still worth a try." Dane said turning to walk ten or fifteen paces back to where Andrew and Sheryl were standing side by side. Andrew looked like a legitimate fat cat, and indeed he was.

"Can you drive me out there"?? David Dane asked his younger sibling.

"What, tonight"?? Andrew asked with a number of creased rolls in his face brought on by his squint against the rain, he looked like a giant porch dog. David observed.

"No, like over the next day or two. I wanna talk to the owner of the bar or the wait. staff. Maybe someone remembers something." The fighter said.

"I have a day off in two days. Maybe we could do it then." Andrew Dane answered.

Suddenly the rain began to shoot from the sky in long straight silver pellets. It immediately reminded David Dane of some of the early days on Ontario Street and he thought of how symbolic the downpour was of those moments, only now, Lilly was gone, lowered into the ground for all of eternity never to return again. Those hazy moments in his head that represented a long standing past were exploding against the earth in atomic rain drops like the frame in the music video HERE WITHOUT YOU by THREE DOORS DOWN.

"I love Lilly." Dane said to the sky above. "I hope on some level that i've made you proud of me. I did my best." He said.

"Let's go." Andrew said stealing underneath a section of Sheryl's open umbrella.

"I guess that we're gonna get wet before the days over." Sheryl said being her usual affable self.

"I guess so." Von "The Icon" responded.

Olend Marx walked below the canopy of a local fresh fruit market on Ontario Street. He hadn't been out for long, but now, in this weather, it did not look like he would get his daily exercise that had been ordered by his physician. He was in good shape for a man of his years however since the stabbing incident Olend Marx was not as spry as he used to be, that, and there were a number of other pain staking complications.

It had only been half an hour since he had left the house, and already here it was raining, coming down in long silver sheets of soaking wet blur. "I'm glad to see you out." Olend said as he came upon Brando from Venezuela bagging a fist full of miniature zuchinis.

"Well, what I mean to say is, it's very good to see you." Brando exclaimed.

"I won't be shopping here again." Etienne Armena said coming from the stores recesses. He now had a cart full of groceries and how the hell was he going to get them home in this silvery mess. "Not only are the prices obscene, but the food is not really all that fresh. This is worse than when I worked at the video store. If you want to watch Von fight with Helena, press one, if you want fight with Yves(Last name omitted), press two, if you want to clean up the urine from the adult section, press three." He went on.

"Well, what I mean to say is, maybe you should call a cab." Brando from Venezuela suggested.

"I don't think I will be calling any cab." … … … … … … …

Just then Olend Marx phone lit up. There was a familiar number on the screen.

"Olend, it's David Dane." The Ontario Street Original said on the other end. "Can you meet me in half an hour"?? The Ontario Street Original requested.

"Where would be the best place for me to meet you David"?? Olend asked politely.

"I'm thinkin maybe outside of Cinema Du Parc at La Cite." David Dane said.

"Okay, i'll be there." Olend agreed, and that was that.

Thirty minutes later a soaking wet, dishevelled David Dane showed up outside the alternative films cinema, he was shivering like a small child who had just been dug out of an avalanche. "Thanks for coming Olend." Dane said as soon as he saw his friend coming toward him.

"We just got Lilly's toxicology report back. She had GHB in her system on the night she died. I'm really fuckin rattled, can't sit still." Dane said. "I'm glad you were available. I really need someone to talk to."

"You know that i'm always here for you. You're a good lad and God has his eye on you. He knows that you're special. I told you before, my Father was a Preacher. My Brothers and Sisters and I, we have a special relationship with God. I know that he loves you. I know that he sees you."

"You're a very good man Olend. I just wish that your son Clinton knew how lucky he was. I've never gotten along with my old man. He always tried to scare me or play mind games with me. He's one of the reasons why i'm so screwed up today. I have paranoia issues that pop up every once in awhile because of him. Very few people know that." Dane said with a rain drop dangling from his nose.

"I've always tried to teach my children to do the right things even in the face of adversity and temptation. Clinton doesn't understand that Jesus loves him. He doesn't understand that if he listens, that if he accepts the lord into his heart that he'll be better off. My Father could have set him straight, but my son doesn't want to accept Jesus Christ as his lord and saviour."

Just then a female security officer walked by, and for a minute, it seemed as though she were frowning at Olend Marx.

"Uncle Von." Kate suddenly shouted from behind him.

"How did you find me here"?? Ontario Streets Last Outlaw asked turning around. He looked almost pathetic standing there drenched to the bone.

"I didn't. I came in to grab a protein shake and I saw you here. Are you okay"?? Shamrock asked looking uncommonly concerned. "Who's your friend"?? She asked of the gentleman that David Dane was having a conversation with. "This is Olend Marx." Dane said making the introductions.

"This is my niece Kate." David Dane said of The Irish Princess.

"It's an honour to make your acquaintance Miss"??

"Kathleen Dane." Kate said extending her hand.

"My niece is The North American Womens Kick Boxing Champion."

"Well then i'm doubly honoured to meet you." Olend said. "You're a prize fighter."

"Olend, I don't know if you've ever followed kick boxing, but if you have then you might have heard of the lady who now stands before you. This is "The Pride Of The Irish" better known to the world and the media as Kate "The Gate" Shamrock.

"I don't watch much television but I believe that if I did i'd remember a young lady as striking as you." Olend said oozing charm as he removed his hat in Kates honour.

"Thank you." Kate said diverting her attention momentarily to her Uncles fixated expression. The last time she'd seen him wearing such a look was during a period where he was being blackmailed by a couple who he had known just a few years ago. The two individuals in question had nearly driven her famous Uncle off the deep end turning his mind both inside out and backward, it had been bad, a full on break down that had caused her Uncle to have to spend a short time in a psychiatric unit.

"Uncle Von, can I speak to you alone for a second"?? Shamrock asked still holding an expression of concern.

Dane nodded, and at exactly that instant Kate knew that something was wrong. Despondence was the quickest way to determine that something was troubling her Uncle, he would have otherwise answered her verbally, however, he did not.

"Olend, please excuse us for a moment." Von said.

"Without a problem sir."

"Let's go." David Dane said leading his niece in the direction of a hallway that led to a bank of Post Office Boxes. "What is it"?? He asked when they had reached a quiet shadow.

Kate frowned, her Uncle was definitely disturbed by something otherwise his reaction to her would have been softer, less brisk, and he was never that way with the niece that he treasured so much.

"Are you alright"?? The female champion asked. "I see the look in your eyes Uncle Von. The last time that I saw you like this was when Abraham and Violet were black mailing you."

"They found poison in Lilly's system. GHB. It looks like someone filled her up before she got back on the highway. I loved her so much." Von "The Icon" said. "I've never done well without her."

"You came here to see Olend or you ran into him"?? Shamrock asked out of curiosity.

"I called him before I got here." Von said as a woman pushing a stroller exited one of the mirrored corridors to his left. "I wanna go back to the early two thousands, I wanna go back to when Lilly and I were first together. I don't know how things got so screwed up. I hate Dad's side of the Family. I loathe and despise Abraham and Violet Morrisey for starting me down this road of phobia's and on going nightmares. If it wasn't for you i'd have no more reason to live."

"I'm proud of you." Kate said with tears welling up in her pretty eyes. "Whatever these people did they should be punished for it." She said.

"I still remember the morning that Jonathan was threatening to share information with Abraham, I was terrified, phobic, so I called Abraham and left a message to try and scare him away from talking to my Father but the whole thing back fired, I ended up doing myself more harm than good. I said something about just acting or behaving professionally if Dad or whoever ever questioned them about anything. I was trying to intimidate them, to scare them away, but instead I made it sound like they knew something that I didn't want them to say anything about. I was to panicked and to F'D up. I didn't know my ass from my elbow until after my anxiety had caused me to do one more stupid thing. I had gone to see a lawyer about the whole blackmailing situation before I went back to Nova Scotia, then I ended up in the hospital." Von said.

"Listen, you will NEVER be alone again. You've been there for me since I was a child. I'm not gonna abandon you through any of this. These people are gonna stop their fucking or i'll make them stop. Let's see what these ass holes do when I send Byron to see them." Byron Richards was Kates Civil litigator. "We'll see who ends up being phobic then." She said. "I love you Uncle Von, and i'll do whatever it takes to protect you. It's my turn." Kate said.

"Thanks Katie." Von said embracing his niece.

"We should try to get some sing started." Abraham Morrisey said. "Maybe zat way we can get his Mozar(Mother) to pay us for za tape." The man from the hot country said.

"We can make his Mother give us some money or her son will go to jail." Violet echoed.

Dane had been standing outside of a door when he had heard all of this. It was all creeping back now, turning his head inside out and playing havoc with his brain.

Trusting Family was a mistake, and trusting the people that you thought were your friends was an even greater mistake, he had done nothing and given everything, he had offered people rolls in books, treated them to free pay-per-views, allowed his friendship to be given unconditionally, showed people that he cared, and the end result was that the people that he did everything for wanted to burn him to the ground.

"Hey, are you alright"?? Kate asked standing a few feet away with a well of tears waiting to spill over in her eyes. She was all heart, and all champion, every breath that she took demonstrated the class that she possessed, and the ethics with which she lived her life. There wasn't an indecent bone in her body.

"It would have been better if I had died on that highway." The Ontario Street Original said breaking down in a sea of tears. "I can't seem to come to terms with Lilly being gone. It was my job to protect her, but I wasn't there this time. I failed her, I failed her." Dane repeated. Everything is in such a goddamn mess that I don't know if i'll ever find the door."

Kate was hugging him now, doing all that she could to console the broken man who was her favourite uncle. "Lilly couldn't have asked for a better boyfriend. You loved her. You would have died for her Uncle Von and everyone knows that. These other people, they've messed up your life. I know that things between you Nana and Papa are extremely rough. I know that you and Papa don't get along and that you don't speak. I know how tough it's been."

"Ye know, I have these dreams where I see Lilly. I had one the other night where she walked up to me on The Stone Park and kissed me, and when she walked away she evaporated." Dane said teary eyed. "It's like being cheated. You really believe that she's there and then the Director of this screenplay or this movie leaves the scene on the cutting room floor. My life is a mess, it's been a mess for a long time. I try to hold on every single day but it just seems to get worse and worse. My old man screwed me up from a very young age. He did everything that he could to hurt me, to try and destroy my future. He never wanted me to be happy."

"I don't know that side of Papa but I know that you two never saw eye to eye. Dad has told me the stories. I guess that when people aren't the same or don't react to things the same way that they end up not getting along." Shamrock surmised.

"What never ceases to amaze me is that when you have a Phobia or an illness that everyone around you will start to capitalize on it, it's like living in a cauldron of bad ethics or evil intentions. One day, much later on i'll write a book about all of this and i'll sell it to the world." Von "The Icon" said.

"And i'll be the first one to buy it." Kate said smiling through her cries. "Thank you."

"For what"?? David Dane asked.

"For being the most special uncle that any girl could have asked for. You were always there for me even when I was still a baby." Shamrock said removing a tear from her own cheek.

"You know, I can still remember the day you were born." Von "The Icon" said. "If it wasn't for you I would never have lasted as long as I have."

"I think you would've done just fine."

Just then a janitor pushed a broom past them, as usual the whole mall had a pleasant chlorine scent that reminded David Dane of better times, in this place, it was ever present. He and Lilly had once lived not far from here, to the South just slightly as Dane recalled.

"I think we should go find Olend. He probably thinks we got kidnapped." Kate said leading her Uncle by placing a hand on his back.

"I never did like him." Jonathan Dane said parking his vehicle against the curb. "He's getting to be the same as his Grand Father, he thinks he can tell everyone else what to do."

"I've never seen two men who were so different in my life." Marilyn Dane lamented as Jonathan Dane

maneuvered his SUV into place beside a set of parking metres that were bound together with wire.

"Hold on, that's him calling now." Marilyn said picking up her phone. "Hello." She echoed into the mouthpiece. She was as usual holding her handset more closely than she should have been, it made for a less clear conversation full of echos and static.

"Mum." David Dane began. He sounded fuzzy, as though he had been upset.

"What is it?? Your Father and I are just going for a Coffee at The Cottage. We haven't been out all day. Your Father's nearly round the bend doing paperwork. He needs to get out of the house."

The Cottage was a frequent haunt of both Jonathan and Marilyn Dane, they had spent many an afternoon or an evening there. It was a yuppie turn over place. They sold such pastries as cake, cookies, croissants, cup cakes, as well as a variety of Expressos and Coffee, and to David Dane who had been there on more than one occasion, the place sucked and had fuck all to offer, period!!!

"I have Kate here with me. She wants to talk to you before she steps into the ring tonight." The Icon said. "I'm gonna pass her my phone. I have to go and see Andrew."

"Where are you"?? Marilyn asked. "There's a lot of noise in the background."

"We're at The Bell Centre, downstairs in a restricted area." Dane said as Kate wrapped her hands only a few feet away. There were already thousands of signs everywhere, each baring a different series of words, but almost all of them had one thing in common, they all extolled a different love or respect for Kate "The Gate" Shamrock.

There were such sentiments across the arena as KATE "THE GATE" SHAMROCK-PRIDE OF THE IRISH!!!! KATE-GATE WAY TO MY HEART!!!!!!!!!! MONTREAL QUEBEC LOVES KATE "THE GATE" SHAMROCK!!!!!!!!!! KATE "THE GATE" SHAMROCK-PRINCESS OF POWER!!!!!!!! KATE "THE GATE" SHAMROCK-COMIN AT CHA!!!!!!!!

"Hi Nana." Kate spoke into the phone as Von "The Icon" left the room to go meet his Brother.

"Jacky Hannah's here ah"!!! Von said when he reached Andrew several minutes later. There were daggers in his eyes.

"Yeah, well don't do anything stupid that's gonna get you arrested." Andrew advised. "The last thing that Kate needs is to see you being carted off in hand cuffs."

"What the fuck are they doing here"?? Von "The Icon" asked as he saw Eva Nicolette and Charles R. Brown slithering their way towards him.

"I have no idea." Andrew said honestly. "Maybe they came to watch the fight." The Barrister surmised unbuttoning the top of his trench coat. It had been wet outside, and Andrews coat still bore the remnants of it.

"Look what the cat dragged in." The Ontario Street Original said amidst smouldering eyes that were his own. He thought about killing them right here, one and done, no more hassles.

"What can I do for you Eva"?? The extreme bad ass asked. He was now more focused than he had been in over twenty four hours, and ten times as lethal.

"Remember what we know about you." The bitch said.

"So you keep tellin me. That information is gonna get you killed."

"The only people you can threaten are defenceless women." Charlie Brown said clinging to the laminated portion of the special back stage pass that he wore around his neck. It had his photo in the centre of it.

"Why, are you afraid"?? Von "The Icon" quipped bringing an irresistible smirk to Charlie Browns lips.

"Twinkle, twinkle little star, how I wonder who the fuck you think you are." Ontario Streets Immortal Legend cracked, if there hadn't been as many people around, he would've cracked Charlie and Eva right across the fuckin head.

"We're gonna get you." The always smug Eva threatened. She had turned her head and was now looking toward Kate who was being lead through the belly of the building by an entourage of security.

"Not if I get you first." David Dane said making a pistol gesture with his hands.

"Get out of my way." Kate said unpleasantly as she deliberately pushed her way past Charlie and Eva who looked unimpressed. "Gotta go." Von said following his niece through the curtain and into the arena that was sold out amidst a spectacle of crisscrossing spot lights, fire works and pyrotechnics that were especially arranged to honour Canadian Kick Boxings favourite Princess.

"Where's Andrew"?? Von shouted over the roar of the crowd that was now deafening.

"He went to speak to the head of security about Jacky. He wants to make sure that she's closely monitored." Shamrock responded.

SHAMROCK!!!!!!!!!!!!   SHAMROCK!!!!!!!!!!!!!!!!!! SHAMROCK!!!!!!!!!!!!!! The chant went out filling the Bell Centre from one section to another. They were rabid as their hero made her way to centre ring.

"GO KATE"!!! Leilani Dane hollered as loudly as she could from her seat in one of the V.I.P. Booths.

When Kate reached the centre of the ring she paused, turned, and asked one of the handsome young ring hands for a microphone. "I'd like to have every ones attention if I could for a moment." The gorgeous and athletic Shamrock began. "Tonight, in attendance as always is a true fighting champion, he is an author, an icon, and a hero to Montreal's east end. He is the uncle who has loved me since before I was old enough to know what love was. He is "THE ONTARIO STREET ORIGINAL," he is my UNCLE, VON "THE ICON" Kate said as tears rolled down her favourite uncles cheeks only a few feet away, he had been deeply moved by his nieces sentiment.

"But hold on, i'm not done." Shamrock said smoothly. There was just one more dedication to make. "I'd also like to take this time to acknowledge another of Montreal's east end legends who recently passed away. She was my Uncles girlfriend, the love of his life, and a fighter if there ever was one. I'd like to dedicate my fight tonight to both my favourite uncle, as well as to the late Lilly "Bad To The Bone" Chicoine." Shamrock said as she readied herself for battle.

"I'm proud of you angel." David Dane said in the direction of his niece.

"Now, for the announcements." The ring announcer began. "In the red corner, hailing from Quebec City, Quebec, weighing in at one hundred and forty five pounds, Theresa Bolduc." Renee Petipas announced as the young girl stepped forward and raised her glove.

"And, in the blue corner, hailing from Montreal, Quebec, Canada, weighing in at one hundred, thirty five pounds, THE PRIDE OF THE IRISH, THE NORTH AMERICAN WOMENS KICK BOXING CHAMPION AND FUTURE HALL OF FAMER, LADIES AND GENTLEMEN, KATE "THE GATE" SHAMROCK!! Petipas hollered.

"Okay, Donovan couldn't make it so i'm in your corner tonight instead. Keep it high and watch out for her right cross, watch that leg. Don't eat the jab, keep movin. Let's go." Von "The Icon" shouted as his niece made her way to the centre of the squared circle. There was gonna be hell to pay.

"I love you"!!! Von "The Icon" shouted just loudly enough to be heard above the chants.

"Love you to." Kate responded as she placed her mouth guard between her lips.

As she stood toe to toe to lock horns with Theresa Andrew showed up and took his place next to Dane at ringside, he was still dressed in his work attire, suit and tie, looked like and was probably wearing a million bucks. "They're gonna watch her." He said.

"Alright, that's good." David Dane answered now throwing short punches in tune with what his niece was doing in the squared circle. "C'mom Kate, let's move." Von "The Icon" instructed unconsciously demonstrating a slip technique, his experience with kickboxing was limited at best, no in ring acumen and no sub crash course, he had been a boxer as well as a street fighter, bar room brawler, that was it.

Kate stood toe to toe with her opponent now not allowing Theresa to cut off the ring. She was fighting her way out, bit by bit. Theresa was an inferior opponent, at least that's what Kate kept telling herself, and to some degree, the psychology was working.

"Yeah, cmon, you can do it." David Dane encouraged.

"She's ready for this huh"?? Andrew thought aloud. "Like it says on her robe- COMIN AT CHA!!!!!!!!!!!!!!!!!!!!!!!!

At that instant Kate struck Theresa with a triple tap, two jabs and a right hand. The right had opened a gash over Theresa's left eye that was now beginning to swell.

"That's good. She's bleedin." David Dane shouted.

"You see why we don't sit her Mother at ringside for these things"?? Andrew Dane asked.

"Yeah, Leilani probably wouldn't understand stuff like this." Von "The Icon" said as Theresa sailed to the mat. "YOW"!!!!!!!!!!!!!!!!!!! VON "THE ICON" shouted as the referee began to count Theresa down. "EIGHT, NINE, TEN." Referee Earl Dominique shouted. The crowd was on its feet now.

"Here is your winner." The ring announcer began. "By way of a knock out." . . . . He went on. "And still, North American Womens Kick Boxing Champion, KATE "THE GATE" SHAMROCK!!!!!!!

Renee Petipas shouted as the crowd at The Bell Centre exploded into cheers.

"She did it again" The Ontario Street Original said.

"COMIN AT CHA Uncle Von"!!! Kate Shamrock yelled.

As soon as the fight was over a menacing looking figure stepped through the ropes as a hushed silence fell over the crowd. To Kate, her face was all to familiar. "Your next fight is with me." Jacky Hannah said closing the distance between she and Kate. "I have three letters for you Kathleen." Hannah went on.

Kates face was like stone.

"G-H-B." Hannah said as the sound of the crowd returned.

Suddenly, everything seemed surreal as Von "The Icon" stood to one side of the ring with an intense frown on his face in an obvious and apparent show of dislike. He had not overheard what Jacky Hannah had said, it was however apparent to him that whatever her message, it was not good.

"What the hell did she want"?? Ontario Streets Last Outlaw asked as Hannah stepped out of the ring and back onto the arena floor. "Your Father told security to make sure that she kept her distance. So much for them doing their job."

"GHB." Kate said in a voice that seemed as though it were emanating from somewhere below the ocean floor. She had not recovered her faculties yet.

"She said GHB." She repeated.

David Dane was looking off to one side of the ring now, to where Jacky had exited. It was as if staring at that one particular part of the ring and its ropes would somehow cause Jacky to reappear but no such thing took place.

"What"??

"You heard me." Kate repeated. "GHB." She said with a look on her face that was serious enough to burn through led as she walked past her Uncle Von and climbed hands over feet out of the ring.

Later that night, as traffic ebbed and darkness fell over the city, five gun shots rang out in succession over Ontario Street with a hollow metallic echo. The first three were fired through the side windshield of a parked car that was sitting on Dufresne and the last two were fired into a man who was walking through an alleyway to meet the woman who had been shot.

The names of the victims would be announced over the radio and television the next morning as Charlie Brown and Eva Nicolette, their vehicle had been found blood soaked to the upholstery sitting awash in ice blue vapour light from the street lamps overhead glare.

"Couldn't have happened to two nicer people." The legendary Von "The Icon" said sitting on the arm of his couch in his apartment. "The next one that should happen to is Jacky Hannah." He said grabbing a handful of Alyssa's ass as she walked by wearing spandex shorts. "Haul ass." He said grinning at the sexy ex strippers figure.

"Wow, you're in a good mood this morning." Alyssa said clapping her hands together inside of two oversized oven mitts before taking them off and laying them on the stove top, face down on their design.

"Yeah, well, good news always puts a smile on my face." The bad ass said switching the TV off with the remote control. If there was anything more worthy of celebration, then Ontario Streets Last Outlaw did not know what it was, and that was a fact.

"Do you want something else to smile about"?? Alyssa asked sitting on the lap of Ontario Streets most eligible stud who was now up to his elbows in I couldn't be happier to hear that two dirt bags just bought it. Fuck em, and everyone who looked like em.

"Whatd'ya have in mind"?? The Thug Life Mogul asked.

"Why don't you come into the bedroom and i'll show you." The seductive Alyssa coerced taking David Dane by the hand. She had several things in mind.

"After you." Von "The Icon" said laying his palm forward in a directive gesture.

"Did Uncle Von just dispatch two people"?? Kathleen Dane pondered aloud later on that afternoon as she watched the grainy footage of two corpses being pulled off a side street in the gloom and rain.

"I don't know." Andrew responded as he poured over his sealed brief case. "I'd like to think that even at his worst that my Brother wouldn't have it in him to do something like this."

"God knows that Aunt Eva and Charlie gave him more than enough incentive." Kate said standing there wearing a black trench coat over an expensive designer suit.

They were in Andrews luxurious suite surrounded by multiple expensive fixtures. It was dark outside, even for the pre dinner time hour, however, the beauty of their surroundings gave sufficient illumination to the otherwise dismal weather outside.

"I'm worried that they're going to file charges against him." The successful Barrister said.

"So you do think that he's involved somehow"?? Kate persisted, her level of fear rising to where it was causing her to feel nauseous, it was a trait that had carried over from childhood, whenever she felt afraid, she would become sick to her stomach.

"I don't know yet." Andrew answered. There was something in his posture that suggested that he might be trying to figure out what to do next. "I want him over here. I wanna talk to him." He told his Daughter. "But quietly. I need you to go over there and pick him up but I don't want him to know why. This is very serious, it's not a joke. I don't want any of what went on in this room leaking. The mindset is that you say nothing to anyone, and that includes your Mother, Nana, Papa, or Evan. NO ONE"!!!!
Andrew commanded.

"Alright, i'll go pick up Uncle Von and bring him over here." Kate said looking at the time stamp on her parking voucher. She still had an hour left.

Five minutes later she had reached the mall downstairs which housed a number of high end boutiques as well as a plethora of expensive eateries, clothing stores, and an art gallery. You would think that only millionaires could afford to shop here however there were less affluent shoppers.

The architecture was state of the art and boasted a triangular shaped atrium style glass sun roof that could be opened or closed when the weather got warmer, or became permissive temperature wise. The mall also served as a ped way to several underground metro systems as well as housed the entrance to four or five extremely bougeoir hotels that often saw a host of famous clientele going to and from its doors such as Robert Deniro, Al Pacino, Brad Pitt and Angelina Jolie, and most recently, Elton John.

"I'm going to my car." Kate reported to the parking attendant who had asked to see her voucher.

There were butterflies in the pit of her stomach. What if Eva and Charlie had actually driven her Uncle to do the unthinkable?? What if the legendary and heroic Von "The Icon" had taken the barrel of a gun to two people. She immediately thought of O.J. Simpsons Daughter Arnelle and realized that this was how she must have felt.

"Hello." Kate said responding to her ringing phone as she moved briskly to her vehicle. It was Evan, he was at Place Des Art and wanted to know if Kate wanted to meet him there for dinner.

"No, I can't." She said. "I have something that I have to do."

"Well, what?? Can it wait"?? Evan had asked setting his briefcase down on top of a food court lunch counter. He was rested up and at least to some degree, back on his feet.

"No, this is urgent, I can't discuss it. I'll have to get back to you later on." She said unlocking the door to her sleek black sports coup and sitting in behind the wheel. "I have to go. I love you." Shamrock said to her fiance.

When she arrived at her Uncles house she found both he and Alyssa in the kitchen making a very late breakfast. "Uncle Von, I need to see you outside for a moment." She told her legendary uncle.

"Alright." He said not in any frame of mind to argue. "What's goin on"?? He asked stepping into the hallway with his niece who looked deadly serious standing there in business casual.

"Dad wants you to meet him at his office, now." Kate said.

"Well, can't it wait until after breakfast"?? The Ontario Street Original asked.

"No, he wants to see you immediately." She demanded.

"I guess the bacon and eggs are gonna go to waste. Just a second." Dane said grabbing a shirt as well as his over coat. "What the hell is up?? Why so urgent"??

"Dad told me that he needs to see you." Shamrock said not wanting to divulge her Fathers reason for wanting to see his Brother.

When they got there Andrew was seated behind his desk mulling over a copy of one of his Brothers former psychiatric reports that he had filed on behalf of his elder sibling. The Report had David Danes name at the top and then a list of opinions that one of his Brothers former doctors had developed over a period of time.

"Kate, could you please wait outside." Andrew requested as his Brother took a seat centre stage before his desk. "Kate just showed up and told me that you needed to see me. What's goin on"?? The Ontario Street Original asked making himself at home opposite his Brother.

"Where were you when Charlie and Eva were shot last night"?? Andrew Dane asked seriously.

"Is that what the fuck you called me over here for, an interrogation"??

"I'm not only your Brother, i'm your lawyer." Andrew Dane said. "That fact alone stipulates that we have what's called lawyer/client confidentiality, but you already understand all that."

"I understand it, and I … … … … … … … … …"

"Did you kill Charlie and Eva"?? Andrew asked. "Never mind, don't answer that." He said making a waving gesture with his hand as if to absolve himself of the request.

"Charlie and Eva were the scum of the earth, whatever happened to them is as a result of their choices in this life, i'm surmising." David Dane said.

"Do you have an alibi for the time of the shooting"?? The suave intelligent Andrew Dane asked. They had come this far, maybe there was hope of getting his Brother to go further.

"I haven't watched the news all day except this morning. When did The Police say that they were shot"?? Von "The Icon" enquired.

"Witnesses reported hearing gun shots around ten forty five and eleven pm." Andrew responded.

At that moment there was a knock at the door, it was Andrews friend and firm partner Alex Whitney who had graduated law school with honours in Cape Breton Nova Scotia.

"I just faxed those papers to the client, so if you hear from him, let me know." Alex requested.

"Will do." Andrew said watching Alex back out into the hallway.

"I left the fight and then I went for a walk, I needed to clear my head." The bad ass responded.

"Was there anyone at all with you"?? Andrew asked taking notes on a small yellow pad.

"No, I was alone."

"Did you stop in anywhere?? A MC Donalds, a Dairy Queen, something"??

David Dane was shaking his head. "I actually felt nauseated so I didn't feel much like eating."

"Do you remember what part of town you went for a walk in, I mean maybe someone will remember you or be able to identify you." Andrew suggested.

"I spent most of the evening in NDG just walking up and down, as I said I needed to clear my head."

"This isn't good." Andrew said. "Two people that you had a beef with were murdered and you have no alibi."

"Yeah, why don't you ask them if they can provide you with an alibi, see if they can do any better." Dane both quipped as well as retorted at the same time. He was busy cutting a thread off of his jacket with a pair of scissors that he'd found in a jar.

"You think this is a joke"?? Andrew Dane asked disbelievingly, his skin was beginning to flush.

"Two dead ass holes. It amazes me that anyone would even bat an eye lash." Ontario Streets Last Outlaw said. "That woman, and I use the term loosely, was a walking bag of pigeon shit and Charlie wasn't much better. She can smirk all she wants now, only now she can smirk from six feet in the ground."

"Well, unfortunately The Police might not feel the same way."

"Yeah, they tend to get a little bent outta shape about these kinds of things."

Andrew could not fucking believe what he was hearing, and at this point he wasn't sure whether his Brother had done it or not.

"I'll see you later on." David Dane said. "I'm outta here."

The next night as the sun died beyond the horizon David Dane stepped onto Ontario Street to a chorus of cheers. They had come out from their homes, taken to the roofs of their cars, stepped onto their balconies, and even made signs and placards for Montreal's east ends favourite hero. VON "THE ICON"-MY IMMORTAL. One of the signs read. VON "THE ICON"-ONTARIO STREETS CHAMPION, VON "THE ICON" ONTARIO STREETS PRODIGAL SON!!! and there were a host of others.

"The emotional favourite." The seductive and alluring Alyssa said standing a few feet away. Then another familiar chant began, its over tones loud and nostalgic.

WE LOVE YOU!!!!! BEAT, BEAT, BEAT, BEAT, BEAT, WE LOVE YOU!!!! WE LOVE YOU!!!!! WE LOVE YOU!!!!! WE LOVE YOU!!!!!!!!!!!!!! WE LOVE YOU!!!!!!!!!!!!!!!!!!

"I love you to." Von "The Icon" said with a warm and genuine smile on his face. He truly adored the people of Montreal's east end and all of the nostalgia that these streets brought about, it seemed that each block held a different memory, a different story, or a different dream.

"It's good to see you." Dane said as Nick Monroe came over to greet him. "I'm glad to see you to Von. I'm sorry to hear about Lilly. I still remember living with you guys and what that was like."

"I still can't believe she's gone yeh know". Dane said sadly. It was on his mind all the time. It hardly ever left. He saw Lilly everywhere, over parked cars, through store windows, walking into houses etc.

"This city's never felt the same without her. She brought a magic to Montreal and to Ontario Street that isn't there with her gone. I felt it before." Von "The Icon" reminisced with a far away look in his eyes. No one and nothing would ever replace Lilly with him. There may be other women who were different, they may come in different shapes and sizes, but there would always and forever only be only one Lilly Chicoine, and she was bad to the bone.

"We should go in the bar and have a drink." Monroe suggested taking a cigarette from his pack. "In honour of Lilly." He said as Alyssa stepped into the back of a cab to meet a previous engagement.

"C mon Chris, let's go". The Ontario Street Original said following Nick across the open street.

Jonathan Dane hugged his youngest son as he walked through the door to his office. "Dad." Andrew greeted letting the "HI" that came before the "Dad" roll off of his tongue without notice as he patted his old man on the back.

"Hello." His Father returned, business casual as Andrew turned away and lifted a notebook from inside of a drawer.

Andrew was wearing a pricy suit and he straightened it as he sat down behind his elegant looking well paid for desk that housed a hand crafted blotter made in England as well as an antique lamp with gold trim running down either side in the shape of byzantine onion spires.

Andrew had always been close to his Father being both similar in nature as well as sharing a number of hobbies that included such interests as computers, the stock market, horse back riding, as well as antique cars. It was a positive that the two had these things in common because their conversations never got tired and could wilfully go on forever.

Andrew had never gotten over the novelty of seeing his Father walk through the door at night as a youngster nor that of being the apple of his Daddies eye having always been determined to please his Father or to achieve highly and make him proud, and in both of those areas, Andrew had surely succeeded. David Dane on the other hand, was the scourge of his Fathers psyche and loathed the ground that his old man walked on. There was no love lost between them, none at all. The two were enemies.

"How was your flight"?? The younger of the two Danes asked raising to his feet again with a gold pen between his thumb and forefinger. He was the picture of sophistication with an under appraised touch of class.

"Oh, it was alright. It was a bit bumpy as we came in for a landing but other than that it was okay." Jonathan casually replied.

"So, the funeral's tomorrow"?? Andrew asked tapping the tip of his pen against the side of his hand.

"Yep. Nine am, at St. Thomas Aquinas." He said.

"Yeah, i'll be there." The suave barrister said.

"Oh, Hi." Alex Whitney said sticking his head in through a crack in the door. He had known Jonathan Dane for many years and immediately recognized him as he walked into the outer office.

"Alex, good to see you." Jonathan said rising to his feet and rendering a steady handshake.

"What's he doin here"?? Von "The Icon" asked appearing out of nowhere, cool as ice. He had just said goodbye to Nick at the bar although the two were scheduled to meet up later on. "Look what the cat dragged in." David Dane said of his old man.

"C'mon you guys, not in my office." Andrew said preparing to get between thunder and lightening.

"When did he get here"?? Von "The Icon" asked gesturing toward his Father by throwing a thumb over his shoulder.

The Ontario Street Original was dressed to the nines, he wore a black leather jacket with an orange pin stripe running the length of each sleeve over dark coloured blue jeans and a black shirt with a V shaped neck over a silver choker. He looked like a stud in a high end porn flick Andrew silently observed, it also reminded him that his elder Brother had once been an exotic dancer.

"What in the goddamn hell are you doing here"?? Jonathan asked openly displaying his contempt for his oldest son. His expression was cold, evil, and miserable, classic sociopath.

"You wanna go rounds with me"?? Von asked legitimately issuing a challenge to his old man. "Oh, that's right, your wife might not like it if I beat the shit out of you."

"No, no. Not in here." Andrew Dane warned. "If you get violent i'm gonna have to call security." He said in the direction of his older sibling.

"It's nice of you to remain impartial." Ontario Streets Last Outlaw said.

"You can't be aggressive in my office. This isn't an alleyway." Andrew scolded.

"I hadn't noticed." Von "The Icon" said sarcastically. "I think i'll come back later. Happy trails." The bad ass in black said turning and walking away.

"Who's that"?? Louis asked stepping out into the dead air rolled morning heat that had drifted in across the old port, turned south and shifted back across the harbour.

"Lean mean Nesrine. How you doin"?? Von "The Icon" greeted as the seductive Moroccan born Montreal bar tender lifted herself from the seat of her Porch carrying an over night bag in her right hand.

"I didn't get out of the house until after ten this morning. I figured we would talk and then go grab breakfast." She said placing a cigarette between her perfect lips and firing up as she looked off in the direction of the writhing sea.

"I think that both of the people at The Vacuum have had quite a party at your expense. I can see why you'd be up set." The Ontario Street Original said.

"The Vacuum," was an all night rave club popularized by a recently shot Montreal movie thats over all bank roll had ties to organized crime, heavy hitters.

"What time is it"?? The irresistible Moroccan Goddess asked removing her over sweater to reveal her voluptuous upper frame, she had never met a man who wasn't eventually in love with her.

"It's half past eleven." Louis responded placing a cigar in his mouth.

Louis and Von "The Icon" had been friends for years, at least during the years that Louis was not in Prison, last time The Bikers had nearly cut his throat. Making it out alive was a talent.

"Which of the clubs two liaisons was open for business this early"?? The Ontario Street Original asked having heard enough from Nesrine (Pronounced Nazarine) on the phone to break both representatives legs, she had been rattled, really worked and they had made it sound like they were going to kill her.

"Um ... ... I think one of them told me his name was Massoud." She said.

Von had screwed up his face already matching her physical description of The apparent Martial Arts whatever to the name that she had just spit out. "Massoud, this dude about five ten, hundred and eighty five pounds, black hair, dimples with an accent"?? The Ontario Street Original asked.

"He wears like a gold medallion around his neck off of a choker." The frightened Moroccan chick went on. She was sitting on the edge of the car seat now with her knees locked together as she puffed away on a cigarette. There were drifts of white smoke hung in a cloud above her head.

Von had stepped close enough to Louis to speak discretely into the convicts ear. "Louis, I know who Massoud is. He's one of Max's friends. We know each other very well." The seasoned street fighter said squinting harshly. He looked like a ticking time bomb, Nesrine registered.

"Max from your old building"?? Louis asked contemplating the retirement of his stogie.

"One in the same." Von said leaning in to kiss the adorable bar tender on the forehead. She was still shaking. "Okay angel, here's what you're gonna do. I need you to go back to the club with us so that you can go inside and get Massoud to open the door. You tell him i'm here, then we're gonna go in and talk to him."

"Why would he let you in"?? She asked.

"Because he knows me." Von said finishing what he had to say as he removed his leather jacket and tossed it onto the seat of the car.

Nesrine had slipped inside the darkness at The Vacuum unnoticed. It was obvious right away that someone had over looked the back door when locking the place up allowing the sexy bomb shell to enter sight unseen right below the clubs rear alley marquee.

In the centre of the room below the visceral drop off there were a cluster of voices marked by a familiar deepening belly laughter that both Von "The Icon" and the beautiful Nesrine had heard many times before. It was unmistakable in both tone and character, sinister laced with sadism.

"Hail, hail, the gang's all here." Von "The Icon" said rising out of nowhere with a 9mm Beretta in his hand. "Max, when the fuck did they hire you on to be their fuckin lackey"?? The Ontario Street Original asked, but the deep laugh had belonged to Massoud.

In secret, Von had always called him the black ninja because he was soulless and seemed to have not a single genuine shred of human emotion or compassion, and even when he purported to, Dane had in all legitimacy never bought the angle. Massoud was to put on, and there was heavy evidence that he had assisted in plotting with Max on several occasions. These people thought they were dealing with a lackey, how their poor judgement had come back to rob them of opportunity and advantage.

Louis was standing in the shadows now still finishing off his cigar, he looked like Robert Deniro on welfare. He wasn't wearing more than ten dollars worth of clothes, and if he was, then he had likely bought them from a thrift store. "I'm glad you brought this to my attention." Louis said. "Now I can go back and tell the ducks in the alley way what I saw." Deniro on welfare said of The Italians that he was associated with. "Don't give me a fuckin way out and i'll have you so dead by tomorrow at breakfast that they'll pour Ketchup on you." He proclaimed.

"You got any paper so I can write that down"?? The Ontario Street Original asked still training the cross hairs of the nine on all four men who sat before him. Massoud made five, but he was still standing, hands on his hips.

"This motherfucker tried to take something from me without asking my permission the other night." Nesrine said of one of the henchmen who was sitting at the table playing cards.

"Yeah, and i'll bet it wasn't a dime bag either." Von replied in a flat voice.

"I'm a fuckin bar tender. I make tips, i'm not a fuckin toy for you ass holes to play with." Nesrine said retrieving a Gloc 9 from her purse.

"Where the fuck did she get that"?? Louis asked.

Von pressed the barrel of the nine against Maxs temple.

"You stupid ignorant Canadians are going to get yourselves killed in here." Papa Persia said. He was all flight, mouth and balls with no common sense. Stupid arrogant son of a bitch!!!

Nesrine pulled her ball cap off and shook out her sexy main of hair. She was in her own right, a bad ass, sexy as hell, pure seduction.

"What the fuck do you want from me"?? Max asked. He was quivering a bit now. No more claims of holding two high end, hard earned black belts. He was a piece of shit.

"You're gonna become a shaheed David." Massoud said as Von began to back out of the room with Nesrine and Louis at his back, in that order.

Shaheed was a symbol of martyrdom.

"You fuckin clowns really think you're gonna do this on my turf and get away with it"?? Von asked. "Come see me tonight and we'll find out." He ended.

As spot lights from distant high rises swirled and swooned over Ontario Street that night David Dane stood alongside his niece, Claude F, and Nesrine who was holding a baseball bat in her right hand. It was dark, and most of Ontario Streets regular traffic had already ebbed for the evening because it was now past eleven o' clock. "We shouldn't have to wait to much longer. Max said they'd be here by eleven." Dane said leaning back first into the grill of Kate's sports coup. "They brought this on them selves." Shamrock said turning to walk toward the window of her vehicle. When she got there she reached in and twisted her keys out of the ignition.

"Ye know a few weeks ago Massoud and I were sitting face to face in a Coffee shop. I think that he wanted me to be afraid. He took a piece of note pad paper and started scribbling on it. He told me to stop saying a certain word, to me it was like a form of trying to gain control. I ended up telling him right to his face that I wasn't afraid of him which didn't seem to suit him to well. I think people like Max and Massoud thrive on fear. They should be booted the hell out of here." The Ontario Street Original said as he looked off into the distance.

"I am sorry that Lilly was go." Claude said during an uncharacteristically sensitive moment. He was usually as hard as nails, and he was here tonight, like himself, as usual, no fear.

"I know you both a long time. It is not good I see you like this." The Man With The Moustache said. "I am sorry." Claude said with great dignity pulling a cigarette from the pack.

"Thanks Claude." Dane said as he stepped slightly away from the grill.

"Here they come." The sexy Nesrine said as a limousine rolled toward them and came to a halt, it's head lights brightened like shimmering diamonds in the night and then died off in the blackness.

"Papa Persia." Dane greeted flatly.

As he said this Massoud made his way around the exterior of the car and came to a halt in front of The Ontario Street Original. "David, I wish I could say that i'm happy to see you but i'm not." He said menacingly and then did his evil ninja laugh thing, the one that should have appeared in an after hours film noir.

Two more henchmen were filtering in around The Founding Father Of The Ontario Street Originals now trying to see if they could rattle him, no such luck, he gave no sign of a response.

"These your goons"?? Von asked as Claude leaned in toward one of them and did that funny thing with his eyes that made him look bloody insane enough to scare The Devil to death. "I think you are go." Claude said to the grimy looking African American gang affiliate.

This was obviously someone that Max had fished out of a local dive bar, one of his Fifty Cent rope chain rip offs, a punk but the best that Max could afford on his salary.

"Max, I should kill you first but that'd spoil most of the fun. Nah, i'm gonna wait, and then i'm gonna drop your ass like a brick covered in blood." Dane said directing his comment to his left.

"Kill him Massoud." Max ordered as Massoud took a step forward in The Immortal Von "The Icons" direction. He was shadowed by a bigger dude with a paunch and a brown suede over coat. Same guy that was in Tim Hortons with him, couldn't walk or something, fat tub of shit!!!

This was going to be no easy mark. Massoud was a highly trained, highly qualified Martial Arts Instructor. He had taught members of The Iranian Military to kill, probably Satanically, brain washing shit. You couldn't trust any one of them, not after that.

Dane on the other hand had never been much of a Martial Artist, but he was an experienced and dangerous street fighter not to mention a boxer.

"Bah"!!! Massoud said as he struck Dane across the face with a crescent kick.

"C'mon Uncle Von, get up"!!! Shamrock yelled as Nesrine swung the baseball bat at the guy in the suede coat. Her ball hat that was pink and blue read "BITCH" in bold lettering.

Max, the blow hard, coward, was watching the whole thing as he smoked a cigarette.

There were people filtering out of their houses now as Von "The Icon" rose to his feet with a gash on his forehead trickling blood, open enough, slightly blinding.

"Fuck you buddy." He said attempting to connect with a failed right cross.

Claude had decked the Fifty Cent rope chain punk with a right hand dropping him to his knees.

Dane swung again, this time connecting with a vicious left hook that sent Massoud sailing against the back door of the limo, his striped white shirt was now speckled with blood but he was far from done.

At that moment Max reached for David Danes collar but Massoud got there first placing The Ontario Street Original in a wicked head lock, tightening his grip.

"He's not gonna give up." Nesrine said eye balling Sayeh who had just stepped out of the limo wearing a grey cloak and jadore over blue jeans and white sneakers.

"The Immortal Von "The Icon" would ne-ver give up, excuse me." One of Danes detractors said from the side lines, invisible to the eye.

"Bring about vengeance for Iran Massoud." Max hollered.

Massoud was behind Dane now holding him in a rear naked choke. It was very easy to die when placed in a hold like this, you could very easily asphyxiate because the hold cut off the oxygen to your brain.

Been here before, Dane said to himself. Step back, which he did and flipped Massoud over the rear of his shoulder and onto his back knocking the wind out of The Black Ninja who immediately stood back up, posture regained. He was like a fuckin cat!!

There were Canadian Flags and Fleur De Lis sailing everywhere now. Dane loved French Quebecers, they had always been good to him, and treated him as if he were one of their own. He would never forget them for that, particularly the ones who had been members of The Ontario Street Originals Street Gang, and there were a few.

As Massoud stood up again he and Dane began to trade a series of heavy blows each fighter landing a number of punches on the other, but this was not about fighting, not about blood, but about national back bone and pride, and in his mind, The Iranians had assaulted his.

Just then Max grabbed Von "The Icon" below the elbows in an attempt to restrain him.

The chants were deafening now, "VON "THE ICON," beat, beat, beat, beat, beat. VON "THE ICON."

As Dane was struggling to break free he looked over his shoulder and saw a friend that he did not expect to see. It was Montreal Wrestling Legend Triple X SEXXXY EDDY. "Whoaaaaa"!!!!! Eddy yelled as he hit Max square in the head with a drop kick.

Von had never seen Eddy look so lethal in his life. They had decimated his friend, decimated his flag and now THE SEX EXPRESS and THE IMMORTAL VON "THE ICON" were going to STAND TOGETHER against this Iranian onslaught.

Now Von "The Icon" and Massoud were toe to toe again. "Thanks for coming to the party." Von said to Eddy over his shoulder. The two friends went back fifteen years to a nostalgic time. Now, here, on this night, they would fight for their country together.

"I just picked up your text an hour ago." Eddy said as Von show boated moving fluidly around Massoud who looked off his mark and completely confused. He had never seen such unorthodox foot work in his life. Dane was dancing like Casius Clay, a technique that had left a number of past opponents confused and off their guard.

At their backs Kate "The Gate" Shamrock delivered a deadly spinning back kick to Sayehs temple knocking her out cold. "Fuck you BITCH"!!! Kate yelled.

"C'MON VON"!!! Nesrine yelled swinging the ball bat into one of the henchmens chest as Massoud sent Dane sailing back first into a line of metal trash cans with a spinning back kick.

As he was lying dazed on the ground all he could see was shadow. Now there was a gleaming as his Uncles image came into focus in the darkness behind his eyes. His medallions were shimmering as he stood there in his well pressed Canadian Military Uniform. "C'mon son. You have to get up." The high ranking Military commander said.

Dane was rising to his feet as Massoud was beginning to walk away.

"Hey yo Massoud." Von "The Icon" said raising a finger in the air as if to halt the martial artist from leaving. "I didn't hear no bell. One more round." Dane said borrowing a line from the legendary Rocky Balboa.

At that instant Massoud began to advance on The Ontario Street Original but got the surprise of a life time when Dane opened up with a series of heavy lefts and rights to Massouds skull opening nearly every section of his face. "FUCK YOU BUDDY"!!! The hard as nails thug hollered in a rugged voice and then chambered his left fist that was wrapped in a fingerless cut glove.

The Canadian flags sailed in the wind again, rippling, flapping at the edges.

"Von "The Icon." King Shit Bad Ass." Someone yelled as Massoud fired back with a series of punches and kicks that sent Dane stumbling backwards at a distance of about five or six feet.

Not done yet. He's a human being. A voice in Danes head seemed to mutter as he almost fell backward against the breweries chain link fence. In his minds eye he saw himself and Lilly standing there on the Sunday morning that she had first decided to come to his house, the morning that had been so hot that neither one of them could breath. It had been sweltering, like the inside of a dream, and it now was.

"You can do it Boo. C'mon." Lilly said appearing out of nowhere through the fever and the sweat. "Do it for me." Lilly said.

As Dane looked up at the big round orange street lamp that stood at the foot of Haitian Claudes building, all of the memories, all of the nostalgia, all of the days and nights in a fever of emotions.

Now Von "The Icon" was swinging over and over for all he was worth. This time Massoud could handle no more as his posture began to weaken. He was deadly, maybe the greatest martial artist that Von "The Icon" had ever known, but he wasn't a hero, and he certainly wasn't part of Ontario Streets legacy.

One more day, one more hour, one more breath.

Through his daze he could vaguely, in dream like whispers, hear the roar of the crowd, of The Ontario Street Originals and Ontario Street regular cheering for him and booing The Iranians out of the neighbourhood. They were not welcome here.

Von "The Icon" was swinging through a blurred haze now as Massoud fired back. Then it dawned on him, one mistake ends the game. Draw his fire and let's go home.

SEXXY EDDY was yelling from the mist somewhere. Not done yet, he had floored two extras that Max had chauffeured in from up North, punk assed gang members. Eddy had hit one with a clothesline before lifting him to his feet and body slamming him to the ground, then he had curb stomped that mother fucker so hard that his teeth had flown out. They called that a smiley.

Dane stumbled back now and then all at once came forward ducking below Massouds guard and hit him full on with a dangerous left hook to the skull. He had thrown it so hard that he had almost knocked himself down losing his balance.

They were cheering now so Dane assumed that he had won. Somewhere in the glowing, orange, white vapour of Ontario Streets misty street lamps Massoud lay bleeding and unconscious as The Canadian Flag and The Fleur De Lis sailed hypnotically in the wind.

"For you Baby Bunny, for you"!!! Dane hollered as SEXXY EDDY came to embrace his tag team partner for the evening. The two Canadian Legends had done it, they had fought for their country and they had won.

"We did it." Von celebrated, blood covered, into The Sex Expresses ear.

Max was lying unconscious behind the limo. Kate had given him a blow to the temple with a crescent kick that had sent him head first into the car door, two black belt wannabe fucker. What a nobody.

Just then Kate came to embrace him as Nesrine watched on from feet away. The gorgeous, seductive bar tender who was a whizz with men was smiling. "Not bad Mr. Icon." She said. "Drinks on the house for awhile."

Dane waved to her over Kates shoulder.

Minutes later "WHEN WE STAND TOGETHER" by Canadian Rock Band Nickleback blasted over the bars loud speakers as THE IMMORTAL VON "THE ICON," SEXXXY EDDY, KATE "THE GATE" SHAMROCK, CLAUDE F, and NESRINE entered The Black Domino Tavern to a round of applause from their countrymen. They were heroes tonight, and if all went well, would still be years from now.

Instinctively, Nesrine took her place behind the bar. She couldn't help herself, it was second nature, very old habits died hard and bad asses died even harder. "What are you drinking Von"?? She asked the battered and bruised world legend who was close to rocking on his feet. "If I had my way, your kisses, but tonight, i'll have whatever you have behind the bar." THE IMMORTAL ONE said as SEXXXY EDDY came over and put his arm around his friend like a brothers neck.

"If you take your clothes off in here we will not be invited back." Von "The Icon" joked as he stoked the fires of Eddys gimmick. "Hold on, my Brother's here." Dane said looking over Eddys shoulder in the direction of the door that had just flown open on the far side of the room as WHEN WE STAND TOGETHER BY NICKLEBACK played on.

The bar was awash in a sea of red and white and white and blue. The Canadian flags and Fleur De Lis were everywhere. National pride was paramount tonight.

"Good of you to come." The Ontario Street Original said embracing his younger Brother.

"Yeah, well, you know how I am about these things. I can't resist." Andrew said ironically. Nothing could have been further from the truth. Andrew hated events such as these and was like his

Father more of a private person. "Alex is on his way over. He should be here soon." The Barrister said.

"Oh, Andrew, this is Claude." Dane said introducing his comrade to his Brother.

On the other side of the bar Kate was carrying on a conversation with Nesrine who was (besy-inside joke) busy making drinks. "This is my Daughter." Nesrine said proudly displaying a picture of the adorable dark haired three year old that she had given birth to.

"Aww … … …" Kate responded. "Little Princess." She said.

Another irony of the evening was that Eddy had once wrestled for a company up north that was run by Smith Hart who was the Brother of Canadian National Icon Bret "The Hit Man" Hart who was Danes idol and hero.

"Thanks Eddy." Von "The Icon" said as he shook hands with his Brother from a different Mother who was walking by with a beer in his hand. "Anytime bro. Glad to have been able to help out." He said turning and walking out of view. It had been a long time since THE IMMORTAL VON "THE ICON" and TRIPLE X SEXXXY EDDY had fought tooth and nail side by side. They were an unshakable team, and one who shared a truly close friendship. Von trusted Eddy, and that was a boast that he made regarding few.

"So, you're Vons niece"?? Nesrine asked pouring Kate a glass of Ginger Ale. "You're Uncle and I go all the way back to 2004." The sexy bar hostess said over the noise of the music and the crowd. "He used to stay with me at the diner all night to protect me during my shift. He always used to go out and buy me Red Bulls when I got to tired to stay awake." The Moroccan Goddess stated.

"Uncle Von is my hero, both he and my Father." Shamrock said taking a pull from her glass of soda.

"What do you want to drink"?? Nesrine asked Claude F who was stalking his way around the perimeter of the bar now. "I'll drink may be one Budweiser." The Man With The Moustache said as he gave the seductive Nesrine a quick once over. "It was may be a good night for us." The French Man said directing his words toward the Canadian Moroccan beauty who had turned away to fill a picture with beer at the tap.

"I think so." Nesrine responded handing Claude an open Budweiser.

The night had gone very well for The Canadians indeed ... ...

Cyril Mathews turned his head to look out the window at his well groomed atrium. He had been waiting all day, this moment, this hour would bring him a financial wind fall the likes of which he had never seen. "When she's brought in the back door I want her lead straight to the chamber. No detours." He said petting his doberman "Max" on the head. "This is her last day on earth. I don't want her to get cold feet."

"I'll see to it." Reland Timmons said obliging his masters orders.

"We have the ether that we need to do the scene. I want Monster wearing gloves because we all know why this girl has agreed to give her life. If any member of the camera crew isn't aware then they should be told that Samantha Wilcox has Aids and is also suffering from an unrelated terminal illness related to the deterioration of the spinal column. Talk about bad luck." He said in his trademark straight voice as he lead the way to the shadowy room where Samantha Wilcox would spend her final moments staring at the blade of Monsters machete, fear in her eyes, clinging to life.

"We're ready whenever she gets here." One of the invisible camera men said from a darkened corner.

At that moment Samantha Wilcox power walked through the back door and rounded a corner with her sister and Danno Santiago in tow. She was obviously high which was evidenced by the recent Coke residue that hung below one of her nostrils.

"Tell Monster that she's here." Cyril Mathews said in an unintentionally sinister voice.

"I'm hard." One of the cameramen muttered as Samantha Wilcox began to disrobe in front of one of the chambers shadowy mirrors. The smoke machines were rolling.

"So, I here you wanna fuck me." Samantha Wilcox said as she read from the script on the teleprompter.

Monster said nothing waiting moments as he took stalk of his prey. He was kneeling on the bed wearing a leather mask and holding a machete in his right hand, his grip like iron. His heart, inside and out, was black.

Breathing coming from the mask.

"Put your penis in his mouth." Cyril ordered.

Samantha did as she was told as most of the camera crew began to jack themselves off periodically stopping so as to pace themselves before the final scene, they wanted to save it, have it ready for the moment when Monster sliced her in half with his over sized knife.

There were clouds of grey smoke everywhere amidst the wicked temperate blackness of the chamber.

"Tell him that you want to die." Mathews ordered in a horrible voice.

Samantha paused for a moment glancing over at Cyril, the Coke had hardened her to any and all sense of her own emotions as Coke usually did. "I want you to kill me." She finally whispered to the close room full of throbbing erections.

Behind a two way mirror on the far side of the shoot was Jacky Hannah who was stroking her boyfriends penis with her right hand, readying him for climax.

"Bring the doberman in. I want the doberman in the scene." Mathews ordered one of the boom operators who was wearing a black ball cap over white runners..

In moments the thin devilish looking K-9 was lead into the room on a shiny silver leash.

"Sit Max." Cyril ordered as Monster terror fucked Samantha as she lay on her back moaning.

"Place the oxygen mask on her." Cyril demanded turning a valve counter clockwise in the far corner of the room in this wicked chamber of nightmares, cranking up, the machine was now breathing.

Monster did as he was instructed placing the mask over the girls mouth and readying his machete as the ether was pumped into her system, into her lungs, into her brain as if the final seconds of Samantha Wilcox's life were being counted down as though on a scale.

"That's enough. HIT HER"!!! Mathews demanded.

In seconds Samantha Wilcox's body was hanging in sections in three different directions. Monster had used his tool of choice to stop the algorithms of life hacking her in several different directions with his weapon of choice that now dripped with crimson fluid.

"Oh God." One of the camera mens voices echoed as he vomited all over the floor.

"At least you guys will be taken care of." Samantha's voice resonated in the recesses of her sisters twisted brain as Danno came in her hand. "Yeah." Jacky responded to the memory from last night. "And now they'll bury you so deep that no one will ever hear from you again." She said as she shook her lovers semen from the palm of her hand.

"Put the pieces in a bag." Cyril Mathews ordered his crew. "We'll burn the rest of her out back after dark." He said as Max teased at the blood with the tip of his long slender tongue.

"Did that turn you on baby"?? Jacky asked turning to view the euphoric expression on her lovers face. If she were to guess she would have believed that was the best orgasm of Danno's life. He was playing with himself now, still limp, but he was holding it.

"Let's go home. I wanna see the tape." Danno Santiago said. "I've never been so turned on in my life."

"Let's go." Jacky said.

"You gonna pour me a glass of Champagne"?? Leilani Dane asked her husband who had just come home from work. He hadn't even put his briefcase down when she'd come to the door dressed up and surprised him, as always, dressed to the nines and fine wine.

"Aw … … that feels good." Andrew said laid out on the couch with his eyes closed. The back of his head was resting comfortably against the back of the sofa. He had had a wicked headache all day and Leilani was massaging his temples, it was doing him wonders.

"I love you." He said. "I love you even more for having taken that acupuncture course. It's weird science, but it helps my headache go away." He said with his arms relaxing on the arm rests.

"I do a special toe and foot massage that I learned from one of my girlfriends as well." She said reacting to the relaxation that her massage was bringing to her husbands brain stem.

"Go bring me the Champagne." Andrew Dane said in a voice that was near sleep.

"Later on. You need to rest."

"Have you heard from Kate today"?? Andrew asked, trying to get in one last verbal stretch.

"Earlier. She called from the gym."

"How is she"?? Andrew enquired reaching forward to grab the channel selector, but in the back of his mind what he was really thinking about whether or not his older brother was going to be charged with homicide, not one, but two counts, a double 187. Had Davids uncontrollable rage finally caused him to kill two people, to shoot them dead in cold blood??

"Kate's fine. She's gonna drive over here in the morning so that we can all go to the funeral together. We'll take my car." She said squatting in heels before her husband. "Get some rest. You had a long day. You can sleep here, i'll see you in the morning." The Oriental Canadian said tucking her husband into his make shift one night only bed. "I love you. Go to sleep." She said switching off the light. "Sweet dreams."

"I saw the video file this afternoon." The altered voice echoed over the computer screen, ending in segments before crackling to life again like a fire that had died down. "It's how many times … … … …"

"You're breaking up." Cyril Mathews said on the other end as he tapped the edge of the monitor. He was wearing a black robe and drinking from a hand crafted goblet that sat atop his luxurious desk. Max lay next to him on the floor.

"When he killed her … … … … … The shadow said attempting to restore the feed on his own end.

"You're the one who owns Night World Productions, so if you liked it then both Monster and I are happy." Cyril said, his wicked smile brightening.

He was wearing ruby red lip stick, like a drag queen, but he was in no way shape or form gay. He wore the shade that he wore to please his master, the one below, that's what all of this was about, saving your servant, kill and receive.

"I've seen both video files on the private server." The owner and financier of Night World Productions said through voice modulation. "I saw him kill the other one, before her." The shadow said of a previous snuff film that Monster had starred in. It had made a quarter of a million dollars in underground revenue, it even had a title-Daddies Little Girl.

"I was in the room when Monster and Melanie shot that scene. She bled out so badly that you could smell the copper all over the walls for a month." Cyril remembered. "The chamber never smelled the same after that. We had to bring a private cleaning crew in and pay them extra. We told them that the room was used for shooting porn and that the copper smell was decay." Mathews said widening his eyes. "I think I said something about the pipes rotting in the walls but it wasn't an easy sell."

"I want to see the figures for this one after it hits the streets and the private sites for a month. We can sell them to the market in New York and Brazil for five thousand dollars each." The sinister shape said clothed partially by a velvet curtain with pleats in it. The voice continued in modulated form.

"I want to see a million dollars ... ... killing was graphic ... ... head off." ... ... The voice of evil came in segments.

The room smelled of sweat on the shadows end.

"Maybe next time we'll fly you in to watch Monster work live." Cyril Mathews said throwing Max a section of raw meat. "I know that the two of you have never met face to face before." He said taking a pull from his goblet of fancy red liquor.

"Not about passion ... ... my money ... ... none of what's done matters ... ... as long as ... ... paid." ... ...

"I get aroused whenever I watch Monster work. Night World Productions wouldn't be the same without him. I love to watch his long cock slide in and out of the girls before he butchers them. It's the fear that's exhilarating. I love the moment just before they breath for the last time, the look in their eyes. I enjoy the terror." Mathews confessed.

He could feel himself becoming erect just imagining it all again, seeing every stroke of Monsters hardened passion, writhing, salavating, and then the blood.

"Monster brings in revenue. His killing ... ... art form." The financier of night said as his thin shadow twisted and distorted in a film like haze that looked like cigar smoke with dust swirling within it, like sunlight underneath a microscope.

"I know each tape ... ... for five grand over seas." ... ...

"We're going to make a killing off of it." Cyril said ironically as he placed an old fashion cigarette between his cherry red lips. He was himself a servant of Satan, even in his day to day life.

"Bring me her blood . . . . sister . . . . worth a lot of money." The shape said as the feed wrinkled and twisted amidst crackling static. "Bring me her . . . ."

"I'm losing you." Cyril said as he again attempted to rectify the technical difficulty.

"I'm signing off." The shape said, and then there was no signal.

Jason Ronin backed his sleek, black sports coup into the car port and killed the sound from its stereo system. It had been a long day and an even longer night, and he was tired. Things weren't going well, business was a struggle and there were more and more restaurants opening up within the neighbourhood providing a steady influx of competition from week to week, many of them had extravagant menus, and employed world renowned chefs, it took money to make money, and more money to keep up with that.

Beyond that there was paying suppliers, waiters, waitresses, bouncers, liquor licence fees and every other goddamn thing underneath the sun. If it wasn't one person looking for money then it was another, a steady fuckin stream of ass holes with their palms out making a nuisance of themselves.

That much worse was the fact that many of these restaurants were owned by Italians some of whose benefactors were questionable. There was always the concern that one might walk out back to dump the garbage and return holding two broken arms or a busted skull. Jesus Christ, what an industry.

Things were not taking shape as he had planned, and beyond that, there had just been two murders, one of which was that of a punk whose ass he'd kicked a few weeks back. Bad fucking karma, if the cops found out, they might start pointing the filthy finger at him.

One two, there's my shoe, three four there's the floor." The tall handsome chick magnet said underneath his breath as he withdrew a cigarette from the pack and fired up.

"It's good to see you." An old friend said coming out of nowhere.

"To what do I owe this honour"?? Ronin asked his long time comrade. "I'll bet that you're not here to provide me with any business opportunities." The tall good looking Martial Artist said.

"Nope, just thought i'd come by before I drop in on Von "The Icon. I haven't seen him in years." The clear blue eyed tough guy said in an upbeat voice. "I checked out his first book, and then his secretary called me and said that he wanted to get together."

"Von "The Icon" has a fucking secretary"?? Jason asked blowing rings of smoke into the sky.

"Yep, he's sure as hell come a long way from the time when he was feuding with that blonde goof with the dimples at The West." Tony D remarked. "I still remember him walking around town with his beard and his spiked hair. That all seems like a million years ago now."

"Yeah I remember that to. I remember every day we'd make these huge fuckin protein shakes in the blender then we'd lift weights and try to come off like a bunch of indestructible bad asses." Jason reminisced.

"Can I bum a smoke"?? Tony D asked enquired sitting down on a box that was set against the wall of the car port. He today, wore baggy jeans over multicoloured runners topped out by a FLORIDA sweater with a ball hat, that was FLORIDA the music group.

Jason handed him one folding himself onto the edge of his car seat. "Such a long time ago." He said and dropped his focus.

A sinister image of Ontario Street by night burned deeper into itself as David Dane tossed and turned inside of sleep, twisting, moaning fitfully, as he attempted to wake up in vein. In the dream there were cold vapour lamps casting their eerie shadow over the abandoned monochrome blue scene as fleeting shadows fuelled the neighbourhood of nights side streets and alcoves watching invisibly as the image burned ominously into itself another time.

"Everything here is closed down." A denim wearing Lilly Chicoine said peacefully as an unconscious David Dane stood before her, dreaming. "I understand why everything appears that way to you." He said with tears welled up in his eyes.

They were standing in front of the bar at the corner of Fullum and Ontario now, the one that Lilly had gone into to gamble on a rainy night so many, many moons ago.

"They won't let me use the slot machines." She said sadly.

"I know." David Dane said with tears streaming down his cheeks. "I love you so much." He said. "More than you can ever know."

"Do you think that they would let me in if I gave them a tip"?? Lilly asked. This had been one of her customary bribes in life, it was usually no more than twenty, but no less than ten.

Dane did not answer her.

"There's no traffic here fuck, how am I supposed to make a customer"?? The dead girl asked.

Dane looked both emotional and serious now.

"I can't see a single car." Lilly said.

Again, Dane was despondent.

"I would have given my life for you on that highway." Dane finally blurted.

Suddenly Lilly looked as if she'd been keeping a secret that had just been discovered. There was sadness all over her face, if not a hint of disappointment and shame. "I knew I shouldn't have come here." She said with a tear streaming the length of her gorgeous face.

"I don't ever want you to leave me again." Dane said releasing all of his tears. He was not giving up on her, not now, not ever. He would stay right here with her.

"Lilly." Dane said as he opened and closed his eyes, but now, he was all alone.

Jonathan Dane starred straight ahead as they carried his sisters coffin out of the church and placed it, chrome first, into the hearse. "Move over to the side just a bit." He requested as Andrew and Leilani did as they were asked making way for another group of people who were filtering out of the church in single file, dressed up, worn down, emotionally spent on nothing.

"Do you wanna take my car to the cemetery"?? Andrew offered standing there in a black trench coat and loafers.

"No, we can take mine." Jonathan decided, his expression full of piss and vinegar. He wondered if his eldest son had just sent two people to their graves in a fit of uncontrollable yet characteristic rage.

Today was a solemn day for Eva Nicolette's Brother, not sad, but solemn, for Jonathan Dane did not become sad, sadness was a state that was not within his range of emotions, he was more over somehow detached, cold or aloof like a piece of wood that had been left out behind the barn on a winter night.

Another of Jonathan's Sisters was inconsolable on the far side of the grave yard. She was with her husband who had white hair and a penchant for sports. It had been a long time since Jonathan, Andrew or Leilani had seen any of them, now here today, they would bury their son, cousin and nephew as well.

"Let's go." Jonathan Dane said heading for the black SUV that he had rented from Hertz Rent A Car.

"I should go over and see Aunt Eleanor. She lost her son today." Andrew said respectfully.

"We don't have time. You can see them at the Cemetery." Jonathan Dane commanded sitting in behind the wheel and keying up.

"Can I help you"?? Jacky Hannah asked turning to meet the figure who had just walked through the doors to her club. She immediately recognized him to be Von "The Icon," and at that moment, her phony as a three dollar smile evaporated.

It suddenly seemed as though all of the air had been sucked out of the room. "You came to see my niece at her last fight." The Ontario Street Original began with a wicked look in his eyes. "You told her that you had three letters for her. Well I have three letters for you." He said. "But they're not GHB. The three letters that I have for you, are D.O.A.." Von "The Icon" hissed venomously. "I'm gonna kill you" Von "The Icon" hissed.

Jacky was expressionless now, taking this all in. She didn't want to show the legend who now stood in her presence that she was afraid, intimidated or even rattled. She said nothing.

"I know that what happened to Lilly on that highway was your fault." Dane said as voices and moans of pain and effort rose around him. The gyms patrons were hard at work, blood, sweat, and tears.

"I'm gonna make you pay for it." He said leaning into her ear. "Your days are numbered." The Ontario Street Original said in as ominous a voice as Jacky Hannah had ever heard, there were blood tones in his pitch, the kind that you never provoked for fear it would cost you your life. He then turned about face and walked casually out of the club.

As soon as Von "The Icon" reached the street Jacky shrieked with anger swiping the contents of the gyms front desk onto the floor with a wild expression on her face. "Yeah. We'll see tonight mother fucker"!!!! Jacky promised.

CHAPTER 8:

That evening as darkness fuelled the night on Ontario Street everyone from Kate Shamrocks camp gathered at The Black Domino Tavern. The street was packed, and there were hundreds watching on from their balconies, patios, and front door stoops, they had brought camera's, made signs and even prepared murals.

As the night grew from dusk to shining blackness Kate and her trainer, Donovan O' Riley sat straight faced at a table in the bar, waiting, watching the minutes go by on the clock. They were expecting Jacky Hannah, and at two minutes after nine they got exactly what they wanted.

"This has gone on for long enough." Hannah said shadowing Kate who was seated in a plastic chair wearing a white tank top with the words- COMIN AT CHA emblazoned on it over green track pants and white runners.

Kate's focus was like iron, there was not a single, discernible human emotion visible anywhere on her face or reflected in her body language.

"I have some footage that I want to show you." Jacky said as Kate continued to stare straight ahead.

After about fifteen seconds Shamrock stood up following her nemesis to a neutral corner and looked her dead in the eye as if to signify that she was ready to view the footage, whatever it may be.

"I want you to pay particular attention to this." Jacky said grinning evilishly as she brought the screen of her cell phone into focus. What Kate witnessed over the next thirty seconds would change her life, give her the incentive that she needed, and haunt her forever.

As the image came into focus Kate saw a masked woman beating Lilly Chicoine to the ground outside of a tavern on the night that she died. The woman, obviously Jacky Hannah, was kicking Lilly in the gut over and over as Lilly lay writhing on the ground clutching her stomach.

Lilly Chicoine may have been a fighter in her own right, but she was no match for a seasoned Professional Fighter the likes of Hannah who was in far better shape and had years of in ring experience on her.

The sign atop the taverns sleazy looking exterior read-THE SNAKE PIT.

"Stop." Lilly yelped in pain as she clutched her wounded ribs. She was obviously in agony.

Kate's eyes were smouldering like The Devils crystals now. She had never been so violent within in her entire life. "You're a dead woman Jacky." Kate said ominously.

"So you're finally gonna step into the ring with me"?? Hannah asked with a trace of a seedy grin on her face, but Kate was stubbornly shaking her head. "Tell me something bitch." She requested. "Who the hell ever said anything about a ring"?? Shamrock asked leading the way to the street.

Outside Kate momentarily flexed her arms by moving them back and forth in an elbowing motion.

At that moment a black Jaguar stopped at the curb and Andrew Dane stepped out, but behind him, there was a shadow still seated beyond the passenger door. At that moment ONTARIO STREETS LEGEND, HERO, AMBASSADOR and KING better known to Montreals east end as VON "THE ICON" stepped into the street and began strolling toward the crowd to an eruption of cheers as he made his way to what would for tonight be called centre ring. Both Kate as well as Jacky's entourages were in attendance, part of which included Danno Santiago who David Dane was now eye balling, her trainer Marty, and the dirty boy who had first appeared at The Black Domino Tavern.

There were signs everywhere. They ranged in sentiment from KATE "THE GATE" SHAMROCK, PRIDE OF THE IRISH, to COMIN AT CHA!!!, VON "THE ICON," FOREVER MY HERO!!!, LILLY "CHICOINE WILL NEVER DIE IN OUR HEARTS!!!, KATE!!! KATE!!! KATE!!!, VON "THE ICON," EAST END LEGEND!!!, KATE AND VON, FIRE AND DYNAMITE, ONTARIO STREET'S LAST OUTLAW IN EAST END'S OLD WEST, BAD TO THE BONE CHICOINE!!!, WE LOVE VON!!!, VON AND LILLY TOGETHER FOREVER!!!!, KATE "THE GATE" AND JACKY'S THE BAIT!!!

"I'm gonna hurt you"!!! Jacky said throwing an opening punch at Shamrock as The Pride Of The Irish ducked and answered with a hook to the skull followed by a front kick.

"C'mon"!!!

"C'MON KATE"!!! A second voice echoed out of the crowd as Alyssa appeared out of the nowhere to cheer her friend on. On the face of it she was mad, but inside Alyssa was furious.

Jacky stumbled backward against the side of a car as Kate side kicked her in the gut.

"Cmon Irish"!!! Hannah taunted as she fired back with a series of jabs and rights to the face of the beautiful and exquisite Shamrock who was now charging her opponent shoulder first onto the pavement.

"Let's go Diamond Doll"!!! Von "The Icon" cheered as his niece crawled on top of Jacky and suspended her in a guard. "How does it feel to nearly have your neck broken"?? Kate asked as she improved the position locking Jackys neck in a scissor lock, pulling weight, putting pressure on the lowlifes neck.

"ARGHHH"!!! Jacky hollered rolling out of the maneuver and rising to one knee as Kate used her shin to skull kick Jacky back into the pavement.

"GET UP"!!! Shamrock demanded in a loud hard voice as as Jacky struggled back to her feet and delivered a wicked back kick opening a laceration above her foes right eye, lacerating her.

There was blood everywhere now as Kate fell to the ground and did a backward somersault into a standing position again. In her minds eye she saw Lilly being beaten to the ground crying and then imagined her being lowered into the earth in a casket. The image seemed to take her to a new place of focus, bringing her back, at least partially, to reality.

As Shamrock raised her left hand Jacky blocked her punch and delivered a standing side kick.

"Fuck." Kate yelped before answering with one of the most evil crescent kicks that David Dane had ever seen. It was five star, impressive, as was his niece.

"Why don't you see how you enjoy it" Shamrock asked as she hit Jacky with a flurry of blows before delivering another vicious crescent kick that sent her enemy face first through the passenger window of a maroon automobile.

The force of the impact was so powerful that it split the bitches right eye in half, partially blinding her and forever robbing her of something that she could never again get back. An eye for an eye.

Somewhere in the darkness "THE NIGHT" from the beginning of televisions MONDAY NIGHT RAW blasted through the intense shadow of the deepening nocturne, giving a big fight feel to the evening that had ended with Kate Shamrock getting her hand raised despite everyone believing that she couldn't lay a glove on Hannah, especially given the environment.

As Hannah turned around she took one more desperate swipe at Kate as Shamrock ducked and floored her opponent with a wicked uppercut sending her sailing head first against the side of The Black Domino Tavern to her defeat.

KATE!!! KATE!!! KATE!!! The crowd roared with approval but Shamrock was waving them off with her first finger. "No." She shouted. "LILLY"!!! She said expressing her love for the legend who had given birth to the night scape that was Ontario Street.

LILLY!!!, LILLY!!!, LILLY!!! The crowd roared.

"WE LOVE YOU BOTH"!!! A woman shouted at the top of her lungs.

As Kate turned around she saw her Father and her Uncle standing before her. As the crowd roared on for Kate "The Gate" Shamrock and Lilly "Bad To The Bone" Chicoine, Kate collapsed into the arms of her Father and her Uncle, the two men who loved her more than any others in The World.

The crowd roared on!!!!

"We did the ballistics report." Sargent Miguel Perez said as he dropped David Danes 9mm Beretta into a transparent evidence bag. "You're under arrest." He said as a second Police officer placed The Ontario Street Original in hand cuffs and then proceeded to read him his rights.

"Do you understand these rights as they've been read to you." Officer Daily asked.

"Yeah." David Dane responded as he was lead out the front door of his unit and into the hallway that was crawling with badges, two members of the media, and four other tenants.

"I didn't bag Charlie or Eva." Dane said as he bumped into Kate who had been on her way up to see him, her face was bruised sporting a heavy shadow that encircled her left eye and ran all the way across the upper bridge of her nose. Last night had been rough, no measure of easy would ever explain the way that she looked.

"Call your Father. Tell him to meet me at the station." David Dane requested.

Kate was to choked up, to emotional and to pain drunk to respond, however she had gotten the message and would do as her favourite Uncle asked.

Now, the Uncle who had loved her all of her life was in serious trouble. The predicament would call for the extravagant, if not the extreme. Her Uncle was an author not to mention a local celebrity. This was going to be heralded as a big media case.

"I love you Diamond Doll." Dane shouted as the two badges held his wrists in wait for the elevator.

By the time that they got to the debriefing room at the station Andrew was already standing outside waiting for him, he had a cup of Coffee in his hand and was texting a non responsive Alex Whitney who was likely still in court or busy dealing with something else that he could not simply excuse himself from, that or he had possibly left his phone in his office.

It had been running through his mind for days, even at the funeral, the spectre of his Brother being charged with the double homicide of his Aunt and his estranged cousin, and now, low and behold, right here below Gods hot sun, it had happened.

"Right in here." Perez ordered as Von "The Icon" was delivered through the doors of the interrogation room. He wore a thin black designer V neck over dark jeans along with an expensive silver choker that gleamed below the sterile Precinct lights. They had already confiscated his shoe laces and his cell phone downstairs.

"Alright, Mr. Dane, is your client prepared to give us a statement"?? Detective Harris asked.

"No, not at this time." Andrew Dane responded in an authoritative voice.

The Police knew all to well who Andrew Dane was, and they were not prepared to cross him.

"Andrew, it's Alex." Whitney said speaking to his firm partner by phone. "I saw your Brothers arrest on television. I'm gonna hop on the metro in about five minutes so i'll see you shortly." The successful barrister from Cape Bretons Whitney Pier said. Indeed, his last name was ironic.

"I'll send my assistant to meet you at the front doors." The esteemed Andrew Dane said spilling the remainder of his Coffee into the water fountain. He now faced the daunting task of having to explain to a jury how it was that his Brothers gun had been taken from his apartment and then returned, for given David Danes personal need for security, he most certainly would have been screaming it from the roof tops had he realized that his gun had gone missing.

"I got here as fast as I could." The heroic Kate "The Gate" Shamrock said forging a path to her Father who looked like he was about to keel over with exhaustion.

"Hi Daddy." She said pecking the sporty looking attorney in the expensive suit on the cheek. Hi." Andrew said with tempered anxiety in his voice. He was about to face the responsibility of a lifetime.

He had always been heralded as a court room hero, to some, a well dressed, poshly groomed court room pit bull minus a studded collar, but this was going to be goddamn difficult if they couldn't find a culprit to pin the gun theft and return on. Who the fuck would have had that kind of opportunity, who would have been in and out of there in a hurry and then back with the smoking gun??

"I don't believe that Uncle Von would do this." Kate said with a tear drop streaming the edge of her left cheek. "It goes completely against the image that he's always projected. When I was a little girl he told me that no matter what he'd protect me, no matter how fierce the monster. He told me that he'd never lie to me and that he'd never let anyone hurt me. That's The Uncle Von that I know" Shamrock said trying to stifle an out pouring of emotion by raising the back of her hand to cover her lips.

"He certainly loves you. He always has." Andrew said putting an arm around his Daughter so as to comfort her. The thought of his Brother going to Prison for the rest of his life was a double edged sword, first it would destroy David himself, and then it would break his little girls heart. Now, there was more incentive then ever. He would not, could not, lose … … … … … …

In the morning Alyssa put her feet up switching on the television with the universal remote control. No sooner had the picture come into illumination then she saw the footage of Von "The Icon" facing arrest right outside of his own apartment, complete with bracelets and a high presence Police escort.

"What the hell is going on here"?? She thought aloud. It was just then that the phone rang and Marcel was at the other end, he sounded vague, tired, and to some degree, out of patience. Star, Alyssa surmised.

"Oh, Alyssa, have I awakened you"?? The short, over sexed Frenchman began.

"No, i've been up for over two hours but I just saw Von getting arrested on TV." She said.

"Oh, well, it is very bad I think." Marcel said with a mixture of kindness and grave reality in his voice.

"I have seen Von in many situations but I don't think that he will do this." Marcel reassured her. "If you want I can drive you to The Police Station to see him." He offered.

"No, that's alright. I don't need to be around cops. I'll wait til they let him use the phone and then i'll see him whenever I can." She said. "I have a jacket, so I might need a lawyer."

"Do you remember me from Halifax"?? Rasta asked as Von "The Icon" was brought in to share the cell next to him. It had been a number of years, but Rasta had not forgotten his old friend. They had once been training buddies at The Y in Halifax. Rasta also knew Von's Boxing Coach Chris Markem as well as Robert and Richard, all had been friends.

"What makes you think i'd forget you"?? Dane asked in a teasingly hard voice. He then gave his comrade of over twenty five years a hug. "It's good to see you." He said.

"Fuck, it's good to see me, of course." Rasta said sucking his teeth jokingly and making his brown eyes wide. He spoke with a Caribbean style accent, but that was not where he was from.

"Where are you from"?? The Ontario Street Original asked. Even though he had known Rasta since they were punks he had never asked his friend his place of origin.

"I'm from all over." Rasta said anointing himself with the possibility of being from anywhere. "You are good boss. What the fuck are you doin here"?? He asked.

"They think I killed two people." Ontario Streets Last Outlaw said.

"Are they right"??

"What do you think"?? The thug life mogul asked. He had sat down on the cot in his cell and was now thumbing through a book that the previous tenant had left. "Cheap junk. He has no taste." Dane commented.

"What are you talkin about"?? Rasta asked gripping the bars with two hands and looking across at his long time comrade who had just stood up and walked over to the sink.

"Whoever was in this cell before I was." He said.

Just then Andrew Dane burst through the doors to Dane's cell block with Alex Whitney in tow.

"We need to talk, now." He said as soon as he came face to face with Ontario Streets most infamous prisoner. "They're charging you with a third homicide." Andrew said.

Danes eyes looked wild hearing this. "What?? Who"?? He asked.

"Clinton Marx." Andrew Dane exclaimed. They found his body a week before Eva and Charlie were murdered. The bullets match your gun." He said.

"I haven't fuckin seen Clinton since the night that he stabbed me." Von "The Icon" said incredulously.

"I don't know what the fuck is going on here, but all of these people were your goddamn enemies" Andrew said. "You're telling me that your gun either disappeared twice and was returned twice or someone had it all that time and then brought it back"??

"I have no fucking idea. All I know is that I didn't do any of this and they're trying to pin it on me." O.S.O said.

"The news papers are calling you The Architect Of Assassination." Alex Whitney proclaimed.

"That so." Dane replied.

"Didn't you have your eyes on your gun on a regular basis"?? Andrew asked probing for answers.

"Every single day I checked on its whereabouts."

"And it was there"?? Andrew questioned.

"Yes, every single day."

"This isn't going to make things any easier on you in court, especially if you testify to that. Tell them something else, tell them anything, that you weren't looking, but don't tell them that you were checking in on the gun all the time."

Alex was standing at Andrews back, taking all of this in.

"You think I haven't already figured that out"?? Dane hollered flipping over his mattress as if searching for what was underneath it, but there was nothing there.

"Okay, Andrew. You need to relax there b'y." Alex said reigning his friend in.

"Fuck, this is unbelievable"!!! Andrew hollered as he fished for ways that this could have all gone down without his Brother, the very man that Sade should have written SMOOTH OPERATOR for being involved.

"Was the gun ever out of your sight"?? Andrew went on with his line of questioning.

"Not for more than a few hours at a time." Dane said. "I have no safety so I checked on it regularly."

"This is the most incredible situation that i've ever been confronted with." Andrew exclaimed. "And my Brother's the one involved." He said.

That night in his sleep Dane saw an image of Ontario and Dufresne by night. It's sinister ambiance was accompanied by a distorted voice that told him of horrible things to come, it also told him that Lilly was in Hell and that she was suffering, in pain, and dreaming the owner of the voices nightmares.

There was a single extension of the glare from one of Ontario Streets vapour lamps and then the words- NIGHT WORLD PRODUCTIONS were whispered from someplace on the other side of darkness.

"You need to ask yourself why all of this is happening"?? The distorted voice asked. It was as cruel and evil a voice as David Dane had ever heard, pure unadulterated wickedness laced with ominous over tones.

"Why is this happening to you"?? The voice asked as an invisible camera made a circular motion around the abandoned street and then came back down again. "I see all that you do." The voice continued. "When you sleep I harvest your soul. One day you'll kill for me." It said as David Dane tossed and turned amongst the sheets.

When Dane awoke about a minute later he was soaked in sweat, bleeding from the lower lip, and badly in need of water. The room around him, was still.

Monica-I know that if you're reading this that you're probably up in Heaven watching over me. This is to some degree, entertainment, and you know that we were both horror fans. Knowing you I know that you'd want the horror element in this book to be as intense and as powerful as possible because that was your nature, there wasn't a lame bone in your body.

I often remember you commenting on Halloweens intensity, and how it was that element that made the series so great that we were able to watch the films over and over again, one night after another during our seven year relationship, and that we never got tired of them.

I miss you, I love you, and I think about you all the time, not just every day, but every hour. You have never and will never leave my heart or my soul forever, you own a very special corner there that is really more like a big huge open field with its own stadium.

I can see you in my minds eye now sitting in a Chapters or Indigo up in Heaven eating a slice of pizza and sipping on an Orange Crush as you leaf through NEIGHBOURHOOD OF NIGHT. This is your series, because without you there would be no URBAN RAIN and no URBAN RAIN II- NEIGHBOURHOOD OF NIGHT.

Because of you, and because of the years that we spent together the world will now have these books to read. YOU, have gone on to become the most famous person in your Family, and not a single soul living or dead can argue with that.

I'll always love you Baby Bunny,

I'll see you in Heaven

Yours Truly,
Von "The Icon,"
From-"The Ontario Street Original" To You
4 LIFE!!!!!!!

As dawn broke the next morning Kathleen Dane stepped into the courtroom behind her Father who was preparing for his Brothers bail hearing, as always he was dressed to the nines wearing a designer suit jacket over pressed dress pants and Italian dress shoes. It had been about an hour since she had heard from him, but Kate was reasonably sure that Evan would also try to make it in support her uncle as well.

Now, at the eleventh hour, Palais Justice in old Montreal was abuzz with everything from Family, to court reporters, to media, to Police Officials who had been involved in the initial arrest. The only person, conspicuous by his absence was The Legendary Von "The Icon" himself.

"All rise." The Judge said appearing before the bench and then sitting down. He surveyed the court room for a moment, and then asked all who were present to please be seated. "Good morning." He greeted fitting his spectacles over his nose as he examined the docket that sat in front of him with great interest.

"Let the record show that Council for Mr. Dane is present without his client." A female court official sighted as the attractive court reporter pounded away on her key pad. Also, allow the record to show that the honourable Judge Adam Williams is presiding."

"Council, will Mr. Dane be attending court this morning"?? Williams asked looking up from his bench in the direction of David Danes younger sibling.

"Ah, as far as I know he will be your honour." Andrew responded.

"You don't know whether or not your client will be attending"?? Williams asked with a puzzled expression on his face. Was Mr. Danes client to busy with a card game over at The Prison to be bothered attending court??

"Ah, i'm receiving word now that he's being brought into the courthouse." Andrew Dane said listening to his investigator who was in his ear.

"I apologize for the delay your honour, but as you know there's quite a media storm surrounding my Brother do to his fame in this city and because of the nature and the severity of the charges." Andrew explained, but in his mind, he was thinking that he was going to kill his Brother for putting him in a position like this to begin with. He was a lawyer, not a soda jockey, such behaviour was not deemed acceptable in the eyes of the court.

As the clock struck ten The Ontario Street Original was brought into the courtroom wearing street clothes below bracelets and leg shackles. They did not have Prison issue with respect to attire in Montreal allowing Prisoners to appear before the judge in their civi's. It was a policy that acted in the spirit of fairness thus allowing someone to be seen as who they were rather than branded as a hardened criminal or a thug, although many of the accused were.

Ron Spencer was also in attendance bringing forth even further media attention as he himself had also been touted as a media mogul as a well sought after legal eagle who had shown up in support of The Immortal Von "The Icon."

"In consideration of the charges as well as the severity of the crime, bail will be set at three million dollars." The Judge said. "Also, i'm imposing a stipulation with respect to the conditions of the bail should bail be posted. The stipulation is that Mr. Dane shall be forced to wear an ankle bracelet and remain under house arrest until the beginning of the trial at which time he will be remanded into custody." Williams said. He then brought the gavel down and adjourned court for the remainder of the day.

At this point I want to address the individual who was on the phone with me during the last conversation that I ever had with Monica. In the grand scheme of things, you're a punk. You crossed a world legend when you decided to turn my life upside down and do what you did. Your cowardice and unwillingness to handle things as a man has cost my Family, myself, and my friends more than we can ever get back. I DON'T RESPECT YOU!!!

You, whoever you are, never lived up to one days worth of what my late ex and I went through together during our seven year relationship. All you are is a lowlife flash in the pan interloper who came and went from Monica's life with all the rest never stopping to consider, even for a moment, all of the people's lives that you might be affecting.

I'm sure that whatever rat hole your in right now it doesn't matter to you that you precipitated one Families nightmare that no matter the circumstances you can't ever repay.

My Mother suffered, my Father, despite our stormy relationship had a massive heart attack, my now deceased uncle suffered, my Brother had to take time away from work to help us deal with the whole mess, and i've developed phobia's so bad that i'll never recover from them. I'm very fortunate that I had the lawyer that I did.

Thank you Ron. You're a star. I'm lucky to have had you by my side.

(Still addressing the punk)-I often wonder though. How could you possibly have so little self respect that you allowed yourself to appear so weak in front of my wife?? You have NO DIGNITY!!!

I'm a very easy man to find. URBAN RAIN is on FACEBOOK. You can always find me there. I'd love to have a conversation with you.

Regards,
Von "The Icon,"
Fr. "The Ontario Street Original" To You,
4 LIFE!!!!!!!

"We need to find the person who's in this photograph." Detective Drew Solomon said displaying a photograph for Roberta Clark who sat before him. It was late, and they'd been attempting to get Roberta to divulge something, anything that she knew for the past eight or nine hours.

"HE'S BAD!!! HE'S BAD"!!! Roberta finally shouted as tears sprung from her eyes.

"Who's he?? Who's bad"?? Solomon who was visibly perspiring asked.

"OLEND"!!! Roberta finally confided. "OLEND MARX." She said.

At the same time Kate "The Gate" Shamrock was stopped by an unfamiliar looking security guard as she walked through La Cites trendy mini mall to get to her vehicle that had been double parked for the past thirty minutes, it was also in a no parking zone so the ticket was likely to be heavy if she hadn't already been towed by The Auto Club.

"I'm sorry to bother you." The attractive blond female officer said. "When you were in here the other day I saw you and whoever you were with talking to Olend Marx. I recognized him right away."

"Okay." Kate responded through a slight frown.

"I'm assuming that you don't know who he is"?? The female guard asked twisting the knob on top of her radio. There had been heavy static, but now it had diminished to the point where it had become almost non existent.

"I used to work at one of the bus depots here in town." The guard began. "Me, everyone who worked there. We all know who Olend Marx is." She said. "Everyone knows The Devil."

Kates frown deepened.

"Olend is a very sick, very twisted old man who is likely responsible for the deaths of several young women and possibly even a five year old boy." Kristen Kyle said.

"Listen, I think there must be some mistake." Kate Shamrock said taking in what the woman had to say, disbelievingly. This was an eerie if not incredible revelation.

"No mistake, Olend is well known among all of us who were around during the time that these disappearances and murders were going on." Kristen continued. "I personally used to watch Olend sit and talk to these strays and runaways as they came off of the bus's from other cities, he'd give them a pep talk and then they'd walk out the door together into the night. It was right around the very same time that these same strays and runaways were turning up deceased."

Kate was shaking her head now with a puzzled expression on her face. "And you're sure this was Olend"?? She asked almost disbelievingly, it was hard for her to imagine that this seemingly sweet old man could really be such a sinister figure.

"The Police investigated him after the bodies turned up. We're the ones that tipped them off, but they could never find any evidence to link him to the crime scenes. As many years as went by we all knew that he had something to do with it. We also knew that there were rumours, folklore, about Olend selling these girls into snuff movies and pornography, then one night a little boy went missing right out from underneath our noses. When The Police did their investigation someone said that they saw Olend giving the five year old a lollipop outside and then walking off hand in hand with him."

"Oh my God." Kate said looking off to one side.

"They found the little boy two days later with his pants down and his throat severed. He'd been sodomized repeatedly. We all knew, we were sure, that Olend did it. As a matter of fact he used to do little things to let us know." Kristen said.

"What do you mean"?? Shamrock asked with astonishment sparkling and shimmering in her eyes.

"I'll give you an example." Kristen said remembering it vividly as if she'd seen it on a movie screen. As the image of Olend walking by her and making a throat slitting gesture with his finger tip ran through her head she explained what she had seen to Kate.

"We all know that he did it. The cops know that he did it. The problem is that no one can prove anything beyond a reasonable doubt." Kristen told her.

"What happens next"?? David Dane asked taking a pull from his can of Diet Coke.

"We try to figure out how your gun could have gone missing and then been returned without you knowing about it." Andrew responded making a lap around the room with a sandwich in his hand. He was starving, it had been at least fourteen hours since he'd had a bite of food.

"None of this makes any fuckin sense to me. I always had my eyes on that thing, how it could have just slipped out of sight and then been returned is as mysterious to me as a Hitchcock thriller."

"Yeah, isn't it"?? Andrew asked as he finished off the baloney and cheese sandwich.

Just then the phone rang. Kate was on the other end.

"Who told you that"?? Von "The Icon" asked as he looked out the big bright windows onto the darkening night outside. The sky in the far off distance, was an alluring monochrome blue amidst a few bruised clouds that seemed nestled to close together.

"Who the hell is Kristen Kyle"?? Von asked sitting forward with a look of bewilderment on his face.

"She's a Security Officer at LA CITE." Kate informed him. "She used to work the bus depots here in Montreal. That's how she knows Olend."

"That's the craziest fuckin thing i've ever heard."

"Where are you, at Daddies"??

"Nope, i'm at his office awaiting a Police Escort." Dane said. "Like they think I might actually get trigger happy with a gun that they've already confiscated."

"Uncle Von, you said you'd never lie to me." Kate reminded him. "Did you do it"??

"What do you think"?? The Ontario Street Original asked as he raised the can to his lips. "Did I go out and pull the trigger on three people?? Did I kill those three pieces of absolute garbage?? No, I did not, but someone sure as hell wants to make it look like I did."

"Is there any chance that you could have done it and blocked it out of your mind"?? Kate questioned.

"Is there any chance that Elvis is being stored in your deep freeze"?? Dane asked.

"Then we need to find out who did it and clear your name as soon as we can." Shamrock said.

"Ya think so"?? Dane asked twisting himself to see Evan Baker walking into Andrews office.

"Your future bow is here." Dane said raising himself from the couch.

"Why don't we try to have dinner before you show me who's in the other room." Cyril Mathews said to the shadow who now sat before him. "What did you do"?? Cyril asked standing up before the large Gothic painting that hung behind him on the wall. "Did you tell her your story, the one about your Father being a Preacher"?? He asked igniting a long thin cigarette. "They never know who they're talking to until they get here and see you wearing the mask." The short man with the long slender fingernails and the slicked black hair said. He wore nail polish, black.

"I told her i'd give her money. Said she was hungry, needed food." Olend Marx said wearing a tawdry brown blazer, pressed dress slacks, a hat, and black leather driving gloves. His expression was a mixture of blank and dreamy, his eyes were however, sadistic. They called him, "MONSTER."

"I know what you did for me that night, what I couldn't do for myself, the night that you killed Kelly."

"Your little girl." Olend said in response, his legs were moving back and forth slightly, as if there was tension between them, gearing up, getting ready, of course no one outside of the inner circle ever saw him like this. They didn't know that he was a pervert, a killer, as well as a child rapist, molester, and killer.

He had taken that little five year old boy down like a Christmas tree, right out from underneath the noses of his Parents who had been looking, and security, then he had done horrible things to him in front of the lens, and left him for dead in a trash bag.

"My Daughter knew to much. She had to be silenced. I wish I could have watched." Cyril said spooning Cocaine from a packet onto his fingernail.

"I touched her down to her most personal area before she died." Olend confessed. "She was very soft and very tender. I didn't rape her though, wouldn't have minded but I was to nervous."

"What did she say?? Did she scream"?? Cyril asked buzzing up from the Coke. "Was it hard when you touched her?? I've always had fantasies about her. She was my Daughter but I had feelings for her." Cyril fantasized. "That's why I had you kill her, because you're an extension of me."

Just then the screen on Cyrils laptop came to life through video distortion. It was again the financier of NIGHT WORLD PRODUCTIONS. There was a hollow sound like air suspended in a metal cage in the background.

"I want to see the figures after tonights performance." The altered voice that emanated from below a billowy black hood began. "I don't care what you do to bring in revenue, it brings me no pleasure, my motivations go far beyond the taste that killing or masochism brings to either one of you." The dreamless sleep said lurching forward. My voice modulator doesn't reveal who I am. You do for me what you do because I bring you money, but i'm not interested simply in money. My ends are far greater and more complex than you can ever imagine, and span a far more vast territory. Tonight, you will hear from me and at the same time I won't answer a single question. I'll contact you again after tonights show." The voice said before the connection died.

"Who are you"?? The eighteen year old girl in the other room asked. There was no one there but she'd been pumped full of drugs and was hallucinating. This would be the final two hours of her young life.

Olend had met her at a Coffee shop downtown fresh off the bus and told her that he would fill her pockets with money. She was a runaway whose Parents had done all that they could to sustain her but things hadn't worked out.

"Somebody help me." The young girl asked. "I need help. Please"!!! She begged as if her torturing had already commenced, yet there was still close to an hour of it to go, and it would be brutal.

Her wrists were bound and her blond hair was fanned out across the pillow that lay beneath her head. She was still, quiet, yet had moments of utter terror and sheer panic as the drugs took her up and down the ladder, in and out, here and there.

"I'm here now." Olend said revealing his fourteen inches of uncut manhood to her as he licked his lips through the straight slit in his bondage mask. "My name is Monster." He said climbing on top of her. "I'm your friend little girl." He said.

Danno Santiago had been contracted to carry out contracts from the time he was fourteen. He had been in and out of gangs such as The Shining Path, MS-13 and had once run drugs for Pablo Escobars cartel. Here tonight, the order was the same, but the man, and the name, who he was, was much different. The order was to cut the mans head off by using a jagged bowing knife at the request of the client.

Danno had been contracted by an unknown source who had solicited him through another associate of his who had asked not to be there when the contract was carried out. The name on the contract, so to speak, was a legend who was known as Von "The Icon," a name, a man whose reputation, Santiago had come to know all to well.

Danno Santiago stood in the hot, quiet shadows outside of Andrew Danes lush condo as he searched for a breaker box or a fuse source so as to cut off the power and kill the lights inside of the house, but in this shadow, he could find none, there simply wasn't enough light.

There was another man with him, waiting in the car. His name was Mohammad, and he'd been hired to keep an eye on The Ontario Street Original months ago.

Danno thought of the shivery impression that he'd gotten when he'd seen a tape of Mohammad, Massoud and four other men standing over an American Soldier as they read passages from The Sacred Koran. Massoud had been the executioner bringing the blade all the way across the soldiers throat as he snickered and sneered at the sight of the soldiers bleeding out like a slaughtered lamb. He was the executioner, the black ninja with the cruel heart. He possessed no remorse and lived for the sake of being wicked.

It was so dark now that you could hardly see the hand in front of your face. This was evil, plain and simple, and to Danno Santiago who had shed blood before, that was just fine.

Now, here in the coiling shadows he waited, but then there was something else, a call from the shape telling him to hold off for tonight with no explanation, he had simply vetoed the order with no rhyme nor reason.

When David Dane entered his Brothers living room the next morning he found Jonathan Dane sitting in the shadows putting away on his laptop. It was six am, and the sun had not risen yet.

Kate and Alex had returned home for the night, and were no longer present. They had all gone their own way, and now it was just the three of them, Dane, Jonathan and Andrew. Leilani was temporarily taking refuge at a relatives house as Andrew was not in favour of her being in the middle of the things that were going on at the condo.

"What the fuck are you doing back in Montreal"?? Dane asked aggressively eye balling his old man, he was not in favour of waking up to the sight of Jonathan Dane lounging in the living room adjacent to where he slept.

"I'll come and see my son anytime I want to you goddamn bastard." Jonathan said dialling in one more key on his computer.

"You trying to electronically impersonate me again"?? Von "The Icon" asked.

"I don't know what the hell you're up to, and I don't really care as long as you're staying out of my affairs, both figuratively and literally." Dane said recalling The Christmas morning with Lilly in the back of the car. "Why don't you go follow a yellow brick road." Dane asked taking a mug from the cupboard and filling it with Diet Coke.

"I mean, what fun is there for you in a house that you have no authority to oust me out of." Dane remarked as he flashed on a night where the Cops had been called to The Dane residence in Nova Scotia. The end result was David Dane being tossed out on his ear with H.R.P.D. in tow, and then when he had returned the next morning Jonathan had told him that in order to get back into the house Dane had to admit, against his own will, that Jonathan was right and that he himself had been wrong, and what a crock of horse shit that was.

"You keep your goddamn mouth shut. I'm so goddamn pissed off by everything that you've done that I could lose it right here." Jonathan said slamming his laptop shut.

"You know what they say about people in glass houses, they shouldn't throw stones, and your house has been made of crystal for a very long time." The Ontario Street Original said glaring in his old mans general direction. "I'll never forget the way that you treated Lilly that morning." Von "The Icon" said.

"I couldn't believe what I was doing down there."

"You had a month to think about it before hand, and then you sat there for the rest of the day after you brought her to tears and stared at her as though she were a sub human piece of trash." Dane said with smouldering eyes, and in them, was destruction for his old man. "You think i'm gonna forgive that"??

Jonathans expression was one of misery and disdain now. "What about all of the goddamn fuckin things that you've done?? You've thrown things, smashed furniture, you've threatened people. What the hell makes you so goddamn above it all"?? Jonathan asked sitting there in his pin striped suit and red tie. "I can remember one morning when I took you to see a Psychiatrist because your Mother and I were so concerned that you were gonna tear the house apart that we didn't know what to do about it. That Doctor cancelled one appointment after another so that he could keep talking to you until you were under control."

"Maybe you and Mum shouldn't go looking for fights with me. I've never created a problem in my life." Dane said returning a five hundred ml bottle of soda to the fridge. He was fed up, agitated, and lacking the patience that it took to deal with his old man this morning.

"You've done all kinds of things. You had everyone in our house living in absolute terror for years and you never showed any remorse for it."

There was a tinge of pale light filtering in through the kitchen window now.

"Remorse"?? David Dane whispered underneath his breath. "Since when the fuck did remorse become your strong suit"?? He asked moving purposefully in the general direction of his Father. Out on bail, no violence allowance, he told himself.

"You smashed things up around our house. You did all kinds of damage. You threw things."

"You want me to throw you"?? Dane asked glaring at his Father from across the room.

"Let's talk about all of the cruel, sadistic things that you did. When we went to The Keg for Hunters memorial dinner you sat there with a smirk on your face as if to say "I got what I wanted. Hunter was put to sleep." Dane said with tears welling up in his green eyes. "He was my best friend, and he was the sweetest angel who ever walked the earth." He said trying not to cave in to his emotions all the way.

"Hunter was sick. We had all kinds of animals when I was a kid and we killed them for profit one after another." Jonathan said flatly. "I've killed plenty of animals."

"Yeah, i'll bet you have. That was probably the genesis of you becoming a sociopath, having a feeling of control over whether or not those animals lived or died. That's why you are who you are today."

Danes Father had been raised on a farm and it seemed that to him animals were simply a means of making a living, but to Dane, killing animals in any venue was repulsive. It was to him, a crime that should have been punishable by lethal injection. There was no excuse, none whatsoever, for killing an animal or hurting one senselessly.

Just then Andrew came striding into the room carrying his expensive briefcase in his right hand. He immediately noticed that there was spilled Coffee on the floor.

"I didn't do that." David Dane said noticing the focus of his Brothers gaze.

"I didn't say you did. I had a cup of Coffee last night, maybe I dropped it there." The legal lycanthrope said.

"Dad was just educating me on the finer points of morality." The Ontario Street Original explained to his younger sibling. "Dad likes to blame me for every altercation that ever took place underneath our former roof."

"You pulled some shit in that house." Andrew said raising an authoritative finger in his older Brothers direction.

This was Andrews general position, that Jonathan and Marilyn Dane were right and that David Dane was wrong, but in Danes eyes, and in the eyes of most of The Mental Health Professionals who had ever interviewed the Family as a unit, David Dane was right.

"I can't believe that you don't see how outta whack you are when you make these statements." Dane argued. "You're as brain washed as a sleeper cell operative and you don't even know it." Von remarked in the direction of his younger sibling.

Jonathan Dane swallowed with his Adams Apple visibly moving up and down. He had become thin, frail, and grey since his heart attack, and it was well deserved.

"Fuck you." Dane said to his Brother who was shaking his head ironically.

"I heard you mention something about being ousted out of the house." Andrew mentioned. "I'm the one who encouraged Dad to kick you out that night." Andrew confessed remorselessly.

"Why the fuck doesn't that surprise me"?? Ontario Streets Last Outlaw asked. "It seems that the one hero in this Family is the one who always catches the brunt of it from his Parents and his younger sibling. How messed up is that"??

"You've got a big ego." Jonathan Dane said.

"Nowhere near as big as yours you fuckin neanderthal." Dane said heading for the plush beige couch on the other side of the living room that sat next to the venetian lamp.

"Now you see why I sent Leilani to her aunts house." The high end barrister remarked scornfully as he took a pull from a hot cup of Coffee. He was wearing a ten thousand dollar designer suit over five thousand dollar dress shoes and a Rolex time piece.

"What never ceases to amaze me is the innate self righteousness of those who deserve to be anything but. I still well remember the times when both you and Mum threatened to send privileged not to mention distorted information to those who had it in for me." Dane said referring to his Father and his Mother.

"You attempted to ascertain the receipt for a lawyers consultation so that you could hand it back to the lawyer because you knew that I was leery of him. As soon as I disclosed that the receipt was hidden in a DVD case in my apartment in Montreal you didn't want me going anywhere near the place. To this day I don't know what that guy was up to, if he was trying to scare me, teach me a lesson about giving people details of my or Lilly's back ground, or what."

Jonathan had reopened his lap top and was entering something on the key board now.

"I got so desperate when I was staying in that house that I ended up phoning a cop out of desperation and telling him my story, and you know me, I never call cops." The Ontario Street Original said.

"You weren't well when you were staying under our roof in Halifax." Jonathan said wickedly. It was as if he some way, some how believed that he could convince David that he was crazy against his own self knowledge and judgement. This was getting absurd.

"You were suffering from paranoid delusions." Jonathan said scornfully past the hanging veil of a raised eye brow.

"You know what's worse then having phobia's"?? David Dane asked. "Having people around you that have no scruples about doing everything in their power to take full advantage of those phobia's." He said retrieving an orange from the fridge.

"If it hadn't been for Mum being willing to fly me out here and get my hands on that slip of paper I don't know where the hell i'd be." Von "The Icon" stated. "I'm lucky that I was getting along with her then. And you're proud of yourself aren't you"?? Dane went on.

"Proud"?? Jonathan asked impatiently.

"Yeah, proud. You had a fax machine, computers, cell phones with internet access on them, etc and you knew that you could use those devices to hang the threat of electronic impersonation over my head while I was living in your house. Then there's the matter of a certain something else that you threatened to attach to a letter or two before in the past. You know which axe that is. I never should have let you file my taxes." Dane commented.

"Are you two gonna keep this up all day or is it safe for me to go to work"?? Andrew Dane asked.

"We're gonna keep this up all day." Dane said peeling a piece of fruit.

Danno Santiago was fuming. He had not only failed in his mission because of a contravening order, failed to collect a paycheck and failed to kill Von "The Icon" but he had failed his wife who was languishing in a hospital bed do to a staff infection, and now, she only saw through one eye.

"This is mine." Danno said licking the tip of his bowing knife. "I won't fail a second time." He said to the shadowy spectre with the electronic voice who now sat on the computer screen before him.

"His head ... ... the motherfucker of wickedness that he's become. No more stardom, no more books, I want him dead." The Dreamless Sleep said lowering his head beneath the shadowy veil of his cloak. "I want him to have nothing, and then to die in solitude. You have to kill him for me ... ... off his head." The distorted voice said breaking up.

"I get my money up front this time." Danno said snorting a line of Coke up his nostril.

"The things that he's done ... ... for him to live anymore. If he lives I only want it to be for a short time, no longer than he has to." The echoing distortion continued. "me the tape so I can watch him die."

"I'll send it to you live streaming if I can. Then you can see all of it. Tell me something. What did Von "The Icon" do to make this happen anyway"?? Santiago enquired with Coke residue smeared across his outer nostrils. "I mean I can't see your face, i've never seen it. Who are you anyway"?? Danno asked of the creepy distorted image that sat before him like a blurred pool of greasy oil.

"Not something that you need to know ... ... what I ask and you'll receive your money." The shape said. The frame was wavering now, as though losing signal. "You have a job to do. I want it done within twenty four hours." The shape said as it became a pin point of shadow and then evaporated.

"Hey, I don't know if I can ... ...

"I haven't had anything to eat since I got off the plane." Marilyn Dane lamented as she traced the line of her cheeks with the palm of her hand. She was dressed expensively, everything boutique purchased down to her designer earrings. She had done well for herself, indeed, and so had Jonathan. They had both bought into diamonds and Rolex's after they left school, the problem was the hanging burden of image that went with it. The things that we marry, the attitudes and guide lines that we felt the need to answer to, sometimes the burden was steep the cross to heavy to bare.

When Marilyn Dane was still dating she had met a man who had made her feel inferior about where she lived and about what her Father did for a living, she had shopped it, moved up in the world as a show of defiance only to find out that this walk of life had to be protected by a glass house. There were problems with kids who didn't agree with your attitudes, shattered the idealism of your image or went against the grain. David Dane had been such a child. He was strong willed and had a mind of his own even at a young age.

There in that vein was a similarity to the relationship that his late girlfriend had, had with her Parents. Linda Chicoine had once remarked that Lilly was out of control that and they didn't know what to do with her.

Lilly had been The Princess of Defiance of all on the planet earth with Dane following not far behind as The Prince, he simply could not, and would not be controlled.

For the Parents of both, it was in a sense like trying to baptize fire, that, and there were other clashing forms of behaviour that stood out against their bougewoire image.

In David Danes mind it was an inherent lack of street smarts that kept he and his Parents from seeing eye to eye on many matters. Danes beliefs, associations and values came from a lifetime of hanging out on the streets amongst drugs and thugs, hustlers and hoods while his Parents had lead a posh life of exclusivity and seclusion from Danes branch of society.

In the end, it was he and Lilly who had become world legends. They were the stars of the show amongst any and all in both their families despite the fact that they two had travelled the hardest road and faced the toughest opposition. The names of both David Dane and Lilly "Bad To The Bone "Chicoine would go down in history. (Authors note:- Credit goes to Von "The Icon" and the late Monica Mayhem).

"I could cook you my famous Lebanese chicken dish." Kate offered as her Grandmother removed her fine over coat and spread it neatly across the back end of the couch.

"Oh, I don't think i'll have anything to heavy before I go to bed. It might upset my stomach." Marilyn answered. She was now looking for her cell phone to call Jonathan who had disappeared from the house just over an hour ago.

"I could cook you some pan cakes." Kate offered as Evan strolled into the room carrying a newspaper in his hand. "Remarkable." He said. "Your Uncle is all over the front page. They're calling him The Architect Of Assassination." He said pecking Marilyn on one cheek and then the other.

"We're trying to do something about that." Alex Whitney said emerging from Andrews study.

"I didn't even know that you were here." Kate said upon seeing him.

"I took a nap for awhile while I was waiting for your Dad to get here but it doesn't seem to have paid off."

"The nap or the waiting"?? Shamrock asked taking a tiny bite from a cracker.

"Neither." Whitney responded incredulously.

"He should be here soon. It's getting late." Marilyn said smoothing her pant legs with the tips of her fingers. "He usually comes in at around seven when he's working late but now it's half past eight."

In one of the bedrooms in Andrews condo David Dane lay sleeping on the couch. In his sleep he saw Lilly Chicoine walking alone through a department store as he attempted to pursue her but he was unable to move, it was as if the moving image was to remain suspended from his touch so as to preserve the moment in whatever form of time or space.

He loved her. There weren't enough words in The English language or for that matter in any other language to express Danes love for Lilly, his eternal private dancer.

Dane had once expressed to his Mother amidst tears that if Lilly could rise from the grave for only a moment and agree to it that Dane himself would be willing to marry, and be monogamous to her memory. The time that they had shared, a moment of seven years that had been so emotional and so special to him would last a lifetime. It was, as Dane had characterized it, something that happened in the darkness of time. Despite everything, and all in all, his favourite atmosphere.

"I'mmm … … … … … … … going, I don't know where." Lilly explained to a store attendant who had noticed her loitering and stopped her. "I just showed up here I guess." She said. "Nothing personal. I just wanted to see what kind of clothes that you guys sold."

A few feet away, Dane wanted to cry out. There were tears in his eyes. Every effort that he made was impossible, fruitless, but not without merit. He could not speak. His vocal cords were not working for him. It was as if a higher force had momentarily silenced him.

"I can leave, I mean, if you guys are offended by my presence. I didn't come here to bother anyone." Lilly apologized dancing on her toes a bit with her hands held behind her back soldier style.

Dane wanted to hit the store attendant with a wicked left hook and drop the motherfucker so that he would leave Lilly alone but his efforts took him to only greater heights of futility. It was no use.

"I once bought a winter scarf in here." Lilly went on. "It was made of some kind of warm material so it kept me warm all winter." She said as though she were trying to strike up a conversation so as to appease him, to say, i'm just another shopper like everyone else.

This was the kind of treatment that she received sometimes, the kind of treatment that turned Dane nearly violent toward whoever it was that was treating her with that level of unkindness, but this time he was shut out of it, unable to come to Lilly's aid as he'd done before in the past.

The forty something man was now scolding Lilly verbally as her eyes started to tear up. Danes fuckin blood was starting to hyper boil. If he could have broken loose from his invisible confines he would have killed this motherfucker, shattered his glass jaw and beaten the son of a bitch to the fucking tile floor.

Lilly was dancing a bit more feverishly now, hands by her sides, out of the soldier posture.

"I love you." Dane tried to call out, but he knew that Lilly couldn't see him.

The store clerk had taken Lilly by the elbow and was ushering her toward the night outside the doors now.

If the scene got any worse Dane would find a way, some way, if possible to break free and commit whatever form of murder existed in this place against the store attendant. He could not stand ANYONE treating Lilly with disrespect, disregard, or disdain because of her struggle with drugs.

He had rolled over on the couch now and awakened himself. There were a battalion of tears streaming his cheeks and soaking into the pillow below him.

"This is akin to some cruel and unusual form of punishment." Alex said as he took another bite out of the stale, dried out sandwich that had lingered in the pocket of his briefcase all day.

He had grown up in Whitney Pier Cape Breton and it had been rough. They had, Alex and his Family once lived without running water for a period of time to the displeasure of he and all of his siblings. In his youth he had been surrounded by drug dealers and ruffians who would roll you for a pair of your shoes if they were the right brand, it had been dangerous, but Alex had survived and was now a success.

Dane had once called Alex the legal version of Marshall Mathers (Eminem). Alex Whitney's was a real life rags to riches story with a happy ending. Without Alex there had been nine Brothers and two sisters. What a house to contend with. They had lived in very modest quarters growing up and now Alex was a sought after not to mention affluent attorney who drove a fifty thousand dollar sports car and wore designer suits, he was also a ladies man.

"How's Von "The Icon" holding up"?? He asked Kate who was sitting on the couch with one knee pulled in to her chin.

"My Uncle is a tough bastard. He's weathered every storm that Mother Nature has ever thrown at him. He'll get through this with flying colours." "The Gate" exclaimed introspectively.

MONICA-As I prepare this manuscript for publication I am going through some of the toughest adversity of my life, I love you more today then I ever did during our time together although to me that now seems impossible.

You were and will forever be the love of my life and the keeper of my soul. We were a great team once and I was always proud to have you on my arm because you were much more to me than just a girlfriend. You were a status symbol.

As I said earlier I can remember a time when everyone wanted you but I had you, to me that was always so surreal because I was never that important to women, especially to a woman who was as gorgeous and as beautiful as you were. It was like I was dreaming as I do every night after I go to bed, and always of you, my number one Bunny!!!

I will never forget, ever, the days and nights that are now immortal and the time that we spent together, all those moments that seem to come from a special place in the darkness of time. When I think of you, I cry, here, there, everywhere as I am now.

I was out with some friends tonight and the Persian girl who was with us kind of looked like you, kind of, and as she sat there next to one of my male friends I thought of how sad it was that it couldn't be the two of us, The Legends Of Ontario Street, who were sitting there together.

I still to this day make our special dish called "Phaghetti Nummy," by two people who always felt a kin ship to rabbits for no discernible reason. I always used to call you-"The most funny of all bunnies."

I can never replace you. You were one of a kind in a time that for me that was strictly about you. No one else could have brought the special atmosphere or flavour to Ontario Street the way that you did.

You are the one who made that neighbourhood special for me, and not just O Street, but Montreal as well. I know that if only we'd met once more than so many things could have and would have been different between us in the end. I miss you so much. I love you forever!!!

I have a lot of regrets about the way that everything ended. I ask myself every day why I am being punished like this and why you are no longer with us, why you are no longer with me.

It all to often seems to me that I am paying for a crime that I didn't commit by being hurt over and over again by life when I only had the best of intentions at heart. I loved you and still do and look at the rotten ending that we seem to have met, you're dead and i'm in a horrible situation.

I thank God each day that I wake up for URBAN RAIN as well as for NEIGHBOURHOOD OF NIGHT that is soon to be upon us. These Books will hold all of our memories, our special moments, and demonstrate once and for all to the world that we had a love and an experience that most will never know, and never share.

I love you Baby Bunny,

In my heart for eternity,

Love always,

Von.

As Dane fell backward into the clutches of sleep he began to see Ontario Street in a similar but not the same form as he saw it in his conscious state, as if the atmosphere was somehow an illusion, or as if it had been altered by an evil and illusive sandman.

In the dream the neighbourhood appeared deeply sinister and had taken on a more threatening and ominous character with the darkness possessing what Dane would have characterized as "A tinge of fall." There were no leaves on the trees that lined the side streets and it seemed as if all evil were somehow about to invisibly break loose setting the nightmare invisibly aflame.

In the shadows of the dream it was well after dark and it seemed that there was no one around however Dane himself was the lone occupant that roamed the inner streets of the more residential part of The Neighbourhood Of Night. Upstairs in one of the houses a girl wearing a white bra and panties rolled out of bed after having sex with her boyfriend and fired up a cigarette.

"Can you see what's in the branches"?? The Dreamless Sleeps voice echoed above the barren tree tops. "It's going to kill you if you don't." The Shadow said circling somewhere above, invisible to the naked eye.

"I don't see anything." David Dane said looking upward at the nothingness overhead.

Sulphur in the room upstairs from the girls cigarette. She must be somehow in The Dreamless Sleeps employ. Dane registered. He hadn't seen her before, nor heard of her.

Downstairs where the leaves had hit the ground there was a small child dressed in pink. She looked to be no more than two. Maybe Kate as a Baby Dane thought hammering his head back to where he thought it ought to be. This child could have been Kate as a toddler. The Terrible Twos. Dane thought and turned down a back alley towards a seedy bar that had been closed down. Not today, not tonight, not in this place but he did not know what he was talking about or why he was having these bizarre thoughts.

Then the focus within him changed and he was entering a noisy strip club that had appeared out of nowhere and where it didn't belong in reality. There was a phony looking blond dancer on stage and she had big boobs, bigger than Dane had ever sucked on. Mammoth tits, gargantuan. Fuck, she must have worn an F cup, no pun intended.

There was a song he had heard before, by DANZIG, called DEEP, but then The DJ in the dream started to play a selection called BODY TALK by THE DEELE that Dane wore in his brain as being from the pilot episode of Miami Vice.

At this point everything stopped going round and round and Dane walked further, darker, and deeper into the club before he found a familiar looking Haitian seated at the table near the DJ booth. It was Olend, and his hands were covered in crimson fluid. His head was down over his shot glass.

Now, all of the music stopped and everything and everyone in the room had gone dead, started not just to lull, but completely ebb.

"Why are you here"?? Dane asked looking for a better way out. A way to wake up.

"Same reason you are." Olend said.

Then the dream ended, and when Dane woke up he found himself in a form of an awakened sleep walk into his Brothers living room. He wore a shirt hanging, wrinkled as fuck, over jeans and bare feet.

This time, as he came to for real Dane found himself face to face with a masked Olend who was holding a butchers knife to Kates throat. Her beautiful eyes were radiant with fear.

"Who are you"?? Kate asked frightfully of the evil demon who had her life in his hands. He was squatting behind her on the sofa like a bull frog.

"Little girls call me Monster." Olend Marx said. "But your Uncle, he calls me Olend."

"How the fuck did you get in here"?? Dane asked squinting in the blaze that the dreamy nightmare living room lights provided.

There was no mistaking his condition. David Dane was awake.

"I dreamt my way in." Olend said simulating a ligature around Kates throat with the blade of the knife.

Then there was a bumping sound from the kitchen, and then another spectre entered the fray, only this time it was someone far closer to home. "I think this is your gun." Evan Baker said tossing a clear plastic evidence bag with a nine millimetre Beretta in it onto the table in front of him with a thud.

"At least it's the gun that you thought was your gun." Baker said in a voice that Dane had never heard come from him before. It was lower, raspier, then that which he'd ever heard from Evan, it had a sleazy if not treacherous quality to it. He sounded like a pimp, Dane registered.

"What do you mean thought was my gun"?? Dane asked never for a second removing his eyes from the knife that Olend held against Kates throat.

Evan stretched his arm out to reach for the bag so as to demonstrate that of which he now spoke.

"Remember the day that I came to your apartment with Kate"?? He asked. "I switched your firearm for this one. Then, that night, I went out and killed Eva and Charlie, and I had your pistol back before you ever even knew that it was gone." Evan explained sinfully. "You should never tell people where you keep your firearm, even if you're only showing it to them." He said.

"Why"?? Dane asked disbelievingly. "Why would you do something like this"?? He asked staring straight at Evan who was using a rag to wipe the blood off of his hands.

"Where are Mum, Dad, and Andrew"?? Dane asked.

"They cut Nanas throat and stabbed Daddy. I don't know where Grand Dad is." Kate said amidst sobs.

"Bring them to me." The Dreamless Sleeps voice came over an imbalanced intercom. It was accompanied by crackling static and the very distant remnant of electronic bleeps.

"Take them downstairs." Evan ordered Monster who was still holding a knife on Kate. Her pretty eyes were shimmering. Fear was all that she had left.

On the way down the basement steps Dane asked if Marilyn and Andrew were dead. Kate said that she did not know and that both bodies had been taken away.

"Do you now know who I am"?? The Dreamless Sleep asked sitting before a bank of live monitors downstairs. His face was shadowed by the overhang of a heavy cloak. The modulator was still filtering the shapes real voice.

"Show me who the fuck you are." Dane demanded with his hands bound behind his back.

On each of the monitors was a display of each room in the house.

As the Dreamless Sleep removed his hood Danes face began to reflect the utter terror and shock of one who has just had the fright of his life. Sitting in the wicked shadow before him was the man who was responsible for his existence on this earth, the creator of sin, and the evil damnation that hell itself had bestowed upon mankind.

"You, are, a mad man." David Dane said slowly as he stared into the face of his Father. The Dreamless Sleep, the voice, was Jonathan Dane.

"Why the fuck would you do any of this"?? The Ontario Street Original asked as Evan held his bindings by the wrists. They were standing at the foot of the stairs.

Jonathan Dane was standing up now, his pale face blank, blue eyes deep set. The only part of his being that seemed alive were his sadistic irises that were aflame with all the evils of history, of all the torture and sin and foulness of the earth. His very existence was now exposed to be vile. He was, in a form, Satan himself, and Evan was smirking.

"You never thought that it would come to this." Jonathan said. "They cut your Mothers throat!! She's upstairs." He said remorselessly, who he was.

"You sick fuck"!!! Andrew Dane hollered from a pool of darkness behind them. He was still breathing, despite having been stabbed and being dragged down a flight of wooden steps. He was lying on the floor with a gag over his mouth and ropes subduing his wrists.

"Why"?? David Dane asked in a rational voice. Kate was being held behind him on the steps by Olend and his sharpened knife. He had still not removed the S and M mask.

"So many people aren't grateful for the years that they have on this earth, and your girlfriend was one of them. My life was cut short by the actions of your girlfriend in 2008." The Sleep explained." My heart will never be the same again, EVER!!! Then came your first book, and you didn't want to give me any respect. You wanted to give all of your respect to your Uncle." Jonathan said twisting his face into a sour grimace, it was an expression that David Dane had seen many times in the past.

"You bastard"!!! Kate managed trying to break free from her wrist bindings, but it was an exercise in futility, the bindings were to strong.

"Let Kate go." Dane demanded of his old man.

"I never meant for her to be here at all." Jonathan Dane said approaching Kate and forcing her into a chair. "But now she is." The Devil himself said as he loosened his Grand Daughters bindings. "I love you." He said to her gently kissing her forehead. "And after I finish dealing with your Uncle forever i'm going to let you walk out of here. But he, has to pay"!!!

"So this is what you do." David Dane said. "What, did you pay these two"?? Dane asked in reference to Olend and Evan who were standing by like two sinister henchmen at the gates of Hell.

"Olend and Evan had their own reasons for doing what they did." Jonathan responded tracing the edge of the monitor console with his finger tip. "The territory that you claim as yours. It doesn't belong to you, it belongs to somebody else." He said dreaming behind his callous blue eyes.

"You came to this neighbourhood as a young man." Olend began. "You walked in here as though you were walking into an ice cream shop." The monster said. "What you looked the other way towards is the nature of all of the things that you saw, of all of the things that these streets truly represent. These streets don't belong to you." Monster went on. "They don't belong to any man, woman, or child living and breathing on this earth. They belong to the one that I dream of, to the one who marks my unconscious mind with his thoughts. The streets, that you claim as your own, belong to Sowen." Olend proclaimed.

"So all this time, all of the things that you said about God and your Father being a Preacher. None of that was real. You weren't really who you said you were on any level"??

Olend was hissing now, twisting and contorting his face into a disease below the mask. "My Father cut up my Mother in front of the five of us, then he hung himself while we watched." Olend said. "My Father was a Preacher, but not someone who preached the word of any God that most of the world that you occupy believes in." Olend responded.

"What about you. What's your story"?? Von "The Icon" asked half twisting himself to look at Evan who stood beside him now. "And you, you killed Olends son"?? Dane slightly demanded.

Evan was shaking his head. "I didn't kill Clinton, did I Monster"?? He asked as Olend jolted Kate slightly forward by the wrists. "Not at all. Olend here killed his own son, didn't you Olend"?? Evan asked rhetorically. "You see, Clinton is the one who put his Daddy in the hospital with those stab wounds." Evan explained with an eerie pitch in his voice. "Apparently Olend here was late making a payment." Kates fiance said.

"Payment on what"?? David Dane questioned out of curiosity.

"Should we tell him what you really do for a living"?? Evan asked smiling at Olend. The blade of the knife was closer than ever to Kates throat, gleaming.

There was blackness and shadow all around them except for the illumination from the monitors.

"You see Olend here, Monster, he kills girls on film, even killed a little boy." Evan recalled with a wicked chuckle.

Jonathan Dane looked up. He was not aware of this revelation.

"But as a side bar, Olend here sells Smack, has for years." Evan said removing himself from Danes direct view as he made a circle around him with his body. "I guess Olend failed to cough up the money for the product that Clinton had fronted him."

"And what about you?? What are you getting out of all of this"?? Dane asked struggling against the grip of his bindings and thus tightening them further.

"Allow me to reintroduce myself." Evan said. "My real name, is Evan Phillips."

Dane shook his head quizzically, he was not making the connection.

"That's Phillips as in Mike." Evan said of the man that David Dane had once fought in the street.(See Urban Rain).

"Oh my God." The Ontario Street Original said as his old man walked in a straight line in front of him.

"Who's Mike Phillips"?? Shamrock asked, her face flush with tears.

Dane tried to turn his head in his nieces direction. "He's an enemy of mine from the past. I fought him in front of Ontario Street." David Dane replied.

"Yeah, and after your Uncle beat him up my Brother was killed for it." Evan went on. "It took me years, and I mean years of planning to come up with a suitable way to pay him back. That's where you came into play." Evan said glancing in his fiances direction. He then spit directly in David Danes face.

"Your Brother put himself in the situation that he was in, no one twisted his arm or forced him to go to work for Manning Robar." The Ontario Street Original said.

"No, but you had to humiliate him. You had to bring him enough shame that he was of no worth to his superiors." Evan said delivering a wicked kick to Von "The Icons" lower abdomen thus causing him to crumple to his knees. At that moment Kate broke free and side kicked Monster in the stomach before delivering a nasty elbow to the child killers jaw.

"BASTARD"!!! She yelled as Jonathan Dane disappeared out a back door.

"Uncle Von." Kate hollered delivering a spinning wheel kick to Evans face.

David Dane had broken from his bindings now turning to strike Olend Marx in the temple with a stiff left hook dropping him to the floor in a heap.

Andrew Dane had risen to his feet, stab wounds and all and was trying to make his way towards his Daughter in order to protect her, fighting, struggling valiantly.

Dane grabbed Evan and was struggling with him over a firearm that he had drawn from his blazer, they were bashing each other around now, going from the monitor board to the walls of the basement. "Say goodnight Evan." Von "The Icon" said forcing the barrel of the Gloc 9 into Evans chest and squeezing the trigger twice. "Fuck you"!!! Dane yelled as Evan slipped to the ground with smoke trailing from his bullet wounds.

"Where's Jonathan"?? Dane yelled.

"He ran out the back door." Andrew managed delivering a knee to Monsters skull as he walked by him and stepped over a fallen chair, nearly tripping.

At that moment Monster rose from his seated position on the ground lunging at Kate with the knife.

"FUCK"!!! Dane hollered as he squeezed the trigger of the gun for a third and forth time in about as many minutes, but this time there were no bullets, the clip was empty, only a morbid clicking sound resulted.

Monster had made it to his feet and had managed to nick Kates flesh with the tip of the blade before Von pistol whipped the top of Monsters mask causing an out pouring of blood to surge from Olends scalp as he went crashing to the cold cement floor of the basement.

"He's down. Tie him up." Andrew hollered looking back and forth for the bindings.

"What about Evan"?? He asked.

"He's dead." Dane said turning to look at the crumpled mess of caked blood and bullet wounds that was Evan Phillips, unbelievably, the Brother of Mike.

"Where's Grand Dad"?? Kate asked out of wind.

"I don't know." Dane responded surveying the basement. "He ran out. I can't believe the sonovabitch was behind all of this." He said in a half disoriented voice. Trickling blood, stains of night.

Later on, after The Police had shown up and taken the bodies away David Dane stood with one arm around his niece and the other holding a cold compress against a gash in his forehead. They had made it out, alive. One more day, one more moment, one more breath.

Andrew and Marilyn had been transported to a local hospital where they, in far separate conditions, were recovering.

When Monster had slashed Marilyn she had lowered her head and the cut had sliced into her chin and the sides of her neck. No major arteries were severed or wounded in the aftermath of the attempted slaying. She would make it out alive, still conscious, although no one had told her about her husbands involvement yet.

"I'm so proud of you Kate." Von "The Icon" said as he draped Lilly's Ontario Street Originals jacket over his nieces shoulders. "I'm so proud of you." He said embracing his niece as he began to tear up.

The Paramedics had seen to Kates flesh wounds and had given her an antibiotic to prevent infection and a clean release. No major damage had been done.

"I love you Uncle Von. Thank you for being there for me last night, and for always being there for me. You're my hero, you and Daddy both." Kate said kissing her Uncle on the cheek as they stood in the living room of her Fathers condo amidst blood stains and Police tape.

"No, you're my hero Diamond Doll." Von said to his niece. "You're my hero." He repeated.

"Let's go see Nana and Daddy." Kate said as they neared the door with their arms around each others shoulders.

CHAPTER 9:

David Dane stood amidst the ground level vapour lamps that lead up the stone pathway toward the two story bungalow that Danno Santiago and Jacky Hannah were staying in. It was just after eleven pm and Dane had been out wandering around old Montreal all night.

He had thought about Danno and Jacky, and how they were responsible for ending Lilly's life with a vile of poison. He had thought about the fact that for Lilly there was no justice and that these two reprehensible scum bags had gotten away with murder, but after tonight, that fact would change forever, he would see to it.

David Dane pulled a ski mask over his head and checked the clip on the Gloc 9 that he'd confiscated from Evan Phillips. Ready, time to die for those who had hurt the love of his life and put an end to the breath of his soul mate.

Now, just a few feet away there were whispers as Dane crept up the pathway unnoticed, like a covert operative on a mission. Now, surveillance, wait and see what happens. Somewhere low murmurs like subdued conversation, secretive, no one supposed to hear what they were saying. Two voices not one and the reflections from a pool of water that sat in seclusion behind the wall of the property line. Rippling liquid shadow. Stream of consciousness. Tonight he would risk his future to earn vengeance for the one that he had loved and taken care of for seven years, the love of his life.

In the distance a dog barking beyond a string of parked cars.

Tonight the darkness was absolute, engulfing. There were almost no passers by. This was an exclusive area. He'd gone walking in old Montreal and ended up in upper Westmount. This was the home of the posh and affluent, Montreals upper echelon, not for those who hadn't done well.

Apparently, Hannah had come into some money.

"You murdered a legend." David Dane said as Jacky Hannah starred directly down the barrel of Evans Gloc 9 with her one usable eye.

"What the fuck are you doing here"?? She asked trembling beneath her mascara.

Danno was standing two feet from her wearing a mask of silence and terror. He knew why Von "The Icon" was here, it was in his eyes. He was going to pay tonight, this was where the road ended. Sleep for all of eternity.

"I have three letters for you Jacky." Dane said. "D, O, A"!!! He said spacing out each syllable for effect before three loud gunshots rang out across the quiet night killing both Danno Santiago and Jacky Hannah and ridding the solar system of Lillys killers for all of eternity.

EPILOGUE:

David Dane sat in a park just off of Ontario Street well after midnight. It was twelve forty five am and the parks wooden foot bridges and bird shaped water fountains were still. It had been ten days since the incident at his Brothers condo and all involved were still trying to recover and get over what they had seen and experienced.

The Police were still trying to locate Jonathan who had been named as the owner of a snuff film company billed as NIGHT WORLD PRODUCTIONS, however they had been unsuccessful. He had seemingly vanished off the face of the earth as men of means often do.

Now, here in the blackness Dane was melancholy and nostalgic as he remembered the legendary Lilly Chicoine and all that they had been through together. This was one more park, the park on St. Alexandre De Seve where Dane and Lilly had spent many days and nights sitting together, but now, Lilly was gone, and Dane was alone.

As he rose from the bench where he had been resting Dane felt an a hand reach out of the darkness and touch the sleeve of his shirt. "Got a light"?? The Spectre asked. As he looked up he saw Lillys face gazing back at him. It was her ghost, and just as quickly as she had appeared Lilly blew out the match flame and vanished back into the engulfing dream like blackness of the night leaving only the scent of sulphur in her wake.

"I love you Lilly." Dane said as tears streamed his cheeks. "I love you." He said breaking down completely.

R.I.P. Monica,
ETERNAL LIFE!!!
FOR YOU BABY BUNNY,
LOVE ALWAYS,
VON

THE END

ONTARIO STREET HALL OF FAME INDUCTION CEREMONY:
CLASS OF 2014:

Authors Note: At this time I want to take the time to acknowledge the participants in this years HALL OF FAME induction ceremony. We are a group of legends who inspired one of the greatest stories in modern history, and in doing so, we made a name for ourselves that will never be forgotten.

We are as a unit better known to Montreals east end as The Ontario Street Originals. As a group, we came together at the turn of the millenium and loved one another with a friendship and a ferocity that is seen in few venues anywhere today.

As the founding Father of The Ontario Street Originals I know that we've been called everything from a band of thugs to the occupants of The Neighbourhood Of Night, and along the way we've lost more than a few friends who I will mention later on, however the closest of those friends was to me my precious ex girlfriend, Monica who will be the first ever inductee. When you died, it tore my heart out, and i've literally never been the same since. I love you. There are so many special moments that I shared with you and if it wasn't for you, there would be no URBAN RAIN or URBAN RAIN II-NEIGHBOURHOOD OF NIGHT. Thank you for giving birth to this odyssey.

So without further ado, let me now present The Ontario Street Hall Of Fame Class Of 2014.

HALL OF FAME SONG BY THE SCRIPT BLASTS OVER THE AUDITORIUM SPEAKERS.

Monica- First of all, before I say anything else, I cannot believe that you are gone.

You were my obsession from the moment that I laid eyes on you, and in the seven years that we were together we loved each other more than words can ever express despite the opinions of a bunch of fools who never knew us, yet feel compelled to offer their two cents worth at every opportunity.

I'll always think of you as the girl who came to stay with me when I had no one else, who filled the void where there was loneliness. You became the love of my life, and then you became all that I had. I miss you so much. There are no words to convey the depth of my emotion for you.

I still remember your multiple bracelets rattling against the couch when you would come to sleep at my place the morning after you'd been out all night. In the beginning i'd just sit there hugging my knees into my chest and watch you with butterflies in my stomach.. I was fascinated by everything that you did, and by your dark and exclusive world.

During the time that we were together I loved you like no other before or after you, I never will.

When I heard about your death almost a year to the day after it happened my world was shattered. As my Mother would tell you i'd never been so emotional in my life. I still dream about you at least once a night and feel jilted when I wake up and realize all at once that it was all just a dream and that you're not really there.

I love you. I don't know how not to love you. I'm attached to you like I can't tell you, you always knew that, and I won't part with your memory or the memory of us together for all the money or gold on the planet, I will fight for that.

As your reputation in the street goes, you are without a doubt a legend. You are easily the most hardcore female bad ass who I have ever had the honour of knowing. I love you Baby Bunny. I'll see you in Heaven.

I now induct Monica Mayhem into the Class Of 2014 Ontario Street Hall Of Fame.

Alyssa M takes the podium-"Our next inductee is a man who needs no introduction to the occupants of The Neighbourhood Of Night. When I first climbed off of the bus from Toronto he was the first or second real friend that I made depending on how you break down the day that I came to this city. From the time that we met each other, he has stood by my side, been a real and loyal friend and never let me down. His was the first and only roof that I stayed under while I was in Montreal, and I was always welcome there.

Ladies and gentlemen, not only a legend in life but a legend at heart. My immortal, the founding Father of The Ontario Street Originals, Von "The Icon."

Von "The Icon" takes the podium dressed in a black tuxedo as Alyssa walks away in the opposite direction, she is wearing an expensive pink evening gown over high heel pumps and red lip stick.

"Thank you angel. Yeh know, when I came to this city I didn't know anyone. It wasn't until sometime into the first week that I got lost and ended up on Ontario Street where I met Monica standing alone in the rain. I'll never forget that moment or the downpour that we got caught in after. Our time together was sacred. I cherish each and every moment that I had with you. There's not a person who knows me who doesn't hear about you from me every day until they've finally had enough and have to tell me to shut up. I've never been the same with you gone.

What those people don't realize is that you gave me the experience of my life. You were an experience. You changed me in more ways that I can tell you, and not having you in my life means that there will always be a part of me that's missing. Somewhere in my heart I believe that your ghost still roams the parks, taverns and alleyways of Ontario Street, our Neighbourhood Of Night. No woman, none on this earth will ever replace you in my heart, of that I can promise you. To steal a line from the legendary Rocky Balboa-"No fighter will hit you as hard as life." He was right about that. I love you Baby Bunny, I know that we'll meet again one day. God Bless You.

Then there are the rest of you guys who were around us every day and night. Alyssa M, Sheryl H, The Casanova Killer Nick G, Suzy/Judy Q, Tiffany whose I.D says Dale Frost, J.P and Valerie, Barbie Blond, Marcel Monduire, but i'll get to you later." (Von "The Icon says smiling).

Angela O, my sister from the streets, Carolyn G, Nick Monroe, (Did you do your little sit ups today)??,

Claude F(The Man With The Moustache), Holly Briggs(Man, if they recalled mouths yours would be the first), Von "The Icon" says smiling, and if i've forgotten anybody then I didn't mean to. I love you all. Thank you for the award, and thank you for being a part of my life.

God Bless.

Von "The Icon" has not left the podium, the auditorium has come unglued with cheers and gang signs, there are thousands in attendance including the reserved section which houses The Ontario Street Originals as well as several Family members. The reserved section is a posh setting furnished with red velvet seats and a varied bar menu. As Von "The Icon" prepares to welcome the next inductee flash bulbs go off and golden cathedral lights crisscross melting into a fused glare. The entire place is a sight to behold.

Our next inductee, is the woman that you just saw a few moments ago. She is the sexy, seductive stripper from the streets of Toronto, and like Monica, she's an enigma. She's also one of the sweetest and most supportive friends that i've ever had. We met each other the very same afternoon that she came to this city, and we've been friends ever since.

She has the singing voice of a thousand angels, yet she's far more beautiful than any angel that i've ever seen other then my legendary ex who's up in Heaven.

She is the person who once wrapped her long shapely stems around me and sang Bette Midlers Wind Beneath My Wings into my ear. She around the same time told a then rival of mine to quote- "Be afraid, be very afraid." And given the intensity of the rivalry at the time, she proved that she was indeed my friend to the bone. There is not an untrustworthy cell in your body, and for the world that we occupy, that's extremely rare. I love you!!!

Her loyalty was again demonstrated only a few days after that when she called me her hero in front of a room full of people whom we both know well, I have never forgotten that moment. Some of you are here today. (Von "The Icon" says smiling and pointing at a specific section of the audience.). Ladies and gentlemen, please welcome Alyssa M into The 2014 Ontario Street Hall Of Fame. (Von "The Icon" claps as Alyssa re emerges and lifts her trophy from the podium smiling, waving, and throwing kisses as the house comes unglued for one of Ontario Streets favourites ... ...
HALL OF FAME BY THE SCRIPT PLAYS ON.

"And now, here to present the next award is a woman that the streets of Montreal, Quebec as well as Halifax, Nova Scotia are very familiar with. Ladies and gentlemen, she is a legend, a hardcore diva, and a woman to be reckoned with, please welcome, my dear friend, The Baddest Woman On The Planet, Judy Q. (Von "The Icon" says clapping his hands at forehead level before exiting stage left as Hall Of Fame by the script plays on as Judy approaches the podium).

She is wearing a long flowing blue evening gown over stilettos. She is an African American woman who is in her sixties, and she has been thought of as The Grand Mother of Montreal's dark and sinister underworld for many years.

"You know I didn't know if security was gonna let me in here tonight." Judy says with a broad grin on her lips as the crowd chuckles in unison). Judy has a raspy voice, low, and you can tell that she has the streets in her blood. "Need to get with the program." Judy exclaims.

"Our next inductee, is a man with a lot of personality. He's a good friend of mine, and I know that he's a good friend of Von "The Icons" as well." Judy says. "The reason why I know this, is because neither one of them has shot each other." She says giving the audience her profile. They are laughing uproariously now, fists clenched at the lips.

"At least that's what they told me." Judy says. "My next guest is my dear friend, Mr. C Monroe(Nick Monroe), Judy exclaims as C Monroe approaches the podium. He hugs Judy, and then she disappears back stage.

"First of all I know that Von would be disappointed in me if I didn't give a speech that tore the fuckin house down." Monroe exclaims in his O.J. Simpson style voice. He is wearing a tuxedo over his African American exterior. He is relatively short with a boxers nose and deep set eyes. He has GANGSTER written all over him. "You guys parked your cars tonight expecting to see a show and that's what you're gonna get"!!! Monroe says charismatically as the crowd roars.

"First of all I wanna thank Von for having me here tonight. The honour is truly appreciated. I still remember the two of us living under one roof." Monroe says with a smile on his face. "Von, I don't know how many days and nights that you fretted over Monica, but you loved her like no boyfriend ever loved his girlfriend and I mean that." Monroe says loosing the comedic temperature. "That girl meant everything to him and you better believe it."

"I think that a lot can be said about my years on the street in this city, from Ontario Street, to The Main, The Point, Lasal and everywhere else that you find guys like me"!!! C Monroe says as spot lamps wash over his face. "If Security keeps doing that i'm gonna have to jam someone up." Monroe says turning to look to toward stage left.

"I know that some of the best times that I ever had were living with Von and Monica when they were together at their first apartment. I remember a lot of days and nights Von and I would come home with food and ten movies from the video store by their building, and we'd all pig out and watch films til the next morning.

When I think about the love of Vons life, I can't believe she's gone." C Monroe says seriously. "The relationship that I had with those two." Monroe says reflectively. "I showed up in a cab on a Friday for dinner, and I ended up staying for three months. Von was very hospitable, of course he and Monica eventually got evicted, but that's another story entirely" Monroe says as the crowd chuckles. "Just before I accept this award, I have just one question to ask. Tracy, Tracy, did you do your little sit ups today, cause I don't want no big bellied woman you know." … … … Monroe says smiling as the crowd roars. "Thank you for this." C Monroe says lifting his statue from the podium and raising it in the air. As he exits to the right he runs into Von "The Icon" who is on his way back to the podium to present the next award. Immediately, the two dear friends embrace for several moments each smiling and pecking the other on the cheek in a mutual show of friendship, respect, nostalgia, and affection.

HALL OF FAME BY THE SCRIPT PLAYS AGAIN.

Von "The Icon" approaches the podium again and looks over the crowd. His jet black hair is slicked back and both his profiles sport long trim side burns. He looks a bit older at thirty nine, but he still manages to maintain his physique to a certain degree.

"My next inductee is very special." The Ontario Street Original says. "He also barked very loudly whenever he saw strangers passing the house or coming to the door. He also occasionally barked at parked cars. He was the kindest, sweetest, gentlest soul who has ever walked the earth, and he had a particular vice for ham and cheese sandwiches as well as blue berry muffins. I have coined his ten year tenure on this earth, a decade of love." Von "The Icon" says.

The crowd is slightly emotional now with several animal lovers dabbing the tears from their eyes with Kleenex, this is a moment that they can appreciate.

"Unlike most people, Hunter loved everyone that he met, both animals and people alike, particularly children, and Hunter had a soft spot in his heart for old people. When my Grand Father Wallace was sick Hunter would go and lay next to him every night and never leave his side. He stayed there until the day that my Grand Father passed away. Somehow, he knew. He was my best friend in the world, and the greeter of all who came to our home. Ladies and gentlemen, please help me welcome to the 2014 Ontario Street Hall Of FAME, my best friend, HUNTER WOOF!!!

The crowd is on its feet now as a custom HALL OF FAME statue in the mold of a gold dog is delivered to the podium and handed to Von "The Icon" who will be accepting the award on behalf of his late great friend HUNTER!!!

HALL OF FAME BY THE SCRIPT PLAYS AGAIN.

Von "The Icon" remains at the head of the podium. "My next inductee, is a man of few words. He is a dangerous and seasoned street fighter, and he's the last person that you wanna find yourself on the wrong side of, truly!!!

If you look up the words "Urban Bad Ass" in Websters Dictionary then you'll probably see Claudes face staring back at you. I know how you think and how your mind works so i'm gonna keep this short and sweet my friend." Von "The Icon" says looking toward at Claude F who renders a mild grin amidst a mimic of his own smouldering demeanour. He then looks back up at Von for a response, and then quits the tease and allows himself to laugh fully.

"I met this guy back in 2002 sitting below the window of a pizza joint on Ontario Street. He was a bad dude then and he's probably an even badder dude now". Von says as Claude laughs out loud.

"Please help me welcome my friend, The Man With The Moustache, Claude F. AKA-The Urban Stud to the 2014 Ontario Street Hall Of Fame." Von says clapping as THE HALL OF FAME THEME SONG BY THE SCRIPT BLASTS THROUGHOUT THE AUDITORIUM as Claude F walks to centre stage in a tux and accepts the award. "Thank you." He says into the mic before using the stairs to exit again as the crowd cheers him on.

Our next inductee is a friend who i've known for many years. She was one of the first people that I met when I came to Ontario Street and is featured many times throughout URBAN RAIN as well as NEIGHBOURHOOD OF NIGHT-URBAN RAIN II. She has a heart of gold and knows what it means to be a true and genuine friend. I can honestly say that since knowing her in 2000 that Sheryl and I have never, ever had an unkind word between us. I love her with all my heart and she is someone that I truly and genuinely respect. She is like as a Sister to me the same as if we were related. Ladies and Gentlemen. Please welcome, my dear friend and confidant, Sheryl H into 2014 Ontario Street Hall Of Fame.

HALL OF FAME THEME BY THE SCRIPT BLASTS AGAIN as Sheryl H takes the podium.

"Thanks Von." Sheryl says hugging her friend of fifteen or so years. She is wearing a long shapely red dress over black stilettos. She is an African American lady with long dreads and a Jamaican heritage.

"Ye know, it's so good to be here." The charmingly self conscious Sheryl begins. "I never in a million years dreamt that i'd be doing this. This is something truly special to me. When I first heard that Ontario Street was gonna have its own HALL OF FAME I was surprised. I mean, I didn't even know if I was gonna make it here or not.

Von "The Icon" is watching Sheryl from the shadows with pride in his eyes. It took a lot of guts for her to do this but she made it.

"Von coached me a lot on the phone. I mean, I was really afraid to come up here but he talked me into it. I don't usually like doing stuff like this, but i'm extremely proud of this award and of Von for coming so far in his life. I remember him when he was a Body Builder up and down the roads taking care of Monica, God Rest Her Soul. I knew Monica well, and she was my friend.

Anyway, i'm gonna wrap it up now." Sheryl says. "Thank you all for the award. God bless Monica up in Heaven, and thank you Von. I love you." She says as HALL OF FAME BY THE SCRIPT plays again.

Sheryl raises her statue above her head as she walks down the steps and resumes her seat amongst The Ontario Street Originals.

As the crowd mulls over their programs, looks at one another, and speaks in the faintest of whispers The Ontario Street Original takes the podium another time. "My next inductee is someone that I truly respect. He is a man of modesty, dignity, compassion and integrity. He is also an MMA Fighter, a band leader, there's a plug for Union Main Nicko, Von says looking off into the crowd at the next inductee. He's a councillor, a ladies man, a role model, and a fitness instructor.

I first met him in my early years on Ontario Street but i'll be damned if I remember how or where we met. People call him a lot of things, but I call him The Casanova Killer. Please welcome to The Ontario Street 2014 Hall Of Fame, my dear friend, Nick G." Von says clapping as the next inductee takes centre stage. Nick G has short cropped hair and tattoos on his arms and looks almost like the dude who played Ryan MCCarthy in Never Back Down.

"Thanks Von." Nick says shaking his old buddies hand and giving him a hug at the same time.

"I've never heard so many nice things said about me in my life." Nick says smiling as Von leaves the stage via the steps. "Before I go any further I wanna thank Von for inviting me here. It's a great honour to be a part of The 2014 ONTARIO STREET Hall Of Fame Ceremony." He says. "I also wanna dedicate the award that i'm receiving tonight to Monica's memory. She and I go back a long way. I as Von well knows, was Monica's councillor of many years. We're all friends. I never thought that i'd be here in the wake of her death, but she's watching us. Belive that. Anyway, thank you all for coming out tonight, and thank you for inviting me to be a part of the 2014 Ontario Street Hall Of Fame." Nick says raising his statue seemingly toward the Heavens as HALL OF FAME by THE SCRIPT plays again.

Von "The Icon" has resumed centre stage and is looking at his cell phone now which bares instructions.

"I'm ready." He says to someone in the back on his mouth piece.

"Alright, my next inductee is one of the hottest, sexiest, most beautiful brunette bomb shells that I have personally ever known, and even though her ID says Dale Frost her street name is Tiffany. She's here tonight, porn star looks and centre fold body. Without further ado, i'd like to welcome Tiffany to The 2014 ONTARIO STREET HALL OF FAME CEREMONY. Von "The Icon" says as HALL OF FAME by THE SCRIPT plays another time.

Tiffany is climbing the steps to the podium now. Her brown hair is tied up in a bun, and her voluptuous body is tantalizing every male in the auditorium from underneath her sky blue, low cut, designer evening gown.

As she reaches Von "The Icon" she kisses him firmly on the lips and wraps her arms around his waist to which he responds with an awesome smile.

"Hey you." She greets him below the sound of the mic.

"Like fire." Von responds.

Tiffany tosses her hair to one side and takes the microphone in her hand.

"I wanna thank you, each and every one of you for coming out tonight, especially all of the Bad Boys and Bad Girls." Tiffany says giving the audience a huge wink as many of the gang members flash gang signs and make cat call sounds directed at the gorgeous and sexy Tiffany whose big blue eyes are sparkling below the bright auditorium lights.

"I see i'm getting a positive response. Maybe I should do these things more often." Tiff says. "I wanna thank The Immortal Von "The Icon" for inviting me to his party. I love you baby." She says. "And tonight, I also dedicate my award to my dear friend of many years, The Incomparable Monica Mayhem who I know is up in Heaven watching the show. I love you Monica"!!! Tiffany said raising her statue in the direction of the Heavens as HALL OF FAME BY THE SCRIPT PLAYS ONCE MORE.

"The next inductee knows me like no other, he is my Brother in arms, my confidant, and my dear friend. We shared our relationships with each other night after night over dinner as well as by phone, we went to war over a woman, we've hated each other, loved each other, and we have on occasion laughed together until we cried. Despite it all, he has always been there for me.

Ladies and Gentlemen, please help me welcome my dear friend, Marcel Monduire to The 2014 Ontario Street Hall Of Fame." Von "The Icon" announces as Marcel walks regally onto the stage with a voluptuous blond on each arm as HALL OF FAME BY THE SCRIPT PLAYS. They are both less than half his age, and they appear to be displaying signs of both exhaustion and after glow.

"Thank you." Marcel says in his quiet French accent as his two escorts leave his side and walk back behind the curtain.

"It is a great honour." He begins adjusting his spectacles below the lights. He is dressed to the nines wearing an expensive tuxedo over designer dress shoes that are so polished that you can see your reflection in them. On his wrist he is keeping time with a one of a kind expensive Rolex time piece that was purchased for him by mail from Switzerland, a gift from one of his affluent sons.

As Marcel turns to Von he embraces him whispering something to him before The Host Of The Show walks away and vanishes through the curtain.

"Thank you." Marcel repeats. "It has make a long time that I am going on Ontario Street." He says. "In the beginning, I was a crazy old guy driving my car to meet Star at Joli Couer." Marcel says of Ontario Streets former infamous no tell motel. "For many years, she has made me crazy in my head." Marcel says with a broad grin on his face. "Especially when she was go at Graem, and that WAS SHIT MONDUIRE"!!! Marcel exclaims as all sections of the auditorium roar with laughter as the grin trails from Marcel's lips. His rugged facial features have turned a slight crimson.

"It has also made many years that I have known Von and Monica." He says more seriously. "I was there for some of what they have lived, and now Monica is not with us anymore. Von was Monica's boyfriend, and he loved her very, very much I think." Marcel said sadly. "Monica was also the best friend of my girlfriend, Star and she and I will also miss her very much. She was a very special person to us. I will also dedicate this award to Monica. Oui, Sevre, it is true." Marcel says in French. "Thank you all for inviting an old guy like me to The Hall Of Fame, and thank you Von." Marcel says as The Ontario Street Original comes from behind the curtain to resume his duties as Master Of Ceremonies.

The crowd roars with appreciation as Marcel raises his award high in the glare of the golden spot lights. "Thank you." He mouths one more time before hugging his old friend and then taking his leave through the back corridor as HALL OF FAME BY THE SCRIPT blasts on.

"Our next inductee is a woman that I have known for many years. She is a bad ass, a street general, and a dear friend. I've often been known to call her The Baddest Woman On The Planet. Ladies and gentlemen, please welcome my friend Judy Q to THE 2014 ONTARIO STREET HALL OF FAME." Von "The Icon" says seriously clapping his hands together above his head.

As Judy stops to hug him he shakes her hand as both smile at each other and exchange words that are inaudible to the audience that is watching on. "Okay." Judy begins in her low raspy baritone as Von "The Icon" steps away.

"First of all I wanna thank everybody for letting me come out here tonight." She begins turning one way and then the other before the raised microphone. "Then again, I dare you to try and stop me." She says bursting into laughter as the audience laughs with her. "I'm a Scotian woman, and you know what they say about us Scotians."

The crowd waits for the punchline.

"WE DON'T PLAY"!!! Judy says resuming her serious facial veneer momentarily. "GOTTA GET WITH THE PROGRAM, KNOW WHAT I'M SAYIN"?? Judy says peeling off another of her familiar lines from an entire book of them that she has kept in her head for a lifetime.

"When you come down the road that I did you learn the hard way up. Aint no parta me that's ever been soft." Judy Q says. "But I must say, I saw love when I lived with Von and Monica. If ever there was a man that was in love with a woman, with his wife, it was him. He took care a her like tomorrow didn't exist. He loved her more than any man that was in love with a woman that I ever knew. Tonight, in my mind, in my heart, deep down inside, is about The two Ontario Street Originals known as Von "The Icon" and Monica Mayhem. He don't play, and neither did she. This award, is for the two a them." Judy says raising her statue above her head before leaning into the mic one more time. "Thank you. I love you all." She says as the crowd roars and HALL OF FAME BY THE SCRIPT PLAYS ANOTHER TIME!!!

The crowd is still buzzing from Judys speech as Von "The Icon" resumes the podium again. There is a light sheen on his face, and his eye lids look heavy and drained.

"The next inductee is a woman who is never at a loss for words. I've known her since 2004, and in that time she's probably said more in a minute than most people do in a whole hour. She is my friend, my street sister, and a legitimate bad ass. Ladies and gentlemen. Please help me welcome the one and only Holly Briggs to The 2014 Ontario Street Hall Of Fame Induction Ceremony."

At that moment HALL OF FAME BY THE SCRIPT BLASTS on as Holly Briggs appears on stage wearing a long flowing gown and earrings. She hugs and kisses Von "The Icon" whispering "My Super Man" in his ear before he walks away and disappears beyond the curtain.

"Good evening." She begins with a slight hint of Devilishness in her voice. "I know we're runnin outta time so i'm gonna keep this short and sweet. You're gonna cut my mic?? I don't think so"!!! She says momentarily breaking into her street persona as a tease and then laughs it off.

"First of all I wanna thank Von for inviting me here tonight. You're my Superman." She says directing her comment toward The Ontario Street Original who is back stage holding a can of diet soda in his hand.

"If it wasn't for you I wouldn't be here at all. This is very special to me. I never spent alotta time on Ontario Street per say, and in all honesty I never knew Monica very well but we have met. I know this night is mainly about her and her contribution to all of her friends lives as well as to THE URBAN RAIN AND NEIGHBOURHOOD OF NIGHT series.

I wanna take this time to thank my dear friends Judy Q, C Monroe, and The Immortal Von "The Icon" for all of their support and friendship. Thank you, I love you, and I dedicate this trophy to the incomparable Monica Mayhem." Holly says as HALL OF FAME BY THE SCRIPT blasts throughout the auditorium that is awash with spot lights as she takes her trophy and exits the stage to a round of applause.

There is a hushed silence over the crowd as they await the next Inductee. Von "The Icon" is standing in front of the mic now keying up, getting ready to introduce the next participant. "Alright, our next Inductee is a man who has a very high profile here in Montreal. He is a Professional Wrestler, a ladies man, a local legend and a dear friend of mine. He is the first ever inductee into the ONTARIO STREET HALL OF FAME CELEBRITY WING. He is my Brother from another Mother, ladies and gentlemen, please welcome THE SEX EXPRESS, TRIPLE XXX SEXXXY EDDY into THE CLASS OF 2014 ONTARIO STREET HALL OF FAME. Von "The Icon" introduces clapping his hands at forehead level. At that moment SEXXXY EDDY appears on stage flanked by ten gorgeous strippers none of whom remember the limo ride over because they were to busy servicing their benefactor.

As Von and Eddy come together on stage they embrace each other in a show of warmth, affection and respect as HALL OF FAME BY THE SCRIPT blasts throughout the auditorium.

The crowd is roaring approval now for two of their favourite local heroes.

"Thanks again Von, for having a place for me not only in your memoirs but here tonight. Kicking ass comes easy for us, but the hardest on going battle is this daily struggle known as life. There is no one else that this wrestling legend would rather have in his corner than The Ontario Street Original. We've known each other for over a decade. Acquaintances are a dime a dozen but friends can only be counted on one hand. It is an pleasure to be inducted into The Ontario Street Hall Of Fame but an honour to be your friend. I've always got your back buddy, now, and 4 LIFE!!!

It is a privilege to be inducted." Eddy closes as HALL OF FAME BY THE SCRIPT PLAYS ON … …

"Our next inductee is not your conventional inductee and what's so ironic about him being inducted into THE HALL OF FAME is that when we first met I was certain that we were destined to be enemies for life.

He is a unique individual who was born along the shores of Haiti. Once bitter rivals, we are now great friends. He appeared in URBAN RAIN wielding a broken bottle that he was threatening to cut me with, but as he once told me, past is past. He is one of a kind, he is also the only human being that I know who would carry a suitcase down the street with a cord dangling out of it just so that people would wonder what was in it.

Ladies and gentlemen, please welcome my friend, we call him "HAITIAN CLAUDE," to THE 2014 ONTARIO STREET HALL OF FAME."

HALL OF FAME BY THE SCRIPT PLAYS in the back ground.

As Von "The Icon" finishes his introduction a short, hunched over, darkly complected male with a shaggy beard, wild hair, and bare feet walks slowly to the podium with a female escort on each arm. Despite his choice of footwear, he is still appropriately dressed for the occasion wearing a tuxedo and bow tie that he has acquired from God knows where.

HALL OF FAME BY THE SCRIPT begins its chorus once more as Claude lifts the podium mic to his lips. He is looking around now, eyes darting in all directions. He looks as though he is about to fly into a Primordial rage, but it is simply a tease to keep the crowd on the edge of its seat.

"I AM RASTA MAN, AND ME NAME BE CLAUDE MON, AND I AM NO AFRAID FOR POLICE"!!! He barks at the capacity of his lungs without breaking a smile. "I come here to accept this award, but I no kill anyone." He says letting a low yet charming laughter escape him, letting the audience off the hook. It is a laughter that Von "The Icon" has heard many times in the past. "Many times we fight for Mon-i-ca"!!! Claude says looking back at Von who is standing by the edge of the stage both smiling and laughing, his hazel eyes are shining.

"But past is past." He says. "I no make big speech. Mon-i-ca is die!!! She's die"!!! Claude says as he begins to sob emotionally as tears well up in his eyes and then begin to make rivers down the length of his round cheeks.

The crowd renders a sympathetic awe, and Vons face has turned serious.

"I accept award for Mon-i-ca"!!! Claude says lowering his head as Von "The Icon" crosses the stage to embrace his former rival who has become a friend.

The two men stay in each others grip for a number of moments before Von leads Claude off of the stage arm in arm as HALL OF FAME BY THE SCRIPT PLAYS ONCE MORE!!!!

The crowd is on their feet now. They are moved by what they have just heard.

Vons head is lowered now as he makes his best effort to pull himself together. Claudes tears have caused him to shed a few of his own as he has over his late love so many times in the past, right up until this very night.

"Oh God." He begins trying to stave off any more tears. He is The Master Of Ceremonies tonight, and he knows, and in honour of Monica, that the show must go on.

"Alright." He begins again, shaking his muscular shoulders out as if to ward off any remaining sentiment that might prevent him from doing his job. "Our next inductee, is a woman who has been like a Sister to me since shortly after I first showed up on Ontario Street. She is sweet, kind, caring and has a strong sense of compassion, but I also know that she'd be disappointed in me if I didn't tell you that she was a crazy bitch as well." Von says chuckling. She is French Italian, and has a ferocious temper toward anyone who might do harm to her or to her friends. She is a staunch protector of those that she loves, and would never let anyone hurt them.

I'll also be very honest. I don't know if Angela is dead or alive, because i've heard conflicting stories. Nonetheless, she is a great friend of mine, and so was it the same for Monica. So on behalf of The Ontario Street Originals, I hereby induct Angela O into The Class Of 2014, Ontario Street Hall Of Fame"!!! Von "The Icon" says lifting Angelas statue off of the podium as HALL OF FAME BY THE SCRIPT plays once more … … … … … … …

The crowd is awaiting the announcement of the next inductee now as a cool breeze blows in from the open front doors. They are in the heart of Ontario Street, and you can smell the stiff scent of yeast coming from The Brewery at Frontenac that drifts in like a wave off of the ocean. It is a scent that most neighbourhood regulars have become acquainted with and frequently associate it with home. If one spends days at a time on Ontario Street, then the scent will soak into their clothes as if it was woven in.

"Ready in 3, 2, … … … … … … a book operator counts down.

Von "The Icon" rises from his chair at the edge of the stage and walks across the floor to the podium that is bathed in the glare of the over lapping spot lights, gold with a tinge of orange, like early summer. He taps the microphone creating a resonating static that is sent across the auditorium. "Alright." He begins.

"Our next inductee, is a woman whose name is synonymous with the words "SEX APPEAL." She is beautiful, kind, sweet, sexy, charming, seductive, intelligent, and she's an impeccable dresser. She is simply put, every mans fantasy come to life, PLAYBOY CENTREFOLD material in the flesh, ladies and gentlemen, please help me welcome my friend, Barbie Blond (Jesse), to THE CLASS OF 2014 ONTARIO STREET HALL OF FAME"!!! Von "The Icon" says as Barbie strolls across the stage, a vision of seduction and beauty, her long flowing blond hair is down to her mid back and her curvy hour glass shape and large chest is drawing whistles and cat calls from the gang members and males alike in the auditorium.

As she approaches Von "The Icon" the forty something goddess embraces The Immortal legend pecking him on the lips as she turns to face the microphone as HALL OF FAME BY THE SCRIPT begins to fade out.

Barbie is all smiles, waves and charisma as her adoring male fan base can't get enough of her. "Thank you." She says in a low husky voice that would make even an impotent male remember his primal roots.

"I love you." She says to the noisy males who love her to death. "I wanna thank everyone for coming out tonight, especially The Ontario Street Originals who have been my Family and friends for so long. I also wanna thank The Immortal Von "The Icon" for not forgetting about me and for keeping me in his heart." She says as Von "The Icon" renders a sentimental expression from the edge of the stage.

"You've all been so good to me." She says as two more gang members flash gang signs in her direction before sticking their fingers in their mouths in the shape of a V to create a high pitched whistle in show of appreciation for Barbie Blonds many charms.

"Keep it comin boys." She encourages as Von smiles from the sidelines.

"On another note, tonight is very special not just because of this award." She says lifting the trophy with her hand. "It's also special because we've come here to celebrate a life, the life of a dear friend of mine who was taken from us to soon. Monica brought a flavour as well as a charisma to these streets that hasn't been seen since the day she left, nor will it ever be seen again.

Who could ever forget the days and nights that Von "The Icon" and Monica Mayhem roamed the shadows and alcoves of Ontario Street together?? I used to say of Von that despite everything he persevered, but in truth, he did far more than just persevere, he brought us all together here today as a unit. You talk about nostalgia, Von and Monica wrote the book on it. Their love is LEGENDARY. You don't see love like that every day." Barbie said emphasizing the final word in the sentence.

"I'm proud to be here tonight. I'm proud to be a member of The Ontario Street Originals, and i'm proud to know all of you." She says smiling. "And Monica up in Heaven, I love you, I miss you, and I cherish you. God Bless"!!! Barbie says taking her award and strutting toward the curtain to a round of applause … … … … … …

"Alright." Von "The Icon" says as the cat calls for Barbie taper off.

"Our next inductee is a man for whom the word suave was created. He is a fashion plate, a hustler, a former night club owner, and an all around nice guy. I met him as well as his girlfriend Valerie in 2002 and we've been friends ever since. Ladies and gentlemen, please help me welcome to THE CLASS OF 2014 ONTARIO STREET HALL OF FAME. My good friend, my buddy and my bro, J.P.." Von "The Icon" announces as J.P. strolls onto the stage flanked by two erotique looking blondes. To The Ontario Street Original, JP would always and forever remind him of legendary actor Richard Gere.

"Thank you" JP said lifting his trophy from the podium and then putting it back down. "I wanna thank The Immortal one for inviting me here tonight and for nominating me as a recipient of this award. You are the man." He said turning to look over his shoulder at Von who was standing a few feet away. "If it wasn't for Von and Monica then none of us would be here this evening. We owe it all to them." JP said to a loud round of applause. "When I heard about Monicas car accident it felt as though someone had hit me in the head with a sledge hammer. What, what, what do you mean she's dead?? I couldn't believe it, very sad.

Her boyfriend Von loved her like no other even when I knew them both, and I know that he would have taken a bullet for her and that's a fact. So, as a token of both my love and appreciation of you both, I dedicate this award to The Immortal Von "The Icon" and The Incomparable Monica Mayhem. Thank you, God Bless, and goodnight." JP said as HALL OF FAME BY THE SCRIPT echoed on … … … … … … … … … …

"Our next inductee, is a woman who definitely has ambivalent charisma. She is a Sandra Bullock look alike, a diva in her own right, and has more sex appeal in her little finger than most women have in their whole bodies, and that's a fact.

I'll be honest, when we first met, I couldn't stand her. I remember her constantly yelling at me and telling me to get off of the street for her own reasons. Once bitter enemies, we became the dearest of friends. I love her.

Ladies and gentlemen, please help me to welcome to THE CLASS OF 2014 ONTARIO STREET HALL OF FAME, Carolyn G." Von "The Icon" says clapping as he turns around to watch Carolyn walk onto the stage to HALL OF FAME BY THE SCRIPT. She is her usual self, straight faced, trim, and gorgeous, but as she reaches the podium she smiles.

"It's good to see you." Von "The Icon" shouts below the cat calls and whistles that the sexy Carolyn is receiving, and he knows, that of any of the diva's who have appeared tonight, that Carolyn will have one of the most interesting stories to tell, because she has a history with Monica Mayhem like no other.

"Thank you sweetie." Carolyn says pecking The Immortal Von "The Icon" on the left cheek.

"It's good to see me." Carolyn says poking fun at her narcissistic reputation as the crowd continues to buzz, literally, not figuratively.

"So." She says gripping her award. "I saw a lot of happy faces in the crowd when I walked in here. I'm like a good movie. You people can't get enough of me"!!! Carolyn boasts with a bright smile stretching from one side of her cute, sexy face to the other. "CAN YOU PLEASE GET THE HELL OFF THE STAGE!!! THEY'RE GOING TO THINK THAT YOU'RE MY PIMP"!!! Carolyn yells in Vons direction. It's a rib and he knows it, a play on their storied past.

"MOVE"!!! Carolyn yells snow plowing the air with her hand while Von watches on laughing from stage left. "He knows that I mean business." Carolyn says drawing the rib out even further. "Anyway." She says, her tone becoming more serious. "First of all, I wanna thank you all for coming out to see me tonight. I guess that you heard I was here and couldn't resist. I have that effect on men. I even made Von kiss me once because of that." The French Quebecer continues. "What a past the three of us have. When Monica first came to Ontario Street we were competing with each other like no two bitches that you've ever met. I wanted everything that she had, and she wanted everything that I had. I can remember nights when we'd be together at The Black Domino Tavern and no matter what we'd keep making a play for whatever attention from the guys who were there, whether they were just bar flies or each others actual boyfriends. It took Von a long time to warm up to me though, as a friend I mean, because at the beginning we really did not like each other, and neither did Monica and I for that matter. At the time, we were the two most popular girls in the neighbourhood so it created a big rivalry, plus she was English and i'm Quebecois which didn't make things any easier. At one point I thought for sure that Monica and I were eventually going to fight, but it never happened. Now, finally, here I am and Monica is up in Heaven." Carolyn said with a touch of both sad and sweet in her voice. "And I miss her." She said breaking down. "Rivals or not, I loved her and she was my friend. So tonight, this award, this trophy is not for me. I dedicate this trophy and my award to The Incomparable, and I mean Incomparable, Monica Mayhem"!!! She says embracing Von as he returns to the podium.

HALL OF FAME BY THE SCRIPT PLAYS ON . . . .

"Our next inductee, is a woman who is not only a physical giant, but she has a giant heart as well. The first time that I met her she stormed into my living room to rescue me from the certain disaster of another female who was well on her way to burrowing herself into my skin, and into my house.

She is as Bad To The Bone as the famous song says. She stands well over six feet tall, has a heart of gold, and I both love and adore this woman for the friendship and kindness that she's always shown me. Ladies and Gentlemen, please give a warm round of applause as we welcome her to THE CLASS OF 2014 ONTARIO STREET HALL OF FAME, my dear friend, Emanuelle R." Von announces stepping away from the podium as Emanuelle takes the stage. She is dressed in a shiny gold top and sequined dress pants over stilettos with silver buckles on them. She looks dynamite!!!

"Thank you everyone." Manny begins clutching her statue. "I've known Von "The Icon" for a lot of years, and I can't tell you enough about how much I love him. He's been like a best friend to me many times when I didn't have one, sometimes he was my only friend. When I was a dancer I used to stay at his house a lot and while I was there I got to know Monica to. She was a sweetheart. It was through C Monroe that I first met Von "The Icon," David Dane, whatever you wanna call him. I was on my way up to his apartment to meet him and that's when I found Tracy causing shit for the hero that you see standing a few feet from me, and that's what Von is, he's a hero, or at least he's my hero." Manny said with genuine emotion. "I wanna thank you all for this." Manny says clutching her award. "I wanna thank Von for always being such a sweetheart, and I wanna dedicate this statue to Monica who's up in Heaven. Thank you guys. I love you." . . . . Manny says as HALL OF FAME plays on.

"Our next inductee is believed to be deceased, and I also believe that to be true in my heart. She was as gorgeous as she was sexy, she was as sweet as she was kind, and the last thing that she ever said to me was "I love you." So tonight, I personally induct my dear friend, Jenny into THE CLASS OF 2014 ONTARIO STREET HALL OF FAME." Von says lifting Jennys award off of the podium and walking away as the crowd cheers below THE SCRIPTS HALL OF FAME THEME SONG ... ...

"Our next inductee is a friend that I know to have passed on. She wasn't a member of The Ontario Street Originals for long but she was one of the most beautiful and alluring urban angels that I have ever seen. Angelica is also very special to me because I was one of the last people to see her alive before Aids claimed her precious life before dawn one morning while Monica and I were on Ontario Street together. Ladies and gentlemen, please help me welcome my late friend Angelica to THE CLASS OF 2014 ONTARIO STREET HALL OF FAME ... ...

Von "The Icon" shrugs off the cob webs that exhaustion has bestowed upon him as he begins to read from the next card. "My next inductee is a very dear friend of mine who I also believe to be deceased as the last time that I saw him he informed me that he had less then a year to live due to Cancer.

He was without a doubt one of the kindest and most sincere gentlemen that Ontario Street has ever produced or known. His name was Francoise, and he had a heart of solid gold.

I originally met Francoise one Friday afternoon as I was in search of Monica, his genuine compassion and concern for my plight immediately impressed me as it was a compassion that you don't often see anywhere. As soon as he saw me he always used to say to me through his thick French accent-"You, you, you are look for your wife"?? He was a truly wonderful human being with a warmth and a kindness that would have made any human being, man, woman, or child fond of him. Ladies and Gentlemen, please help me welcome my dear friend Francoise into THE CLASS OF 2014 ONTARIO STREET HALL OF FAME ... ... Von "The Icon" says

with tears welled up in his eyes. HALL OF FAME BY THE SCRIPT
PLAYS ON … … … … … … … … … … … …

"The next Inductee has been a dear friend of mine ever since
we first met in 2002. She's from Whitney Pier Cape Breton, and
she has a heart of gold. Ladies and gentlemen, please welcome to
THE CLASS OF 2014 ONTARIO STREET HALL OF FAME, my
friend and street sister Ann Marilyn." Von "The Icon" announces as
he steps away from the podium and crosses the room.

HALL OF FAME BY THE SCRIPT again begins to play as the
short, adorable Ann Marilyn makes her way onto the stage flanked
by her dog Princess and one of the many male escorts who are
seated back stage.

"Hey, first of all I wanna thank everybody for coming out
tonight. It is appreciated." Ann Marilyn states for the audience.
"I've been one of THE ONTARIO STREET ORIGINALS ever
since the summer of 2002, and i'm very proud of that.

Our host." … … … … Ann said pausing as she turned to smile
over her shoulder. "Our host is a very near and dear friend of mine
as was The Incomparable Monica Mayhem." Ann says turning her
gaze downward to look at her well behaved black Pitt bull Princess
who is sitting quietly by her side. "If it wasn't for The Immortal Von
"The Icon" and The Incomparable Monica Mayhem then none of
this would be taking place. I love you." She says in Von "The Icons"
general direction. "As I accept this award I also want to thank my
K-9 Princess who was good enough to accompany me all the way
over here without so much as a whimper."

At that very instant Princess took it upon herself to bark in
acknowledgement of her presence as if to signify to the audience
that she was indeed there.

"I love you sweetie." Ann said petting her K-9 companion on the
head. "In closing, I want to thank The Immortal Von "The Icon" for
his years of friendship and loyalty, and I also wanna dedicate this
award to my dear friend of many years, Monica Mayhem." She said.
"Goodnight everyone."

HALL OF FAME BY THE SCRIPT PLAYED
ON … … … … … … … … … … …

Von "The Icon" again strolls toward the podium and turns his lips downward in the direction of the microphone. "Alright, our next inductee is a gentlemen that i've known for many years. He is kinder than the meaning of the word itself and possesses a generosity that is second to none. He was born and raised in Venezuela but blessedly came to Canada to join us. He is supportive, a terrific human being, and more worthy of being noted for his heart than most people that I have ever known.

Ladies and gentlemen, please help me welcome to THE CLASS OF 2014 ONTARIO STREET HALL OF FAME, MY DEAR FRIEND, BRANDO." Von "The Icon" says clapping as his friend makes his way onto the stage with a lovely blond escort on each arm.

"Thank you everyone." He begins. "What I mean to say is that it's very nice to be here. I know that even though this is a great honour, we are still gathered here amidst tragic circumstances. I myself used to know Monica. She was up and down ONTARIO STREET with her boyfriend, my friend, Von for many years. He was always concerned about her and not once did he ever let her down, not ever." As I stand before you here today I can swear to that." The Venezuelan says. "I won't speak for long, but just long enough to thank The Immortal Von "The Icon" for remembering me and to remember "The Incomparable" Monica Mayhem to whom I dedicate this award." Brando said raising his statue above his head in a token of thanks to the hundreds who sat before him as HALL OF FAME BY THE SCRIPT PLAYED ON … … … … … … … …

"Our next inductee is a gorgeous angel and a dear friend of mine that i've known for many years. She is as beautiful and as sexy as she is sweet and kind. Ladies and Gentlemen, please help me welcome to THE CLASS OF 2014 ONTARIO STREET HALL OF FAME, Mary Andre." Von "The Icon" says clapping as the short haired French bomb shell is escorted onto the stage by two well dressed male escorts. As she reaches the podium Mary Andre embraces The Immortal one and pecks him on both cheeks.

"Merci Beaucoup."(French for thank you), Mary says lifting the statue and exiting stage left as HALL OF FAME BY THE SCRIPT plays on … … … … … … … … … … … … … … … … … …

"Our next Inductee has been a member of "The Ontario Street Originals since the year 2000. She is very kind hearted, a good listener even when she's struggling to understand, and she's a dear friend of mine. Ladies and Gentlemen, please welcome to THE CLASS OF 2014 ONTARIO STREET HALL OF FAME, M.J.."" Von "The Icon" says clapping his hands above his head as the tall slim MJ Walks onto the stage wearing her ball hat in reverse fashion over a trendy womens business suit which is a far cry from her usual attire. "Thank you everyone." MJ says as she takes the podium. "It's and honour to be here." She says in a low voice. "Thank you Von." She says in her limited English before lifting her statue from its mantle and exiting stage left as HALL OF FAME BY THE SCRIPT PLAYS ON ... ...

"Ladies and Gentlemen. Once again I wanna thank you for coming here tonight. I also wanna thank all of our inductees for participating in tonights HALL OF FAME INDUCTION CEREMONY. WELCOME TO THE HALL OF FAME"!!!! The Immortal Von "The Icon" says as he waves to the crowd as Spotlights crisscross one another in a dazzling array of glare and gold.

HALL OF FAME PLAYS ON AS THE CEREMONY COMES TO AN END.

WELCOME TO The HALL OF FAME, And THE WORLD'S GONNA KNOW YOUR NAME!!!

MONICA-When I think of our relationship it's as if i'm seeing it in my head one frame burning into another to Patti Austin and James Ingrams Baby Come To Me from the 1980's. The two of us coming together in front of The Black Domino Tavern for the first time, you standing near the corner of Ontario and Dufresne on that hot Sunday morning when you came to my house for the first time. The two of us laughing hysterically when I said that we could blame everything on our twins, the evil Don and Monicrap. That was one of your favourites. The Police bringing you to the door in the middle of the night and you looking into my eyes with love when I defended you. The two of us walking down a darkened Ontario Street together after hours flanked by scattered members of The Ontario Street Originals.

I miss you so much Baby. Von always loved you, no matter what, and against all odds, but now I have to say goodbye to you forever. Your accident, and the way that we ended has broken my heart and it can never be repaired. I must go on living, but without you it was never the same, it was never anywhere near as worth it.

I love you Monica!!!

You are and always will be my number one Bunny. I'll see you in Heaven.

Love,
Von
4 EVER!!!

R.I.P. MONICA,
ETERNAL LIFE!!!
LOVE ALWAYS!!!